THE FALLON PRIDE
A novel of history, adventure and passion

She dropped the blunderbuss. "I am sorry, captain. I did not know who had won—you or Murad's pirates." Her breasts still heaved with agitation. Sunlight through the sterncabin windows surrounded her with a halo. "If there is so much difficulty in going to Spain, I begin to be glad I did not make you take me directly to France."

"We're not going to Spain." Robert Fallon was looking at her fixedly, but he missed the dangerous light that came into her eyes.

Her voice was soft. "I do not understand, captain."

"I'm sailing for Charleston. For South Carolina. I'm sorry."

"Cochon! You promised me! You lie in your teeth, you—"

He took an involuntary step toward her. "Be quiet!"

"—Lying, filthy, despicable—"

Almost of their own volition his arms slid around her, and his mouth fell on hers fiercely. For a moment her hands fought him. Then she pressed against his back, pulling him closer. Wordlessly he scooped her up in his arms and carried her to the bed.

ATTENTION: SCHOOLS AND CORPORATIONS

PINNACLE Books are available at quantity discounts with bulk purchases for educational, business or special promotional use. For further details, please write to: SPECIAL SALES MANAGER, Pinnacle Books, Inc., 1430 Broadway, New York, NY 10018.

WRITE FOR OUR FREE CATALOG

If there is a Pinnacle Book you want—and you cannot find it locally—it is available from us simply by sending the title and price plus 75¢ to cover mailing and handling costs to:

> Pinnacle Books, Inc.
> Reader Service Department
> 1430 Broadway
> New York, NY 10018

Please allow 6 weeks for delivery.

_____Check here if you want to receive our catalog regularly.

THE FALLON PRIDE

by

Reagan O'Neal

Volume II of The Fallon Chronicles

PINNACLE BOOKS   **NEW YORK**

THE FALLON PRIDE

A Tom Doherty Associates Book

An original Pinnacle/Tor Books edition, published for the first
time anywhere.

First printing, June 1981

ISBN: 0-523-48002-4

Cover illustration by Elaine Gignilliant

Printed in the United States of America

Distributed by

PINNACLE BOOKS INC.
1430 Broadway
New York, New York 10018

TO
James Oliver Rigney, Sr.
and
Eva Mae Rigney
Without whom the first word
would never have gone on paper.

THE FALLON PRIDE

BOOK ONE

I

The wind out of the desert scorched across Tripoli harbor, carrying no hint of November with it. Sweat beaded Robert Fallon's face as he gained the deck of the brig *Osprey*. Six feet tall and stocky, he had the hooked nose, high cheekbones and coloring of the Black Irish, belied by cobalt blue eyes. He ran those eyes over his ship, lying anchor in four fathoms, just beyond range of the guns of the fort in the city, or those of the old pile across the harbor called the English Fort.

All eight of *Osprey*'s guns were double-shotted and run out. Two swivels were mounted on the forecastle, and two on the quarterdeck, a crewman at each with a slow-match in his fist. Occasionally a lateen-rigged polacca or xebec slowly circled the brig, swarthy crew staring unblinkingly. The brig seemed to attract every triangular-sailed pirate in the harbor, and eyes from the launches and bumboats darting over the water as well.

One other Western-rigged vessel was there, a three-masted ship anchored close in behind the long, stone mole that served the harbor as a breakwater. None of the Tripolitans gave her a second glance.

Robert took up his spyglass. She puzzled him. Her crew was still on board, and not in chains, so she wasn't a prize. In fact, boatloads of turbaned men went aboard often, and seemed on good terms with her officers.

Three times he'd caught one of the other ship's crew watching *Osprey* in turn. No doubt it was only curiosity, but it made him uncomfortable all the same. He didn't like being in Tripoli, he decided, not even for twenty-four hours. And especially not now.

"Mr. Crane," he called.

"Yes, Captain?" His first mate's long legs and bobbing walk as he crossed the quarterdeck reminded Fallon of the

3

man's namesake bird. His voice held a hard Massachusetts twang, and his manner was as fussy as a clerk's. "No sign of that water barge, yet, sir. That Hamid fellow said it would be here at daybreak, and it's near noon."

Robert scowled at the city, the palace and fort looming over it from the harbor side, the desert stretching in endless heat beyond. He'd never have stopped if the water he'd taken on at Rhodes hadn't been tainted.

That fall of 1799 few ports in the Mediterranean were more than nominally open to American ships. Half of Europe was at war with the other half, and the Barbary pirates seemed at war with everyone. Even America was involved in a war with France, though neither had declared it or admitted it. British captains were seizing ships right and left for trading with French-held ports. The Barbay pirates at least had treaties of a sort with the United States; they were supposed to allow watering. And he had to get back to South Carolina as fast as possible.

"I'll have the launch over the side, Mr. Crane," he said. "And issue a cutlass to each oarsman."

"Pistols, sir?"

"God, no! I'm hoping cutlasses will make any trouble-makers back off." He grinned sourly. "If we shoot, we'll likely none of us make it back alive."

"You're going back to that heathen Hamid, sir?" His mouth was drawn up in disapproval.

"No. If he doesn't deliver for one bribe, I'll not give him a second. I've heard President Adams was going to send consuls to the Barbary states." He took a deep breath. "See to the boat, Mr. Crane."

"Aye, sir."

Six oars made the launch skitter across the harbor like a waterbug. Dark eyes followed their passage; Robert had eyes only for the other Western ship. They passed her stern; no name or home port was painted there. He shrugged. That was common enough these days.

They neared a boat landing at the quay, its slime-covered stone steps running down into water with a greasy film on top. The smell of the city drifted to him, pungent spices and rotting garbage, the smell of not-quite-arrested decay.

Berbers, Arabs, Turks, and men from inland tribes in a dozen variations of long flowing robes jostled on the quay. They eyed the men in the boat as they might exotic animals. Only a few paused in their rapid, sharply pitched speech, though, as the launch grated against the stone steps. Robert hopped out.

"Miller," he said, "Thompson, come with me. The rest of you back off, and wait till I return."

The two largest oarsmen climbed out after him, settling cutlasses awkwardly at their waists. The others backed oars to move away from the quay. Miller, looking like a balding bear, had a paunch that was belied by sunken knuckles and scarred hands. A wicked scar ran diagonally the length of Thompson's face, giving him a sinister air. It was rumored he'd sailed with pirates in the Caribbean, and Robert could believe it.

With the two men at his heels, Robert set out into the town. He had no idea which muddy stone or stucco building might be the consulate. Someone in the nearest market would surely know.

As they left the harbor area, the narrow, twisting streets became emptier. A handful of people stared suspiciously, or darted out of the way into even narrower alleys. Robert felt eyes on his back from every arched door and window. Moisture-leaching heat made the air shimmer. The low, stuccoed buildings seemed to be closing in. Then, as they rounded a bend, a sigh of relief escaped him. They were in a large square. At last, life that didn't disappear at their coming.

A public tank of stagnant water stood in the center of the square, veiled women filling jars from it. Scattered scraggly palms gave no shade at all to peddlers displaying their wares on blankets. People swathed to the eyes in robes bargained in a swift cacophony of high-pitched chatter.

"Not a bloody thing worth stealing," Thompson grunted. Miller, running a contemptuous eye over the square, nodded agreement.

Robert approached the closest cluster of peddlers, holding up a Spanish-milled dollar. "Do you know the American consulate? The United States?" They stared at him blankly. *"Los Estados Unidos? Les Etats-Unis?"* There wasn't a flicker of understanding. *"Die Vereinigten Staaten?"* he added without hope. All he had left was a little harbor-and-tavern Greek, useless here.

The next group he spoke to gave him the same looks of non-comprehension, and the next, and the next. Then a wizened little man with a black-toothed grin looked up at his voice.

"Ah!" he said. "You English?"

"American," Robert said. "I want—"

"I speak English plenty much good. You want buy plenty fine gold cup? English cup. No? Ring. See? Fine ring."

"I don't want any rings. I want the American consulate."

"No ring?" The little man rummaged among his wares. "You want plenty fine pin?"

"What I want is the Ameri—" Robert's voice trailed off as he focused on the cameo pin the wrinkled peddler held in front of him. The high-cheekboned face was exotically beautiful. And a twin for his half-sister, Catherine.

Slowly he took the pin, running his thumb around the cameo. It wasn't right, he thought, that any woman could so affect a man without trying. It was all that much worse that she was his half-sister.

He shoved the cameo back at the peddler. "I don't want cameos. If you don't know where the American consulate is, that's an end to it."

The old man eyed him shrewdly. "Plenty fine pin. Plenty fine amber. For good English friend, ten pound your money."

"Five pounds," Robert said suddenly. "For the pin, and directions to the American consulate." Why in the devil's name was he buying a cameo? *This* cameo, in particular.

The peddler frowned. "American? What? I do not know." He added plaintively, "I know English. Men like you."

"Yes, men like me. Men who talk English, but are not English."

The peddler looked at him reproachfully. "Eight pound?"

"Five. For the pin and the information." Robert took a deep breath. How? "The flag. Listen carefully. Have you seen a flag with red and white stripes?"

"Seven pound?"

"I said listen. In one corner it's blue, with white stars. Sixteen of them, it should be, but stars anyway."

Creases in the old man's face deepened with pleasure.

"Yes," he said suddenly. "Yes." He pointed to a street leading off the square. "Go there. Three street. Turn right and walk. You will see. Flag is there." He glanced hopefully at the pin. "Six pound?"

"Five." Robert dug Spanish and Turkish coins to approximate five pounds from his coat pocket, and shoved the cameo in. "Miller, Thompson, come on."

Of course, the man could just be making up his directions to sell the pin. Robert didn't believe it, though. One street, two streets; he'd know soon enough. Three steps after turning to the right, a smile appeared on his face. Ahead, on a pole in a courtyard, was an American flag.

The gate was barred by a scowling man in a turban. "I'm here to see the American consul," Robert announced.

The scowl deepened. "Who?"

"The American consul. I'm Captain Robert Fallon of—"

"Who?"

"Here, sir," Thompson growled. "I'll bash him so he knows who."

"No need," Robert said drily. "*Baksheesh* is one word I *have* learned in this part of the world." He tossed an English half-crown through the bars of the gate.

The gateman scooped it up and made it disappear. His scowl giving way to an oily smile, he pulled open the gate and discovered some thick English. "Come in, *sidi*. Come in. I will tell my master." Ducking and bowing his way across the slate-tiled courtyard, he disappeared through a stuccoed arch into the house.

Fig trees gave shade, and a fountain bubbled and splashed in one corner. Except for the American flag, it could have been any of ten thousand courtyards along the North African coast.

"Captain," Miller rumbled, "begging your pardon, but you think this fellow here will help? This consul, I mean. Mostly they don't."

Robert nodded. Every nation had consuls, though the United States hadn't for long, but they were usually men chosen because they were on the spot. They were also usually more interested in feathering their own nests than in sailor's problems. "He'll help us," he said grimly, "or I'll—"

"Captain—Fallon, is it?" A hook-nosed man with the

coloring of the Black Irish appeared in the doorway. He was big, with a broad, open face, but his dark eyes measured shrewdly. "I'm James Cathcart. The American consul."

"Robert Fallon, Captain of—"

"Of the *Osprey*. Bound for South Carolina with a load of trouble."

After a moment, Robert said, "Yes. Of the *Osprey*." He took the hand Cathcart offered and was surprised to find it hard with callouses. The consul's bearing and well-cut russet coat bespoke a gentleman. But he *did* speak with an odd precision, like a man who had learned proper English as an adult.

"If you'll come to my study, we can talk."

"Miller, Thompson," Robert flung over his shoulder, "wait for me here." He nodded for the consul to lead the way.

Inside, Cathcart stopped to speak in rapid Arabic to a servant who murmured in reply. "I'm having tea sent out to your men. With a dollop of rum, if that's all right."

"Certainly." Cathcart nodded; the servant scurried away. Robert went on: "Now, I'd like to know how you know about my ship. And my trouble."

"In here, captain. Away from prying ears." His eyes shifted as if he were actually watching for listeners.

Robert followed him into a room that, except for a mosaic tile floor, could have been in any house in America. The furniture, the rugs, even the pictures on the walls and the curtains at the windows had obviously been shipped out. The consul stopped in front of a sideboard topped with decanters. His manner was smooth again.

"Brandy, captain?"

"Yes," Robert said shortly. Cathcart was obviously going to take his own time. He took the brandy the other man handed him.

"I knew your ship because there's only one American ship in port. *Osprey*. Last port Rhodes. Silk, olives, olive oil, salt, oranges, pepper, cloves, ginger, other spices. What else, I don't know."

Robert's jaw tightened as he listened. "That's a deal more than *anyone* here should know."

"Common knowledge, Captain Fallon. Talked on every

street corner. Also, you need water. And you have paid bribes to get it.''

"Damn!''

''It's not as if it was something unusual. You can't get anything done without bribes in a Mediterranean port. But this time the Bashaw has been stirred up over it.''

Cathcart sipped at his glass; Robert tossed his brandy down in one gulp. "The Bashaw himself? In God's name, why? You had the right of it. Bribes are as common as fleas in the Mediterranean.'' His mouth twisted mirthlessly. "Damnation, our entire country bribes these pirate bastards.''

"Not exactly,'' the consul sighed. "Besides, nearly every nation in Europe pays the pirates to be left alone. England does it. France has been trying hard enough to be allowed to. Do you think we're near as strong as *they* are? Or would you rather have to fight your way through every time you pass the Pillars of Hercules?''

Robert scowled. This was getting nowhere. "I need to sail as soon as possible. *That's* the only thing that's important. Now what's to be done? Is there a fine to pay?''

"Another bribe, rather. To the Bashaw.'' He smiled thinly at Robert's stunned look, and refilled the glasses. "Perhaps it will help if I explain a bit.'' Robert nodded numbly; Cathcart went briskly on. "Does the name Murad Reis mean anything to you?''

That jolted him out of his daze. "It does.'' About the Bashaw he knew little more than the name. But Murad Reis was known to any ship's captain, the most infamous of the Barbary pirates. The Mediterranean was too small to hold him. He had seized ships in the English Channel, taken a Spanish treasure ship in sight of Cartegena, raided an Irish town and enslaved all the inhabitants. "What does he have to do with this? Or with me?''

Cathcart frowned worriedly. "I don't know. Or at least, I know only a little. When you began passing bribes around, Murad whispered in the Bashaw's ear about the insult of all that gold being passed and not a coin going to him. Or so my informants tell me. As to why?'' He shrugged, and his frown deepened.

"This is insane. Heads of state, even pirate ones, don't get bribed by ship captains. They're bribed by governments, with thousands of dollars of gold and square miles of land.''

"It won't take that much." Getting down to the mechanics of the problem seemed to have relieved the consul's worry. "Yusuf Karamanli might be a prince, but he's still a pirate. Buy a girl in the slave market, dress her properly, and—"

"I don't own slaves," Robert said shortly.

Cathcart's eyebrows raised. "But you sound like a southerner. Well, I'll leave it to you, but it must be something that will catch his eye the way a slave girl would. I should be able to arrange an audience inside the week."

"A week! I can't wait that long. I need to sail today, tomorrow at the latest."

"Impossible. You ought to know how long dealing with princes takes."

Robert hesitated. It was instinctive not to tell anyone what he knew, but he couldn't afford to delay his return to Charleston by one unnecessary day. "The Spanish and French signed a secret treaty about four years ago. Some time this coming year the French will take control of Louisiana, including New Orleans. With our frigates fighting every time they meet, it's not likely they'll continue to allow us to trade on the Mississippi. The Americans there won't know until it's too late, until their goods are seized, and they're thrown into prison.''

"You are invested in the Mississippi trade?" Cathcart asked shrewdly.

"I am. But that doesn't change anything I've said. And there's the matter of having the French for neighbors.''

Robert thought the French had too many problems in Europe to cause any but economic troubles in Louisiana, but he could see that Cathcart was thinking furiously. There was still some support for the French Revolution in America, but even its most ardent supporters might not like the possibility of guillotines and French armies in North America.

"No," Cathcart said finally. "It's impossible. Such a treaty couldn't have been kept secret so long. Word would have gotten out. Someone would have talked."

"Someone did. A Spaniard in Rhodes who was too drunk to be making up lies. Apparently he'd been caught in the wrong bed by the wrong husband. He was bitter that all his good friend Godoy could do was help him get out of Spain before he was murdered.''

"Godoy!"

"That's right. A powerful name in Spain. As I said, the man was too drunk to lie, and the stories he told bore out his being close to men in power. Palace intrigues. Political dealings. One was this treaty. I believe him, Cathcart. I believe every word.''

The consul seemed caught up in Robert's intensity. "Yes. Yes, I can see. This information has to get to the President.''

"Then you'll help me get away as soon as possible?''

Some of the enthusiasm went out of Cathcart. "I'll try, captain. At the best, though, it will take two or three days.'' He set down his glass and seemed to summon briskness from somewhere. "I had best get started. And you must see to your gift for the Bashaw. Is there anything else I can help you with, captain?''

Robert paused on the point of leaving. "There is one thing. There's a three-master in harbor, painted black. What do you know of her?''

Cathcart eyed him. "Why do you ask?''

"The crew seems too friendly with the pirates. Makes me uneasy.''

"Um. They've been making me uneasy since I got here. Four like this one have called in that time, all owned, I believe, by the same man. Their captains deal directly with Murad Reis, and that makes the dealings both large and foul. I'd advise you to steer clear of that ship.''

"I intend to.''

"Then I'll send word when an audience is set. And Captain Fallon,'' Cathcart's voice was suddenly intent, "in *this* harbor, keep your eyes open for treachery.''

II

The consul's closing words stayed with Robert across the harbor on his return to *Osprey*. As he neared the brig, they took on immediate force. A launch, its rakishly curved sternpost proclaiming Tripolitan origin, was lashed against *Osprey's* side. A score of scruffy men in turbans, arrayed with daggers and scimitars, lazed at their oars. Their dark eyes caressed the brig hungrily.

"Keep your cutlasses handy," Robert ordered quietly. "But don't start anything unless I give the order."

The rowers muttered assent. Miller growled and spat tobacco juice over the side. Robert had no worries about the men fighting, if it came to that. Officers might be held in hopes of ransom, but seamen would sweat out their lives laboring on the mole.

The boat bumped against the brig. Robert scrambled up the side, ready for anything. Only his own crew were in sight, working at their usual tasks. The swivels were still manned, their gunners eyeing the boat full of Tripolitans nervously, and the only sound was the creak of the rigging. The first mate came bobbing forward as soon as Robert's feet touched the deck.

"Mr. Crane," Robert grated, "what's that launch doing alongside? I left orders—"

"He says he's the High Admiral of the Navy of Tripoli." It was a measure of Crane's agitation that he interrupted. He licked his lips incessantly. "When he demanded to come on board—. Well, he *is* an Admiral. And he did come alone. I put him in your cabin, sir."

"My cabin? And you left him alone?" With an oath Robert darted down the companionway. He flung open the door to

12

his cabin, and stopped.

At the table in the center of the cabin sat a man in a green turban, the color signifying a pilgrimage to Mecca. He was sipping a glass of Robert's best brandy. Snowy white robes glistened as he shifted, and the jeweled hilt of his scimitar caught the light. Cold blue eyes watched Robert above a sandy blond beard.

"You seem surprised, captain." A faint Scottish brogue clung to the voice.

"I understood the High Admiral of Tripoli was on board," Robert said.

"He is, captain. I am he." He flashed a mocking smile. "Before I took the turban, I was an infidel of a Presbyterian Scot named Peter Lisle. Now that I am of the faithful, I am called Murad Reis."

Robert turned to the liquor chest to hide his confusion. None of the stories he'd heard of Murad Reis mentioned him being a renegade. He didn't doubt it, though. What was the man doing on *Osprey?* He lifted a decanter.

"May I offer you a drink, Admiral? Oh, I'm sorry. I forgot your religion forbids—" he stopped with a frown at the sight of the glass in Murad's hand.

"Not exactly, captain." The mocking note was stronger. "Brandy and whiskey didn't even exist when the Prophet lived. How could his prohibition apply to them? I'll have a drop more of brandy."

Robert kept a tight rein on his temper as he filled the pirate's glass and one for himself. It was plain enough Murad enjoyed putting him off balance. So he'd refuse to get off balance. He sat across the table and watched the other man silently.

Murad eyed him in turn, his face still derisive. "This is a tidy vessel you have."

"It is."

"Heavily armed for a merchantman."

Robert let a touch of sarcasm into his voice. "Sometimes there are pirates."

Murad didn't seem to notice. "Very fast, I expect."

"Very."

"You can't outrun the xebecs. Even if you *are* fast, there are monstrous calms, and you have no sweeps." He smiled at one beringed hand as if amused by the gems.

Robert felt the touch of real fear. *What* was the man doing there? "I trust I won't have to outrun them."

"Not unless you're a fool, captain." Murad paused. Robert made no response, and the Scottish pirate continued. "For reasons that need not concern you, the Bashaw has decreed that no ship leaving Tripoli may carry passengers without his personal approval for each passenger."

Robert was so startled he blurted, "Is that all?"

Murad frowned. "Were you expecting something else?"

"No. No, of course not." He'd been having wild ideas that Murad's visit in some way concerned the bribes, and even wilder thoughts about the treaty news, but if it touched either it was a deeper game than he could fathom. "I've no intention of taking passengers."

"See that you don't."

"A moment, Admiral," he said as Murad rose. "I trust the other ships in harbor have also been told of this. I wouldn't like to think one of them could take someone board and I get the blame."

Murad shook his head scornfully. "What you mean is, how much chance is there of *you* sneaking someone aboard and someone else being blamed? None. The only ship here that doesn't sail for Tripoli is the *Caribe*. Her captain knows of the edict, and no Fourrier ship will flout an edict of the Bashaw."

Fourrier. The name shook Robert to his core. Until he was sixteen, Robert Fallon had been called Robert Fourrier. He existed, it had seemed to him, only to be the target of one act of cruelty and violence after another from the man he thought was his father, Justin Fourrier. Only when his mother was dying had he discovered the truth. He was a bastard, the son of Michael Fallon, the man who had bedded Fourrier's wife and married his sister, the one man Justin Fourrier hated with every ounce of passion in him.

When she was dead, he'd run away, realizing he'd only been kept alive as a means to torture her. But Justin hadn't been content to let the symbol of his shame live beyond its usefulness. Nearly fourteen years had passed since that running away, but men still appeared when least expected, with Fourrier gold in their pockets and a promise of more when

Robert died.

The presence of a Fourrier ship couldn't be a coincidence. But how could it be more? Justin's henchmen *might* have arranged for the tainted water. But how would they have known to be waiting in Rhodes? How would they know he'd go to Tripoli? It sounded impossible. Besides, he didn't even know for a fact it *was* one of Justin's ships.

He kept his voice carefully emotionless. "Admiral, that's not a common name, Fourrier. I once knew a man, in Jamaica, named Justin Fourrier. Could *Caribe*'s owner be the same man?"

Murad's eyes were suddenly intent. "Yes," he said slowly. "The very same man." It was clear he was reevaluating Robert. A man who knew Justin Fourrier might be many things, but seldom an honest merchant.

To Robert that reevaluation was comforting. If *Caribe* had been sent after him, her captain would certainly have told the High Admiral what he was up to. Especially if, as Cathcart implied, Fourrier ships were regular visitors. But Murad had been surprised at even a faint connection with Fourrier.

"It was just a brief acquaintance, of course, but it *is* an odd chance, running into one of his ships like this."

"Of course."

Murad was still watching him closely. Robert sought for a change of topic. "Is it enough to refuse passage, or do you want me to report anyone asking?"

It seemed to work. Murad's mocking smile reappeared, more contemptuous than ever. "There's no need of that, captain. Just don't take any passengers. That's all you must do."

He swept out of the cabin without another word. Robert hurried after him, eager to see him over the side and gone. At the top of the ladder he almost ran into the pirate Admiral, who had stopped dead. Murad's attention was on the ship's rail, where a young woman was being helped on board. Robert found himself staring, too.

She was slender, and no more than five feet tall, wearing a high-waisted blue silk dress in the fashion of Italy and France. Without corsets, her dress clung to the lines of her body, and the tops of her small breasts quivered at her bodice. A bonnet shaded her face from the sun, but she still carried a parasol on one shoulder. Raven-black hair framed an ivory face with a turned-up nose and large melting brown eyes. A tiny mole high on her left cheek set off her beauty rather than diminishing it.

As she turned from the rail she stopped, eyes widening at the sight of Murad. Spots of color appeared on her cheeks. After a moment she pulled her gaze away to stare out across the harbor toward the sea.

Murad glared at her back, then at Robert. "No passengers, captain," he snarled. "See that you remember." With a swirl of his white robes he disappeared over the side.

Robert listened to the boat pull away with only half an ear. His attention was focused on the young woman, little more than a girl, really. That she was the object of the no-passengers order was plain enough. But why would the Bashaw go by such a roundabout way to stop one girl from leaving Tripoli?

"Miss?" he said. "I'm Captain Robert Fallon, of the American brig *Osprey*. Can I help you?"

She whirled with a start, as if she'd forgotten he was there. She took a deep breath, and her delicate chin was suddenly set with determination. "Forgive me, captain. I was thinking." Her English was exotic with French flavor. "I wish to book passage on your vessel for any port in France."

He shook his head, reluctant in spite of himself. "I'm sorry, Mademoiselle." He paused, but she didn't supply a name. "I'm sorry, but there's an order from the Bashaw forbidding passengers. Even if there wasn't, there's still the matter of a near war between the United States and France. How long do you think I'd keep my ship in a French port?"

She sniffed, and brushed away his question with a small white hand. "My family is high in the service of France. You will have no trouble. Now. I will pay you fair passage now. When I am ashore in France, you will receive five times as much again."

"No. I've explained why."

"Ten times as much again."

"No." He sighed. She seemed to refuse to understand. "No matter who your relatives are, you can't get me much of safe conduct. Papers like that are good with one set of officials, and just paper with another. No. No, I said, and there's an end to it."

Her brown eyes had taken on a harried look, darting around the deck. Some of the crew had slowed in their work to watch the captain and the lady. The sour smell of the harbor hung in the air, and the hollow echo of the muezzin's call to prayer drifted out from the city.

"Captain—" her voice faltered. "Captain, could I speak to you in private?"

He'd meant to keep her on deck. That way he could make their talk short. His refusal would come easily, and she could be put back on her boat and sent ashore. When he looked into those large, melting eyes, though, he felt the villain. Somehow he found himself escorting her below.

He muttered to himself even as he held a chair for her in his cabin. Whatever her problem, he couldn't afford to get entangled. It wasn't just the delay in getting his news to Charleston. He could lose *Osprey*. He and the rest of the crew could end up in chains, working on the mole. He'd give her a minimum of civility, and that was all.

He turned to the decanters. "Would you care for a glass of wine, Mademoiselle? You still haven't told me your name."

"I am Louise de Chardonnay. My father was Georges Phillipe Marie de Chardonnay." She paused as if waiting for a reaction. When he continued to look at her without changing expression, she frowned. "He was cousin to de Talleyrand-Périgord, the Foreign Minister of France. The Directory themselves asked his advice. Even Napoleon Bonaparte, the foremost general of France, felt honored to call him friend. He was a great man. A great man."

He shook his head. She was on the verge of breaking, but he couldn't afford to humor her. He made his voice deliberately hard. "If you're trying to convince me you really can arrange a safe-conduct, it won't work. Even I know Talleyrand's been out of power, and favor, since July. And your General Bonaparte is in the same way. He's been recalled to France."

"Recalled! But he is a hero!"

"That's as might be. But I've been told by men I trust that he's left Egypt with only a few officers for company. That sounds to me as if he's been relieved of command."

She jerked her head fiercely. "That does not matter. I must get—get back to France." He was certain it wasn't what she'd started to say. "If you cannot land me in France, then an Italian port will do, or a Spanish one."

"Italy's as bad as France. If *Osprey* wasn't seized by officials favoring France, those opposing France would notify the British blockade within the day. It's no better being taken by British than by French. Spain, now—." He stopped abruptly. What in God's name was he doing? Figuring out how to put her ashore in Spain, that was what. Damn it, for a fistful of reasons he *couldn't* afford to get involved with her. The anger he felt at himself, he turned loose on her. "You say you have to get back to France? Or just out of Tripoli? Why is the Bashaw going to all this trouble to stop you?"

She wet her full lips. "I—"

"Damn it, girl, don't try to play me for the fool. A blind man could see the way you and Murad Reis reacted to one another! Now tell me the truth, or stop taking up my time."

She clenched her fists in her lap, then regained her outward calm. "I think that I will take that glass of wine now, captain."

He eyed her with new respect, and poured a glass of Madeira. "Start at the beginning."

She took a tiny sip and set the glass on the table. Her hand and voice were steady, but she avoided looking at him. "My father was sent by the Directory to negotiate treaties with the Barbary states."

"One man?" he asked incredulously.

"One man would not attract English attention. I have traveled with my father since my mother died, when I was very young. This time there was only my father, myself, his valet, Tomas, and my maid, Marie. In Morocco, and again in Algiers, he achieved some success. They would sign a secret treaty if all of the other Barbary states did also. Here, with the Bashaw, he was almost so far. Then, three weeks ago, at bed-time, he complained of a headache." Her voice quavered. "The next morning my father was dead."

"I'm sorry," Robert said gently.

Her back stiffened pridefully, and her voice steadied. "The man, Murad Reis, looked at me often. He desired me." He grunted in astonishment at this flat statement, but she went on without noticing. "Usually there is some pleasure in knowing this, unless the man is old or ugly. In his look, though, there was something savage. I began to feel fear in his presence. While my father lived, he did nothing. But then—" she took another sip of wine. "The day after my father died, Murad offered me his—protection. He was amused at my refusal. He would be there, he said, when I changed my mind. Four days later Tomas disappeared."

"Murad Reis?"

"Of a certainty. He came again to our house with his offer. When I confronted him with Tomas' disappearance, he affected surprise. Servants often run away. I was lucky he had not taken my valuables. It was dangerous for a woman alone. Marie was so terrified it became all I could do to get her to do the marketing." She sighed heavily. "Poor Marie. Perhaps she knew best. Ten days ago she did not come back from the market. I became frantic. I ran into the streets and spent the entire day searching for her."

"Surely one of the consulates would have helped you."

"No, Captain Fallon," she said softly. "Either they are at war with France, or they do not want to offend those who are at war with France, or they do not want to offend the Bashaw's High Admiral. When I returned to the house that evening," she went on, "Murad was there. There had been a most regrettable incident, he said. Marie had been seized—quite by accident, he insisted—and was already on her way to Turkey as part of the tribute to the Sultan. I offered money, my jewels, but there was no way to get her back. He would only say that the same could happen to any beautiful woman without protection. To me. Marie was only a year older than I. Now all I could do for her was cry. The woman who cleans for me, watches me for Murad. He appears when I least expect him, in my bedchamber, even in my bath. He does no more than look, and talk, but I feel dirty afterwards. When the other ship came, I had myself rowed to it. Murad was there before me, with the captain. They laughed and said vulgar things before I was allowed to leave. And now your ship arrives. I fear you are my last hope, Captain Fallon. You must help me."

Robert took a deep breath. The woman had a way of making him forget the risks. Her soft brown eyes seemed to shimmer hypnotically. But it was still a bizarre story. "Forgive me for being blunt, Mademoiselle de Chardonnay, but if Murad wants you so badly, why is he playing these games?"

She smiled, womanly wise tinged with bitterness. "At twenty I know more of men than you do at, at whatever. You all enjoy playing games. Murad knows I cannot escape. He can reach out for me when he wishes. So he plays, like the cat with the mouse. It will inflate his pride to make me go to him and submit myself."

He cleared his throat in embarrassment, uncertain of what to say next. A knock at the door saved him. "Come."

Mr. Crane stuck his head into the room. "There's a gentleman topside, captain. Says he has to see you. Urgent."

"If you've let another pirate on board, Mr. Crane—"

"Not an Arab," the mate said hurriedly. "A gentleman, captain."

"Very well. Tell him I'll be there in a moment." Crane disappeared. "If you'll excuse me, mademoiselle."

She put a hand on his wrist as he turned to leave. "Captain, you will help me?"

"I don't know," he said, and tried to ignore the way she slumped. "We'll talk when I get back."

He wasn't surprised to find Cathcart on the quarterdeck, but he was surprised to have the consul round on him, frowning. "Fallon, I understand you have a woman on board. Is it Louise de Chardonnay?"

"It is," Robert said slowly. "What do you know of her?"

"I know she's trouble. And considering the problems you have already, too much trouble for you. Your information is important, but it'll be too late to be any good if you end up in the Bashaw's prison."

"God, man! Then you *didn't* try to help her. How could you leave a woman to the likes of Murad?"

Cathcart colored, his back rigid. "To smuggle her out of the city I'd have had to use favors that—let me finish, Fallon. There are forty-one American seamen in chains in this city, despite the treaty. With those favors, and time, I'll get those men free. I'm the *American* consul, Fallon, and the choice was between one Frenchwoman and forty-one Americans."

"I see," Robert breathed heavily. "I apologize."

The consul seemed mollified. "If a ship had come in, I might have been able to sneak her aboard in the night. But yours is the first, and there's no sneaking, now. Do you want to take the risk? Murad will never forgive you for taking something he wants. You'll be lucky to make a day's sail from here. Well?"

"You didn't come out here to tell me about Mademoiselle de Chardonnay," Robert said quietly.

Cathcart drew a breath and nodded. "You're right. Well. You have your audience, Captain Fallon. This afternoon at six."

"This afternoon?"

The other nodded grimly. "Yes, this afternoon. I was wondering what had happened to bring such haste. Perhaps the de Chardonnay woman is the answer. In any case, you can wager there's trouble in this."

"Mr. Cathcart, I've seen nothing but trouble since I dropped anchor. Now what do I do about this audience?"

"Present yourself about half past five, with your gift, at the main gate of the palace. Wear your fanciest rig. I'll meet you there and do what smoothing of the way I can. Now, about the de Chardonnay woman—"

"I'll take care of that." Robert held out his hand. "Until five thirty?"

Below, he found the girl still seated at the table. When he entered, she tried to pretend she hadn't been staring intently at the door.

"Do you need to go ashore for your things?" he asked suddenly. "It might be dangerous."

A slow smile bloomed on her face. "Then you will help me? No. No, I do not have to go back. I have a few things in the boat that brought me, and my money and jewels are in pouches sewn to my petticoats. The rest I will leave. I promise you, when we reach France—"

"I said nothing about France. I'll try to put you ashore in Spain. And I do mean 'try.' The British Navy takes being in

European waters as proof of trade with France, often enough, when it comes to American ships. If I sight a British frigate, I'll have to run. God knows where you'll end up then. Are you willing to risk that?''

"I have the fullest confidence in you, Captain Fallon."

He looked at her, sitting primly with her hands folded in her lap, and grunted sourly. "Yes. Well. That's as may be. For now, would you mind going on deck? I must dress for an audience with the Bashaw. And decide what sort of gift to give him."

She had risen smoothly at his request, but now she stopped at the door. "Animal, captain. A peacock, or a hawk, or a leopard. With expensive trappings, of course."

"Animal," he said flatly.

"Yes, captain." She seemed amused at his slowness. "I saw my father deal with these people. Unless you wish to give a sack of gold, or a slave. But that would be much more expensive." She smiled, and disappeared up the companionway.

For a moment he stared after her. "Animals," he said. Then he began digging out his best suit of clothes.

III

The chimpanzee at Robert's feet stirred, and he flashed a grin. Merchant captains didn't run to gold braid. The best suit he could come up with for this interview with the Bashaw was plain blue superfine and silk stockings. The ape, though, met the Frenchwoman's admonition for fancy dress. It wore a red vest, held with gold chains across the front, and a red hat sporting a long feather. The chain to lead it by was gold, too. By the price the animal trainer had charged, the chains should have been thick enough for an anchor.

The door to the anteroom opened, and a turbanned guard put his head through long enough to gesture for Robert to follow.

Still no Cathcart, he thought sourly. The note delivered just before he left *Osprey* said the consul would be a few minutes late. What was keeping him? Chain in hand, Robert led the chimp after the guard. Toward the Bashaw.

The guard hurried through ill-lit corridors to a pair of huge double doors. Two more guards stood there, scimitars in hand, but they ignored Robert and his escort as the Tripolitan opened one door just enough for the two of them to squeeze through.

Inside, Robert stopped at a scene of barbaric splendor lit by flickering braziers on tripods. A score of fluted columns supported the high domed ceiling above an obviously ancient mosaic floor of a man on horseback killing a leopard with a spear. Three girls in transparent silks and jewels danced to a motley group of musicians playing a shrill tune on flutes and odd, stringed instruments. Serving women, dressed more like the shrouded women in the street, moved among two dozen robed and turbanned men seated on cushions on the floor.

Murad Reis, scowling through his beard, sat at the right hand of a man whose pile of cushions, higher than the others, was on a dais at the far end of the room. This, Robert realized, must be Yusuf Karamanli, Bashaw of Tripoli.

Karamanli was a dark man, with grasping eyes set in a thin, foxlike face. When Robert entered, he tossed a half-eaten orange over his shoulder and motioned him to come forward. Conversation stopped, and silence fell, except for the music, as he walked forward leading the ape.

"Your Highness," Robert began slowly, "I do not speak your language. Mr. Cathcart was to—"

"I speak English," the Bashaw interrupted in a thick accent. "Also French, Spanish, Italian and others. It is well to know the language of your prey." A ripple of laughter went through the room. Only Murad failed to smile.

Robert paused while the mirth died. Without Cathcart he felt sure to put a foot wrong. "Your Highness, I brought you a gift, a token of my gratitude for the use of your harbor." He dropped the chain and tapped the ape on the shoulder the way he'd been shown. Immediately the ape doffed its hat and sprang into the air in a forward somersault, then another, and another.

Karamanli giggled, a startlingly high-pitched sound. "I thought that it was your first mate. I will promote him. I will call him my American Captain." He cut his eyes at Murad. "American captains are very much like monkeys, getting their paws into things that do not concern them."

Robert colored, and tried to ignore the laughter that swept the room. "I'm glad Your Highness likes my gift."

"Your gift," the Bashaw said absently. "Yes." He carefully selected a date from a tray and popped it into his mouth. "You have a woman on your ship, do you not, Captain?" He darted another glance at Murad.

"There is a woman visiting my vessel," Robert said carefully. Sweat began to plaster his shirt to his back. "I'm certain Your Highness realizes few western vessels touch here. Such a ship would seem like a breath of home to—"

"Home, captain? A Frenchwoman? An American ship?" He paused. It was a long, uncomfortable moment. "No matter. The woman may visit where she wishes. Go where she wishes. There have been rumors that she may not take passage without my approval." Again his eyes cut to Murad. "I have issued no such order. Have you heard of such an order, captain?"

Relief warred with the feeling that he was caught in a maelstrom. "No, Your Highness," he managed. "If I had heard, I would have obeyed."

Karamanli's face drew into an angry frown. "Yes. Not knowing it was a lie." He glared from Robert to Murad. "The water you need," he said suddenly, "is at this moment being loaded onto your vessel, captain. By my order. *My* order."

"I thank Your Highness." Yusuf seemed to be working yourself into a towering rage. Robert didn't want to be there when it broke. "If Your Highness will excuse me, I have duties aboard my ship."

The rage melted, and the high giggle erupted again. "Of course not. You are my guest. Sit. Eat. Enjoy." He seemed to forget Robert immediately, turning to talk with Murad Reis in low Arabic, but there was no doubt it was an order.

Robert was guided to a place between two men who frowned at him and edged away. One of the serving women put a tray of fruit in front of him and filled a handleless cup with strong syrupy coffee. The dancing girls gyrated to the shrill music. He settled in with a muttered curse. Why wasn't Cathcart there to guide him? He'd have to stay there until it was over.

The servants kept his cup filled, but the rest seemed to ignore him, murmuring among themselves and occasionally breaking into raucous laughter. The dancing girls were replaced by acrobats, then more dancing girls appeared. He sipped his coffee and waited, while the night dragged by in inches.

Just after ten o'clock, Yusuf suddenly rose. Murad ducked through a curtain behind the dais. The others rose and bowed toward the dais. At last, Robert thought. He stood and bowed in imitation of the others.

"Captain."

Slowly Robert straightened. The Bashaw regarded him from the dais. "You are my guest, captain. It is late. I will have you shown to a room." He clapped his hands and issued a swift stream of Arabic. There was nothing for it but to obey.

As soon as the door to his chamber closed behind him, Robert began a vigorous search. The door had neither lock nor bar. The walls behind the hangings were solid, and the floor was unbroken tile. The lone window had no bars, but it opened on a fifty-foot drop to the water below, glinting in the moonlight.

What was Yusuf planning? This was too much attention for a simple merchant captain. With an oath he turned back to the window and strained his eyes in the direction of his ship. Unless they were trying to steal the girl back. The pirates might believe watchfulness on the *Osprey* would slacken with the captain gone.

He couldn't hear or see a thing. The harbor was a mass of indistinguishable shadows. He refused to believe his ship could be taken in silence. There would be fighting, and noise. For the night, though, he must trust to Crane to hold *Osprey*. There was nothing for him to do but wait.

Ignoring the low bed in the center of the room, he extinguished the lamps and settled himself in a corner. From under his coat he took a pocket pistol. If there was treachery, he'd exact a price for it.

In the dark silence the night passed slowly. The sound of his own breathing was the loudest thing to be heard. His legs and back began to ache, but his watchfulness never wavered.

Then, after hours, his patience was rewarded. The door slowly opened, and a single figure slid through. Robert cocked the pistol; the sound was loud in the dark. The figure froze.

"That's right," Robert said. He got softly to his feet and moved closer. "Don't move."

"Not so loud, Fallon." The answer was a hoarse whisper.

Robert pulled the man to the window, into the moonlight. "Cathcart!"

The consul gestured vigorously. "Keep your voice down. I bribed some guards to let me get to your room, but others can hear too." He took a deep breath. "Why are you still here? The audience was six hours ago.'.'

"I'm the Bashaw's guest," Robert said drily. "He said water was being sent to *Osprey*. Is that true?"

"Yusuf doesn't have guests. And water? Man, I've had no time for your problems. News arrived from France. Abbé

Sieyès, one of the Directory, has overthrown the government. The National Assembly's been dispersed by soldiers. Sieyès, Pierre Ducos, and Napoleon Bonaparte have taken the title Consul and set up to rule. I expect the governments of Europe are going mad. Will they stop the war? Expand it? God!''

"Bonaparte," Robert murmured. "Maybe she could have done it after all."

"What? Never mind. There's no time. What's this about being Yusuf's guest? Tell me everything that happened."

Robert complied, but before he was done the consul was shaking his head. "That's the way it happened," Robert insisted. "Everything that was said or done."

"It just doesn't make sense. It doesn't."

"Anything that lets me sail with Louise de Chardonnay—"

"That's what doesn't make sense, Fallon. Murad's too important for Yusuf to slap him down like that. Besides, Yusuf's fond of games. I think he's playing one with you, now, and one with Murad. He lets you think you're getting away, and lets Murad think so, too. In the morning, when you sail, he'll let Murad go after you. I'll bet on it."

"Unless I don't sail tomorrow."

"What? You can't just wait him out."

"I could sail tonight."

Cathcart gave a low whistle, cut short when he remembered where he was. "You're mad," he whispered hoarsely. "This harbor's no Sunday stroll. You'll be aground inside half a mile, and lucky not to rip your hull open."

"It's that or Murad Reis, now, isn't it? Can I get out the way you got in?"

"Mad, Fallon. Oh, very well. Stay close, and keep silent." He cracked the door to peer out, then slipped into the hall. Robert followed.

The palace corridors were dimly lit by scattered braziers, and torches stuck in wall sconces. Pools of light were interspersed with flickering shadows. Robert waited for someone, anyone, to appear. A dozen times, it seemed, he started at a will-o'-the-wisp shifting on the wall. Then one of them resolved itself into a guard.

He bit back an oath and tensed to fight, but Cathcart stepped forward and murmured with the insubstantial figure in the darkness. Something changed hands; the consul motioned Robert to follow. Hesitantly, he did, keeping a close eye on the guard. The bearded Tripolitan stared fixedly over their heads, seeing nothing. Cathcart hissed and jerked his head down the hall, and the two men hurried on.

Twice more the consul did business with a guard in the shadows, and twice more the guard looked the other way as they passed. Then they were in the cobblestone street outside. The city lay dark except for the moonlight, dimmed by clouds pushed along by an offshore wind.

"At least you have the wind," Cathcart said. "But you'd better hurry."

"There's room for another on *Osprey*. I mean, you did say your position was shaky, and this—"

"The guards won't talk. You vanished like smoke. Believe me, I'll know when to go. For now, I've work still to be done. God be with you, Fallon," he finished gruffly. They gripped hands, and then Cathcart was gone in the night.

Robert moved toward the waterfront, drifting from shadow to shadow, keeping a wary eye out. Except for an occasional half-starved dog, though, or more frequently, a boldly scurrying rat, his was the only movement in the streets. Abandoning the shadows, he began to trot.

At the quay he hurried to the water. He'd told Miller to wait there. If the boat was gone, he'd have to swim. He felt his way down the slime-covered steps.

"Miller," he called. Then a little louder, "Miller."

"Captain," came a reply, and he heaved a sigh of relief.

With the creak of oarlocks the launch moved in. As he scrambled aboard, a babble of questions started, but he silenced them all. "The ship. And quickly."

His urgency communicated itself to them, and they sped across the black night water. Miller stood with a boathook to catch a deadeye, but Robert leaped for the rail and clambered aboard. Crane hurried up to him.

"Captain, we were getting worried. The water came, but when you didn't—"

"It's aboard, then? What about the lady?"

"In the starboard passenger cabin, sir. Asleep, I think. What's going on?"

"As soon as the boats aboard, assemble the crew. And quietly."

Crane's Adam's apple bobbed furiously, but he asked no more questions. He dove into the forecastle himself, and in five minutes the crew was gathered in the waist, grumbling sleepily.

"The pirates," Robert began quietly, "will overrun us at dawn." That woke them up. A murmur of fear rose.

"Damn," Miller said softly. "Begging your pardon, sir." Thompson grunted sourly and began to test his cutlass' edge.

"We can't fight them off here in the harbor. So I don't intend to be here at dawn." Silence fell. "Mr. Crane, I'll have staysails and jibs on her. Eadie, stand by to cut the anchor cable." His orders began to come faster, and men began running to obey. "Miller, take the wheel. Thompson, you'll be in the head to heave the lead. Lookouts aloft and on the bowsprit. Move. I want to be long at sea come dawn."

The men set to, and Robert climbed to the quarterdeck. Long at sea, he thought. Or aground.

"All's ready, captain."

"Cut the cable, Mr. Crane," he ordered, "and loose the sails." Crane relayed the orders, and from forward came the chunk of an axe severing the cable. It's done, he thought. "Miller, steer northeast by north." He'd watched the pirate ships; all took that heading out of the harbor.

"Aye aye, captain," Miller rumbled. His gnarled hands gripped the wheel firmly.

The wind caught the sails with a snap, and *Osprey* heeled over and began to move. From the bow Thompson's voice drifted back.

"Four fathoms. By the mark four. By the mark four. By the mark four."

Robert began to relax. Could it be he'd blundered into the middle of the channel? Then Thompson's cry took on more urgency.

"By the mark four, less a half. By the mark three. By the mark three. Three fathoms, less a half."

Shoaling, Robert thought. But which way to safety, and which way to put *Osprey* hard aground?

"Light water to starboard," the lookout sang out from the

foremast. Shallow water.

"Starboard your helm a point," Robert ordered.

Slowly *Osprey*'s course curved to port. Suddenly a jolt threw Robert against the quarterdeck rail. The masts swayed, and the rigging hummed. Men shouted, seizing whatever was handy to cling to. For an instant the ship shuddered to a halt, dragging bottom. Then she was free and moving.

Robert muttered a short prayer as he straightened. It had been the luck of inches and seconds that she hadn't gone hard aground. As it was— "Cousins," he called, "sound the well. Thompson, take up the count."

There was a definite shake in Thompson's voice. "By the mark three, less a half. By the mark three. By the mark four, less a half. By the mark five. By the mark six. By the mark six."

"We're out," Crane breathed.

"Wait," Robert said.

"By the mark six. By the mark six. By the mark eight."

"Ripline!" the foremast lookout screamed. "A point off the port bow! Close!"

Robert whirled to peer futilely into the dark, shouting, "Port your helm! Hard!"

The ship heeled violently. Tackle clattered, and the sails cracked like whips as the wind took them differently. Then he could see it, passing close to port. Moonlight glittered on a line of heavy ripples and miniature breakers where two currents warred over rocks just below the surface.

"God." Crane's voice was a bare whisper as the ripline dwindled astern.

"By the mark eight. By the mark eight. By the mark ten. No bottom at ten. No bottom at ten."

Robert made an effort to keep his voice calm. "Now, Mr. Crane, I think we're out." He flexed his hands to work away the ache of his grip on the rail. "Steer northwest by north. With this wind she'll not make more than eight or ten knots, but we should clear Cape Bon by morning. I'll be in my cabin. Wake me when the masthead sees first light."

A crewman's rap at the door wakened him. Robert allowed himself just an instant to lie awake in the darkness. Tripoli might be behind them, but Tunis and Algiers still lay ahead, not to mention Morocco. And the pirates of all three. He dressed quickly and hurried on deck.

Crane, his collar turned up against the night chill, stood peering astern. Only a rim of light showed to the east.

"Lookout thought he saw a sail, captain," he said by way of greeting.

Robert looked toward the growing dawn. "Thought?"

"It's hard, looking into the sunrise. I sent another man up, but he wasn't sure either."

"Make sure they keep a close eye. There are other pirates beside Murad Reis."

"Yes, sir."

"Good morning, gentlemen." Louise appeared suddenly between them, smiling at the dawn. To Robert her lowcut pink dress seemed more suited to a party than to a ship's deck. "I do so love sunrise. But we must have sailed very early to be so far from land." She looked at Robert abruptly. "Did I hear you speak of Murad Reis?"

Robert was uncomfortably aware of her eyes. "There may be a ship behind us," he said shortly.

"Not Murad!"

"Of course not," Crane broke in. She turned her smile on him, and he grinned till it seemed his narrow face would crack. Robert was astonished. This was a complete departure from Crane's usual clerkly ways. "Why, Miss de Chardonnay, we left Murad behind at Tripoli like a baby. Reefs and rocks on every side, but we sailed out with no charts and no pilot in the middle of the night."

Robert noted irritably that her eyes widened in seeming admiration. He didn't see her smile widen at the same time. "Oh, la, Mr. Crane! You must tell me of it."

"Well—"

"Mademoiselle de Chardonnay," Robert surprised himself by saying. Both she and Crane looked to him expectantly. What was he going to say? "Would you dine with me this evening?" he blurted. "Our earlier meals are rough things at sea, and—what I mean is, I would enjoy the pleasure of your company." He cleared his throat furiously. Damn it, he was *never* awkward with women.

This time he saw her smile widen. "Of a certainty, captain. If Mr. Crane can join us, also."

"I'd be delighted," Crane said, and immediately began preening himself, it seemed to Robert.

He opened his mouth to remind the mate that he would have to remain on duty, when the lookout called, "Sail astern! No, two! No, three! And another two points on the starboard quarter!"

"The total, man," Robert shouted. "How many in all?"

For a long minute the lookout counted. "Ten, sir!"

Robert and Crane looked at one another in consternation.

"A British squadron?" the mate said hesitantly. "The French haven't had that many at sea since Aboukir."

"What kind are they?" Robert shouted.

"One full-rigged ship," the lookout answered. "The rest lateen-rigged. Xebecs or polaccas. Sir, the ship's the one that was in Tripoli."

Robert felt frozen. "Damn," he breathed.

"It can't be," Crane said. "They'd have had to sail no more than two hours after us. How?"

"Maybe someone checked my room at the palace," Robert said wearily. "Maybe someone saw us sail. Maybe a hundred things. But they're out there, all right."

"Talk of the devil's luck."

"Well, I hope he's used it all."

"God, yes. To be caught now—"

Louise caught at a full lower lip with small white teeth. "I will not be taken, captain. I will not be."

Robert glared at Crane over her head. "Of course not." Didn't the man know enough not to frighten her to death? "We have a goodly lead on them. They'll never catch us."

Her eyes were uncertain. He managed a confident smile, and the corners of her mouth perked up. "If you say it is so, captain, I will believe."

"I do say it." How to convince her there was no danger? "I look forward to our dinner this evening, mademoiselle."

Her smile regained some of its vivaciousness. "But of course. If you will excuse me, though, I will return to my cabin. The sunrise seems no longer so beautiful."

As she went below, Crane said quietly, "That's all well and

good for calming her, sir, but wherever we touch port, they'll be waiting for us to come out.''

Robert's smile faded and his voice hardened. ''I don't intend giving them the chance. We should clear Cape Bon by six this afternoon.''

''Yes, sir,'' the mate said cautiously.

''Once we do, we'll turn to the northeast.''

''Sir?''

''It's a likely enough move, so they'll follow us. But they won't know whether we're making for Palermo, or Messina, or even Naples.''

''Yes, sir,'' Crane said, sounding bewildered.

He tried to mask his impatience. ''There'll be no more than an hour's light left when we change course. Dark will add to their confusion about exactly where we're going. An hour after dark, we'll reverse course, and leave them sailing into the Tyrrhenian Sea after nothing.''

Crane laughed. ''Why, it's wonderful, sir! We'll teach these Barbary pirates to try their hand against Americans.''

Robert grunted and turned to watch the sea behind.

The sun rose higher. On *Osprey* men worked as they did any other day, but occasionally one would pause to look astern, or another would see to a cutlass. Louise de Chardonnay stayed in her cabin. Robert and Crane kept to the quarterdeck. Behind, the pirate ships clung like leeches. Slowly, the sun began to sink.

IV

Before the first light the next morning, Robert was on deck. A light mist floated in the darkness, not heavy enough to be called fog. His plan had worked perfectly. The Tripolitan ships had followed as *Osprey* changed course toward Italy, and had still been there when night fell. One hour later he'd doubled back on his course, and an hour after that sat down to a dinner Louise de Chardonnay had described as a celebration of his victory over Murad Reis.

Victory celebration! He growled deep in his throat. She'd managed a good job of deflating his feelings of victory. First, she'd insisted that Crane be there, and the mate had continued his idiotic behavior, Robert thought sourly. And she hadn't helped. She's laughed at the mate's sallies, batted her long eyelashes at him, made calf-eyes at him. He growled again. It had been all he could do not to throttle the both of them.

And then there had been her dress, diaphanous, almost transparent. It hid almost nothing, and she'd worn almost nothing under it. He'd heard how daring the Continental styles had become, but seeing was something else again. She lit fires in his brain every time she moved. The dinner had passed like a fever dream. Her gently pear-shaped breasts. Her tiny waist. Her gently flaring hips.

"Four sail astern!" At the masthead lookout's cry, he colored as if the man had heard his thoughts. "Lateen rigged, sir!"

"How far?" he shouted. Dawn had come; the mist had burned away, leaving a cloudless sky.

"About ten mile, sir."

He pulled his thoughts away from the night before. "What lies forward?"

The lookout's reply was frantic. "Two sail forward, sir! Xebecs! About fifteen mile, and turning this way."

Robert leapt for the ship's bell. "All hands! Man the guns! Mr. Crane! All hands!"

At the clangor of the bell, barefoot sailors boiled out of the forecastle. Crane appeared, coatless, his shirt hanging loose around his scrawny frame.

"Get men to the guns, Mr. Crane. Grapeshot on top of the ball. We've two of Murad's ships ahead, and four more astern."

"But we lost them last night!"

"Evidently not. Now move, man. We have less than twenty minutes."

Crane turned to shout at the men hauling on gun tackle, and Robert straightened angrily. Much as he hated to admit it, Murad had outthought him. The pirate had thought of what *he* would do if he was being chased, then thought how to counter it. At dark, Robert was sure, Murad had sent some of his ships to wait beyond Sardinia, then later he'd turned more back. Robert was done with underestimating Murad Reis.

"Captain," Louise's voice came suddenly over the rumble of gun-carriage wheels, "what is going on? Are we in danger?"

Standing at the head of the companionway, wearing the same blue silk she'd worn the first time he saw her, she was watching the bustle on deck curiously. Abruptly all the rage and frustration in him exploded. "Get below! I said, get below! We're going to fight a battle! Now get below, or I'll have you carried."

For a moment brown eyes fixed him icily. Then she turned, and flounced back down the companionway with exaggerated dignity. He was conscious of the crew's eyes on him but when he looked, each man had turned away. Crane alone stared openly.

"Well, Mr. Crane?"

The mate's thin lips worked. He swallowed, then spoke. "I've never fought these African pirates before, sir. What can we expect?"

Robert raised his voice so everyone could hear. "There'll be a hundred men on each of those ships, or maybe half again that. They'll try to close, and swarm over us like ants.''

Crane's mouth dropped open. Two or three crewmen stopped work and looked up, frightened. It was those Robert wanted to get to. He raised his voice again.

''But we're more nimble than they are, and they've no taste for an ordinary sea fight, being terrible gunners. We'll keep them away, cut them to pieces, and leave them for Murad to find.'' A half-hearted cheer went up; the men went back to work. Robert spoke for Crane's ears alone. ''To make sure, see to mounting the swivels. And fix your shirt, Mr. Crane.''

The two vessels ahead were in sight from the deck, now, one a point off the starboard bow, the other two points on the port. The one to starboard was a little ahead. It wasn't likely they had any real plan, Robert thought. Murad might be a cut above the rest, but the average Barbary captain just tried to come alongside, with no regard for anything else. He might be able to make use of that.

He would have to. He couldn't afford to let them close. *Osprey* had a larger crew than most merchantmen, but she wasn't a warship. With the necessary crew at the guns, he had two men and a boy aloft. With luck, though, it would be enough. It had to be.

The lead xebec was two hundred yards ahead of the other, its crew covering the decks and rigging in a solid sheet, screaming and waving scimitars. In minutes they expected to scrape along the starboard side of *Osprey*.

Robert smiled grimly. ''Port your helm, hard! Crane, fire by guns as they bear!''

Osprey heeled over in a sharp turn to starboard. One by one the four guns of the port battery belched fire and smoke at the pirate ship, less than fifty feet away. The port swivels added their barks to the roar, until a solid wall of smoke hung between the two ships. Already Crane was ordering the guns back in to reload.

''Chain shot and grape,'' Robert shouted. ''Chain shot and grape.''

As the brig glided on, the pall of smoke began to clear. The xebec lay wallowing, dismasted. Some of her crew were in the water, clinging to the tangle of rigging draped over the side. The imprecations they'd shouted had turned to moans and screams.

Quickly Robert looked for the other ship, and swore when he found it. The other captain had broken out his sweeps and changed course. *Osprey's* turn to present her broadside had given him his chance, and now there was no time to avoid him. Robert took a cutlass from the rack by the quarterdeck rail and tested its edge with his thumb. He felt unnaturally calm.

"Mr. Crane, hold your fire till I give the word. On my command only."

The xebec knifed down on them, bow on, its crew howling for blood. Men huddled around two cannons mounted on either side of the long bowsprit. Inexorably it rushed across the last hundred feet. Fifty. Thirty. Ten.

"Fire!"

Osprey's guns roared as one, and a sheet of smoke hid everything. The xebec had chosen the same instant to fire. Lanrage whistled through the air, scrap iron, rocks, broken glass. The man at the quarterdeck swivel suddenly slumped against the rail, blood running down his arm.

Coughing, eyes burning from the acrid powder smoke, Robert snatched the man's slow-match. The xebec's bowsprit thrust through the smoke to tangle in the rigging over his head. He pointed the gun into the smoke at its base and touched the match down, sending thirty-two one-ounce balls screaming across the pirate's deck. Shrieks answered from the smoke.

Before he could turn from the swivel, a pirate ran along the bowsprit and dropped in front of him. He snatched up the dropped cutlass and ran him through. Another scrambled aboard to have his skull split by Miller.

Suddenly Robert realized that the pirates weren't boarding in their usual overwhelming numbers. As the smoke thinned, he could see why. The bowsprit had tangled in such a way as to keep the xebec end-on to the brig. The bowsprit itself was the only means of boarding. Now. But as the brig moved forward, the pirate ship, a fire blazing amidships, was twisting. In minutes it would be alongside.

At the toolchest under the quarterdeck ladder, Robert exchanged his cutlass for an axe. Leaping to the shrouds, he scrambled up to the xebec's bowsprit. Lacing his legs in the rigging, he began to chop, awkwardly, but steadily. The spar was well seasoned, but he soon had it more than halfway through.

"Captain!"

At the scream he jerked his head up to find a scar-faced Tripolitan almost on him. Desperately he flung up the axe to catch the pirate's scimitar blow. The blade struck the handle, and he found himself holding the head by a foot-long stub. The pirate raised his sword again. Using every ounce of strength, Robert swung what was left of the axe. The head knifed into the pirate's chest. Mouth twisted in a soundless scream, the man fell, wrenching the axe from Robert's hand.

He stared at the half-severed bowsprit. There was no time to go down for another axe. Flames were leaping up on the xebec, and its crew was massing for a desperate rush. A pirate started along the spar toward Robert, but a musket shot from the deck took him. Others crawled out, flat against the wood.

Suddenly, loud enough to be heard over the uproar, there was a crack. In disbelief he watched the bowsprit twist. The brig's forward motion forced the xebec back. Then, amid howls of rage from the pirate ship, the timber parted with a violent jerk.

The rigging hummed like guitar strings. Lines and blocks fell, pulled loose by the shock. But, clinging there like an ape, Robert couldn't stop grinning. The xebec was drifting behind, flames running up its rigging. The other had put out sweeps and was running away, leaving its fellows to their fate. From his own deck a cheer rose. He started down.

On the quarterdeck, Crane was flapping his arms, a nearly hysterical grin on his smoke-blackened face. "We did it, sir! I don't believe it, but we did it!"

It was all Robert could do to keep from cheering himself. "How many wounded, Mr. Crane? How many dead?"

"Eight or nine wounded, sir. Dead?" The mate looked about dazedly. "There aren't any, sir. If Miss de Chardonnay—"

Robert didn't wait. He leaped over the quarterdeck rail to the waist and darted below. "Louise!" He pushed over her cabin door—empty. "Louise!" He bolted down the short passage, hurled open the door to his cabin, and stopped.

She stood behind the table, fear and determination on her

face, a blunderbuss at her shoulder. It took a moment for her eyes to soften; then she dropped the blunderbuss with a self-conscious laugh. "I am sorry, captain. From the noise, I did not know who had won." Her words were calm, but her breasts heaved with agitation. Sunlight through the stern windows seemed to surround her with a halo. "If there is so much difficulty in going to Spain, I begin to be glad I did not make you take me directly to France."

"We're not going to Spain." He was looking at her fixedly, but he missed the dangerous light that came into her eyes.

Her voice was soft. "I do not understand, captain."

"I'm sailing on for Charleston. I'm sorry."

"*Cochon!* You promised me! You lie in your teeth—"

He took an involuntary step toward her. "Be quiet!"

"—Like a bastard English barbarian. You—"

"Shut up!"

"—Lying, filthy, despicable—"

He had her by the shoulders, shaking her. "Damn it, woman, I've just fought a battle for you! Now you shut up and listen! Murad still has ships behind. Close behind. If I go into port, they'll be waiting when I come out. I can't lost any more time, and I won't lose this ship. Not for you."

Almost of their own volition his arms slid around her, and his mouth fell on hers fiercely. For a moment her hands fought him futilely. Then she pressed against his back, pulling him closer. Wordlessly he scooped her up in his arms and carried her to the bed. Her large brown eyes watched him, moist and without expression, as he hurriedly undid the catches of her dress. The blue silk slid down to reveal her delicate breasts. When he caught one pink nipple with his lips, she gave a startled cry, half shock, half pleasure, and her slender fingers tangled in his hair.

Hastily he stripped his own clothes off, and hers. His roamed the ivory satin of her skin. She murmured soft, half-formed protests, but her eyes had become heavy lidded, and her hands clutched restlessly at the sheets. As he moved over her, her eyes opened wide in almost frightened fascination. He entered her, and a long "Aaaaah" escaped her.

She was a virgin, he realized in surprise. Then lust chased out thought as he began to move in her. Tentatively, her small hands caught him, and she met his thrusts, her shuddering coming in rushes, until she stiffened, eyes staring in disbelief, and stifled her open-mouthed scream against his chest. In the same instant he went rigid, clutching her to him with a savage growl, fading into heavy panting.

After, she lay in the crook of his arm as he dazed on his back, her breasts soft against him. She played idly with one finger in the silky hair on his chest. "You will marry me, yes?"

She said it so casually, he wasn't certain at first what he'd heard. "Marry! No."

She made a small determined noise. "You carry me away to a savage land without my consent."

"No."

"You ravish me."

"No!"

"You must marry me."

"I said no!" It made him angry, and uncomfortable, that her tone stayed conversational. "Now let's stop talking about it."

"But we must talk of it. If you do not marry me, what will you do? Will you abandon me on the docks? Ruined, with no money for passage, or to live?"

"Of course not."

"Ah!" She sat up, crosslegged, and looked at him disconcertingly. "You mean for me to be your mistress."

For a moment he was startled. He hadn't intended any such thing. But why not? She was beautiful, intelligent, witty. Few men had a mistress to compare. "Any why not? I'll be good to you, see you have your own apartments, the best clothes Charleston has to offer."

"No," she said firmly. A secretive smile played on her lips. "If I am to be a mistress, I will be a respected mistress. I will have my own house and servants. There must be a carriage, and a horse to ride. I must be able to order the latest fashions from Paris. I must—"

"Your own house?" Robert said. He felt thunderstruck. "Paris?" Suddenly, in spite of himself, he began to laugh. He pulled her down on top of him. "We'll talk about it." It began to look as if the second half of the voyage to Charleston might be as interesting as the first.

V

Michael Fallon left the large white single house he rented on Tradd Street and walked to his carriage with his head down. For once he didn't even pause to wonder if Decembers were getting colder in Charleston, or if he was just getting older. He had the same high cheekbones, hooked nose and icy blue eyes as Robert, his son, but years, wars, and tragedy had left their marks on his weathered face.

Unmindful of the chill wind whipping down the street toward the Ashley River, he climbed into the open carriage. "The Bridge," he said, and the green-and-white-liveried slave on the driver's perch started the horse.

As the carriage rolled down the street people waved, or motioned for Michael to stop for a word, but he saw none of them. His mind was wrapped around a letter that gave him the feel of a road with no turning back. If he took it. And if the facts of the letter were straight, he had no choice.

My Dear Mr. Fallon,

I take pen in hand to write you, and at the same time take advantage of our meetings last year in New York and Philadelphia. We seemed at that time to hold some ideas in common. Foremost among these was your opinion of Alexander Hamilton, our respected Inspector General of the Army. For this reason in particular do I write.

As you know, sir, it begins to seem that I am assured of being the Vice Presidential candidate for Mr. Jefferson in next year's election. I have made no secret of wanting this, nor of wishing to one day become President, and Mr. Jefferson now wants me because he needs New York in the election. And if the rich of New York heed Clinton and Livingston, I may say

41

without boasting that the common people of New York listen to me.

Of late, however, it has come to my attention that George Clinton, DeWitt Clinton, Robert Livingston, and others, in the south, who follow the republican path, have entered into close contacts with Hamilton himself. To have the leading Federalist closely touching some of the leading men of our party is more than worrisome.

I would think little of it were it not for one thing. Though it is known that Hamilton and I have no love for one another, it is less well known that Livingston and the brothers Clinton wish me no better than does Hamilton. Indeed, they are incensed greatly that one of them was not chosen to guarantee New York for Mr. Jefferson. Given their contact with Hamilton, I now fear that they will let their hatred of me, and more, of my receiving the nomination, lead them into doing harm to our party's cause. You know my reluctance to speak ill of anyone, but I do fear this.

I ask you, sir, not to aid me, but to try to thwart them. Who are the southerners whom Hamilton has touched? I do not know. One, at least, I do know, lives in Charleston. Discover for yourself what it is they plan. I am certain that once you do, you will see that you must oppose them.

I remain, sir,

> Your Most Humble and Obedient Servant,
>
> Aaron Burr

Aaron Burr. Though he'd not met the man above six times, Michael couldn't forget him. A small man, with a lively face and dark, magnetic eyes, he was a lawyer who championed the common people. He should have been a general, though, or a pirate. He was that full of energy, that hypnotic in personality. That was why some people distrusted him. It wasn't that he'd ever done anything to merit it. He simply frightened men with less electricity in them. He hadn't frightened Michael. In fact, Michael rather liked his frankness.

Hamilton was another story. He'd met that cold, arrogant bastard more often than he cared to. Bastard he was, not only by birth, but by actions. Hamilton hated his shortness, hated larger men, larger physically or otherwise. He seemed to want to sit on a throne so he could look down others. Indeed, he was as close to a royalist as it was possible to find in America. He disliked what he called "the common, vulgar herd," and he distrusted democracy. To Michael, who had bled for the Revolution before most men even knew there *was* a Revolution, that was enough reason to oppose him.

Michael had thought he'd left all that behind, the politics, the intrigues, the machinations, when Gabrielle, his wife, died. He'd left it for a quiet life where his only worries were fur prices on the Mississippi, the sailing times to China, and the rice crop from Tir Alainn. But to oppose Hamilton again, to oppose the Federalists again—it shouldn't be hard to find those men.

"The Bridge, Mr. Fallon, sir."

With a start Michael looked up at the warehouse at the foot of Carver's Bridge, a long wharf stretching into the Cooper River. The sign on the front said FALLON & SON. The rumble of barrels and crates being shifted on the wharf, the shouts of men hoisting bales out of ships, rivaled the noise of the street, with its cotton wagons clattering on the cobblestones. With Christmas close, peddlers with toys and gewgaws vied with hawkers of berries and popcorn for the attention of passersby.

"Thank you, Saul," Michael said. "Go on back to the house. I'll walk back later."

The driver tipped his tall hat, but Michael was already heading into the relative quiet of the warehouse. A bell rang as he entered, once, then again.

The bell of *Hussar,* he thought, his privateer during the Revolution. She'd burned when Charleston fell to the British, with little but her bell saved. Now it rang when a Fallon ship made harbor safely.

A one-armed gray-haired man in severe clothes came down the steps from the bell with a sheaf of papers in his hand. "Good morning, captain," he said.

"Good morning, Mr. Petrie. What ship's arrived?"

"The *Swift,* sir. Just crossed the bar. English spun goods and cutlery." He squinted at the sheaf of papers. He had spectacles, but refused to wear them. "*Catherine's Hope* is in the harbor. Morrison says he got his Madeira and port cheap enough, but the Portuguese in Brazil raised the price on coffee again."

"Damn. Well, make delivery at the prices we promised, but let them know we'll have to raise it in the future."

"Yes, sir. There's one other. The *Speedwell* tied up this morning. From the Baltic. Norwegian fur and spruce, iron stock and cloth from Germany, Danish porcelain, and some good smuggled French brandy. She's unloading now."

"Good. I'll take a look in a minute." He hesitated. "Petrie, do you still know men who can ask questions without being noticed at it?"

"Why, yes, captain." Petrie drew himself up; he looked surprised.

He could see Petrie was curious, but he intended to err on the side of caution. He told Petrie a little of what he was after, without mentioning Burr's name. "Now I'll take that look at the *Speedwell*. And tell me the latest news from New Orleans."

"Tensions seem to be higher, sir, but no one knows why, exactly. The Intendant talks against the right of deposit, but he still allows us to store our goods for reshipment. As for fur prices—"

Michael listened with only half an ear. He was still thinking about Burr and Hamilton as they walked through the dark warehouse, and once he reached the dock, his mind was on the ships. There was the *Speedwell*. Some of her spars had been swayed as booms for the unloading. Great ropes lowered crates and bales and huge bundles of timbers. Every time he saw the scene, a bolt of disbelief went through him. How could a penniless Irish farmboy rise to this? He'd come to America thirty-five years before, looking for a fresh start and hoping to someday own a farm. How had it all come to this? The last part of Petrie's report broke into his reverie. "What was that last again, Mr. Petrie?"

"I said Lopes, the man who manages the warehouse in New Orleans, reports that he spotted a Frenchman snooping about. He says the same man has been snooping at other warehouses, too. It's his opinion the fellow isn't a spy for pirates, but he doesn't know what else he can be. It's not important, sir. I was down to the gossip, so to speak."

"Did he say Frenchman, or French Creole?"

"His letter said Frenchman."

Michael nodded slowly. To Lopes, that meant someone *from* France, not a French resident of the city. His judgment was good, or he wouldn't be managing the Fallon warehouse. But why would a Frenchman be poking around warehouses in a Spanish colony?

"Petrie, get a letter off to Lopes today. Send it by courier, on the best horse we have. I want more information about this Frenchman." He saw Petrie's look, and chuckled. "I know, but my hunches are usually good ones."

Petrie nodded. "Yes, captain. He'll be gone before midday."

"Excuse me, please," came a thickly accented voice from the *Speedwell*'s gangway. "I am a stranger here. Could either of you give me directions?"

Michael looked up to see a fair young man. He was well above six feet, with a jutting jaw, dark blue eyes, and curly blonde hair. He had a stiff way of standing, but he smiled at them easily.

"Certainly," Michael said. "I'm Michael Fallon, and this is Donald Petrie. Where can we direct you?"

"Excuse me for not introducing myself. I am Karl Holtz." He met them at the foot of the gangplank, and they shook hands. "Would you be, sir, the same man who owns the ship on which I have arrived?"

Michael smiled. The young man's open manner was an amusing contrast to his stiff speech. "I am."

"Then perhaps, sir, you will direct me to a good banker. I have letters of credit from Leipzig. I wish to open an account here, and to purchase a house."

"Purchase," Petrie said. "Then your visit's a long one?"

"Oh, no," Holtz said. "It is not a visit. Perhaps I should explain. I come from a family which owns woolen and cotton mills in Saxony. I was much in the mills, but when my father died, they went to my older brother. It is the way, you understand."

"I do," Michael said. "It was once the way here, but we changed it."

"I have heard as much. A year ago, when my uncle died, he had no children, and so left his fortune where he would. To me he left enough that I might come to America and start my own mill."

"A mill!" Petrie said.

Holtz looked on in confusion while Michael stared, then spoke. "You'll have to forgive us, Mr. Holtz. We've milled our rice in South Carolina since before the Revolution, but I don't believe anyone has even thought of a cotton mill. You can sell raw cotton, but you can't sell rice in the husk."

"So," said Holtz with a smile, "there will be little competition for my mill. Yes, Mr. Fallon?"

"Yes, Mr. Holtz," Michael said. "I like your idea. Would you be my guest at dinner this afternoon?"

"I would be pleased, sir. The captain said that my bags could be held for me at the warehouse until I have lodgings."

"Certainly. Come along to my office. We can have a glass of wine while I write an introduction to Jacob Todd. He's a good banker and an honest man."

Michael was holding the warehouse door for Petrie and Holtz when Catherine, his daughter, appeared around the corner of the tall wooden building. She wore a simple-seeming dress of white that he knew from the modiste's bill was far from simple, and carried a matching parasol. Her mother, Gabrielle Fourrier, had had the same oval face and large, hazel eyes, but Catherine had inherited his own high cheekbones. She was exotically beautiful. Her lower lip was a trifle too full. Michael sighed. She was— he winced at the word—too sensual appearing for her own good. Even for Charleston she was extraordinary looking. In Boston she would never have escaped censure.

She picked her way toward Michael, the longshoremen ducking their heads respectfully as she passed. "Good morning, papa." Her smile brought an answering one to Petrie's usually stiff face. "I do hope my lace, at least, has arrived. Marie positively refuses to work with American dress goods."

The smile faded from Michael's face. "Imported," he growled. "Everyone assumes if it's not imported, it's no good. Damn it, are we independent, or are we still a colony?"

"Papa, you're beginning to sound like Robert. I vow, he should have been a Yankee."

There was a bite to her words that worried him. As a child she'd refused to accept Robert as even her half-brother. He'd hoped she would outgrow it, but at nineteen she was tenser than ever about the boy. No, not boy. The man. He was ten years older than her in age, and a hundred in wisdom.

"Child," he said, "that's no way to talk about your brother. As for your lace—" He broke off as she suddenly stiffened, angry color flaring in her cheeks.

"I am not accustomed to being stared at, papa."

Michael looked around in confusion. Holtz colored to his eyebrows. "I am sorry," the young German said miserably. "I did not mean to—" He took a deep breath and went on in a rush. "It is just that you are the most beautiful woman I have ever seen. No man can see a goddess without staring."

Catherine seemed stunned, caught halfway between preening under the compliments and upbraiding him for his rudeness.

Michael suppressed a smile. "Catherine, this is Mr. Karl Holtz, of Saxony. He's come to settle in Charleston. Mr. Holtz, my daughter, Catherine."

Holtz made a passable bow. "An honor, *fraulein*. I hope to have the same honor again soon."

A faint smile had begun to play around Catherine's lips. "Perhaps we shall meet again, Mr. Holtz," she said grandly, but not unkindly. "And now, papa, I must see to my lace."

"Of course, my dear," he said.

Petrie cleared his throat with a rumble. "If you don't mind sir, I'll show Miss Catherine where her packages are. And I *do* have some other work. Some *letters.*"

Michael nodded. Catherine took Petrie's arm, and swept away with as studied a job of ignoring Holtz as Michael had ever seen. Holtz stared after her.

"She is not married?" he said suddenly, a touch of worry in his voice.

"No, she isn't," Michael replied. "She'll marry the man she wants to marry. Arranged marriages are something else we've done away with."

"Of course—" His face went red again. "Forgive me, Mr. Fallon. I was presumptuous."

"It's all right," Michael said. "As I said, she'll marry the man she chooses. Whoever he is. Now come along and have that drink."

As he was leading the young man to his office, he

remembered when it was that *he* had been so stricken with a woman at first sight. Elizabeth Carver had consumed him like a flame. He forced the thought away angrily. His daughter was nothing like the woman who had married Justin Fourrier. Nothing.

Before the brief meeting with Holtz was over, Michael rewrote the introduction to Jacob Todd. He made it into a letter recommending Holtz and asking Todd to give him every help. He thought about the young Saxon as he walked back toward Tradd Street.

Holtz was a personable young man, and a man with ambition. It was seldom enough the two went together. The mill was a good idea, and he wasn't one of those Europeans who came to America with an idea and no money. He had enough to start without help. If he and Catherine *did* hit it off—

He strolled down the Bay—East Bay Street, they called it now; he never could remember—deep in thoughts of Karl and Catherine, of Catherine in particular. She was too self-willed for her own good. If only she would marry, have children. That would settle her down. Tall cotton wagons lumbered past him on the cobblestones, piled high with dingy white bales of the crop that had already replaced indigo in South Carolina's economy, and was fast challenging rice. Marriage would settle her down.

"Michael! Michael Fallon!"

He came to his surroundings, blinking. He was opposite Vendue Range, a short street leading to the river. A crowd was gathered in front of one of the platforms, set flush with the fronts of the buildings along the street where slaves were sold. A short, stout man with a red face was beckoning. Michael walked over to him.

"What is it, Arnaud?" he asked. Arnaud Beamer was a cotton planter, a slight acquaintance, and a huge bore. How such a fussy man, always on the lookout for others' wrongdoings, had managed to grow up in Charleston, was beyond his understanding.

"You can see for yourself what it is," Beamer huffed. "Just watch. They're bringing out another, now."

On the platform a weedy-looking auctioneer peered at a

sheaf of papers in his hand and called in a thin voice. "Lot One Hundred Thirty-Seven." A muscular black man, scowling with defiance and fear, was prodded onto the platform. He was manacled at wrists and ankles, and wore only a pair of ragged pants. Chevron-shaped ridges marched across his cheeks. "One prime field hand," the auctioneer went on. "Age, about twenty-six. Had the smallpox as a child. Born in Georgia. A little slow, so he don't speak much English that can be understood, but he's strong, and a willing worker. Do I have a bid of four hundred dollars for this prime field hand?"

"One hundred," someone called.

"Prime field hand," Beamer snorted. "Look at those scars on his face. Those are tribal markings. If he was born in Georgia, it's on the west coast of Africa. Can't speak much English, indeed."

Michael sighed as he studied the man on the platform. He had been smuggled in, that was sure. And it was men like Beamer who'd made the illegal slave trade profitable enough to exist. Part of the first rush to cotton had occurred because it took fewer slaves per acre to make a crop than rice did, and fewer slaves was something almost every planter wanted. It wasn't humanitarian feeling; it was economics. Slaves cost money to buy, and the northern factors who handled most of the South's trade already took enough of that. Many men with fine plantations found it hard to put hands on cash without getting an advance on their crops from the factor. Fewer slaves meant more cash, so any crop that needed fewer was welcome.

But there was much more land that would support cotton than would support rice. Men who planted cotton began to expand, and to expand they needed more slaves. Soon cotton planters owned more slaves than any rice planter ever had, and as mills in the North and in England demanded still more cotton, there was a need for still more slaves. It had been southerners who got the foreign slave trade stopped in the first place. Now they needed it; their need kept it going illegally.

"Two hundred dollars," the auctioneer called mournfully. "Gentlemen, that's insultingly low. This is a prime hand. Now, do I hear three hundred?"

"What do you intend to do?" Michael asked.

"It's got to be stopped," Beamer said. His pudgy lips

worked in and out. His indignation seemed to get the better of him. "Illegal slaves. Got to be stopped. Out in the open like this. Disgraceful. Oughtn't to be allowed."

"You could ask the Federal Customs to investigate."

Beamer stopped in mid-bluster. His voice took on a cautious tone, as if he was no longer sure he was dealing with someone who would be reasonable. "I, ah, I don't think I could do that, Fallon. After all, a man in my position has to, ah, be careful. I can't go carrying tales like common spies. Perhaps—"

"Yes, yes," Michael interrupted. He was tired of the man. In spite of his puritanical streak, Beamer only wanted the illegal sales hidden, not suppressed. To Michael it was a measure of just how far things had gone that today's sale of illegals was being held openly. "You do what you think is best, Arnaud. Now, if you'll excuse me?"

Michael turned away with a grimace. He wouldn't do anything. It would be a great deal of effort for very little effect. Today's sale could not have been held without some connivance from the Customs.

A familiar black face at the back of the crowd caught his eye, and he worked his way to it. Jeremiah, the eldest son of Daniel, his chief boatman, stood watching the platform closely, his leather carpenter's apron rolled and tucked under his arm. He had little of his father's looks. His mother, Callie, had given him his features, including the proud eyes that made him seem nearly as untamed as the cheek-scarred man being sold.

"Jeremiah," he called.

For a moment the black eyes that swung to him were empty of recognition or friendliness. Then they softened to mere wariness. Michael blamed his mother for that. She'd put her stamp on his mind as well as his face, and she had no trust of whites.

The boy came to stand in front of him, poised as if to dodge. He was going to be a slender man, Michael thought, and tall.

"Good afternoon, Mr. Fallon."

"Good afternoon, Jeremiah. Shouldn't you be at Millward's? He's not the man to like his apprentices being off and about."

"No, sir. He give me the day." A small grin flickered on his face. "He give me the day more than any of the rest get it."

"Does he, now?" Michael frowned thoughtfully. "Come along, lad. I have to see Mr. Millward. You walk with me. This is no place for you."

Jeremiah looked back at the platform—a woman had replaced the man—and quickly tore his eyes away. "No, sir. No, sir, I guess it ain't."

Millward's shop had a neat sign out front, THOMAS MILLWARD, FURNITURE MAKER, and a smell of shavings and wood stains. The walls were finely paneled, and highly polished furnishings were displayed on a well-waxed floor. The work was done in the rear, behind a partition. Millward himself was bluff and broad. He frowned worriedly as Michael entered with Jeremiah.

"I come back to leave my apron, Mr. Millward," Jeremiah called over his shoulder as he darted up the steps at the back of the shop. His sleeping quarters were in the loft above.

From the rear came the tapping of hammers, and boys' voices. Millward rubbed his hands on his shirt. "Ah, Mr. Fallon."

The man looked nervous, Michael thought. "How's the boy doing, now, Millward? Does he still show an eye?"

"Uh, yes, Mr. Fallon, he does. About the boy, though—"

"I'd be thinking you'd keep him hard at work, then. If he's the eye for furniture, he's still needing the practice of it, now."

The bigger man shifted, and wiped his hands again. Michael kept his tone pleasant, but a touch of iron crept in. "Or is it that after only a year he's better than boys who've been with you four and five years? Is that why you give him the day so often, and keep the rest at work? But that doesn't make sense, does it?"

Millward's eyes flickered around the shop, resting now on a wardrobe, then on a sideboard. He glanced to the back of the shop, and then, as if afraid the apprentices behind the partition might hear, stepped closer and lowered his voice. "Mr. Fallon, you know, I really have more apprentices than I need. More than I have work for. I can't afford—"

"You told me all that a year ago. That's why I paid you one hundred dollars to take on Jeremiah. That's why I give you a sum to cover his room and board. Now tell me again what you can't afford."

"Mr. Fallon—sir—I've had complaints, sir. From my customers. From other craftsmen."

"What kind of complaints?" Michael asked sharply.

"The other cabinetmakers don't like me apprenticing a freedman when there are white lads about. They say we've already enough competition from plantation-trained blacks, without we train them ourselves. To tell the truth, I see their point. And the finer sort of people, sir. Why I haven't sold a stick to any family from Santo Domingo since Jeremiah came here. And they favored me more than any other, before. But after seeing their friends and relatives, sir, butchered in a slave rising, then come to me and see a *free* black as my apprentice—well, sir, how else can they feel?"

"Maybe they've cause for their feelings," Michael said, "but I don't see that you've suffered for it." He looked pointedly around the shop, at the tables and desks, sideboards and highboys, before fixing Millward with his gaze. "Would you be wanting to know what it is you *can't* afford? You can't afford to go back on your deal with me. Do you think getting rid of Jeremiah would bring back the French? You're marked in their minds already. But suppose I withdrew my custom from you? Suppose I just let it be known that I can no longer, in good conscience, buy anything from you?"

"Sir!"

"How much business would you lose then? How many men who know me would go elsewhere?"

Millward seemed to sink in on himself. His voice was almost a whisper. "Sir, they'd think I was a thief, or—God knows what they'd think. I'd lose everything."

"Then you'd better be standing by the deal you made with me. You said the lad could be a master craftsman. I expect you to make him such." Jeremiah came running down the stairs, and Michael lowered his voice. "Not another word of this, Millward."

"Yes, sir," Millward said dully.

Michael nodded. "Jeremiah, where are you going? If it's my way, I'll walk along with you."

The boy's face closed. "I be going to see a friend, sir. Down the Bay.''

"Then I'll keep you company. Come along, now.'' At the door, Michael took a last look back. Millward was still standing slumped in the middle of his shop.

The incident bothered Michael as he set off with Jeremiah. It took him a while to realize why. He'd bullied the man. No matter that he'd deserved it, he'd used his position to frighten Millward. He'd used Michael Fallon the merchant planter to face Millward, not Michael Fallon the man. For the first time he realized just how much he *had* changed in thirty-five years. He wondered if he'd ever again be able to think of himself as an Irish farmboy.

Jeremiah, fidgeting at Michael's silence, had begun to chatter. Now his words caught Michael's ear. "What was that, Jeremiah?''

"I said he won the East Bay Lottery, sir, and bought hisself free.''

"I heard about that. Name's Vesey, isn't it?''

"Yes, sir. Denmark Vesey. He a carpenter. He work on houses and ships and such.''

Michael realized they were in one of the small alleys that had sprung up below the Exchange Building with the expansion of the warehouses there. "Where is this Vesey's place, Jeremiah? This is a rough area for a boy alone.''

"Over there, Mr. Fallon.'' Jeremiah pointed to a one-story shop, little wider than the doorway in front, that had obviously been built between two buildings already there. "He going to use the rest of his money to buy a house. Can't afford no better shop.'' He paused awkwardly. "Sir, could I introduce him to you?''

Michael was surprised, but he nodded. "Certainly. I'd be glad to meet him, if you want.''

A real smile—the first Michael had seen in a long time—flashed across Jeremiah's face. "Oh, yes, sir!'' He darted into the shop, shouting, "Denmark! Where you be?''

Michael followed. The shop was dark and narrow. It had the same smells as Millward's, wood shavings and resin, but instead of furniture there were only a few sawhorses standing against one wall. A half-dozen adzes and saws hung on pegs, and a battered toolchest sat on the sawdust-strewn floor.

"Mr. Fallon," Jeremiah said, appearing out of the shadows in the back, "this is Denmark Vesey." A tall, muscular man, above thirty, followed him.

Michael barely contained his surprise. Except for the tight black curls on his head, Vesey could have passed for white. People born in Virginia or the Carolinas were used to such things. Michael, after all his years there, was not.

Vesey stood with his hands clasped in front of him, head down, but the eyes that watched Michael were far from servile. "I am honored to meet you, Mr. Fallon, sir. Jeremiah has spoken of you often." The deep voice was a second shock, cultured, educated.

"He's spoken well, I hope," Michael said. "And I hope you're a good friend to him. There are things around here a boy his age shouldn't get into. Gambling. Drinking. Worse."

"I try to show him the right way to be." Vesey flashed a smile of real affection at Jeremiah, but there seemed to be something mocking in his tone.

"Yes," Michael said slowly. There was no reason for Vesey to mock him. "I'll be going now, Jeremiah. I have much to do. You take care, and work hard for Mr. Millward."

"Work hard for Mr. Millward," Vesey mocked bitterly as Michael disappeared up the street.

"He a good man," Jeremiah insisted.

"Good man? How many slaves does he own?"

"Well, he be good to me, anyway."

Vesey deliberately broadened and thickened his voice. "Boy, white folks is always good to they pets." He turned away and busied himself with makework in his toolchest.

Jeremiah stood looking at the floor. Occasionally he peeked hopelessly at Vesey's back. He didn't want the man to turn away from him. "Denmark," he said after a while. "Denmark, I decided."

"Decided what, boy?"

"My name." He stood as straight as he could. "I—I'm Jeremiah Carpenter, now."

Vesey grinned over his shoulder. "Carpenter, huh? You're a furniture maker, or will be, not a carpenter. How did you set on that one?"

Jeremiah shifted uncomfortably. "I don't know. I just—what be wrong with it?"

"Not a thing. It's a man's name." His voice became intense, and he gripped Jeremiah's arm. "Remember, boy, when you only have one name, you're nothing. One name is a dog's name. Jeremiah is just one step from Mr. Fallon's Jerry. But Jeremiah Carpenter is a man's name."

"I understand, Denmark." His arm hurt under Vesey's grip, but he didn't let the pain show. "I be Jeremiah Carpenter, now."

Vesey studied him hard, till Jeremiah thought the man's eyes would bore holes in his thoughts, then nodded. He released his grip, and Jeremiah tried to rub his arm unobtrusively.

"All right, boy. I have something back here for you."

"Is it a book?" Jeremiah asked eagerly. "You got another book?"

"No, it's not a book. It's something better." He took an oilskin packet, slit on one side, from his toolchest, and pulled a pamphlet from it. "Here, boy. This came on a ship from Philadelphia. You read it yourself, then you read it to some more people, or give it to somebody who can read himself. Just don't let any whites see it."

Jeremiah read slowly, his lips moving, until he came to a word he didn't understand. "Denmakr, what do a-bo-li-tion mean?"

"It mean there aren't going to be any more slaves." Vesey said. "Aren't going to be any more slaves."

VI

Thomas Martin ignored the November cold and drew a careful bead on the deer foraging among the snow patches. He was tall and lanky, with large hands, but he handled the rifle surely. Just as he squeezed the trigger, a branch behind him snapped. As the rifle roared, the deer leaped, staggered, and darted into a stand of Judas trees. He could see a red splotch on the snow where the deer had been.

"Well, Sam," he drawled, "we got us a wounded deer."

The Houston boy, still three months shy of his seventh birthday, stared at the ground, scuffing a patch of snow clear with his foot. "I'm sorry, Thomas. I didn't think it'd break. Honest! I was just holding on." His face twisted as if he were trying hard not to cry, he looked up at Martin. "What do we do now?"

"I don't rightly know what you do in Virginia, Sam, but in Tennessee we don't let wounded animals run off to die. It isn't right, and besides, it's wasteful."

"You going to track him?"

"In a little bit." He began reloading. Despite his farmer's homespun, he had a knife, a tomahawk and a brace of pistols in his belt. After three years working cotton with his father, the habits of three trips to the Western Lands, one all the way to the Great Mountains, remained. "First we give him time to stop running," he said. "He'll do that sooner if we're not chasing. Time we find him, he'll be too weak to run far or fast."

Sam nodded sagely, taking it. "Then you've time to tell me again. About Mexico," he announced.

Thomas hid a smile, checking his priming. "What about it, boy?"

"The missions," the boy said eagerly, "and the priests in the long robes and the soldiers with their lances and the Indians, the Comanches, and—"

"Hold on there, boy. Who's going to tell this? You just hold your horses, and I'll see if I can remember where to start." He grinned as the boy shut his mouth firmly. Sam liked the stories about Mexico, that was a fact. When he went back home to Virginia, his folks would likely think them a pack of tall tales. "Well, Sam, I wasn't more than fifteen when I heard that Captain Benjamin St. Simon and Mr. Julian Raiford were going to Mexico. They were taking a trading party down through what the Spanish call Bexar, and some folks call Texas, to Mexico. I'd never been more than fifty miles from pa's farm, and the thought of going all that way just made my feet itch for it."

Something floundered in the brush and fell heavily.

"Thomas?"

He slapped a hand over the boy's mouth. People were beginning to think of this end of Tennessee as civilized, but it wasn't that far to the Indian lands. And there were white men about who were worse than any Indian. He pulled Sam behind a tree and motioned him to stay there. With a cupped hand to shield the sound, he cocked his rifle. Whatever it was had gotten up and was coming closer.

Suddenly a figure lurched through the brush and fell. For a moment Thomas froze. Then he was running. It was his sister. "Sary! Sary, girl, what's the matter?"

He dropped to the ground beside her, rolled her over gently. She uttered a choked scream and tried to struggle loose. He caught her wrists to keep from being clawed.

"Sary! It's me, Thomas! It's Thomas!"

"Thomas?" she said hesitantly. Suddenly she buried her head against his chest, whimpering in a way that made his hackles rise.

An ugly purple knot was growing on her temple, and one of her eyes was blacked. A trickle of blood on her temple, and one of her eyes was blacked. A trickle of blood ran from the corner of her mouth. Her dress was torn and rumpled, as if it had been ripped from her, then hurriedly put back on. He forced the thought away. She was seventeen, but he could never think of her as nearly grown. In his mind she was still the toddler who'd trailed about the farmyard after him.

"It must have been a bear," Sam said breathlessly.

"Shut up," Thomas said. The harshness of his own voice surprised him. "I'm sorry, boy, but be quiet." He swallowed. "Sary, tell me. Tell me."

Her hold on his arms eased, and he realized for the first time that she'd been gripping him hard enough to hurt. "I was taking some honey to old Mrs. Hodges. Mama asked me to. She likes honey, Mrs. Hodges does, and since Mr. Hodges died—" She took a deep shuddering breath. "They came riding up on me while I was crossing Parson's Hill. Samuel Applegate, and his brother Ben, and William Cole." Her voice rose to the edge of hysteria. "They—oh, God, they hurt me, Thomas. They—"

He pulled her head tighter against him. "It's all right now. It's all right, Sary." He held her, rocking back and forth, crooning meaningless sounds. Bit by bit her breathing lost its panic. "Sam," he said softly, "can you do a man's load of work for me?"

Sam tried to stand straighter. "I can do it, Thomas."

"Good. Then you see that Sary gets home." He pulled her to her feet. She came unresisting. The blank look in her eyes frightened him. "Take her hand, Sam. Get her to mama, then you tell mama she was hurt. Hurry."

"I can do it, Thomas." Sam took her hand and started in the direction of the Martin farm. She followed, stumbling, eyes focused on nothing. "I'll do it," Sam called back over his shoulder.

Carefully, with almost exaggerated precision, Thomas saw to his rifle and pistols. Then he set off in the long, ground-covering lope he had learned in the west. Samuel Applegate. Ben Applegate. William Cole.

He crossed the village road under the noses of a wagon team, and never heard the farmer's curses chasing after him. He crossed a corner of the Rogers farm, where Tim Rogers and his sons were digging out stumps, clearing more land for cotton. He saw them, vaguely.

And then he was trotting up the drive of the Applegate plantation, toward the white, three-story house with its wide verandas. He remembered when it had been the Applegate farm, when the Applegates had worked like the Martins and the Rogerses, every man and woman working to plant and harvest a crop of cotton. Then the Applegates suddenly had money. From where, no one knew, though it came at the same time William Cole had. The farmhouse was replaced with this plantation house five times as big. Fifty slaves appeared to work the cotton, and a half-dozen more for the house.

Thomas trotted steadily up the steps of the big house. He pounded the door twice.

"Yes, sir?" The slave stopped at the sight of the gun.

Martin pushed the man aside. "Be quiet, and you won't be hurt. Where's your master? Where's Applegate?"

The slave pointed silently to a door down the hall, then shrank against the wall.

Thomas walked down the hall softly. Cocking his rifle, he pushed open the door and stepped in.

All three men he sought sat around a table, silver cups in hand and a bowl on the table. Cole had a pipe in his teeth, his usual sneer on his long sallow face. A laugh froze on Ben's wide red face, and sick fear seeped into his eyes. Samuel, too broad and burly for his fine clothes, had scratches down both cheeks. His cup fell, splashing wine punch across the table. "It was her fault," he screamed. "She asked for it!"

"God damn it all to hell!" Cole shouted, and clawed a pistol from under his coat. Thomas' rifle ball took him in the head, knocking him backwards out of the chair.

Thomas dropped the rifle, pulling his pistols, as the others surged to their feet. Guns appeared in their hands, but he took the extra tenth-second to be sure. His first shot caught Samuel in the chest. He smiled as the man screamed and fell. Something struck him a fearful blow in the side, and he realized he'd been hit. He hurried his shot at Ben, but the big man left his feet in a low dive at him, and the shot hit only wall.

They went down, rolling on the floor, kicking, biting, gouging. Ben fought from desperation, but Thomas fought from cold rage. He managed to free one hand long enough to get to his knife, and Ben rolled away screaming, blood flowing from a long slash across his face. Before the other could move further, Thomas slammed the blade through his ribs to the heart.

A scrambling noise caught his ear. He looked up to see Samuel, his shirt bloody, trying to climb out the window. Thomas didn't even realize he'd moved, but suddenly his tomahawk handle bloomed between Applegate's shoulders. For a long moment the rapist clawed at the window, still trying to drag himself through. Then he fell inside the room.

Thomas staggered to his feet, the blood rage still on him. He tugged his knife from Ben Applegate's chest and coldly cut the throat of each man.

He could hear murmured voices and shuffled feet in the hall, and more voices through the window. The blood trickling down his side came from more than a scratch, but the ball had gone on through. There'd be no need for probing. Hastily he reloaded his rifle and pistols. Slowly, with the rifle barrel, he opened the hall door.

The house slaves, clustered at the foot of the stairs, drew back as he stepped into the hall. Cordelia Applegate, Samuel's wife, showed no fear at all.

She was a tall woman, beautiful, with pale skin, fiery red hair, and green eyes. She wore a dress of shimmering black, cut to show more of her breasts than any dress he'd ever seen. And she was watching him as coolly, as if he'd come begging for a handout.

"Mrs. Applegate," he began.

Abruptly she turned to face the slaves. "Go outside and stay there till I send for you. Pomp, don't let anyone in. Tell them there's been an accident, but they're to stay outside. Now go." She clapped her hands, and the servants began to file out.

Thomas opened his mouth, then closed it again. "Ma'am, I won't hurt you. I'll just go."

She started toward the door behind him. He put out a hand to stop her, but she brushed past. Calmly she surveyed the room, then turned her head toward him. "You certainly meant to kill them, didn't you?" Her eyes were level and unblinking.

He stared at her. Could she have gone mad with the shock? "Mrs. Applegate, I reckon I ought to send one of your women in."

"I'm not mad, Mr. Martin." Her smile made the hair on his

neck bristle. "You see, I've been planning to kill those three for over a year."

He took a step toward the door. "Uh, yes, ma'am."

She didn't seem to notice. She sneered at the three bodies through the door. "Sam wasn't much of a man, even before William Cole showed up with his story of a land pirate's cache. I'll wager no one ever suspected this plantation was started with gold stolen on the Natchez Trace. There was murder done for it. After that, he was no kind of man at all. And his brother was worse, as bad as Cole. For freeing me from them, I will give you one hour, while I have the vapors, as a proper lady should at such a scene. Then I regret I will have to identify you. Good luck, Mr. Martin."

He watched her make her way regally up the stairs, his mouth open. "Christ," he muttered.

He eased open the front door and peered out. The house servants were huddled together under an oak a hundred feet from the house. Three white men stood nearby, arguing among themselves, as if undecided about what to do. He didn't know any of them. Perhaps he actually had that hour Mrs. Applegate had promised.

The thought of her sent a shiver through him. As he sauntered down the drive, the three men frowned at him, but none of them came after him. When he was out of sight, he began to run. He stopped among the trees above his father's farm. The wound in his side burned, but the bleeding had stopped. He studied the house, a single rambling story with a broad porch. Beyond lay the snow-patched forty acres they'd broken their backs over the past three years, putting in cotton for a cash crop, and the gardens that put vegetables on the table. There were two horses tied out front; one his father's bay, the other a gray he didn't know. After a moment he went on down.

His father was sitting in a straight chair on the porch, a clay pipe in his fist. The old man's weathered face was stoic, but he ran a worried eye over Thomas. "You all right, son?"

"I'm fine, pa." He shifted his coat to make sure the blood on his shirt was covered. "How's Sary?"

"She's with your mama," he said shortly.

Thomas let it go. He jerked his head toward the gray.

"Whose horse?"

"Mine," said a hawk-faced, graying man from the door. The cut of his long black coat was too fine for a farmer, and his eye had a permanent fierceness about it.

"This is Andy Jackson," his father said. "He's a judge on the Superior Court. I've known him near twenty years. You can trust him."

"Mr. Jackson," Thomas acknowledged. A judge, he thought. The only person who could be worse was the sheriff himself. "Pa, I have to talk to you. Alone, if Mr. Jackson doesn't mind."

"He knows, Thomas," his father said.

Jackson nodded. "I assume you've done what had to be done."

"They're dead, if that's what you mean."

"I figured that," Jackson said drily, "or you wouldn't be standing here. Now, did they have weapons?"

"Of course they did. Pa, what's this all about?"

"I'm trying to help you and your pa," Jackson answered instead. "Particularly your pa. Like he said, we go back a long way together. You're lucky I was passing through."

"I still don't under—"

"If you'll hold still, I'll tell you. I'm a judge, or didn't that sink in? I'll convene a court as soon as I can get twelve men for a jury, and under the circumstances I can guarantee you'll walk out a free man."

"Under the circumstances," Thomas said softly. He shook his head. "It won't work. It won't work, pa. Three on one, weapons or not, it all boils down to me killing them in Applegate's own house. Folks are going to ask why."

"Thomas," his father began.

"If I run, though, they'll never guess the reason." He shook his head. "Folks can be pretty mean to a girl who's been—I mean, some folks would act like it was her fault. But I can pull the dogs off the scent."

His father nodded slowly, and walked down the porch to look out at the bleak fields. "Don't seem to be much fairness or rightness, anymore. A poor man kills himself trying to make a living, and rich folk with their slaves . . . . " He sighed. "I expect you've got the right of it, Thomas. I don't like it, but I expect you've got the right of it.''

It'll change, one day,'' Jackson said. ''But in the meantime, your son *is* right. Thomas, I'd like to shake your hand.''

Confused, Thomas took the offered hand. It was surprisingly hard for a judge's. ''I don't understand, Mr. Jackson.''

''There aren't many men of honor left in the world.'' Abruptly Jackson's grip tightened, and his voice grew hard. ''You realize this will make it murder, heinous and foul. Three men butchered, the sanctity of the home violated. If you're caught, you may hang before anyone even thinks of a trial.''

Thomas swallowed. ''I know.''

Jackson studied him, then nodded. ''All right, then. Where will you go?''

''West, I suppose.''

''No,'' the other snapped. ''Your pa's told me of your trips to the Western Lands. It's a fact known about you. That's where you'll be expected to run. You must head East, instead.''

''East! The cities? What do I know about the East? At least to the West I can make a living.''

''You know cotton,'' his father said slowly. ''You've done a sight of reading and studying on it. Those big plantations back East, the owners don't run them themselves. They hire men.''

''He'll need references,'' Jackson said. Quickly he untied a lap desk from behind his saddle and sat down with it open across his knees. He dipped a quill. ''You can write one in a moment, Mr. Martin. He'll need two. Now, what name will you use? They'll be looking for Thomas Martin.''

''Martin. Martin Caine.''

Jackson wrote hurriedly. ''You didn't kill your brother, but rather for your sister. Still, it will do.''

''You'll need a horse,'' his father said suddenly. ''I suppose I knew when I saddled Wing you'd be going.''

''Going!'' The word was a gasp. Thomas' mother clutched her apron with both hands as she came onto the porch. The usual twinkle was gone from her gray eyes, and for the first time he realized her face was lined. ''Judge Jackson and your pa, they said you'd go free.''

Thomas took one of her workworn hands. ''It wouldn't be

good for Sary. You can see that, can't you?''

For a time she was silent. Then she looked him in the eye. "I always hoped I'd get to watch your babies. This ain't right, Henry Martin. It ain't right, Judge." Suddenly she swallowed and turned away. Her voice was husky. "You take care of yourself, son." She disappeared into the house, and he thought he heard a sob as she went.

Jackson cleared his throat. When Thomas turned, the judge held out two folded sheets. "These say Martin Caine oversaw cotton for me, and for your pa. They should be enough to gain you employment." He frowned at the sky. "It may snow by nightfall. I wouldn't wait—Mr. Caine."

Thomas took the letters, and untied Wing's reins. With one foot in the stirrup he stopped, staring across the saddle toward the cotton field. "Goodbye, pa. Tell ma—oh, hell." He swung into the saddle and rode out, heading West. In the night, after he'd left a trail, he'd turn back to the East.

VII

Neither the chatter of her slender black abigail, sewing on a footstool by the fire, nor the book open on her lap had any interest for Catherine Fallon. *Castle Oliandro* might be all the rage in London, but it seemed to Catherine that most of the heroine's problems were caused by her own stupidity. Her large hazel eyes had a dreaming look as her thoughts drifted to the balls and dances of the coming Christmas season. She'd wear out a pair of slippers a night, beginning that very evening at the Manigaults'.

Something in the serving woman's talk caught her ear. "What was that, Mary?"

"Why, it's Mr. Cheves, Miss Catherine," the abigail said. "He done brought in three horses from England, for the racing in February. Folks say—"

"Not Langdon. There was something else. Before."

"Only Mr. Robert. His ship get in this morning. It must be tied up to the Bridge, by now." Mary glanced at Catherine out of the corner of her eye and took a deep breath. "Miss Catherine, you shouldn't brush over Mr. Cheves so light. He a fine gentleman, and it high time you think about getting married. Young lady get to twenty without getting married, she done let herself sit on the shelf too long. You—"

Catherine didn't bother to shush the familiar harangue. She didn't even hear it. Robert was back. She hadn't exactly hoped his ship would sink, but there had been pleasant daydreams where he never came back. He had no right to be in Charleston, forcing himself on her father. He had no right to look like a young version of her father, to be so handsome. He was a bastard. He should be marked by it. A hunchback, or a clubfoot, perhaps. Instead he managed to inveigle his way into

65

the best homes. Girls who should know better flocked around him.

She shut the book with a loud thump. "Tell Saul I want the carriage. I'll be going to the Bridge." Mary stared at her, open-mouthed, and that somehow irritated her beyond reason. "Well? Are you going? Or must I stifle indoors all day?"

The abigail set down her sewing with a sigh. "I'm going. Mighty cold out there for driving, but I'm going." She stumped out the drawing-room door, her mutterings fading down the stairs.

Catherine fingered her dress, frowning. The sprigged silk would do. It was, after all, merely a ride for the air.

As the carriage turned onto the cobblestones of East Bay Street, Catherine pulled her shawl close against the wind off the river. Saul, on his high driver's perch, and Mary kept their own silence. There was noise to spare from orange sellers and roast-chestnut vendors, and peddlers of a dozen Christmas gewgaws, but none of it impinged on Catherine. Her mind was on Robert, and the effect his arrival would have on her Christmas.

There was no doubt he'd attend most of the balls and dances. He liked the gaiety. Her mouth twisted. And the attention the women paid. Well, she wasn't going to let him spoil her fun. In fact, she was going to be around him as little as possible.

There were levees and at-homes in the afternoons as well as balls at night. And Langdon wasn't the only one who wanted her company for carriage rides of an afternoon. There were the Pinckney boys, and Thomas Howe, and Louis Manigault, and Karl Holtz. Most particularly Karl Holtz. The tall Saxon's almost doglike devotion was a source of constant amusement to her. He was so stiffly formal, and at the same time so—worshipful was the only word—that she couldn't help but he entertained.

"Mary, did Mr. Holtz leave his card this morning?"

"Why, yes, ma'am. I told you that. He say it be his pleasure for you to go riding in his carriage this evening."

"Hush, Mary, and let me think." She buried her chin in her hand, ignoring Mary's protest that that was no way for a lady to sit in public. If she waited too long, Karl would be about other business. A note from the Bridge *might* reach him in time.

Just then a cotton wain lumbered in front of them. Down the alley it had come from, a group of young blacks, teenaged boys, huddled by some stacked crates. And the one they were all listening to was Jeremiah. He could carry a message.

"Jeremiah," she called.

"Lord, Miss Catherine!" Mary hissed, "don't you go shouting in public!"

"Hush up, Mary. Saul, stop the carriage. Jeremiah, come here!"

At the first mention of his name Jeremiah had stared at her, mouth open and eyes wide. At the second he turned and ran, his listeners scattering like quail. In seconds not one was in sight. She peered after them in consternation.

"What was that about? He looked frightened."

"I don't know, ma'am," Mary intoned flatly.

Catherine looked at her sharply, but all she got back was a blank, impassive gaze. If she didn't know better, she'd think Mary was keeping something from her. In any case, she had more important things to worry about. Since Jeremiah wouldn't be carrying her note, it was all the more important for her to reach the Bridge quickly.

"Saul, drive on. The Bridge, and quickly."

She sat back as the horses started off again, studying Mary. The black woman endured the gaze quietly, neither acknowledging nor ignoring it. Mary had been with her since she was little more than an infant, yet she realized that she knew little of the woman. She didn't even know how old Mary was. Thirty? Forty? Not older, surely. And what went on behind that face? Not the smiling, chattering face she saw every day, but the carved ebon face she saw now. *Did* Mary know something about what Jeremiah was doing? Was it something she shouldn't know about, something wrong?

"The Bridge, Miss Catherine," Saul said, and Catherine gave a start. The carriage had stopped.

"Thank you, Saul. Come along, Mary." She started toward the warehouse with the black woman at her heels. She would ask her father to look into Jeremiah's doings.

As she put a hand to the door of her father's reception room, she paused. A softly French-accented woman's voice was drifting through.

"Robert," the voice caressed, "you have not told me you are so wealthy. Why do you let me think you own only the ship we came on?"

"Because, Louise," Robert answered, sounding amused, "I'm not wealthy. My father is. I own *Osprey,* and part interests in three other vessels. That's hardly wealth."

Catherine pushed the door the rest of the way open. "And you won't get any of *my* father's money, Robert. I'll see to that. Somehow."

Robert and the woman—Louise, he had said—were standing in the center of the room, cloaked as if they'd just come in. She was pretty, Catherine admitted grudgingly, but she'd bet she played on her tiny size, acting the child with men. Scornfully she turned her attention back to Robert. He watched her warily.

"I hope you're not intending to make trouble," he said.

"Trouble?" she asked gaily. "Why should I make trouble for my father's byblow? He did tell you he was a bastard, didn't he—Louise?"

Robert's face darkened, but Louise spoke first. "Ah, child. Have you had your tonic yet today? You must be, how do you say, colicky."

Catherine's smile froze. Why, the little snit couldn't be a year older than she. "Aren't you at least going to fetch me a glass of wine, Robert? Or have you become too interested in stealing French children?"

"Catherine," he began warningly, then broke off in a mutter. "All right. You'll get your wine. Just—Christ, just keep a civil tongue in your head."

He shrugged off his cloak and tossed it on a couch as he headed for the wine cabinet against the outside wall. He looked out of the windows at the traffic on East Bay; from the way he stood, Catherine thought he was longing to be out there. Ridiculous, she thought, turning toward Louisa.

The French girl had let her cloak slide to the floor. Her blue silk was cut revealingly, proving she was no child. A glitter in her eyes, she sauntered dangerously towards Catherine.

"In my country, there is a custom with unruly children," she said. She held up one hand, flat. "The hand, so, is applied across the *fesses*." Catherine gasped. She could feel the red flooding across her face. "If you anger me just a little bit more, I will myself administer it."

"Why you—you threaten me? I'll—" With a growl, her fingers curling into claws, she took a step toward Louise. Only to find that something was holding her back.

"God's bones, Catherine," Robert snapped, "come to your senses! Do you think you're some tavern wench?"

She stared at him blindly. "Come to *my* senses?" she hissed. "She threatened me!"

"And I'll be doubly damned if you didn't deserve it," he said. "God, girl, you were slashing and cutting like a harpy." He drew a ragged breath, and she realized he was having difficulty containing his own anger. "Now. I'll do the introductions, and we'll start over. Louise, this is my half-sister, Catherine Fallon. Catherine, Louise de Char—"

With all her strength Catherine slapped him across the mouth. In the shock of it he released her, and she darted out the door.

Mary, waiting just outside, scurried after her into the street. "Miss Catherine! What's the matter? Are you all right, Miss Catherine?"

"Home," Catherine snapped, falling back into her seat. Saul took one look at her face, suffused with rage, and the carriage lurched into motion.

Mary half fell to a seat beside Catherine. "Are you all right, Miss Catherine?"

Catherine let her eyes close. "I have a monstrous headache."

"I'll make you a nice posset when we gets home," Mary crooned. Her fingers began to work gently at Catherine's temples. "You lie down and forget about that Manigault ball tonight. You can miss one night's dancing."

"I will not," she answered fiercely. "I will dance at the Manigaults. And I will ride with Mr. Holtz. I want a note taken to him the minute we get home. You understand? The minute!" She slumped back in her seat. Damn the man! How did he always manage to rouse such anger in her? God rot his eyes!

Through the window Robert watched the carriage roll away, swallowed up in the stream of cotton wains and carter's wagons. He rubbed his mouth reflectively. He'd never seen her so violent before.

"She is your sister?" Louise asked quietly.

"Half-sister."

"So!"

He looked at her her his shoulder, and she returned his look levelly. "What's that supposed to mean?"

"She is very—emotional."

He frowned at the street outside. "She is that," he said. "Louise, would you mind waiting here a few minutes? I have to speak to my father. Then we can see about a house for you."

She gave a very Gallic shrug. "So long as you remember the house, I am content to wait."

When he opened the door to his father's office, Michael rose from behind his desk a broad smile deepening the lines in his face. "Robert! Come in, man. Come in. I knew *Osprey* was in, but it completely escaped me that you must be docked by now. The work, lad. The work. Sit down. Madeira?"

"Thank you." He settled into a chair and took the proffered glass. "If it piles up too much, let Petrie handle some of it."

"Ah, it's too much fun is the thing of it," Michael laughed. "New England rum for Sweden, and Swedish iron for Pennsylvania. Coffee from Brazil. Cocoa and sugar from the West Indies. And look here." He turned to a large globe by the wall, one hand spinning it, the other tracing routes as he spoke. "I'm sending the *Catherine* around the Horn to here, north of Mexico. A place called Oregon. They trade for furs there, then across the Pacific to China."

"China!"

"Yes, China. If those damned New Englanders can do it, so can I. Porcelain and silk, ivory and spices. And speaking of spices, the *Trueheart* ought to be outbound by now from Sumatra with a load of pepper."

Robert held up a hand. "Enough. It's too much for one sitting. And besides, I've news that's not so good. Some time next year the French are taking back Louisiana."

Michael's lips pursed for a whistle, but no sound came out. He sank back into his chair. "Are you certain?"

"I'm certain." Quickly he explained about the Spaniard in Rhodes.

"He could have been lying. Bragging to make himself seem important."

"He was too drunk to lie. And he just threw out the part about the treaty. I think he was just what he said he was, one of Godoy's intimates who got into trouble Godoy couldn't get him out of."

Michael laughed mirthlessly. "Lopes reported a Frenchman around the warehouse in New Orleans, but I never expected this. Damn. And not a chance the French will let us keep using the port."

"Just how much do we lose if they do cut us off from New Orleans?"

"Oh, they will," Michael snorted. "We're at war, remember, or as good as. Lose? With beaver pelts selling the way they are, maybe a third of our business. Maybe more."

"A third! I didn't know we were in that heavily."

"You've not shown much interest, lad, but we're bidding to become one of the biggest fur dealers out of New Orleans. Or we were. It won't finish us, Robert, but it won't help, either." He squeezed his eyes shut and pressed the heels of his hands into them. "God's teeth. If it's not one thing, it's another. I just found out Cruz sold a thousand stands of muskets to the Spanish Quartermaster General in Caracas."

"Cruz? I thought he wanted to start a revolution. The George Washington of Spanish America. Isn't that what he said he'd be?"

"That's what he said, but it was good English muskets *I* sold him at cost for that purpose that he sold to the Spanish. And then there's Burr. Lord, I'm getting too old for all of this."

"Aaron Burr? What about him?"

"Nothing. A small thing compared to your news. Listen, Robert. I think we must close down the warehouse, clean it out. Then, instead of sending a Fallon ship to load our furs, we ship on whatever's available, whenever a consignment comes downriver."

"That cuts the profit down considerably. Still, I suppose

there's nothing else to do, until we're sure.''

"Damnation, no, there's nothing else to do. And it's still better than having a full warehouse, and maybe a ship, seized.'' Michael slammed a hand flat on his desk. "Damn it, it's not right. We can trade the length of the Mississippi in American water, but we can't get in or out the mouth without permission from the Spanish, or the French, or God knows who. New Orleans should be ours. The United States ought to be everything clear to the Mississippi.''

Robert smiled. He'd heard this before. "Including Florida?''

Michael laughed and sat back. "Well, I admit I can't see much use for Florida. But the rest of it should be ours. Now, bucko, enough of this folderol. We've a day or two to decide what to do, and New Orleans will no doubt settle itself. Will you dine with me this evening?''

"I'd be pleased to,'' Robert said. He finished his wine and got to his feet. "For now, though, I must see about renting a house. I acquired a—friend, this trip.''

"A friend, is it?'' Michael grinned. "Well, get on with you, and settle this—friend—in. *I* wouldn't waste time with an old man if *I* had a friend. Get on with you.''

Robert laughed, too, but as he closed the door behind him, his laughter faded. Michael was already back at the globe, frowning, one finger on New Orleans. It was just as well he'd decided not to bring up Justin Fourrier. Michael had enough on his mind. Whatever the reason a Fourrier ship had been in Tripoli, it couldn't affect them. He put on a smile and went down to meet Louise.

VIII

The hired horse from Kingston dropped his muzzle to the water trough even before its sandy-bearded rider dismounted. The rider mopped sweat off his face with a huge handkerchief, then stopped to rub his buttocks.

"Damn," he muttered. It was ten times as muggy as North Africa, the roads in Jamaica were bad, and he was no horseman. "Damn," he said again.

His gait had a roll to it as he walked up the steps of the tall brick manor house and knocked on the door. He mopped his face again until the door opened.

"Yes, sir?" a black butler said. His tone was deferential, but his face showed disdain; he had already classified the caller by his clothes.

The bearded man brushed past the startled butler into the marble-floored entry hall. "You go tell your master that Peter Lisle is here. Go on. Be quick about it."

The butler shifted his feet, then hurried up the broad stair. The man who had indeed been Peter Lisle before he was Murad Reis shook his head. The hall was spacious, with its mural-painted domed ceiling, its crystal chandelier and its fine, delicate furniture. Justin Fourrier had done well from their dealings in piracy and slaves. Perhaps even better than Murad had. Suddenly he needed a drink.

It wasn't hard to find a drawing room, and, most important, a row of decanters atop a sideboard. He filled a glass with brandy and drained it. He was filling it again when the door to the room slammed shut.

"What in hell are you doing here?" came the rasping question.

Carefully Murad restoppered the decanter, set it back in

place, and sipped from his glass. Then he turned. "And good afternoon to you, too, Fourrier."

Sometimes Murad found himself wondering what kept Justin Fourrier alive. He was tall, and he might have been handsome, once, but now he was sepulchral. All the juice had been burned out of him. His eyes were flat, black, and lifeless, and his mouth had a permanent twist of distaste.

"I said, what are you doing here?" Fourrier said. "You were never to come near me. Never."

"Never come near you," Murad snorted. "You act as if you were some bloody king. What would your fine friends say if they knew you were the biggest slaver on the African coast? What if they found out just how the notorious Murad Reis knows to slip through the Pillars of Hercules when there's an especially rich cargo about? Don't come near *you*, indeed."

"Is that meant for a threat?" Fourrier asked flatly. For the first time, though, light flickered in his eyes.

"Of course not," Murad said quickly. It was a long way to Kingston. "I've taken too much out of this to ruin it now. Especially when we're just about to double the take from the blackbirding."

"The Ashanti business? That does call for a drink." Justin filled a glass and raised it silently toward Murad. "It's something to own a king. Even an African one."

"That fat bastard Osei Bonshu doesn't think he's owned. In six months he'll be on the throne, but all we'll get will be our pick of the blacks and reduced prices. Anything more and some other slaver will overthrow him, the way we finished that poor sot before him."

"It should be more. It should be—" He stopped suddenly, his eyes pinning Murad. "You didn't cross the Atlantic to chat about that black savage. For that matter, how *did* you get here?"

Murad shifted uncomfortably. "The *Caribe* brought me."

"The *Caribe* was supposed to load with blacks at Cormantine."

"I told Nash to bring me here instead."

"You told him." Fourrier's voice was expressionless. "I would be very interested to know why."

"There's a man I'm after."

"A *man*?"

"That's right."

"You diverted the *Caribe,* left the slaves we bought to be stolen no doubt by some other ship, and crossed the Atlantic, all for a *man*?"

"Damn it, he stole a woman from me and sank two of my ships." Murad took a deep breath to calm himself, then gulped the rest of his brandy. "I want him. I *need* him."

Justin's lip curled further. "You're a fool. Whatever you do to his man won't get your ships back. And there are plenty of women. Find another one."

"You don't understand, Fourrier. Even if I wanted to let it go, and I *don't*, I couldn't. The reason I'm high Admiral of Tripoli, the reason I can deal with men like Osei Bonshu, is that I'm Murad Reis, unbeaten and unbeatable. Where I point, the lightning strikes, and my enemies fall dead from my glance. Well, that's what they believe, anyway. If I let this American scum get away with this, I'll have my own captains plotting to replace me."

"Yes," Fourrier said thoughtfully. "I see. But why come to me?"

"Because you've men in Charleston. This Robert Fallon is from—"

"Fallon!" Fourrier's hand closed convulsively on his glass. Broken glass, brandy, and drops of blood fell to the carpet. Fourrier pulled out a handkerchief and dabbed at the gashes, but his body shook as if from silent laughter. His eyes blazed, and his voice was a hoarse whisper. "Fallon, you say? *Robert* Fallon? Oh, yes. I'll help you, Lisle. Michael Fallon dead. Robert Fallon dead. You don't know how good that sounds. Or how long I've tried. Oh, yes, I'll help."

Murad listened disbelievingly. Who in hell *was* Robert Fallon? And Michael? For the first time he began to wonder if Justin Fourrier was insane.

IX

The study of the rented house on Back Street was filled with builder's plans. Maps and plats lay on every available surface. Karl Holtz often wondered if one day he would find there was no place left to sit. On New Year's Day of 1800, though, he felt too good to worry about clutter.

With Michael Fallon's letter of introduction, Banker Todd had acted as if he were an old and valued customer. Money had been advanced almost on request for what he needed beyond the letter of credit. The house he was in had been rented, and servants hired. With Fallon's advice, and Todd's, a tract of land on Johns Island, south of the city, had been bought, and another up the Ashley River, for his mill.

That had caused a few raised eyebrows, but once he explained what he wanted to a man who built rice mills, the plans had been drawn. Construction would start in the spring.

He chuckled as he remembered the to-do over the house he wanted for the island. He had told the builder to draw plans for a cottage, thinking to build larger later, when he could better afford it. But the plans he was handed were for a two-story house with large, high-ceilinged rooms and wide porches. To these Carolina planters, a house of wood and less than three floors *was* a cottage.

He dug the rolled plans out of the pile on his desk. He had accepted them, but not because his ideas of a cottage had changed. It was Catherine Fallon had made him want the larger house. He had to school his thoughts carefully when thinking of her, or images would come that were not proper. She was exquisite, a goddess, a Venus like the pagan statues he'd seen in Italy. He shied away before he began thinking of her as undraped as those statues. Of one thing he was certain.

In less than a month he had fallen in love.

There was a soft tap on the door, and his butler entered. "A Mr. Propman to see you, sir."

"Propman?" It was an effort to shift from Catherine to more mundane things. "It must be about my advertisement for an overseer. Show him in, Ezekiel."

The man was short, with a crooked nose. Hat in hand, he ran a quick glance over the room, giving the unpleasant impression that he was putting a price on the furnishings. On the spot Karl decided he didn't like him.

"Mr. Propman?" he said curtly. "I would like to see your references, first, and to know a little of your experience as an overseer."

Propman reared back. "Overseer? No. No, sir, you got the wrong idea. I ain't no overseer."

"Then why are you here? You will pardon my bluntness, but I have much to do."

"Oh, sure. Sure. You bought some cotton land. On Johns Island."

Karl frowned. "I did not believe that it was common knowledge, but yes, I have."

"You'll need blacks to work it."

Comprehension dawned. "I understand, now. Mr. Propman, I am sorry you have gone to this trouble. I am buying field hands who are trained through Mr. DeSaussure. If you will excuse me?"

Propman waved his hat violently. "No, sir. You don't understand. You'll need common niggers as well as trained hands. Men to do the ditch digging and the like. They'll cost you maybe three hundred fifty dollars apiece from Mr. DeSaussure. I can see you get them for two hundred."

"So," Karl said. "These blacks are illegal, then? Do not bother to deny it. I know the significance of the low price. What I do not understand is why you have come to me like this. Even in the short time I have been here I know that the smuggling of slaves thrives. But whether they are sold openly or in secret, I do not think they are sold by men going from house to house. Perhaps you are attempting a swindle."

"No, sir." Propman's voice was pained. "No, indeed. You don't have to lay out a penny till the blacks is in your hands.

It's just that the folks bringing these in want the sales arranged before times. Me, I think they're scared, and want to land the niggers and sail quick. So I get told to find people who want to buy them, starting with folks on Johns Isl—'' His mouth snapped shut, and he began to worry his hat.

"So this ship will make its landing near Johns Island."

"I didn't say that, sir. Do you want to buy? I've got to go."

"I will need perhaps thirty of the sort of laborers you talk of. But I will bring a doctor to look at them. I will take none who is sick or maimed. Now, where—''

"I can't say, sir. That is, you'll be told later."

"Come, man. I already know it will be near Johns Island."

"I never—'' He shoved his crumpled hat onto his head. "I got to go." And he darted out of the room.

From the hall came shouts, and the thud of someone falling. Muttering to himself, Karl strode to the door. The door to the street stood open, and a stocky man with a sun-darkened face was helping Ezekiel up off the floor.

"What happened here?" Karl asked.

The stocky man shook his head. "Fellow seemed to want to leave in a hurry. Just knocked your man here down and ran off up the street."

"I'm sorry, sir," the butler said, brushing himself off. "This gentleman, Mr. Caine, came about the overseer's position. That Mr. Propman was in a powerful hurry, sir."

"That's all right, Ezekiel. Mr. Caine, I am Karl Holtz. Will you come into my study?"

Karl's eye was caught by the strange, gliding way that Caine walked. After a moment he remembered where he'd seen it before. In Germany, *jaegers,* huntsmen, walked that way, as if feeling for the twig underfoot before it could snap.

"Sit down, Mr. Caine. You have been a huntsman?"

Caine paused perceptibly in lowering himself into the chair. "I was. For a time. But I've worked a sight of cotton the past few years. Here are my references."

Karl read the pages carefully. "Excellent," he said at last. "Both Mr. Martin and Judge Jackson think you a man of sterling character, Mr. Caine. It makes me wonder why you left them."

"Cotton planting's a small thing in Tennessee," Caine said

slowly. "Here on the coast I hope to better myself."

"A good reason. Now, as to the treatment of slaves. How do you propose to get the most productivity from them?"

"The same as with any man, Mr. Holtz. Treat them fair. Feed them good, clothe them good, and see they have houses that keep the rain off and the cold out. Seems to me people who're treated good, work good."

"Remarkable," Karl said. "Would you care for a drink, Mr. Caine?"

"I would, thank you kindly. I don't see what's so remarkable, Mr. Holtz."

"You are the first man I have interviewed for the position who has mentioned fair treatment. The rest have ranged from saying one cannot expect much from blacks, to a man from Massachusetts who proposed sermons on the rewards in heaven for good workers. These to be supplemented with a most severe set of punishments for being less. Perhaps you would like some of this whiskey? It is from Kentucky, just north of your Tennessee, I believe. It is called bourbon."

"I would indeed." Caine took the offered glass and drank. "This is almost as smooth as what we make in Tennessee," he said finally. "About that Massachusettser, though. There are some folks, Bible-thumpers, mostly, who think the only way to get good from anybody is to force it out."

"Exactly. In my country there are serfs, peasants tied to the soil, who are no more free than black slaves here. They may even be sold as easily. But some landowners make certain their peasants are well fed and housed. They allow the peasant a piece of land off which he may sell what he does not eat. Invariably these men get larger crops than those who gouge and starve."

"You aiming to do that? Let your slaves farm, I mean, and sell their surplus."

"I do," Karl said gravely. "Does that shock you?"

"No. It's surely not a common thing, but I've heard tell of it before."

"Good." Karl became suddenly brisk. "Now. I am told the usual wage for an overseer is twenty dollars per month. I believe that we shall make more cotton per acre than others, and I do not wish you hired away by men thinking to learn how it is done. Therefore I will pay you thirty dollars per month. And a house, of course. This is agreeable?"

Caine stared open-mouthed over the top of his glass. "You mean I'm hired? Now? On the spot? That surely *is* agreeable, Mr. Holtz. Like two blankets on a cold night."

"Very good. Now, I have a map of the land I have purchased. We will speak of my plans for it."

Karl and Caine stayed bent over the map for nearly two hours. The Westerner had a quick mind, Karl found, grasping the way the plantation was laid out and making good suggestions of his own. He was curious. How had a woodsman—and certainly Caine was one—come to be an overseer? That there was more to it, Karl was certain, but he decided to dig no deeper. Caine already believed in the way he wanted his plantation run. They would work well together.

"—And so you see," Karl finished, "barges will take the raw cotton the rest of the way to the mill."

Caine nodded. "But couldn't the cotton be loaded closer to your plantation? That would cut down—"

The chiming of the clock on the mantle pulled Karl's attention away from what Caine was saying. Ten o'clock. Suddenly his jaw dropped.

"Gott in Himmel!" he shouted. A startled Caine, cut off in mid-word, stared at him. "You will forgive me, Mr. Caine, and find your own way out. I must go. I am late." He dashed into the hall without awaiting a reply. "Ezekiel! Ezekiel, *Gott verdammt,* where are you?"

The butler appeared at almost the first shout.

"Have my carriage made ready," Karl said, snatching up his hat and walking stick. "Immediately!"

"Yes, sir. Shall I tell you when it's brought round, sir?"

Karl stared at him, wondering why the man didn't understand. "Brought round? No. Send it to the Fallon house. And hurry!" And he dove out of the house.

He dashed down Back Street, rounded onto Tradd, and raced toward the Fallon house. The first thing he saw was ominous. The Fallon carriage stood in the drive with grooms scurrying to harness a team. He trotted up the steps and knocked on the door to the porch. The Fallon butler opened the door. His wrinkled black face creased deeper with a genuine smile.

"Why, Mr. Holtz. Come in, sir. I'll tell Mr. Fallon you're here."

"Thank you, Caesar, but—" Over the gray-haired butler's shoulder he saw her, gliding down the porch in a russet gown, her abigail trailing behind with her parasol. He brushed past Caesar. "Miss Catherine, may I say how much that color becomes you."

She checked the buttons on her gloves. "Mr. Holtz, it is customary that only a *close* gentleman friend may comment on a lady's gown. Mary, see if the carriage is ready."

"Miss Catherine . . . Catherine . . . you cannot simply leave me because I am a trifle late. I was involved in an important business dealing." A glint appeared in her eye. Suddenly he wished he had made some other alibi.

"Business?" she said softly. "You are late, and for business?"

"Catherine, you must understand—"

"I understand that you find *business* more important than you do me."

She started toward the door, but he moved in front of her. "Catherine, I love you."

"Get out of my way, Mr. Holtz. I am going shopping."

"Did you not hear me?" he asked distractedly. "I love you. I do not mean the casual affection that frivolous young men apply to every girl they meet. I *love* you. With every ounce of my being I have loved you since the first moment I saw you. I worship you like a pagan before the idol of his goddess. I wish to marry you. I can conceive of marrying no other woman. Only you. Only you."

The flood of words ran out, and he stood wondering where he had found the eloquence. At least, he thought, Catherine seemed to be affected. She stared past his left shoulder, a strange smile on her face. Slowly she lifted her hazel eyes to his.

"You truly love me, Karl?"

"I do," he said stiffly. The easy words seemed to have fled. "I love you. I wish the honor of your hand in marriage."

Suddenly she was in his arms, and they were kissing. All rational thought fled before the soft tenderness of her lips beneath his. His arms tightened around her, and his mouth became roughly possessive. After long moments she pulled free of him. They both were breathing raggedly.

"I apologize," he said. "I . . . I became carried away."

"You love me," she said. She was looking at him quizzically, as if she'd never seen him before.

"Is it so hard to understand? I love you, and I wish to marry you."

She continued to stare, then, half to herself, she breathed, "Yes." Suddenly she shook as if waking up. Her eyes widened, and she darted past him down the steps.

"Catherine," he called after her. "Where are you going? Catherine!"

Unheeding, she climbed into the carriage, Mary scrambling in as her command sen the equipage rolling down the street. Karl could only stare in consternation. She had said yes. Did she mean yes, she loved him, too? Yes, she would marry him? Then why had she run like that?

Suddenly he realized he was not alone. Robert Fallon stood at the foot of the steps looking at him with a raised eyebrow. So that, he thought, was why she fled. He cleared his throat.

"Ah . . . you may wonder, Mr. Fallon, about what you have seen. Let me assure you, there has been no impropriety."

"What, none? Seems to me I heard love mentioned more than once." Abruptly, maddeningly, he began to chuckle.

Karl stiffened. "That is correct. I love your sister. I have asked her to marry me, and she has done the honor to say yes."

"Well, don't be so grim about it. There are many things worse than marrying Catherine."

"You do not disappove?" He felt the rigidness draining out of him. "I have known her less than one month. If I speak the truth, I will say that I would have waited some months yet, so that propriety would not be offended. But I could not help myself." Abruptly he became anxious. "You are certain that you approve?"

Robert's face broke into a huge grin. "Why not? You're presentable enough, and you don't spit on the carpets."

"Spit on the carpets? Of course I do not spit on the carpets!"

"Whoa, Karl. I'm just trying to say you're perfectly acceptable to me. If Catherine wants you, that's good enough. You *have* spoken to our father, haven't you?"

"*Mein Gott!* No, I have not. This came on me suddenly. He will not refuse me? I am willing to wait a proper time."

"He won't refuse anything that Catherine wants," Robert said. "Come. I'll walk you to the Bridge, and you can speak to him."

"I thank you." At that moment he spied his carriage, making its way down the street. "But there is no reason to walk. Let us ride." As they climbed into the open carriage, St. Michael's began to toll in the chill air.

"Why are the bells ringing?" he asked. "It is just past the hour."

"Someone must have died," Robert said. "Someone important. I don't know of anyone who was sick, but my father would."

Karl gave orders to the driver, eyeing the younger Fallon. He was in many ways a frivolous man, almost the buccaneer he looked. Yet he was a shipowner, and the son of a shipowner and planter, a man of position and respectability. Awkwardly he cleared his throat. "As you are Catherine's brother, it is fitting that I tell you what I am able to give her."

"That's not necessary."

"Not necessary? But of course it is. I have the land on Johns Island bought. Three thousand acres to put in cotton. By next summer the mill I am having built on the Ashley River will be complete."

"That mill, now," Fallon said, interest lighting his eyes, "I understand you'll be taking the cotton all the way to cloth."

Karl nodded. "Yes. The mill will gin, card, spin, and weave. Of course, the cotton may be removed at any stage. I will sell the ginning service to those planters who have no gin. My own cotton will be made into cloth."

"Yes. That's what I find interesting. Everyone else ships it off to England, or New England. With a mill here . . . . " His voice trailed off as other church bells joined the first. And not only church bells. The bell at the Customs tolled, and the fire warning bell. Peddlers huddled in knots, talking instead of selling, and people ran in all directions as if panic were sweeping the city.

"What is it?" Karl shouted over the noise. "Is the city under attack? Wild Indians, perhaps?"

"Of course not," Robert shouted back. "I'll soon find out. Driver, stop the carriage." He leaned over the side as soon as their motion slowed, and collared a boy in bare feet and a tattered shirt.

"Let go," the boy squealed, wriggling. "I ain't done nothing."

"What's all the commotion?" Robert said. With his free hand he held a coin in front of the boy's suddenly fascinated gaze. "Why the bells?"

"You don't know? He's dead. Washington's dead." With a twist the boy grabbed the coin, broke free and dove into the crowd. Robert stayed as if frozen.

"Washington," Karl said. "He meant George Washington?"

Fallon nodded dully. "The only one he could mean. The only one . . . " Suddenly he opened the carriage door and leaped to the cobblestones. "I'm sorry, Karl, but this is the wrong time to speak to my father about Catherine. I'll go with you tomorrow. I'm sorry."

Robert disappeared into the alleys leading to the docks, and Karl stared after him. In an upper-floor window a shopkeeper's wife wept openly, and two blowzes huddled at a street corner did the same. A man in a well-cut coat of superfine and a tall hat walked down the center of the street, unmindful of the filth being splattered on his trousers by passing wagons. He looked as if he'd heard something he'd never thought to hear.

Karl sank back with a sigh. They looked as if they were mourning a king. "Home, Noah," he said. He would have to find a funeral wreath.

X

February Race Week was annually a time of gaiety, a week of horse races every day and balls every night, culminating in the St. Cecilia Society Concert. That year there was no gaiety for Michael Fallon. His horses had won their share, and at the balls he had shown he wasn't too old to dance with the best. But the most important ball of all, to him, was at that moment going on downstairs. In a little while he would go down to announce Catherine's betrothal.

He poked at the fire and grunted. A man should be happy announcing his daughter's betrothal. And he didn't disapprove, despite the short time they'd known each other. But in the past few hours other matters had come to a head. Information he had been weeks gathering and finally fit together.

Tonight he would learn the whole story of what Hamilton intended. Roger Hilton was coming. Hilton had been his friend during the Revolution, but now the man, for his punctillious honor, would not associate with Michael. He saw Michael's opposition to the Federalists as a betrayal of Washington and worse, to his mind, of the aging Christopher Gadsden, who had begun the Revolution in South Carolina almost by the force of his will. And brought Michael into it. That made it a personal betrayal to Hilton. It had been all he could to do persuade the man to come.

A tap came at the door. "Yes?" he said.

Caesar put his head in. "It's Mr. Hilton, sir. You said to show him right up when he came."

"Very good, Caesar. Come in, Roger." When the door was closed behind the butler he spoke. "Will you have a pipe, or a cigar? I have these things from Cuba, tobacco wrapped in paper. They're called cigarettes."

Hilton was a short man, and broad, with the air of a bantam rooster. He stood with his chest thrust out, and his voice was cold. "I did not come here to smoke, Michael."

"Then a drink. We weren't always on different sides of the political fence, Roger. Surely you can still drink with me."

"Well . . . ." Some of the stiffness went out of Hilton. "I'll have a brandy, Michael. This meeting is damned odd, you know. It's an open secret you're announcing Catherine's marriage tonight. And we've been political enemies for ten years now."

Michael handed Hilton his glass and took one for himself. "Thirty years ago we weren't enemies."

Hilton shook his head. "Lord, has it changed since then." Suddenly he raised his glass with a sardonic laugh. "The Revolution! Do we know yet what we were fighting for?"

"The Revolution," Michael echoed. He was certain now that Hilton was his man. "We may not be certain what we were fighting for, but most of us know what we *weren't* fighting for."

"Michael, you haven't asked me here for political talk? Man, we're so far apart—"

"I've heard Hamilton's taking an interest in the election of Aaron Burr."

Hilton choked on his brandy. Michael waited patiently while he regained his breath. The smaller man seemed to choose his words carefully. "You must know that Hamilton hates Burr."

"Of course. There's no saying what sort of interest it is. But I've heard the rumor. And I've heard your name mentioned with it. Roger, we may be opponents in politics, but I can't believe you'd lend yourself to anything underhanded. And this smacks of Europe, of court intrigues."

"God, doesn't it," Hilton sighed. Michael held his breath while the other peered into his glass, then set it down. He looked less the rooster, now. "By God, I wish I'd never listened. But the men came from Hamilton. It was what he wanted. Damn me, but I've always thought Hamilton knew what was best for the country."

"What was it he wanted?"

"For Federalist votes to be cast for Burr, if Hamilton said the word."

"What?"

Hilton made a sound halfway between a laugh and a sob. "Michael, I listened to it. Talk of your backstairs intrigues." The words began coming faster. "Hamilton is sure South Carolina will vote Federalist. After all, what better guarantee could he have? Our own Pinckney is John Adams' Vice-President. I'm certain to be one of the electors. That's why I was asked. Asked to be ready to betray Pinckney and cast my ballot for Burr."

"Roger, Hamilton hates Aaron Burr. And even if he didn't, why would he want Adams to have a republican Vice-President?"

"I don't know, Michael. I was told that when the electoral college meets, there might be cause, for the good of the party, that I cast my vote for Burr. I know it makes no sense, but there it is. God help me. Washington warned us against political parties, and he was right. We're falling into the same muck that fouls Europe."

"Perhaps not," Michael said soothingly. He studied Hilton. The little man was indeed sensitive of his honor. What he'd been asked to do pricked that honor deeply. "Even if the muck pit's been filled, Hilton, there's no need for us to leap into it."

"What?"

"You could be telling what you know to the rest of the Legislature in Columbia."

"My honor—"

"Is it honorable to keep back what you know?" He waited, holding his breath, for Hilton to speak.

The small man's head came up slowly. "I must vote my beliefs and my conscience," he said slowly. "I believe that John Adams is the best man for the Presidency, with the possible exception of Hamilton. I shall vote that way." Michael began to marshal his arguments. "However," Hilton went on before he could speak, "I will hold conversation with as many legislators as I can, and I will tell them what I've been asked to do."

Michael's breath let out with a rush. "Good. It's the honorable way, Roger."

"Honorable," Hilton laughed. "It will be the breaking of the Federalists in South Carolina. We've had enough trouble in the legislature from William Alston, as it is. This will give South Carolina to Jefferson.''

"Perhaps not, Roger.''

"Of a certainty, Michael. But what am I to do? Am I to let the Almighty Party rule my life?''

"Of course not, Roger. You're not the first to find the men he supported something less than he supposed. Sit. Have another glass, and we'll talk of the old days.''

"I am sorry,'' Hilton said stiffly. "I must be going.'' He looked right and left, as if he couldn't see clearly, before he turned to the door. "And Michael,'' he said without looking back, "I should prefer not to see you again.''

Michael watched the door close behind Hilton without speaking or moving. Then he lowered himself into the chair at his desk. For a moment he frowned at the glass of brandy, glowing amber in the firelight.

"Damn it all to hell,'' he growled, and hurled the glass into the fireplace. The fire flared high for an instant.

The things men did for causes, he thought. Even when they weren't sure their cause was right. And he realized he wasn't certain whether he was thinking of Hilton or himself.

There was a soft knock at the door, and Caesar looked in. "Mr. Fallon, sir, you told me to tell you when it was nine o'clock.''

Michael nodded silently and rose. On the stairs he straightened his coat and put a hand to his high white stock.

The drawing room had been cleared for dancing. Two violinists and a cellist were crowded into one corner, and the rest of the room shimmered with ladies in silks, satins, and diamonds, and men in the plainer colors now fashionable. There were Manigaults, Middletons, Rutledges, Pinckneys, the cream of South Carolina aristocracy, come to see a former bondservant give his daughter away. He picked out Robert against the wall in conversation with young Langdon Cheves, and there was Catherine standing with Karl. The string trio fell silent; he turned to face the crowds of smiling, expectant faces.

"My friends,'' he began . . . .

Catherine listened to the announcement with only half an ear. When her father had asked if she wanted to marry Karl, she had said yes, and yes when Karl had carried out the formality. And she still wasn't sure why.

Karl would certainly be a devoted husband, and she had no doubt she would be able to manage him, but she had always thought there would be more. Strange. It had begun with that kiss on the porch. Or perhaps it had climaxed then. In any case, the odd thing was, she had only kissed him because she'd seen Robert, past his shoulder, coming up the walk.

And that *was* odd, she thought. It had had her in such confusion that day she couldn't think straight, and she still couldn't understand it. Why would she want Robert to see her kissing Karl? It made no sense however she looked at it. She hated Robert. That was the plain and simple of it.

Her eye sought him out where he stood talking to Langdon. He was smiling, at ease. Damn his eyes. He looked so much like her father, so exactly like Michael as a young man, that she wanted to scream. God, just the sight of him made her boil with emotion. She hated him.

Suddenly she realized her father was finishing.

" . . . and felicity. And so I wish to announce that my daughter, Catherine, will marry Mr. Karl Holtz, late of Saxony, now of South Carolina."

"So," Karl said, smiling down at her. "it is official." He swept her into a kiss, and she was dimly aware of laughter and applause from the onlookers. When he backed away there was a smile of fatuous pleasure on his face.

Before she could so much as draw a breath the assemblage surrounded them. The women drew her off toward the back drawing room, while the men closed in around Karl, escorting him toward the punch bowl.

"Come along, Karl," one of the men shouted. "A good drink and a smoke over your betrothed any day."

Laughter ran through the men as Karl tried to pull free, looking woefully back to her. "But it is not proper. Catherine . . . . "

"None of that," Robert laughed. "You'll have more of her company than you want once you're married."

It was supposed to be a great joke, keeping them apart for the rest of the night. With a slight shock Catherine realized she didn't care. In fact, the rest of the evening away from Karl might be more enjoyable than with him. In the back drawing room, chairs had already been set in a circle, and a maid stood by with ratafia and lemonade. Flora Middleton shut the door as they sank giggling into their chairs. "Just think, Catherine," she said, "soon you'll be able to talk of all the things unmarried women aren't supposed to mention." She was a thin-faced girl with an infectious smile.

Most of the others laughed, but Elizabeth McCants pulled her dour, eighty-year-old face into a frown. "And what might those be?"

"Why Madame de Staël, for instance," Flora answered pertly.

Instantly everyone except Elizabeth and Catherine was chattering. The French novelist was a favorite, if disreputable topic of conversation. Was it true she'd borne two children for the lover she left her husband for? Had she actually left him in turn? Just to lure a married man away from his wife?

After a time they realized that Catherine wasn't joining in, and the conversation drifted to a halt.

"Catherine," Flora asked, "is something the matter? You haven't said a word."

"I'm all right," Catherine said vaguely. Her mind was still on that kiss on the porch. "It's just that I don't care for novels."

Flora shook her head. "What do you mean? You read as many of them as any of us." A murmur of assent ran through the room.

Catherine looked around the circle in surprise. "Well, there's nothing else to do. One can't dance or shop all the time. But the heroines are so insipid. And so stupid. If one of them had the brains God gave a goose, she'd be over her difficulties by the end of the second chapter."

"Brains," Mrs. McCants snorted. "Women don't get husbands by having brains, in books or in real life."

"How can you enjoy seeing women portrayed as brainless fools?" Catherine asked. "We have as good brains as men, and that's how it should be shown."

"Oh, dear," Flora said.

Elizabeth McCants snorted again. "That's an idea you'll do well to get rid of."

"And why should I? I'll help Karl run his plantation, as I should. I can hardly do that without thinking."

Mrs. McCants mouth twisted with exasperation. "That is an entirely different thing. Seeing to the house and the kitchen farm, schooling children and looking after servants are a wife's place. This wild talk of brains is wrong. Next you'll be complaining because girls aren't sent to William and Mary or Harvard, like their brothers."

Before Catherine could answer, Flora broke in. "Let's all stop this talk of brains. We are supposed to be enjoying ourselves. Not arguing. Now, how many of you will go to see *The Secret Marriage?* The singers have come all the way from Italy."

Catherine let the talk of Cimarosa's opera wash over her. Women weren't supposed to have brains, were they? Well, wait until they saw what she did with Karl's plantation. He was so wrapped up in his mill, she'd be able to do as she pleased. And she would show these chattering magpies that a woman could think for herself. Idly she wondered if mistresses were allowed to think. If so, what did Louise de Chardonnay think of?

Robert heaved a sigh of relief as the women swept Catherine away. The last few weeks had been hell. To know he desired his own sister, even a half-sister, was bad enough, but for weeks he'd had to fight jealousy as well. And yet he'd recognized it as a salvation, too. Once she were married, he would surely be able to control his feelings.

He put his hand in his pocket and stroked the cameo he'd bought in Tripoli. Bringing a mistress home should have made him forget the amber pin, but still he carried it.

On sudden impulse he pushed through the crowd around Karl. "Karl, I want you to have this." He put the cameo into the surprised Saxon's hand.

"Why, it is Catherine," Karl said with a smile.

Robert nodded. "It looks like her, at least. I bought it in North Africa. You should have it."

Karl ran his thumb over the likeness. "No. You must keep it. I will soon be married to the original. Here."

"No, Karl. I want—"

Holtz pushed the pin into Robert's pocket, and then Charles

Clark, a young planter, had the bridegroom-to-be, pulling him away. "Karl, did you see *Wind Devil* today? Did you? Finest horse in America. In the world. I won five hundred dollars on him. Wish I'd bet more."

Karl gave an apologetic shrug as he was pulled back towards the punchbowl, and then was surrounded by jovial men forcing drinks on him. Robert turned away, and bumped into a short, dark man, spilling some of the man's drink down his sleeve.

"Your pardon," Robert said.

"Granted," the man replied. Robert was certain he'd remember that Roman nose and pointed chin if he'd seen them before.

"I don't believe we've met, Mr. . . . . . "

"Stanwyck," the dark man said. "Peter Stanwyck. Mr. Holtz invited me to accompany him tonight."

"Do you know him from Saxony?"

Stanwyck hesitated. "No. We have some business together. I didn't catch your name."

"Fallon," Robert said. "Robert Fallon." Stanwyck's hand jerked, and more punch spilled.

He frowned at the cup, then carefully set it on the table. "It appears I've had a little too much to drink. You will excuse me?" He turned, and found himself entangled with Charles Clark, now with even more wine-punch in him.

"Sorry," Charles chuckled. "I've had—don't I know you?" He peered intently at the dark man. "Yes. I remember. How're things at Cormantine and Quashie's Town?"

"You must be mistaken," Stanwyck said. "I need some air." Roughly he pushed Clark aside and hurried from the room.

Robert looked after Stanwyck, then turned to Clark. "Charles, who is this Stanwyck?"

Clark's cheeks colored. "I—I was mistaken. You heard him." Suddenly he looked ill. "Lord. I guess I've drunk too much. Will you make my apologies, Robert?"

Clark stumbled out of the room with surprising speed. Robert followed and caught the young planter on the porch. "Charles, I need the truth. You sailed on a slaver, didn't you?"

The young man slumped against the porch railing. He

scrubbed at his mouth with the back of his hand. "I did. God help me. It was hell, Fallon. They crammed those poor beggars in like fish in a barrel. The screaming. The moaning. The stench. Halfway back a fever broke out. It spread like a fire. They started bringing them all on deck every day. And if they showed the slightest sign of the fever, they were thrown over the side. Women. Children. It didn't matter. I tried to stop it. Before God, Fallon, I tried. But I was just the super-cargo." He began to weep into his hands. "How did you know?"

"Cormantine," Robert said. "And Quashie's Town. They're slaver's ports. There's not a sailor doesn't know the names, but not many else. This Stanwyck was on your ship?"

"No, another one. A big, black-painted ship."

Robert felt the breath seize in his throat. It had to be just a coincidence, but . . . . He dashed back into the house shouting. "Where's my father? Has anyone seen my father?" The dozen men drinking in the hall looked at him in open-mouthed surprise. He grabbed the nearest by the shoulders. "Jeffcoat, have you seen my father?"

"Why, yes. He went up to his study. What's—"

Robert leaped to the stairs without waiting for the rest. Before he reached the first landing the sharp crack of a pistol shot echoed down the stairwell. A second followed on the instant. From below a woman screamed, and a man yelled from outside, "What's going on? Someone just dropped off the second-floor veranda!"

The door to Michael's study was ajar. Robert flung it open and rushed in. Michael lay crumpled near his desk.

"Oh, God," Robert breathed. Gently he rolled the old man over. Two red blotches stained the snowy shirt front, but his icy blue eyes flickered open.

"Never—expected—it—at—party—here."

"Be quiet," Robert said gently. "Where's Dr. Warren?" he shouted toward the door.

Michael coughed. "Was—in room—before—I saw. Getting old."

"Nonsense," Robert said. Michael's eyes closed, and his breathing turned ragged. "Damn it, where's Warren?"

"I'm here," Thomas Warren said as he pushed through the crowd clustered around the study door. His round cheeks and paunch testified to his weakness for food and drink, but he was known for a sure hand and for dragging patients back from death seemingly by nothing but his will. He bustled to Robert's side and jerked his head toward the door. "You might as well wait outside."

Robert got to his feet. "Will he live?"

Warren forced his hand under Michael's back, and brought it out covered with blood. "They both went through. No need to probe, thank God." He spared one exasperated glance for Robert. "Live? He's as good a chance as any man. Now will you get out of here? And tell those women to stop caterwauling and boil some water. And tear some sheets for bandages." Tugging his coat off, he wiped his bloody hand carelessly on his fine lawn shirt. Gently he began tearing Michael's shirt away from the wounds.

Suddenly Langdon Cheves was inside the door. The slender lawyer took Robert by the arm. "Come on, Robert. We're waiting for you, as many as are sober enough to ride. We all have horses, and Tom Hall's chasing him afoot."

Robert took one last look at Michael, then pushed his way grimly through the people crowding the hall. Women and the older men, he saw. His gaze flickered over Catherine, and she started toward him, but he had no time. He went down the stairs at a run, Cheves at his side. "Guns?" he asked shortly.

"We all have pistols," Langdon answered, "and there are even a few cutlasses. Your father—your father keeps near an arsenal."

From the veranda Robert could see a half-dozen horsemen in the drive, ill-lit by the moon and the windows of the house. Charles Pinckney, a United States Senator and the republican brother of the Federalist Vice-Presidential candidate, was at their head. Young Clark, looking as if he'd sworn off drink for life, sat a horse beside him. All who were sober enough to ride, Langdon had said. Robert hoped it was enough. A horse whickered, and saddle leather creaked as a rider shifted impatiently.

"Robert! Langdon!" Louis Middleton called. "Hurry up. He'll be getting away."

"A minute more," Robert said. "Karl? Where's Karl Holtz?"

"Here," came the accented reply, and one of the horses moved closer to the veranda. The light from the windows showed Holtz' grim face clearly.

Robert vaulted the railing and grabbed Karl's bridle. "That man you brought tonight, the slaver. Where's his ship?"

"His ship?" Karl asked in surprise.

"What's this about a slaver?" Middleton asked.

"Let's get after him," John Calhoun shouted. He was barely old enough to be at the party, and full of the impatience of brandy and youth.

"Karl," Robert persisted, "he was the one who shot my father."

Langdon gasped. "Are you sure, Robert? No one saw—"

"I'm sure. It'd take too long to explain why, but I'm sure. Now, Karl—"

"A small river behind Johns Island," Karl answered immediately. "The ship is there."

"Good," Robert said. A horse had been brought forward for him. He swung into the saddle. "Now we know where he'll run to. Which way did he head?"

"Straight down Tradd toward the Ashley," came the answer, and they galloped down the street in a knot.

Before they'd gone a hundred yards, though, a man appeared out of the dark, running the other way. "Hold up," he shouted. "It's me. Tom Hall."

"Where did he go?" Robert asked. "Did you lose him?"

Hall leaned against a brick wall, panting. "Went straight to the public landing at the foot of Tradd. There was a boat waiting. Headed off down toward the harbor."

"A boat!" Robert growled. "Damn it! We'll follow him anyway."

"But a boat," Middleton protested. "There'll be no boats for hire this time of night. We have to go back to the docks."

"We'll steal one," Robert snapped, and spurred away. The rest followed without hesitation.

At the landing, there *was* a boat, a battered launch tied with a frayed rope. A small black boy in patched shirt and breeches hopped out and stood wide-eyed as they clattered up and dismounted on the wet cobblestones.

"How much for the hire of your boat, lad?" Robert asked.

"Louis, see if the oars are in her. If not, try to find some."

"Mister," the boy said. "Mister, I can't hire you this here boat. It Mr. Putnam boat. He say for me to watch it."

"The oars are here," Middleton shouted from the boat. "This thing leaks like a sieve, Robert. We'll have to bale the whole way."

"Mister." The boy's voice was tense. "You can't take the boat. It Mr. Putnam boat. He say . . . . "

The boy's words trailed off as Robert upended his purse, coins ringing on the landing. "There, boy. There's enough to *buy* Mr. Putnam's boat. And he'll get the boat back, too. Senator Pinckney, Langdon, everybody, let's go."

They scrambled into the bed, shedding their coats, and settled at the oars, white shirts gleaming in the night. As they splashed away from the landing, the boy, crouched to gather the coins, shouted, "You gots to bring back the boat by morning."

Robert had an oar in the bow of the boat, with Karl beside him to show the slaver's location. For the half hour it took to pick their way across the black harbor to Wappoo Creek, no sound came from the Saxon except the heavy breathing of exertion. As marshy ground rose on either side of the boats, though, and the sour smell of pluff mud filled the air, he spoke.

"I must offer my deepest apologies, Robert. I had no idea."

"Of course you didn't," Robert said shortly. He peered over his shoulder into the darkness ahead, where the moon glinted on the water and made fantastic shapes from oaks close to the creek.

"Still," Karl persisted, "I should never have introduced a slaver into your father's house. He seemed very much a gentleman, though, despite his profession."

"Doesn't signify. There are plenty of gentlemen in the business of selling slaves. Middleton, DeSaussure, a half dozen other old names. In fact, there are those who think selling slaves is less demeaning than selling other kinds of—merchandise. Not many are involved with the ships, though. Those are nearly all from Boston, or Philadelphia, or England."

Karl nodded. "Yes, the crew of this one seemed English. And this Stanwyck was the only one of them who appeared to have the slightest culture.''

"Even so, how did you come to ask him to your betrothal party?''

"The entire thing was most strange, now that I think on it. He had almost exactly the number of slaves that we wanted to buy, and they were all in remarkable health for having been transported from Africa, so the sale took only a short time. As the auction went on, Stanwyck circulated among us, talking for a while to this man, and then to another. He spoke to me, and was about to move on, when I mentioned my betrothal.'' His voice became suddenly excited. "Robert, I mentioned your father's name. That is when he stopped. Do you suppose he always had the intention of shooting your father?''

"Go on," Robert said harshly.

"There is little more. We spoke longer. He mentioned his delight in dancing, and that his life on a ship meant associating with those who thought a party was a drunken brawl. I do not remember exactly when, but I inivted him to come. *Mein Gott,* what have I done?''

Robert muttered under his breath. "I should have killed you long ago, Justin.''

"Justin?" Karl asked. "Who is Justin?''

"A dead man," Robert said, his voice so grim that Karl left him in silence.

Now the boat rode the Stono, the river behind Johns Island. Occasional lights spotted the shore, but the area had never been favored by rice planters, and cotton planters didn't need to hug the shore. Then, in a small inlet, a creek mouth just wide enough and deep enough for a vessel to be kedged in almost under the trees, sterncabin lights twinkled as if from the forest.

Robert motioned for the rowers to stop. The oars splashed as the rowers backed water. The quiet was broken by night birds, the scuffling of feet, and an occasional cough.

"Robert," Cheves whispered hoarsely, "exactly how do we go about this? It's come to me that none of us have ever boarded a ship in anger except you.''

Robert raised his voice just enough to be heard by everyone in the boat. "We'll go to port, to the left, that is. There's just enough room on that side to get a boat between the ship and the bank. I'll go aboard first. If you hear fighting, come swarming over the side. Otherwise, sit tight till I call you up."

"Shouldn't we hail them?" young Calhoun asked. "Just explain the situation? I'm sure they don't want a murderer . . . ." His voice trailed off uncertainly.

Boarding was risky enough, with only seven men, but if it was a Fourrier ship, as Robert suspected, they'd never give up a Fourrier assassin. "If we hail them, they'll likely think it's a Customs' trick. We're liable to get a load of grapeshot into us."

The boat crept forward again, disappearing into the shadows alongside the slaver. A foul odor hung about the vessel, excrement, urine, vomit, and the sour sweat of fear.

Now was the time for silence, but it seemed to Robert that the scraping of indrawn oars was twice as loud, that there were twice as many muttered curses as men bumped into each other in the dark. And yet there was no response from the ship. He motioned the others to stillness, then pulled himself up to the ship's rail, just enough to see over it.

The moon cast pale shadows of the rigging on deck, covering it with shifting shapes and masses. One cannon, a long twenty-four, sat mounted on a turntable between the two masts amidships, a typical slaver mounting, and there were fittings for swivel guns all along the rail. But there wasn't a crewman to be seen.

"Follow me," Robert called softly. "One at a time, and quietly."

He took the pistol Senator Pinckney handed up to him and slithered over the rail. Still the only sign of life was the light from the stern-cabin windows. The rigging creaked slightly as the ship shifted on the tide, and a freshened breeze brought the welcome smell of the salt marshes.

Stealthily he started toward the stern, wincing as Middleton followed him aboard with a thump. Discipline was lax on slavers, he knew, but surely they should have a deck watch. His foot hit something soft, and the deck watch woke up with a jerk.

He gave another jerk at the pistol Robert presented to his head, and his gap-toothed mouth fell open in a soft moan. "For God's sake, Trask, wait a minute! I only had a drop!"

Robert clapped a hand over his mouth; he gave a muffled shout as a shift in the clouds revealed Robert's face.

"Karl," Robert hissed.

"I am here."

"Take Louis, Clark and young Calhoun to the forecastle. I think they may be sleeping off a drunk."

Turning his prisoner over to Langdon, he eased down the aft companionway. The door to the stern cabin stood ajar, letting a stream of light and a murmur of conversation into the passage. He raised the pistol and put his eye to the crack. A tall, lean man with bushy black whiskers sat at a table across from Stanwyck. A wine bottle stood open between them; another lay on its side. The tall man swayed slightly as he spoke.

"I always let my men drink their fill once the niggers are off. All except the watch." He had a broad English country accent. "Aye, and they deserve it, having to ship with those murderous black beggars. Had one of them bite a chunk out of my leg, once. Bite it right out."

"Damn it, Trask," Stanwyck began.

"Aye, Aye, I know. You want to be gone. Well, they'll be sober by daylight. They'll be sober or I'll kick it out of them. And we can't sail till then, anyhow. Tide's wrong, and I'll not try these bloody Carolina creeks in the dark. Bad as the slave coast, they are."

Stanwyck growled, then took a deep breath and went on in a calmer tone. "You knew I might have to leave at any time, and you were supposed to be ready to sail on the moment. This sodden lot will never make the first tide in the morning."

"I tell you—"

There was a crashing thump in the passage behind Robert. He whirled, pistol at the ready, to find Louis Middleton getting up from a heap at the foot of the ladder.

"What in hell was that?" Trask shouted.

Robert kicked open the door and went through it pistol first. Stanwyck skidded to a halt halfway to the door. Trask still sat, blinking his watery blue eyes, at the table. "Who in hell are you?" the slaver captain thundered.

"I'm Robert Fallon, and I'll put a hole through the first one of you to move."

Louis Middleton stumbled into the cabin, a pistol in each

hand. He peered around, wrinkling his patrician nose. "I was coming to tell you the crew is all drunk. Passed out, mainly. God, this ship stinks. How can they stand it? Don't they ever wash anything?"

"It goes with their business," Robert answered harshly. "All right, Stanwyck, get on deck. And you, too, Trask. You'll be facing charges for the attempted murder of Michael Fallon."

Stanwyck looked disbelieving. "You'll never hang me."

"Murder!" Trask gasped. "I don't know nothing about no murder. Stanwyck here just bought a passage, that's all." Fear seemed to have burned the alcohol fumes out of his head. He watched Robert with a crafty eye.

"Don't take me for a fool, Trask. Fourrier wouldn't spend money hiring somebody else's ship for his killer."

Trask spat contemptuously. "Fourrier! Cut me out of half-a-dozen good cargos, he has. This here's my ship, not his."

Robert smiled grimly. "It's no matter. Smuggling slaves is enough to hold you. We'll ferret out your connection with Fourrier."

"Smuggling," Trask said slyly. "Well, now, your friends there maybe might have something to say about that. I mind me seeing a few of them before. Buying smuggled slaves."

For the first time Robert realized that Karl, Langdon, and Pinckney had joined Middleton by the door. Langdon glanced at the rest and spoke.

"Robert, look at their faces. Some of our friends do indeed recognize Captain Trask. Even so, if you've proof that Trask is involved in the shooting of your father, I have no doubt they'll testify to a man to see him held." There was a murmur of assent. "But be sure, Robert. Buying smuggled slaves is as illegal as smuggling them. It isn't something to admit lightly before a magistrate. Now you say Trask doesn't own this ship?"

"That's right. It's Justin Fourrier's ship. I'd swear to it. And he's tried to kill my father before."

"She's mine," Trask barked. He lurched out of his chair toward a cabinet against the hull, and froze under five pistols. Easing himself back down, he pointed. "In there. The top drawer."

Louis Middleton jerked it open and rummaged among

papers and old logbooks. "Here," he said finally. "Says Jasper Trask is owner, under the British flag, of the brig *Skua*, two hundred ten tons burden."

"See," Trask said. "I've nothing to do with Fourrier."

"It's a trick," Robert insisted. "Maybe in case his papers were examined, so we wouldn't hear of a Fourrier ship here. Just look at the slaves you brought. Karl told me how good they looked, considering the voyage from Africa. They were in such good shape because they'd only come from Jamaica, where Justin Fourrier lives."

He could tell he hadn't convinced them. Even Karl looked doubtful. Langdon shook his head. "Think straight, man. We're to convince a judge Trask was involved because this is a Fourrier ship. And it's a Fourrier ship because the slaves are too fresh to have come all the way from Africa. It's too thin. We need something on paper, but if this Fourrier put the papers naming Trask owner aboard, there won't be a scrap with *his* name on it."

"Well, Stanwyck," he said, "you've heard what's going on. If you don't speak up, Trask gets off. You'll go alone."

Trask's gaze darted warily to Stanwyck, but the other refused to look at anything in particular. "I was a passenger," he snarled. "That's all. And you can stuff yourselves trying to prove different."

Rage flared up in Robert. That Stanwyck might try to take Trask with him had been his last hope. If he couldn't convince his own friends with the rest, he'd never convince a magistrate.

"At least we have this one," he growled, indicating Stanwyck. "We'll take *him* back to hang."

Stanwyck darted toward the stern windows; Langdon and Karl had him before his second step. Throwing him to the deck, they roughly bound his hands behind him, then pulled him to his feet. He glared about him ferociously.

"I'll never hang, damn you! Never!"

Robert ripped a blanket off the bed and dumped the contents of the cabinet drawer into it.

"Here! You can't take that," Trask protested.

Robert ignored him, tied the blanket into a rough sack and hoisted it to his shoulder. "Some one find Stanwyck's cabin. Bring everything in it. There may be evidence."

Trask's eyes flickered to Stanwyck. With a care for the pistols, he got slowly to his feet. "Here, now. You can't go looting—" Robert rounded on him, and he stumbled back.

"You, Trask. I want you to take a message to Justin Fourrier."

"I told you, I don't know Fourrier."

In one move Robert jammed his pistol under Trask's chin. The slaver's whiskers twitched, and a bead of sweat rolled down his forehead. "I said," Robert grated, "you'll take a message to Justin Fourrier." Trask nodded infinitesimally. "Tell him if Michael Fallon dies, I'll cut his heart out. Do you have that?"

"Yes," Trask gasped.

Robert shoved the pistol back into his belt. "Throw any guns you find over the side," he told the others, "and let's go."

Trask watched sourly as the contents of *Skua's* arms chest, and even her swivels, were dumped into the soft mud of the inlet. The rest of the crew remained sunk in their drunken stupor. Stanwyck glared wildly, but was easily hustled into the launch. As the boat glided away Robert saw Trask, standing on the quarterdeck, staring after them. He turned his attention to Stanwyck.

The dark man lay where he'd been thrown, in the bottom of the boat. Water had soaked his coat, and the cold wind of a February morning had him shivering. Robert watched him unblinkingly.

"You could save yourself a lot of difficulty, Stanwyck," he said finally. "You might even save your neck. Talk. Look what keeping quiet back there got you. You're here, and Trask is going free."

"You'll never hang me!"

Robert nodded. "Perhaps not. Perhaps there's a better way. There are men in this boat who own plantations, with overseers who'll do what they're told. Have you ever seen a man whipped to death?"

Several of the rowers missed their stroke, but Stanwyck didn't notice. He licked his lips nervously. "You wouldn't do that to a white man."

"Keep your silence," Robert said, "and find out."

Stanwyck twisted around, peering through the dark at the men at the oars. The few faces he could make out in the moonlight were stark and grim. "All right," he said finally. "All right, I'll talk. It was Fourrier paid me, God rot his soul. I've done a job or two for him, but I never killed no muckety-mucks before. I should've known it was going to go bad, right from the start."

"I'm not interested in your troubles," Robert said coldly. "Stick to the facts. Fourrier sent you to kill Michael Fallon."

"I was to get both of you if I could." Some of the men nearest him shifted away, as if afraid of being dirtied. "After that sugartit man-milliner saw me, though, I knew it wouldn't be long before he told somebody I worked Fourrier slavers. I saw the old man going upstairs by himself, so I took what I could and ran."

"Gott in Himmel!" Karl growled. "So casually he speaks of it. This is not a man. It is an animal."

"What do you know about it?" Stanwyck snarled. "You pretty lads with your fine clothes and your fine horses. You've never had to fight your way out of the gutter."

" Shut up," Robert said, "and answer as you're asked. Was Trask in on it?"

The bound man laughed mirthlessly. "God, yes. He knew what I was here for. Those blacks spent a month getting fat in the Jamaica holding pens while Fourrier arranged things. Oh, yes, he knew."

"Then we will go back for him," Karl said. He looked up out of the boat, and his month fell open. "A fire!"

Everyone peered back down the river. Above the trees a red glow, reflected off the drifting clouds, colored the night horizon red.

"Fourrier will have his hide," Stanwyck muttered.

"It is the ship?" Karl asked.

"It is," Robert answered. "There's no need of going back now. Trask will be long gone."

"But the crew," Karl protested. "They were dead drunk. How could there be time to get them off the ship." Silence answered him. After a moment he breathed a fervent, *"Mein Gott!"*

Suddenly Stanwyck, hands still bound, surged up from the

bottom of the boat, lurching into the staring men. All went down in a shouting heap. Stanwyck managed to gain his feet again, and putting one foot on the gunwale, he leaped into the river.

"Grab him!" someone shouted.

"Where's my gun?"

Robert fumbled in the bottom of the boat until he found a pistol, whose he didn't know. He ignored the others, concentrating on the phosphorescence on the black water where Stanwyck was strongly kicking his way toward shore. He took careful aim, drawing a steadying breath. The pistol cracked, and with a hoarse cry Stanwyck arched up out of the water and fell back. His dark head slipped under, and nothing more disturbed the surface.

"It seems he was right about hanging," Robert said. Dropping the pistol, he moved to his seat in the bow and sat staring toward the city. If Michael died, he thought, he *would* cut Fourrier's heart out.

"The body—" Karl began hesitantly.

"Leave it to the crabs," Langdon said, with a look toward Robert. "To your oars. I think we all need to get back to a warm fire and a stiff drink."

As dawn was breaking, Robert sat at the desk in his father's study. The curtains were still drawn against the night air, and the fire burned low in the fireplace. Two whale-oil lamps on the desk cast the only other light.

The blanket containing the ship's papers, still unread, lay in a wing chair. The contents of Stanwyck's cabin, from clothes to books, lay scattered on the floor. The most interesting part of it, though, sat on the desk. Two hundred fifty pounds sterling, in English coin. And a like amount in Turkish gold.

Idly he fingered one of the large coins covered with a strange script, and with a hole in the center. It made him think of Murad Reis, and of the *Caribe* sitting in Tripoli harbor. How far did Justin's tentacles reach? However far, it was time they were cut off.

The thought made him smile, a grim rictus-like snarl. It would be suitable if the very money Justin had paid for Michael's death was used to finish Justin himself.

The last time he'd been back to Jamaica, Justin had had

thugs waiting. Robert had barely escaped with his life. There would still be men who knew what he looked like, but they'd be looking for a ship's captain. He could go north, ship before the mast on a Yankee trader bound for Jamaica. Once there, he could jump ship. The money would buy information, buy him a way to Justin. And then . . . .

The door banged open, breaking into his thoughts. Catherine stood in the opening. Her face bore lines of tiredness, and she still wore the dress she'd worn the night before. Even so, he thought, she was beautiful.

"Doctor Warren says he'll live," she said wearily. "His exact words were, 'your father's tougher than a man of his years has a right to be, so he'll pull through.' But it'll be a long hard fight." She frowned at the clutter on the floor. "What's all this mess?"

"It belonged to the man who shot father." The tension that had kept him going began to run out. Michael would live. He let his eyes close.

"You caught him? Thank God. The magistrates have him, then, and he'll hang."

"He's dead already. He tried to get away, and I had to shoot him."

"You killed him."

Her tone made him look at her. She had one hand to her throat, and she was looking at him with horror. "For God's sake, girl. He shot our father. And he was trying to get away. It was either shoot, or let him escape."

"Of course," she said hollowly. "There was no other way. I wanted him tried and hanged, Robert. Not hunted down like an animal."

He shook his head in exasperation. He was too tired to explain to the fool of a girl. "I have to go away. I may be gone three or four months."

"Go away! Are you trying to kill my father?"

"What are you talking about? You said he'll be all right."

"I said he'll have a long, hard fight. And you're going to go gallivanting off. Damn you, Robert Fallon! He needs you. He called for you tonight."

"I'll go to him."

"He's asleep, now. Doctor Warren gave him laudanum. But

he'll still need you tomorrow, and the next day, and for months to come. Damn your eyes, you can't go off and leave him."

She was quivering with emotion. He realized how much it had cost her, saying that Michael needed him. Normally she'd have liked nothing better than his going away.

"Very well. My—business can be put off. Catherine," he added as she turned to go, "about your marriage . . . ."

She stopped, not looking at him. "What about it?"

"It will have to be delayed, of course," he finished lamely.

"Of course. Is that all?"

"Yes. No. Catherine, do you love him?"

"Why else would I be marrying him?"

Had there been a slight hesitation? "Nothing else, of course." She stared at him, tight-faced, clutching her skirt with both hands. She was lovely enough to make his thoughts blur. Abruptly he realized that she had been up all night, too, and under as great a strain as he had been. "I'm sorry. I didn't mean to keep you. You must be exhausted."

"Am I dismissed, then?" she said bitterly. Before he could say another word, she was gone, her footsteps sounding up the stairs.

He turned back to the Turkish coins, blinking against the fatigue stealing over him.

His business could be put off for a little while, until Michael was back on his feet, but then he had to get on with it. He knew now that even Catherine's marriage would not control his desire for her.

Exhaustion claimed him, and his head dropped to the desk. Clutching a coin he slept, dreaming of Fourrier.

And Catherine.

XI

Michael Fallon mended slowly through March and April of 1800. By May he was well enough to write to Burr of what he knew, but with summer came a fever in his lungs. Cold compresses and New England ice, brought packed in sawdust on a fast Fallon coasting schooner, saw him through, but just. He was barely able to leave his bed in November, when the presidential election was held.

South Carolina, to the surprise of many, repudiated Adams and Pinckney for Jefferson and Burr, and Michael smiled in his weakness. Hilton had done as he said he would.

Jefferson and Burr carried enough states to win, but then the electoral college met. Federalist electors, bound by law to no candidate, cast just enough votes for Burr to create a tie with Jefferson for the Presidency. And then, with the election thrown into the House of Representatives, Federalist votes went just heavily enough for Burr to keep Jefferson from getting a majority. Through ten ballots it went. Twenty. Thirty. And through the letters he received, Michael could see that Jefferson was beginning to distrust Burr. After all, who else could be behind it?

By February of 1801, almost a year after he was shot, Michael was on his feet, with the aid of two walking sticks. He was able to stand beside his daughter on her wedding day.

As the carriage left with the last wedding guests, Michael laboriously made his way back into the house. Caesar fussed around him, trying to help.

"Go away," Michael said irritably. "Go on. You're so old, if I fall and you try to catch me, we'll both break all our bones."

"Yes, sir," Caesar said, continuing to hover in the background.

In his study Michael dropped into his chair with a sigh of relief. He propped the canes against the desk and rubbed at his chest with one hand. It hurt when he walked, hurt when he breathed, hurt just sitting. He made a sour noise when he realized Caesar was still watching him. "Stop acting like my mauma," he growled. "Go away. No. Wait a minute. Go find Robert. Tell him I want to see him."

"Yes, sir." The old butler gave a doubtful look at Michael, but he went.

Michael began rummaging in his desk. All of them—Warren, Catherine, Karl, even Robert—tried to keep him from working. How was he to do the things he had to do? Strain himself, indeed.

Robert came in without knocking, and immediately began shaking his head. "You know the doctor's instructions."

Michael continued to sort the papers. "Bugger the doctor. The lot of you will have me hobbling on those sticks ten years from now, if you have your way. Well, I haven't got ten years. And I don't have those sticks, anymore. Tell Caesar to take them away. And I'll have good red beef tonight, and none of that broth."

"Father—"

"Now to business. Are you still sure about—"

Robert's voice rose. "Father, are *you* sure? About the sticks, I mean. If you want beef, I say let you have it, but you can hardly make it the length of the veranda without those canes."

"If I can walk so far today, I'll walk further tomorrow. But not if I use those damned sticks. They go. Now, are you ready to hark to business?" Robert nodded, and he went on. "Then I'll ask you again. How certain are you of what you told me about the French and Louisiana? Before you answer, I have a letter here from Lopes. As of the last week in December he doesn't mention the French at all. And some damned assistant to an assistant clerk wrote to tell me the government knows all about the situation in Louisiana, and the French have no intention of seizing it. Damn fool wrote as though he was calming a hysterical woman." He fixed his son with a piercing gaze. "Well? How certain are you?"

Robert hesitated. "I was dead certain at the time, but if the French haven't made a move . . . . I suppose that Spaniard *was* nothing but a drunk."

Michael snorted. "Well, I'm still certain."

"But those letters . . . . "

"Son, I'm still alive, *and* I've made something of a fortune, because I played the hunches other men called foolish. All I have are your Spaniard and the Frenchman Lopes saw, but I'm playing them for all they're worth."

"And what does that mean?"

"It means I want you to go to New Orleans. What's the matter?"

Robert had opened his mouth, then shut it again. "I had intended to go north for a time," he said slowly. "I thought I might go to New York, or Boston. Just for the visit."

"Now why in God's name would you want to do that? You've got more thieves than Charleston in one, more Bible-thumpers in the other. Nothing else."

"I just thought I'd make the trip, go as a passenger. Let someone else have the worries."

Michael stared. This wasn't like Robert at all. "Well, I wish you'd think again. Man, I need you for this. We must convince those dolts in Washington City that something is happening. For that we need evidence, and with me banged up you're the only one I can trust to go get it."

"New Orleans has waited a year. Why can't it wait a few more months?"

"My hunches say you don't wait. If the French were supposed to take over this year, why didn't they? I smell danger, and where there's danger, there's profit for the man who keeps his head."

"Profit?" Robert asked shrewdly. "Or perhaps something to do with your dreams of an American New Orleans?"

Michael chuckled drily. "And what if it does? I'm not the only one believes New Orleans should be ours. Jefferson, Burr, even Hamilton. Not a man of importance and intelligence in this country but believes New Orleans must and will be ours."

"But you intend to do something about it."

"I intend to find out what's going on before we find a French army in New Orleans, that's what I intend. Will you make the trip for me?"

He held his breath while his son frowned into the fireplace. Finally Robert spoke. "I'll go."

"Good."

"I'll sail as soon as *Osprey* is ready. I need to get away from Charleston in any case."

"What's troubling you, Robert?"

"Troubling me?"

He chose his words carefully. "At the ceremony I noticed you in the back with a long face. And after, you shook Karl's hand, said two words to Catherine, and disappeared into the garden while the rest of us were toasting the bride and groom. Now this talk of getting away. Is it trouble with Louise?"

"Louise?" Robert grinned. "No, I've certainly no problems with her."

"No complaints about the places you don't take her? I thought perhaps she might have wanted to come to Catherine's wedding."

"Lord, no! In fact, she has a better sense of where it's proper for me to take my mistress than I do."

"Then I don't understand. Something's bothering you."

"I just need to get away. That's all." Abruptly he seemed to come to a decision. "In fact, I think I'll start getting ready. With luck I can sail for New Orleans by tomorrow. If you'll excuse me, father."

Michael watched him go sadly. Something *was* troubling him. But he'd already dug deeper than was proper between two men. Whatever the matter was, and he feared it was something big to trouble Robert so, he would have to let him find his own solution.

Digging back into the papers piled on his desk, he began muttering to himself. Without him to watch every minute a thousand things went undone. Part of last year's rice crop from Tir Alainn was still unsold. Nothing more had been done about the China venture, though he'd had it all laid out before he was shot. Another Spaniard, one Luis Ruiz Hidalgo, wanted guns, wanted to overthrow the Spanish Viceroy in Mexico.

Furiously he threw himself into it, scribbling instructions on how to handle this, initialing an approval of that. Despite the months' accumulation he felt he was beginning to make headway, when there was a commotion in the street out front.

He got up, scorning the walking sticks, and made his way slowly to the window. He threw up the sash. All along the street, on doorsteps and in clumps on corners, people stood with their heads together. A few men, under the disapproving eyes of their wives, were cheering.

"What is it?" he called. "You, there, Sam Bradley! What is it?"

Bradley, a rotund merchant, peered up at Michael's window with a broad smile. "Fallon? Haven't you heard? Jefferson's won. After thirty-five ballots, he's won!"

"But what of the Federalists?"

"It's said Hamilton himself talked some of them into voting for Jefferson."

"Hamilton!"

"Yes. For the good of the country. Seems we may have misjudged Hamilton, don't you think?"

Michael pulled his head back in without answering. *Hamilton* had talked *Federalists* into voting for *Jefferson*. After he'd set up the whole situation, he'd be remembered as a selfless hero, who talked his own party into voting for his chief opponent in order to spare the country any more strife over who would be president.

He rubbed his chest. Hamilton was more devious than he'd imagined possible. And modern politics was too devious for him, too. Not like the simple revolutionary sort. He walked slowly back to his desk, vowing never to mix in politics again. There was work and plenty for him there. He began to apply himself to it. The price of Barbados rum . . . .

Jeremiah trotted into Vesey's shop, chuckling to himself over all the music and the color of the wedding at the Fallon house.

"Where have you been, boy?"

He looked up in surprise at the harsh tone. Vesey stood in the back, in the shadows.

"I was just down to Mr. Fallon's, Denmark. For to throw

rice at his daughter's wedding.''

"Still can't get over being the bucra's nigger, can you?"
Vesey asked scornfully.

Jeremiah shifted his bare feet on the sawdust-covered floor.
"Mr. Fallon, he been good to . . . . " For the first time he
realized there was someone else in the shadows with Vesey.
"Who that with you, Denmark?"

"No one," Vesey answered quickly. "No one to concern
you."

"Nonsense," said a rasping voice. "I am concerned with all
of my colored brothers and sisters."

A white man stepped out of the back of the shop, and
Jeremiah started. He had seen white men there before, hiring
carpentry done, *but* this man seemed alien. His suit was of the
severest black, and plainly cut. He seemed paler, drier, and
more angular than the men of Charleston. There was no hint
of a smile about his thin mouth, and his eyes held a look
Jeremiah had seen in preachers' eyes when they got caught up
in their own sermons.

"This boy isn't one of—" Vesey began.

"I say that all of them are," the man said. "This is the
Lord's work, and He will not let us rest while one man is held
in bondage by another. From your words to this boy, he
knows of your beliefs. What better for the first than a child
who—"

"*This* child," Vesey broke in, "is not a slave, Houghton.
He's free, an apprentice cabinetmaker." He glared at
Jeremiah. "He was supposed to help me distribute pamphlets,
today. And you'd better learn not to give confidences just
because the skin is black. There are many, those who take old
clothes from the whites, who would turn you in at the first
opportunity."

Houghton did not seem to like being lectured. "I have
labored long to free your people, Denmark. You must let
yourself be guided by me." Vesey's face had a look of disgust,
but Houghton hardly seemed to notice. "You, boy," he
thundered, and Jeremiah jumped as he leveled a bony finger at
him. "Do you want your people freed from the iniquitous
bondage in which they are held?"

"Uh, yes, sir," Jeremiah said. He cast a worried look at

Vesey, who had folded his arms and had a frown on his face.

"Good," Houghton said. "Good. I am the Reverend Hezekiah Comfort Houghton, boy. I know your friend Denmark through the letters he has written to men in the North. In a new day, he will be one of the leaders of your people. And I have come to help bring that new day. I can tell from your words that you, too, believe. And you can help the new day come, too, in a small way. You can help those less fortunate than yourself make *their* way to freedom."

"Damn," Vesey said softly. Then louder, "Damn it all, Houghton, will you be quiet?"

The reverend's face slowly suffused with red, and his eyes goggled. "I am not," he said hoarsely, "accustomed to being addressed in that manner by—"

"By a nigger?" Vesey broke in sharply.

"I did not say that. I was going to say, by anyone."

"Then listen to me, and I won't have to talk that way. If too many people know too much, there's bound to be a betrayal, even if it isn't intended. Look at Gabriel."

Houghton's thin lips thinned even further. "I prefer not to look at Gabriel. Nor to think of him. Violence is never the answer. The sin of slavery cannot be wiped out by the sin of murder."

"And that's not what we're after. But you have to have a little discretion. Jeremiah won't talk of what he's heard. Will you, Jeremiah?" Vesey's eyes burned into his; the older man didn't need to wait for his denial. "For the rest, we must be shrouded in secrecy, or we'll end in the city jail."

The New Englander produced a tall hat from somewhere in the shadows and dusted it with a frown. "I have spent ten years of my life helping your people flee their servitude in Virginia. I do not need to be instructed by . . . by you. I will return when you have had time to calm yourself." Without another word he put on his hat and left.

Jeremiah let his breath out slowly. "Denmark, that man going to get you a Moses' dose."

"*Is* going," Vesey said absently. "*Is*, Jeremiah."

"You better stop worrying about teaching me to talk proper, and start worrying about yourself."

Vesey laughed ruefully. "If thirty-nine lashes were all I had to worry about—you know why Houghton is here?"

"To help runaways get north."

"You're quick, lad."

"I don't have to be quick, the way that man was talking. I read all the pamphlets you get. And I knows about that Fugitive Slave Law."

"So?" Vesey scowled. "You want to leave black people as slaves because the white folks pass a law?"

"Denmark, this law goes all over. Massachusetts or South Carolina, it be the same."

"*Is*, boy. Not *be*."

"Denmark."

"All right, all right. I know it better than you, boy. It's against the white man's Federal law to help a slave run away, or to feed him if he does, or to hide him or do anything at all for him. You're even breaking the law if you know about him and don't tell the sheriff. That's the worst of it in a lump. Now," his voice grew harder, "let's see if I know the worst about you. You hand out pamphlets and read to slaves, but if you're caught you can just claim you're a poor dumb nigger who doesn't know what he's doing. This other, now, helping runaways; there are no excuses if you're caught then. And that's why you're afraid of it, because you're only willing to risk a little bit for your people."

"Denmark, I . . . ." He shifted uncomfortably. "Yes, I'm scared. I don't want to go to jail. But I'll help. Any way you want me to. Honest."

Vesey nodded glumly. "There won't be anything for you to help."

"But that Mr. Houghton . . . . "

"He thinks he's still in Virginia, with safety an hour away by horse. No, the best thing for runaways here is to join the Maroons."

Jeremiah frowned. "The Maroons? My mama makes out like they some kind of heroes, but my papa says they nothing but killers and thieves."

"Your papa," Vesey began angrily, then cut off with a glance at Jeremiah. "Your papa," he went on in a milder tone, "is mistaken. The Maroons are just men and women. And children. They're escaped slaves and the descendants of escaped slaves.'' His voice became fervent. ''There are thousands of them, Jeremiah. Nobody's sure *exactly* how many, but thousands, anyway. They kill because they can't afford to let anyone betray their villages in the swamps. And if they steal, it's from the whites, and less than the whites stole from them.''

Jeremiah stared. The silence dragged on, and he began to fidget. Finally, he said, ''Denmark, who is Gabriel?''

Vesey paused. When he answered, his voice was low and sad. ''He was a hero, Jeremiah.''

''A hero?''

''He got a thousand blacks together last summer, boy, free and slave. A thousand men ready to follow him against the whites in Virginia. Some say he was going to attack Richmond. Some say other thing. It doesn't matter. He was betrayed.'' His voice became bitter. ''By blacks. The sort who pull wool when they see a white man. The kind who suck around white folks' back doors for a handout. He was arrested and hung, and his army ran away without firing a shot.''

''But I never heard nothing, anything,'' Jeremiah protested. ''Or saw anything in the papers, either.''

''Well,'' Vesey said drily, ''the whites don't exactly want it spread around that black men are fighting for their freedom. It might give other blacks ideas.''

''You sound like this has happened before.''

''It's dangerous talk,'' Vesey muttered half to himself, ''even among friends. Still,'' he went on, louder, ''maybe it's time you know. Jeremiah, in the last thirty years in this country, there've been nearly twenty slave uprisings that I know of. Some were big, and some weren't more than a score of men, but there they were. And there must be some I haven't heard about.''

''*I've* never heard *anything* about them. And my mama was always telling me stories about the uprising in Santo Domingo. Tales from slaves whose masters refugeed to Charleston.''

''I told you; it's dangerous information. Even whites like Houghton, who say they want to help, don't want the news to get about. Because no matter what they say, they're still white. Remember that, Jeremiah. White is white.''

He didn't see any point in saying again that he thought

Michael Fallon might be different. "Denmark? Would you do it? Revolt, I mean?"

Vesey took a deep breath. "Boy, you surely do ask a lot of damn fool questions."

"You said I should. You said I should ask you about anything I didn't understand."

"I suppose I did." Vesey bent to pick up a handful of shavings off the floor and bounce them on his palm. "Well, the answer is no. In the first place you're got no place to go, even if you win. And the whites will send an army to put you down. And in the second place, no matter how carefully you plan, there'll always be some white man's faithful nigger to betray you. Now, if that answers your question, let's get to work. Houghton did at least bring some pamphlets from Philadelphia."

"Uh, Denmark?" Jeremiah said diffidently.

Vesey was rummaging in a waste barrel. "What, boy?" he said absently. "Lend a hand here." He began to lift out oilskin packets.

"Denmark, I . . . I was coming to tell you I wouldn't be able to help you this evening." His voice trailed off as Vesey turned, still bent over the barrel, to look at him.

"And why not?"

"Well, you see, it's Delilah. She belongs to Mr. Middleton. Louis Middleton, that is. And she was passing by the Fallon house while I was there. She was on her way to Mr. Middleton's house."

"Spit it out, Jeremiah."

He took a deep breath. "She said she'd be walking up the Neck about an hour from now, on an errand, and wouldn't I like to walk with her." He shivered, remembered how soft she'd felt when she leaned against him.

Vesey seemed to be biting his lip. "Jeremiah," he said at last, "how old are you?"

"Fourteen."

"As I recall," Vesey said with an open grin, "that Delilah is about two years older. But you're tall for your age." Jeremiah wondered what that had to do with anything. "And," Vesey went on, "I'm the last man in the world able to tell you to stay away from women."

"Does that mean you don't mind?"

"I suppose not. And Jeremiah," Vesey added as he started for the door, "if she suggests a side trip—take it. And follow her lead."

"Side trip? What are you talking about?"

"Nothing, boy," Vesey laughed. "Go, or you'll miss her."

Jeremiah didn't need a second telling. He dove through the door and darted down the street, Vesey's laughter still booming in his ears. Briefly he wondered what he could find to laugh about with Mr. Houghton around, but the thought of Delilah pushed that away. Side trip, hmmm?

XII

The carriage ride up the Neck in her wedding clothes seemed interminable to Catherine. There was a light breeze off the Ashley River, harbinger of an early spring, and she was grateful that she and Karl would honeymoon in a rented house away from the dust and bustle of the city. Karl. But it was Karl who was making the trip seem so long with his rambling talk.

"The bulbs come from the Lowcountry," he was saying. "That is, of course, not the Lowcountry here, the coastal plain, but what is called the Lowcountry in Europe, Holland. They must be imported anew each year, for they will not survive the summer here, but—"

Why was he babbling? His blonde, square-chinned face didn't look nervous. An irritating thought struck her. Did he think that she was nervous? Was he trying to calm her with this drivel, as one would soothe a nervous horse with a drone of meaningless sound?

Her lips pursed, and she frowned at him, but his only reaction was to pat the hand he'd held since leaving her father's house. Did he think she was going to try to get away? She eyed the driver's green-clad back and thought of telling him to drive faster. Only the story of Anne Wallace's wedding, and the humiliating way her request for haste had been misunderstood, stopped her.

"—and Mr. Caine assures me that all is in readiness at Seven Oaks for the first planting—"

He was on to something that interested her, now.

"But, of course," Karl went on, "the planting would not interest you. In your compassion as a woman, though, perhaps it will interest you that the matter of manumitting slaves has been complicated by the Legislature. There must now be a hearing before a magistrate. It will no longer be as easy to reward faithful service with freedom. Mr. Caine believes it will have an adverse effect on the labor and morale of slaves. Taking away one of their hopes, as he says. Your brother, Robert, believes that it was inspired by the number of free blacks who took part in that business in Virginia last summer."

She had resigned herself to being bored, but the mention of Robert was too much. "Pooh!" she cried, and raged inwardly at the inadequacy of the word compared to what men could say. Karl's mouth fell open, and even the driver jerked, but she rushed on before her husband could speak. "It's obvious why the law was passed, Karl. Anyone who can read the letters in the newspapers knows, if they can think as well. Part of it was craftsmen, and the men who hire out their slaves to work. They always complain about the number of free blacks competing with them. They certainly don't want more. And then there are people who free a slave if he's crippled, or too old to work. All those can do are steal or beg. They're a charge on the public. Well? Haven't *you* read the letters in the newspapers?"

He stared at her, even after she stopped, then patted her hand in an irritatingly comforting manner. "Yes, my dear," he said finally. "I can see where you could form such an opinion from reading the papers. But you must realize that your brother and I have more direct contact with—"

"Damn it, Karl!" Lord, how satisfying it felt to say that. Even more so to see the shock on Karl's face. "Don't talk down to me. I'm not a child. My opinions are every bit as good as yours. Or Robert's."

His hand-patting increased. "Of course, my dear," he said soothingly. "I should not have suggested otherwise. You must forgive me for upsetting you."

Upsetting her! He thought she was just showing her nerves on her wedding day. Her slow burn flashed into flame.

"Don't you dare patronize me. And stop patting me! I'm not a horse!"

"Of course not, my dear."

Her voice rose dangerously. "Damn, damn, double damn. Will you stop talking that way? I'm perfectly calm!"

"Certainly, my dear." His voice was becoming tinged with panic, and sweat beaded his brow. "I know that you are all right," he said with false earnestness. "I know that."

She took a deep breath to flay him, then let it out again in frustration. The more she tried to convince him she wasn't hysterical, the more he'd believe that she was. God, what a mess. She jerked her hand away and glowered at the coachman's back.

From the corner of her eye she could see him, still watching her worriedly, as if he were seated next to a wild creature. At that moment she hated him.

He took her hand again. Visibly he cast around for something safe to say. "You will like the house where we are having our honeymoon. It is very like the house at Riding Green, I am told. Very cool."

"And what," she snapped, "is Riding Green?" She was too out of sorts to let him smooth things over. He was sitting there looking dumbfounded. "Well?" she said impatiently.

"I was not supposed to mention it," he said softly.

"Not supposed to mention it? Do you mean it's some sort of secret? Karl, I won't have secrets between us. Especially not on the first day of our marriage."

"Your father said I should not speak of it until after the honeymoon."

"My father! Karl, what in heaven's name is this?"

He looked at her anxiously. "Well, there can no longer be any surprise, so I shall tell you. Your father has given us a plantation as a wedding gift. It is, he said, a sort of dowry."

"Dowry," she said eagerly. Surely if it was a dowry, she would have a say in running it. Perhaps she could even get Karl to let her run it completely. "What sort of plantation is this Riding Green?"

"It is fine. The house, as I have said, is much like the one we are going to. It is of brick, and three stories tall, with a front veranda of granite brought by wagon from the Blue Ridge Mountains. The front drawing rooms on the lower floor open on the entry hall for dances and balls. The grounds are magnificent. There is a formal garden. The stables are extensive, and the riding area from which it takes its name—"

"I don't care about the riding area," she broke in. "Is it a rice plantation, or cotton? How many slaves does it have? How many acres, and how much in cultivation? What sort of crop does it produce each year? The important things, Karl, the important things.''

"I do not understand why . . . . Oh, very well. Riding Green is a cotton plantation of three thousand one hundred acres. It has one hundred and ten slaves for the fields and the crafts, and seventeen for the house. Catherine, why are you so eager to know these things? The number of servants for the house, yes, but the rest makes no sense.''

"Karl, if Riding Green is my dowry, I shall of course run it. How can I do that if I don't know these things, and a thousand more about the place?''

Karl looked more stunned than ever. "Run it?'' he said incredulously. "You?'' Abruptly relief washed across his face, as a drowning man might look at a raft close to hand. "We are here.''

She realized that they had left the road up the Neck, and were riding down a drive. As Karl finished speaking the carriage stopped in front of a three-story brick house with large windows and a veranda across the front.

A groom in her father's livery ran to seize the team's bridles as soon as the carriage stopped, and the butler appeared from the house to hold open the carriage door.

"Karl,'' she said hastily, "we must talk about this.''

"But my dear, your woman Mary is waiting for you upstairs. And my man Zeb is no doubt waiting, too. An amusing name, Zeb, is it not? Come my dear.''

He handed her down, and she was suddenly too cold inside to protest further. It had come to her that she was nearly at the very moment. So very soon the man next to her would . . . .

Hazel eyes wide, she stared at Karl as he led her into the house. This blond giant she hardly knew *owned* her. The rector of St. Michael's had pronounced it so, and very shortly Karl would come to her to claim that ownership.

She moved in a haze. She realized he was speaking to her, but she didn't hear. He frowned and spoke again, questioningly. Mary. Mary was upstairs. She turned to the broad curving stair.

Somehow she found her way to the second floor. And there

was Mary, a broad grin on her face. Catherine wanted to speak, but there were no words. But Mary seemed to understand. Her smile became sympathetic.

In the bedroom a huge canopied bed seemed to loom over everything. Her gaze fixed on the turned-down coverlet, the white sheets, as Mary spoke words that she heard only as vague, comforting sounds. But they didn't comfort.

Now Mary was undoing the laces and hooks of her clothes, undressing her. For a moment she shivered with cold as she realized she was standing naked, then the maid slipped a white cotton nightgown over her head.

And then Mary was gone. She was alone. With the bed. She couldn't take her eyes off it. She knew what Karl was going to do to her. She knew the mechanics of it. But the actuality . . . . Her daydreams had never gone beyond a few kisses, followed by a beautiful future in which she and her husband talked by the fireplace of an evening and gave wonderful parties. But in minutes he was going to put her on that bed. She couldn't face it. She couldn't.

She turned to run. And he was there. Silently he stood closing a door on the far side of the room, watching her gravely. She wanted to giggle at the long white gown he wore, so much like her own, with buttons all down the front, but no sound came. He moved to her. His fingers stroked the line of her cheek.

"Do not be afraid," he whispered.

He bent to put an arm beneath her knees and straightened with her in his arms. In spite of herself she leaned against his hard chest. It seemed to be a haven of a sort. And then he bent again, and she realized he was laying her on the bed. She lay there stiffly as he fumbled with the buttons on the front of her nightgown.

"*Liebchen,*" he murmured.

She felt cold across her breasts, and knew that he had opened the gown that far. His head bent to the opening; his lips found her nipple. What in God's name was he doing that for, she thought, then gasped as her nipple went hard and erect.

He moved to the other nipple, and she tried to find words

for the feelings that boiled in her breasts. She put a trembling hand out to touch him. It came down on a hard, bare shoulder.

Bare! Her gaze flickered to him, then hurriedly, ashamedly away. He had managed to remove his own nightrobe. He was naked, and the image of the flat hardness of his body remained burned into her thoughts, bringing a blush that even his touch had not.

She went rigid as she felt him unfastening the rest of her buttons, heard him whispering.

"*Liebchen*. My little flower. Do not be afraid. I will be gentle. Ach, you are so pink and white. So perfect."

Then she, too was naked. His hands roamed over her, caressing her breasts, stroking her, driving her to distraction. She moaned and shifted as his hands traced fire over her body.

"Yes," he whispered. "Yes, my *Liebchen.*"

Dimly she was aware of him moving over her, and then a scalding pain seemed to rip her in two. She put up her hands to push him away, but they could only clutch weakly at his shoulders. She shouted for him to stop, but only a strangled moan came out. He was killing her. She was being murdered by his writhings.

Oh, God, it hurt. It burned. It hurt so that she could barely breathe. And then, suddenly, it didn't any more. It didn't hurt. It still burned, burning that spread through her limbs, but it was a burning she didn't want to stop.

"Karl?" she cried out. "Ahhhh?"

He seemed to redouble his efforts, as if spurred by her cry. Delicious flames licked at her. She seemed to be drifting away from her body, going off where there was no sensation but pleasure.

Images flickered in her mind. Karl, naked. Karl, bending over her. Robert. No. It was Karl, her husband. Karl, naked. Karl, caressing her. Karl. Robert, naked. Robert stroking her. Robert, sending fire through her. Desperately, she tried to push the wicked thought away. She hated Robert. She hated him with every ounce of her being. Karl was her husband. It was Karl who lay with her.

But against all her efforts the image of Robert came back, unbelievably clear. The hard plane of his lean cheek. His hooked nose and piratical, piercing blue eyes. The scar at his temple. The one curl that always seemed to fall across his forehead. Inwardly she writhed in shame as she tried to picture his body, his hard, naked body. And to her horror she realized that the tongues of pleasure that lapped at her bored deeper when the image in her mind was Robert.

Suddenly she became aware that Karl was grunting as he moved against her. She opened her eyes in time to see his face go into a red grimace. He stiffened against her, his breath rushing hoarsely past her ear.

Slowly his breathing returned to normal, and he rolled heavily off of her. He patted her cheek and gave her peck of a kiss. "It had been a long day, my dear, yes? We will nap before dining." And he rolled over and promptly began to snore.

Wide-eyed she stared at the canopy over the bed. It was over. She felt suspended on a precipice. Her breasts felt painfully tight, her belly burned, and her thighs trembled with need she didn't understand. God, there had to be something more. There had to be.

Hesitantly she put a hand to her still swollen breast. She gasped. The touch of her own fingers was magical. They felt as good as Karl's, perhaps better. Unbidden, her other hand crept downward to the juncture of her thighs. The flames leaped high once more, and she wanted to cry. She wanted to cry; she wanted to laugh; she could barely find air to breathe. She was sure she should stop. What her hands were doing must be sinful. It felt too good not to be. But it felt too good to stop. It felt too good. It felt . . . .

The world exploded; fire raced along her limbs and through her belly. With gaping mouth and staring, unseeing eyes she arched up from the bed, and a low shriek ripped out of her. "Roberrrrt!"

Karl stirred beside her, but didn't wake. Exhausted, she fell back, and immediately dropped into a troubled sleep, filled with dreams of her half-brother.

Robert stepped aside to let two crewmen carry a crate up the gangplank to *Osprey's* deck, then turned back to Crane.

"Then everything will be ready. I want to sail on the first

tide in the morning.''

His first mate looked near distraction. "It'll all be ready, sir. But I don't understand the need for such haste. New Orleans is a ragtag little place, except for the river trade.''

"The river trade's why we're going, Mr. Crane. There's a warehouse full of Fallon-owned furs to pick up. And we're hurrying because I say to. I expect *Osprey* to be ready the moment there's light. Is that understood?''

"Yes, Captain,'' Crane said stiffly.

Robert nodded and headed toward the street where his carriage waited. The driver took one look at him as he climbed in, and the smile faded from his face. Robert was a study in glowering. At the small house on Queen Street he'd bought for Louise, he hurried inside and immediately began shouting up the stairs.

"Simon! Cloe! Esmerelda! Where are you? I want my bags packed! Stir your stumps or I'll fire the lot of you.''

With a clatter and rush the three appeared on the stairs above. Simon, the dignified black butler, who also acted as Robert's manservant, was slender in his long coat of dark blue. Cloe, plump and round, was the housekeeper, while Esmerelda was Louise's abigail. Louise had been surprised when he'd hired them, along with a cook and a groom, instead of buying slaves, but she'd kept her peace.

"Simon, lay out my razor, then begin packing my seachest. Cloe, tell Lerner to prepare a light collation. Esmerelda . . . . ''

He became aware that Louise was standing in the drawing-room door. "La!'' she said lightly. "There is such a commotion that I think me there is perhaps a bull-baiting in the house.''

"I'll be sailing in the morning,'' he said slowly. God, what a fool he was, he thought. To let a woman he couldn't have chase him away from one he could!

Her face fell for just an instant, then recovered. "Is one permitted to ask when you will return?''

He took Louise's arm and led her into the drawing room. Nervously she smoothed the front of her pale yellow dress, then knotted her hands together. He watched her, frowning.

"What's the matter, Louise? You knew all along I'd sail

sooner or later. I'd never have stayed in port this long if my father hadn't been shot."

"I know that." She sat quickly at a writing table by a window, her back to him, and ruffled through letters laid out on its surface.

"Then I don't understand," he said after a minute. "You don't think I'm going to abandon you, do you? Even if I never came back, Todd will see that your expenses are paid and your allowance continued. He won't cheat you."

"You are one big fool, Robert Fallon," she said quietly.

"Perhaps you'd better explain."

She smoothed a letter on the table, then refolded it. "I have written to my father's *advocat*. I had very much desire to discover how papa's affairs were being handled."

He felt a chill. He couldn't lose her, not on top of the rest. "And what did you find out?" He thought his voice was remarkably calm.

"There was not much money," she said, still not looking at him. "Papa was not a rich man. But there is a small house in Paris, and two farms, one in the south and one in the north, near the Pas de Calais. Also there is some land in Louisiana, I do not know how much, not large. I am the *héritier*, the heir, Robert."

"So," he said after a bit. "I suppose you'll be leaving, then."

She looked over her shoulder at him. Her lips were tight, her eyes flashed. "You are one big fool. I tell you this so you will know I do not worry that you will leave me destitute. And so you will know that I do not stay with you just because you give me a house and money."

"I'm sorry, Louise." He touched her face, and she let her cheek rest against his palm.

"Why don't you come with me to New Orleans? I'll be gone for months at the best, and there's no need for you to stay here." He said it on impulse, and regretted it instantly. He'd never seen anything but trouble from a captain carrying wife or mistress on a voyage. But there was no way to back out now.

"New Orleans!" She made a face. "I will admit that I was mistaken about Charleston. It is a city of charm, and even sophistication. But New Orleans, Robert? La! It is truly on the edge of the wilderness. Besides, if I go with you, there will be no *belles femmes* for you." She looked at him with exceeding casualness.

"Louise—" he said hesitantly.

"Hush, *mon cher*. You are Irish, like your papa, and emotional. I am French, and practical." She smiled. "I do not think I am the only woman to whom you make love, but I will not try to change you. Now. When do you sail?"

"In the morning." He remembered the reason for his haste, and it made him sound grim. "At the first tide."

"So! Tonight, then, we will make love, no?" She held her arms up to him.

"Yes," he said thickly.

He picked her up out of the chair and carried her toward the stairs. Her face was turned up to him, her large eyes twinkling, a mischievous smile on her lips. For a little while thoughts of Catherine would be buried deep in his brain.

XIII

The early August heat from the Mississippi rolled along Rue Dumaine under a burning sun, bringing the dank smell of the cypress swamps around the city. Robert mopped at his face. He wondered how it could possibly be hotter in his room than in the muggiest South American port, but it did seem so. It was just as well Louise had stayed behind.

He checked his watch. Two hours short of noon. Lopes, the manager of the Fallon warehouse, was due any minute. And unlike most men of business he'd met in Spanish colonies, Lopes could be counted on to be prompt. Robert shrugged into his tight-fitting coat of dark blue superfine, checked his high white stock in the mirror, then took his walking stick and tall beaver hat and went down to the street. Lopes arrived at the front door at almost the same instant he did.

The Spaniard was a slender man of medium height, with small, carefully edged mustachios and a tiny triangle of beard. He bowed over his walking stick. "Good morning, *Señor* Fallon I see you are recovered from the wine and the ladies of last night, and once more eager for your search. Whatever it is for."

"The heat's worse than any head from wine," Robert answered with a smile. "And my rooms are more like an oven every day. It makes a man eager to be up and out."

Lopes smiled. "At least it is better than the cabin of your ship, no?"

"It is that," he admitted. Frowning, he thought of *Osprey*, and of his crew. "If I don't sail soon, though," he muttered to himself, "I may not be able to root my men out of the taverns."

Lopes arched an eyebrow, and murmured, "There *are*

attractions in the *cantinas*. But your *Señor* Crane," he went on, "he will not be joining us?"

Robert grimaced. Crane was sodden in his rooms across the hall from Robert's. "No. He was a bit shocked to find out the lady he'd been squiring was married. I'm afraid he took it out on a bottle. Don't you think we should get on to this meeting you've arranged? If there's any chance these men know something about the French privateers who've been giving us trouble . . . . "

"Of a certainty," Lopes said smoothly, "we must find the French privateers who are troubling the Fallon ships." His tone was a trifle patronizing; Robert saw that he didn't believe the story for a minute. "I think it is very possible these men will know. But tell me," he added as they started down the street, "were you also shocked to discover that your so delightful companion was married?"

He threaded his way through the foot traffic and sedan chairs behind the Spaniard. Carmella was a lush brunette with misleadingly demure eyes. "Not enough to stop me from taking her to the Théatre de St. Pierre tonight."

"Alas, the *señora*'s husband came home unexpectedly from patrol, and she will be unable to join us. Such are the vicisitudes of a military marriage."

"Yes," Robert said drily. "I can see that." He had been shocked at first, he realized. Not so much that the women who so eagerly accepted an invitation to the theater, and more, were married. That had never stopped him before. But the men of the city seemed to assume that every wife, except their own, was unfaithful. Lopes had explained that many women, raised under the close chaperonage of a *duenna*, found their first opportunity for dalliance after they were married, and no few took advantage of it. As he could testify. He realized that Lopes was talking again. "I'm sorry. I didn't catch that."

"I said that you will not even miss the lovely Carmella. There is another woman, one who has been making inquiries about you."

"Inquiries!" Robert stopped, letting the throng pass around him.

Lopes looked bemused. "Why so surprised?"

"I have enemies," he said carefully. "I'm leery of strangers asking questions about me."

"Oh, no. No, it is nothing like that. This is a widow, an *Americano,* who saw you at the opera and has asked for an introduction. You will enjoy her. She has beautiful *seno,"* he made a cupping motion in front of his chest, "and I tell you she is a woman who enjoys men."

Robert shook his head doubtfully. "Perhaps. We can speak of her later. Right now I want to get to that meeting."

"But we are there," Lopes said, and gestured to a tavern across the street.

A sign proclaimed the *Cantina El Alhambra,* but for all its fine name it was another seafarers' inn. Lopes ignored the inn-keeper behind the bar and the plump girls carrying drinks to the tables, and led Robert to the back and up a flight of stairs.

The paneling was handsomer there, and there was carpet on the floor. Here were the private rooms, for those who had more money than the patrons below. Lopes opened a door without knocking, then gestured for silence as soon as they were inside.

Two men awaited them. A dark, slender, smiling man watching an older, gruffer man bent over a billiard table. The older man shot, and the object ball caromed off a cushion, struck the red ball, and missed the second white ball widely. He flung down his cue and glared at Robert and Lopes.

"*Oncle,*" the slender man said soothingly, and bent over the table in turn. There was a sharp click-click as the object ball came off the cushion and struck each of the others in turn. His smile broadened, and he held out his hand. Scowling, the older man slapped a wad of paper money into it.

"*Señor* Fallon, this is Renato Beluche," Lopes said, indicating the older man, "and this is his cousin, Alexandre Lafitte. They are smugglers. Among other things."

"You," the younger man snapped. His smile disappeared. "Here I am called Dominique You."

"Of course," Lopes said. "*Señor* You."

Robert looked at the two men warily. They were both French, but from the colonies by their accents. "Gentlemen, I am seeking information."

"I hope you can pay for it," Beluche grumbled. You's smile reappeared, and he ostentatiously tucked his winnings into his coat pocket.

"I can pay," Robert said cautiously. "Within reason, for solid information."

"If you have the money," Lafitte, or You, said, "We have the information. But old Lopes would not tell us what it is you want." Lopes sat down, fanning himself with his hat. He looked amused.

Robert eyed the Spaniard, wondering once more whether he was playing some deeper game. "My name is Robert Fallon."

"That much he told us," Beluche rumbled. "The information, *monsieur?* I am not so comfortable on Spanish soil as to wish to linger."

"Very well. I want information about Frenchmen around New Orleans. My family's ships trade heavily here, and there's been trouble lately. Attacks. Ships shadowing ours. If you'll forgive me, gentlemen, we have reason to believe our troubles are caused by French pirates. Since they must know sailing times from New Orleans . . . . Well, you can see my need.

For a minute Beluche and You stared at him. You's smile slowly widened to split his thin face. "My *oncle* Renato and me," he said, "we are French pirates."

Beluche winced. *"Merde,* Dom! Not pirates. Privateers. We have the commission."

The slender Frenchman shrugged. "It does not matter, *oncle*. But, *Monsieur* Fallon, we have never taken *any* American vessel. Only those of England and its allies." He finished with a defiant look at Lopes, as if daring him to say they'd ever touched a Spanish ship.

"Our countries are, of course, allies," the Spaniard said blandly, but his blandness faded as he turned to Robert. His dark eyes became intesne. *"Señor*, I do not work only for your family. Also I labor for myself. In the weeks, the months, that you have been here, I have become convinced that I must know the true reason for your visit." He held up both hands as Robert started to speak. *"Por favor*. Do not deny it. No French privateer has attacked an American ship, but you do seek the French, and from the time you have spent at it, it is important that you find them. It is important for me, too, I think. Tell us the true reason you seek Frenchmen in a Spanish colony, and I will help to my last breath. As will *Señor* You and *Señor* Beluche.''

''*You* helped him,'' Beluche grunted. ''Why should we?''

Lopes looked at Robert before answering. ''Because his family has supplied arms to help over throw Spanish rule in the Americas.'' He made a shrugging gesture with his hands. ''Forgive me, *Señor* Fallon, but it will help you get the information you desire.''

''How do you know about that?'' Robert asked gruffly.

''Because I, too, aid in my small way, *Señor*. And I have helped your father. I was born in Caracas. That makes me what is called a Creole.'' He grimaced. ''I would rather be a citizen of my own country than a second-class Spaniard.''

''A very nice speech,'' You said drily. ''Hey, Fallon. Is this true? You sell guns to *les revolutionnaires?* Why?''

Robert answered carefully. ''My father fought in our revolution. He doesn't like colonies. Anybody's colonies.''

''And you, eh? What about you?''

''If people want their own country, then I believe they ought to have it. Now you answer a question. Why would this make any difference to you?''

''I was born in Port-au-Prince,'' You said. ''I am French enough to fight for France, but not enough for other things. So I don't like colonies, either. Besides, I don't like the Spanish government too much. If you help somebody fight them, then I like you. What you want to know?''

''The money, Dom,'' his uncle protested.

''We talk later, *oncle*. *Monsieur* Fallon?''

They all looked at Robert expectantly. He hesitated, then took the plunge.

''I have information that control of this city passed to France some time last year.''

Lopes merely stared at him. You laughed, and Beluche grunted.

''*Señor*,'' Lopes said carefully, ''the flag of Spain still flies here.''

''I know it sounds crazy,'' he said calmly, ''but the treaty itself was secret, signed maybe five years ago. It's possible the transfer is being kept secret, too.''

You looked at him thoughtfully. Beluche crossed to the sideboard and poured himself a drink, gulped it down, and belched. "You ready to go, Dom?"

"Yes," You said regretfully. He picked up his hat and walking stick, avoiding looking at Robert. "Perhaps we do business again sometime, *Monsieur* Lopes. *Monsieur* Fallon."

"A moment," Lopes said thoughtfully. "Think you carefully, the pair of you. I know enough of the intrigues of governments not to dismiss *Señor* Fallon's story out of hand. I, for one, should not like to suddenly discover that I am not only a Spanish Creole, but a Spanish Creole in a French colony. And you, *messieurs*. Would you like to suddenly discover a French naval base here? Perhaps there would be no need for privateers? Perhaps there might be some, shall we say indignation, when it is discovered that some among those privateers are known to smuggle brandy and such into the territory?"

"Is still crazy story," Beluche said.

"Be still, *oncle*," You said. He still held his hat and walking stick, but he had not turned to go. "Lopes, in truth France would like the return of New Orleans, but why would it be kept secret?"

Lopes shrugged. "This Bonaparte of yours, he does things no man has done before. And he likes very much for what he does to come as a surprise. So?" He shrugged again.

You put down his hat and sat down.

Beluche appeared dumbfounded. "Dom, they are both crazy. Let us get out of here and back to the ship."

"*Oncle*," You said, "you are one fine smuggler, and you are maybe even better with the cannons than I myself, but when you get on dry land your brains don't work so good. You want to risk our government finding out we been smuggling? They will hang us damned near as quick as the Spanish. Sit down. We can afford to waste a few days. Now, *Monsieur* Fallon, what do we look for?"

"I don't know," Robert said, and for a moment he could see them slipping away again. "After all, I'm talking about something the French want kept secret. Maybe even the Spanish authorities here know nothing. So you needn't expect a French flag."

"*Non*," Beluche snorted. "We look for the ghost of King Louis. I want some more rum."

Robert ignored him. The other two listened closely. "Look for anything, anything at all, that even seems to indicate official French interest. The French community is the likeliest place for it, but I'm afraid *Señor* Lopes doesn't have any contacts there."

Lopes gestured apologetically. "There is little, how do you say it, intermingling."

Beluche, filling his third glass, laughed. "By damn, there is not. They may say we are allies in Paris and Madrid, but—"

"Peace, *oncle*," You said. "*Monsieur* Fallon, my *oncle* Renato and me, we will take in the French *quartier*. If there is something to know, we will discover it. But it may not come quickly."

"I don't expect it to," Robert answered. "But we each have our own reasons for wanting to know before the whole world does. We'll meet here at ten each day until we have what we need."

"Done," You said. "Come, *oncle*. Let us begin."

"Species of a . . . ." Beluche's mutter faded into inaudibility. "I come here to shoot a little billiards, drink a little rum . . . . " He followed the younger Frenchman out.

Knowing what they were about vitalized Lopes. That day the Spaniard ferreted out pepole they hadn't been near before, asking about French Canadian fur traders come down the Mississippi, French commercial interests in New Orleans, French naval activities anywhere in the Gulf of Mexico or the Caribbean. At times Robert thought he was going too far, beginning to arouse suspicion, but always Lopes drew back at the last instant. Still, in tavern after tavern, on wharf after wharf, men from high-born Castilians to venal Customs men to rum-ridden sailors told what they knew. And they knew nothing.

As darkness began to fall, the streets emptied. Robert called a halt.

"It's getting late, *Señor* Lopes, and I am getting tired. Perhaps Beluche and You will have something in the morning."

"It is possible." Lopes took out an ornate watch and snapped open the painted lid. "Aiee! It *is* late. And we have lovely ladies to escort to the opera."

"You escort them. I'm going back to my rooms, to bed."

"But the ladies, *señor*. They are waiting. They are expecting us."

Robert sighed. Perhaps he was simply discouraged. "Very well. Perhaps wine and pretty women are just what I need."

"*Bueno.* Your *Señor* Crane, I suppose he will not wish to join us."

Robert had to smile. "I don't expect he will."

"Then I must find some story for the lovely Juanita. No matter. I will send her a note. In any case, I will be at your rooms with my carriage in three quarters of an hour. We must make haste. *Buenas tardes, señor.*"

Lopes disappeared into the twilight, and Robert turned the other way, back toward his apartments. As he went up the stair to his rooms, he met Crane leaving. The mate looked unsteady, as if there was still a feel of greenness in his belly.

"Ah, Mr. Crane. Feeling better?"

Crane's queasy face settled in lines of glum disapproval. He drew himself up to his most priggish. "Captain, I have often upbraided Charleston for its wickedness. The gambling, the consorting with loose women, the horse racing and cock fighting even on the Lord's Day. But this city is infinitely worse." His voice dropped to a near hiss. "New Orleans is the Whore of Babylon incarnate."

"Mr. Crane, you need a dose of salts. Or," he added with a straight face, "try a little half-cooked salt pork, floating in its grease."

Crane's mouth snapped shut. His eyes bulged. The disapproval on his face was swept away by a wave of pale green. With a noise like a choking goat he hurriedly fumbled his way back into his rooms.

Robert, grinning, listened to the retching sounds from inside and shook his head. He'd often wondered how such a good seaman could be such an unholy bible-thumper. God knew, this couldn't have been the first time Crane had been exposed to the temptations of the flesh.

But then he had no more time to think about his mate. He made a hasty wash in a basin of cold water, and hurriedly got out fresh linen. By the time Lopes' closed carriage appeared in the dark street below, he was attired in a long, plain black coat, cut tight across the chest and shoulders, and soft gray trousers, which were beginning to replace breeches for all but the most formal occasions. With his hat on his head and walking stick in hand, he went downstairs.

Lopes stepped down from the carriage into the pool of light from the windows. "Come, *señor*. Hurry. We must not miss the opening curtain."

Robert allowed himself to be bundled inside, and Lopes tapped on the roof as soon as he was seated. The coach lurched into motion.

He knew the heart-faced girl seated next to Lopes, Carmen Estevar, whose husband was a confidant of Morales, the Intendant. But his attention was focused on the other woman seated beside him.

He had an impression of upswept, elaborately coiffured hair and a great expanse of pale skin above her decolletage. Cool eyes watched him from the shadows above a catlike smile.

"*Señor* Fallon," Lopes said, "this is *Señora* Cordelia Applegate. The *señora* is a widow from your state of Tennessee, but lately moved to our city. *Señora* Applegate, *Capitàn* Robert Fallon."

"Ah," the woman said. "A ship captain. I should have known." She moved closer to press a full breast against his arm.

Remembering his earlier suspicions, he said, "You're a widow, Mrs. Applegate? My condolences. I'm surprised you left Tennessee, though. The comfort of family and friends can be a great help."

She frowned slightly. "I had no family in Tennessee, Captain Fallon, and certainly no friends among our—neighbors. They were farmers, dirt poor and dirt ignorant. It was the comparative elegance and sophistication of New Orleans that first attracted me." With a sudden smile she took his hand in both of hers. "Now, captain, do we truly have to talk of Tennessee?"

He darted a glance at Lopes and Carmen, but they were engrossed in each other, whispering and giggling. "Mrs. Applegate—"

"Cordelia."

"Cordelia, we've just met."

She laughed throatily. "You think me forward, over-bold?"

He took a deep breath. There was nothing to be found out tiptoeing around the edges. "Yes. I do find you forward. Incredibly so for a woman of your background. I want to know why."

He'd made his voice deliberately cold, but she simply laughed again. "Well, you're right. I am bold. Captain . . . Robert . . . my husband left me fairly wealthy. I don't need a man to support me, and I don't care what people think, though *that's* hardly a problem here."

"That still doesn't explain why you were asking questions about me."

She let his hand fall. "Very well," she said, an edge to her voice, "if you must know, I saw you in the boxes at *Lenore,* and then again the next week at some Italian thing by Cherubini. I don't recall the name. You're a handsome man, Robert, with broad shoulders and quite an air of command about you. Each time I saw you there was a different woman on your arm, and they all looked . . . contented. In this city, my money allows me to pursue men the way you no doubt pursue women. I *had* intended to pursue you."

"You intended to . . . pursue me?" In the shifting light he couldn't see her face. "Have you ever heard the name Fourrier?"

"No," she said sharply. "I don't have many friends among the French here."

"You'll have to forgive me," he said slowly. "The last time a woman, ah, pursued me, for no reason I could see, she was employed by Fourrier. To kill me."

"And you thought I . . . . " She sounded caught between amusement and anger. "Well, at least it makes you more interesting. I can believe you are a man other men want to kill."

"Just one man."

"And what did you do to make this one man want to kill you?" The flirtatious note was coming back into her voice.

"He had his reasons. I suppose he thinks they're good ones."

"A man of mystery." Her voice was warm again, and throaty. His hand was restored to its former place. "I like men of mystery."

The box Lopes had secured for them was close to the stage, with an excellent view. Every sound from the singers could be heard clearly. Still, when the opera was over, Robert knew only that it had been called *La Clemenza di Tito* and written by the German composer Mozart.

He spent the entire opera looking at Cordelia. She was beautiful, with flaming red hair and cool green eyes. Her round and almost fully exposed breasts shimmered like satin in the light of the opera house. Her flesh seemed to call for his touch. His experience told him red-haired women didn't wear red, but Cordelia wore scarlet and carried it off with aplomb.

After the opera, as they reentered the coach, Cordelia suddenly spoke. "Captain Fallon, *Señor* Lopes, I'm afraid you'll have to excuse me from our dinner. I seem to have come down with a headache." Her eyes closed, and she put a hand to her forehead.

Robert looked at Lopes, who shook his head and shrugged; Carmen smiled at him mockingly.

"Of course, Cordelia," he said. "We'll take you home."

"Of a certainty," Lopes said. He opened the trap and gave orders to the driver.

Cordelia sat with her hand hiding her eyes until the coach stopped in front of a three story house with white-plastered walls and wrought-iron balconies. Robert got out to hand her down. As he did so, she caught at his wrist.

"If you would, captain. I have a fear of coming home late alone. Would you enter with me?" She turned to the house door, not waiting for his answer.

Lopes stuck his head out. "Of a *most* certainty *Capitàn* Fallon will not leave you, *Señora* Applegate. *Capitàn* Fallon, it is but a short walk to your rooms from here. Until tomorrow." He tapped on the coach roof, and it lurched off into the night.

Robert stared after it for a minute, then hurried after Cordelia. Her butler bowed, and closed the door behind him.

A maid was taking her wrap. "You may go, Lucinda," she said. "And you, Augustus." The two slaves withdrew, without a glance at Robert. Ignoring him, Cordelia started up the stairs. Then she turned, with a mischievious, and slightly malicious, smile. "Captain. You must learn not to be so ungracious toward a lady who favors you."

He took the stairs three at a time to seize her shoulders. "Don't play games with me," he said angrily. "When I don't know the rules, I make up my own." And he pulled her up into a kiss.

He straightened to find her watching him with calm, self-confident eyes.

"Well," she said with a slight breathlessness. "Perhaps you can stay after all."

"I never intended anything else," he growled, and scooped her up in his arms.

Still wearing that infuriatingly calm smile, she pointed the way to her bedchamber. He kicked the door shut behind them; she murmured, "Let me down," and immediately began to undress.

He looked at her a moment, then shrugged out of his coat and began loosing his stock. He had never yet bedded a woman in rage, yet he realized he was close to it. That hint of coldness in Cordelia Applegate, that feeling that a hair's breadth beneath her surface she was watching it all calmly, stoked his anger. But it didn't quench his lust.

She faced him, hands on hips. Her pale skin was satin smooth, her breasts large, but shapely, and so milky white as to seem tinged with blue. He could nearly span her waist with his hands. It made the flare of her hips even more enthralling. Her long, slender legs were a challenge to any man. And then he was upon her.

Their coupling, on the floor, was more a contest than an act of love. She spurred him, goaded him, as if her insatiability would wring him dry. Yet he gloried in meeting her challenge, in the moments when, wide-eyed as if with surprise, she screamed her exaltation. He lifted her onto the bed, and she returned to the caresses and strokings, the murmurs and soft cries, until both were sweat-slick and panting.

Then the door burst open. Robert knew a moment of panic. He pulled free of her entangling arms and legs, dove for the pistols in his coat. Even as he did so, he knew he'd be too late. And yet no shots came. His hands found the pistols; he swung up to one knee with the guns presented.

Renato Beluche and Dominique You stood grinning at him from the doorway. "Is that how you greet your *amis?*" the younger Frenchman asked in mock horror.

"He should put on some pants," Beluche snickered. "The pistols, they don't cover too much."

"What in hell are you doing here?" Robert growled. "And how the hell did you find me?"

"You know these, these . . . . " Cordelia's shriek burbled off into incoherence. The sheet she had pulled up to half-cover her breasts, and her damp hair, clinging in ringlets, made her the picture of a wanton in the middle of the bed.

"That one nice bit, Fallon," Beluche said appreciatively. He ogled her, and gave her a wink.

"God damn it," Robert began.

"Easy, *mon ami*," You soothed. "Lopes told us where you were. And I must say he was as angry as you about being pulled away from the sultry Carmen, or whatever her name is. Now put on your trousers, *s'il vous plait*. I have myself found what you are looking for."

"Couldn't it wait till morning?" Robert said, but he was already getting dressed.

"Augustus!" Cordelia screamed suddenly. "Call the watch!"

Beluche shook his head in exasperation. "I had a woman with a mouth like you, I whip her *derrière*."

"If you please, Captain Beluche," Robert said. "Cordelia, be quiet. These are my friends. There's no need to call the guard. You, whatever you found had better be good."

"How about an encampment of French Army Engineers?" You said. He adjusted his cuffs, smugly.

Robert froze with his shirt half on. "Are you certain?"

"*Certainement*. I did not come here on the errand of a fool."

"You bastard," Cordelia hissed. She scrambled from the bed, still holding the sheet around her. "You're leaving me to go after some, some . . . . " Words failed her for a minute, then her face twisted and her fury redoubled. "Damn you! Goddamn you! Which one of them's going to bugger you? I thought you were a man, but you're nothing but a mewling—"

Beluche's broad hand clasped her mouth. His other arm encircled her waist and lifted her feet clear of the floor. "Only way to shut them up," he said. The sheet fell away, and she writhed and kicked in naked rage.

"For Christ's sake," Robert said. "Put her down. She won't cause any trouble."

"I know," Beluche said. Before Robert could move, he went swiftly to the clothes press and pushed her in, pulling a chair over to jam under the door handle. "There. Now she don't cause any trouble."

Robert hesitated, but the muffled shrieks and imprecations from the clothes cabinet decided him. He winced as the howls grew louder. "She's sure to wake the servants, and then we'll have the guard to contend with."

"We will be long gone," said You. "Besides, will she really wish them to know she has been locked naked in her own clothes press?"

Robert took a last look at the cabinet, but the undiminished fury of Cordelia's shouts gave him no incentive to let her out. Instead, he put on his coat and followed the two Frenchmen out.

For all the Frenchmen's reluctance to be in Spanish New Orleans longer than necessary, they seemed to know a great number of people. A weedy Spaniard with one eye produced horses for them, and when the three men rode east out of the city to the edge of the cypress swamp, a whispered conversation with a black man in a rundown shack led them to a dugout canoe. The narrow strip of black water they took, wending its way under moss-covered trees, cypress knees jutting like posts out of the water, was, You told him, Bayou Vienvenue.

Robert knew that on his own he would have been lost in five minutes. At times the bayou seemed to disappear, and they poled through the simple swamp. Always, though, the way cleared again. The stream widened, and they poled on through the miasma of rotting vegetation, with no sounds but the cries of night birds, the buzzing of mosquitos, and their own breathing. The day was so new that there was no hint of light or dawn.

At last, Beluche stopped poling and raised his hand.

"What is it?" Robert asked. You motioned him to silence.

At last the older Frenchman nodded. "There is someone ahead, by damn."

"I don't hear anything."

"Trust *mon oncle*," You said quietly. "Put water under him, and there is no one better. If he says there is someone, there is someone."

Slowly they began to pole forward again. Once more the cypress trees closed in. Then, abruptly, there were lights ahead. Expertly, Beluche and You slowed the canoe with their poles.

Set among the cypress ahead was an island, the first truly dry land they had seen since entering the swamp. A number of canoes lay drawn up by the water. A half-dozen campfires, screened from most directions by the trees and brush, lit an ordered array of tents, ten small ones and one large. Beyond the fires, in front of a mound with the regular angles of stacked crates, a man in rough civilian clothes paced with a musket in the even stride of a sentry. There was no other movement.

"Damn," Robert muttered. "I didn't think there'd be anything this big."

"So," Beluche grunted, "you going to give up?"

He studied the island for a moment, then shook his head. "No. I can get by that sentry. Let's go in."

They poled closer, until the bow of the canoe struck the dark island. Quickly they hauled it ashore and concealed it in the low bushes.

"Where do we begin?" You whispered.

Robert pointed to the big tent and he moved forward in a crouch. The other two followed at his heels, but he didn't spare them a glance until he was flat on the ground behind the tent. He lifted the edge of the tent slightly. Beluche moaned.

A lantern, turned low, hung from the center pole of the tent. There were several chests, a table, and two cots, one of them holding a sleeping man.

"One man," Robert whispered. "Knife."

You produced a knife; there was a tearing sound as Robert made a long vertical slit in the canvas. He went through as soundlessly as possible, and headed straight to the table. It was a jumble of papers. Beluche and You slipped in after him.

Suddenly the sleeping man sat half up. "Etienne?" he muttered sleepily. Beluche's fist hammered into his jaw, and he sprawled back onto the bed, one arm swinging over the side.

Robert let out a long breath and unrolled a paper. He almost shouted in triumph. It was a map of the area east of New Orleans, with notations on likely sites for fortifications. He began hurrying through the rest of the papers. "Dominique," he said, "help me look through these."

Beluche, who had opened one of the chests, looked up with a grin. "Surveyor's instruments. With the crest of the Armé de la République."

"Take one," Robert said. He stuffed the maps under his shirt. "Dominique?"

"Nothing. A report on food expended." You said. He was scanning sheets rapidly. "Another on gunpowder. *Sacré bleu*, do they do nothing but write reports? Wait. Here is something with a seal." He began to read. "'You are hereby ordered to carry out a survey of the approaches of the city of New Orleans preparatory to the city being occupied by the government of France.'"

"That's it," Robert said. He matched You grin for grin.

Beluche said, "I think maybe it is time to get out of here."

"Hell, yes," Robert began.

"Aux armes! A moi! Aux armes!"

The officer had suddenly lurched from his cot, shouting. Before they could move he threw himself on Robert.

Robert, struggling to free himself, shouted, "Get going! I'll follow."

Instead, Beluche grabbed the officer, and You hit him on the head with a pistol. Then they all tumbled through the rear of the tent and ran for the boat.

The camp boiled like a kicked antnest. Rapid-fire commands were shouted; men poured out of the tents, grabbing muskets as they came, taking aim at any shadow.

Robert ducked as an errant ball clipped a twig by his head. Wrestling the boat into the water, they tumbled in. Beluche grabbed a pole immediately, but Robert took a moment to look back at the chaos behind him. Muskets were still being left off at random.

"That officer must still be out," he said at last. "Do you think they'll get a boat after us?"

"Never," You said.

"They are shooting themselves in the feet," Beluche laughed. "*Hé!* You two going to let me pole back to the city by myself?"

Robert and You turned to, and the canoe sped away from the cacophony on the island.

Back in the city, the first hint of dawn was on the horizon as Robert invited You and Beluche by his rooms for a drink. At the top of the stairs Robert stopped with an oath. His door hung by one hinge.

"What the hell!" He brushed past the canted door and stopped again, staring. Every drawer had been pulled out and emptied. Every piece of clothing had been ripped and strewn on the floor. Even the bedding had been thrown down, and the mattress split open.

"I think somebody does not like you," said You from the door.

Robert picked up a ruined coat and let it fall again. "Yes, but who? And why?" He darted across the hall and pounded on his mate's door. "Crane! Crane, are you in there?"

"You think this Crane did this?" You asked.

"No. He's my first mate. Crane!"

The door opened an inch, and Crane's eye surveyed Robert from the crack. "So! You have come back. With all of your sins on you, you have come back."

"*This* is your mate?" Beluche said doubtfully.

"Crane," Robert said, "what happened here? Open this damned door!"

The door opened further, and Crane stuck his head out, Adam's apple bobbing furiously, eyes darting along the hall. "The soldiers came, hunting for you."

"For me!"

"They knew your name. They knew you were a ship captain. I could hear them talki..g. I should have told them about you, but then they might have imprisoned all of us. The innocent in the crew should not suffer for your evil."

"Crane," Robert said grimly, "why did those soldiers want me?"

"Blasphemer!" Crane cried. "You come with your sin fresh on you, and you blaspheme the Lord's name. You know your sin. Rape! Yes, rape. And not some Spanish doxie. An

American woman, and a widow.''

"*Parbleu,*" You breathed.

"Crane, do you mean Cordelia Applegate?"

"Yes, *captain*. Mrs. Applegate. I heard the soldiers speaking of how you broke into her chambers, and forced your attentions on her.''

"Damn," Robert said. "We'll have to sail immediately. Is the crew aboard, Crane?''

"You intend to flee?" Crane asked. "Justice will follow you, captain, and the vengeance of the Lord."

"Crane, is the crew aboard?"

"The vengeance—"

"Oh, shut up. I did not rape Cordelia Applegate."

"My friend," You said, "You had better go quickly now. The soldiers may return at any time." He took Robert's hand in a firm grip. "As I do not wish them to find me, either, I will go too. If you are ever in New Orleans again, mention my name. It will either help, or get you shot. Come, *oncle.*"

The two Frenchmen faded down the hall, and Robert seized Crane out by the collar. "I should leave you, Crane. Hell! You'd better pray I can get all the crew aboard before we sail.''

He headed down Rue Dumain for the levee, little caring whether Crane followed or not. The city was beginning to stir to life, black women with their heads wrapped in kerchiefs heading for the morning markets, workmen shouldering their toolchests. Here and there an American trapper from upriver, in leather leggings and hunting shirt, made his way home from a night's drinking. Robert counted on the bustle to hide him.

As he reached the levee, a sharp whistle stopped him. Miller, his boatswain, had poked his head just above the long mound of earth. He whistled again and beckoned.

Robert hurried to him. Miller, and four more of his crew, were in a launch. "Miller, am I glad to see you. Help me round up the rest of the crew, and quickly."

"Heard some talk in the *cantinas,* captain," Miller rumbled, "about three, four hours ago. Something about the *garda* wanting to arrest you. There was already soldiers at your rooms when I got there, so I just gathered the crew up and got them aboard. I figured if you made it free, you'd come this way.'' He hesitated. "Uh, sir, begging your pardon, but with things the way they was, well, I took the liberty of getting the lads to warp *Osprey* out into the channel. Sorry if I overstepped my bounds, captain.''

"I'm damned glad of it,'' Robert said with a baleful look at his mate. Crane avoided his eye and climbed down into the boat. "Let's get out to *Osprey*. We've a sight of river yet to navigate before we're at sea.''

Cordelia Applegate. He pitied any man who ever ran afoul of her.

XIV

Martin Caine mopped at his face with a kerchief as he rode Wing past the cotton fields at Seven Pines. Was it actually hotter in September than it had been in August? His attention turned to the fields he was passing, snowy with black-seed cotton, the kind that was coming to be called sea island cotton.

It was a fine growth, some of the plants towering nearly high as his head as he rode past. The harvest had been going on for three weeks, and would continue for three months, but there wasn't a black in the fields that Sunday. That was Karl Holtz' idea, and a good one, he thought. Let other planters make their hands put in half a day after church services during harvest. They still wouldn't match Seven Pines' two bales an acre.

The thought of the slaves' church services made him turn toward the quarters. The regular service, given by a white Baptist minister after he finished at his church, was long over, but Martin was certain what he'd find.

He heard the sound long before he reached the rows of small, neat, white-washed cabins. Drums were forbidden by law, but the rhythmic beating of sticks on a hollow log was unmistakable. The chant that came to him in the still air was unrecognizable at first; gradually he realized that the words were those of a Baptist hymn. He reined in short of the cabins, far enough away not to intrude.

In a stamping shuffle two circles of blacks, women on the inside, men on the outside, moved in opposite directions, chanting the words to the hymn. The hymns changed from time to time, but the chanting, varying little in pitch, left little but the occasional "Lord" understandable.

At the sound of hooves behind him he looked around. Catherine Holtz, seated sidesaddle in a pale yellow riding dress, galloped up to him and jerked her gray gelding to a halt.

147

Her eyes were cool beneath the brim of her feathered riding hat as she watched the dancing, but her gloved hands were tight on the reins and her voice was angry. "Are you going to allow that to continue?"

"Yes, ma'am," he said quietly. She jerked as if struck.

"That dance is blasphemy. And even if it wasn't, everyone knows slaves shouldn't be allowed to dance. They become inflamed. Anything might happen. Remember Santo Domingo."

He looked at her petulant frown and wondered what Holtz saw in her. More trouble than her beauty could be worth, he thought. Her brother's woman, now, that Louise de Chardonnay, that was a woman worth having. All he said was, "I don't reckon this is going to lead them to kill us in our beds."

"*You* doubt!" she gasped. "You're not paid to have doubts. You're paid to obey orders. And I'm ordering you to stop this at once."

He kept his voice neutral. "I'm paid to obey your husband's orders, ma'am. And he says to let—"

"I told you to stop this disgusting thing at once, Mr. Caine."

"Ma'am, if you'll just talk to your husband."

For an instant he had the idea she was going to slash at him with her quirt. Abruptly she wheeled her horse around and galloped off toward the main house.

He sighed as he watched her go. She'd find ways to make his life difficult. But it was too fine a Sunday to worry about Catherine Holtz. He'd take the launch to town. With Robert Fallon gone to New Orleans, Louise de Chardonnay must be lonesome. Perhaps he could hire a carriage and take her for a drive.

Catherine galloped up to the main house of Seven Pines, leaped off her lathered horse, and absently tossed the reins to a waiting groom. As she hurried up the broad front steps and into the house, she flicked her quirt at every step. She ignored the butler's bow and swept into her husband's study.

"Karl, you must dismiss that Caine man."

Karl looked up from the ledgers spread on his desk and

blinked. "And good afternoon to you, also, my dear. If what you wish him dismissed for is not too serious, could it wait until I am less busy?"

She began a slow burn at his tolerant smile. Tolerant! "Isn't it enough that I want him dismissed? I'm your wife, Karl. Damn it, stop treating me like a not-too-bright child."

"My dear, when you ask me to dismiss Mr. Caine simply because you are my wife, you act like a not-too-bright child." He shook his head suddenly and cut her off as she tried to speak. "No. I am sorry, Catherine. I should not speak to you so. It is just that I am tired. What is your problem with Mr. Caine?"

Problem. He still saw it as trivial. "I gave him an order, and he refused to obey it."

"And that order was?"

"I . . . I ordered him to stop the slaves from dancing."

Karl looked bewildered. "But *I* have told him to let them dance. I cannot dismiss him for obeying *my* order."

"Karl, don't you see? It's blasphemy, *and* it's likely to stir them up to run away. Or worse. Besides, it's wasteful allowing them all that time. Everyone works their hands half a day on Sunday during the harvest. Everyone but you."

Karl lifted his hand, and held up one finger. "It is worship, not blasphemy." He raised another finger. "Second, they are more likely to be content, not less, if they are allowed to worship in their own way." Another finger. "And third, I am making two bales to the acre, while everyone else is making one."

"All the more reason not to waste Sunday," she insisted. "You'll have *one* bale an acre rot in the field because you won't listen to me!"

"Always it is the same, Catherine. I make a decision, and no matter what it is, you try to insist on a different course. I love you, *liebchen,* but I will not be ruled by you."

"You must fire Caine. He . . . he's disrespectful to me."

Karl slapped the desk in exasperation. "Enough, my dear. *Bitte,* enough. I cannot believe Mr. Caine has given any intentional offence. He is perhaps not so subservient as you think proper, but he is a *jaegar,* and subservience does not come easily to such men."

"A what? He's not respectful. There shouldn't be any excuses." He let his eyes close, and she prepared another argument, but before she could begin he spoke again.

"My dear, have you thought of visiting your father in the city? I realize you are not used to coming to the country until October. Perhaps I made a mistake bringing you out so early. And you will no doubt wish to see your brother."

Suddenly all thoughts of Caine, slaves or cotton, were swept away. "Robert is back?" she said numbly.

"Yes. Mr. Rivers stopped by. He saw the *Osprey* crossing the bar while he was coming from the city this morning. No doubt Robert will have many stories to tell of New Orleans. You will go to the city?"

"Yes." She licked lips suddenly gone dry. Robert was back. "Yes, I will. I . . . I'll go change immediately."

"All for nothing," Robert said in a near laugh. "It's funny. It really is. I went sneaking around in the swamps, nearly got hung for rape, and it's all for nothing. Oh, hell, it doesn't matter. I wanted to get out of Charleston anyway."

His father turned from the liquor cabinet in his study and handed him a brandy. "Your trip was hardly useless, now. Here. Take a sip of that. I don't hold with this new fashion of not drinking before noon."

"How was it not useless? I went for proof the French are taking over New Orleans, and I return to hear it being talked on every street corner."

"Rumors, lad. You have proof. There's been precious little of that. Will you drink the brandy, lad? And sit down. You look as if you're ready to run off on the instant." Robert sipped his drink and took the wing chair by the fireplace. "That's better," Michael went on. "Even Jefferson will have to be convinced, once you take your evidence to Washington City."

"I'm not going near the Federal City," Robert protested.

Michael frowned slightly. "I prefer Washington City to that, that abomination of a name. In any case, though, why not? You have what you went after. The logical thing now is to be taking it to the President. Can't you see?"

"Send it. But I'm not going with it. Listen, father, I went to New Orleans running away from my problems. And I found new problems. So I'm going to stay here a while, and face things." Away or at home, the problem of Catherine remained. It *was* better to face it.

"Is there . . . is there anything I can help with?"

Michael's look of fierce protectiveness made Robert want to reach out to the old man, but he only said, "I can take care of it." There was an uncomfortable silence. He changed the subject quickly. "What's this I hear about us being at war with Tripoli? I've heard they declared war months before we heard it."

"Robert—"

"Something about chopping down a flagpole, I believe. I met Cathcart, you know. Hope he got away. Petrie—"

"Robert—"

"—says Jefferson's announced his war is all to be at sea. No action against the ports. What kind of war is that?"

"Robert, will you—"

He sighed. "I'm not going to Washington City, and that's that. I intend to spend Christmas here. And the New Year."

Michael bristled. "You must go. These papers are all very well, but they'll have ten times the impact with a man there to say 'I saw it.' All right. I'll not ask you to go now. But after Christmas? For God's sake, three months should be long enough for anything."

Robert opened his mouth, then closed it again. Michael had always believed the United States must acquire New Orleans. Now he was certain Robert's presence could tip the scales. And who could say he was wrong? He had so often been right when everyone else insisted differently. Besides, three or four months *should* be long enough.

"All right," he said. "I'll go. But after the first of the year. And there's no use trying to convince me to go earlier."

Michael rubbed his hands together briskly. "No, no. I'm happy enough that you're going at all. I'll give you a letter to Burr. I did give him *some* help. He can pay me back by getting you to Jefferson."

"Yes." A sudden thought came, something that had played on the edges of his mind since New Orleans. "Lopes says he's helped you with getting guns to the Spanish Americas. How many more are helping you that I don't know about?"

For an instant Michael looked the privateer he had been twenty years before. "Lopes talks a great deal more than he should."

"He's discreet enough. He had to tell Beluche and You to make them work with me."

"Yes. Well, I suppose sometimes I carry the secrecy too far."

"It won't work, father. When enough of them want a revolution, they'll start one. Then's the time for us to send arms."

Michael snorted a laugh. "Lad, when our own revolution began, there was less than one man in three supported it, or anything it was about. It took ten years of hard work to get that far. And as for starting on its own, why, some of our best people, de Kalb, maybe even Franklin, were being paid by the French to stir up trouble here for the British."

"Franklin!"

"I said maybe. I'm not sure to this day. And if he was, it doesn't take an inch from what he did. The Revolution must be exported, lad, that's our trust."

"Your trust, father. Not mine. I help, for your sake. But I see it as giving guns to men who set up as bandits, or sell the guns and run off with the money. You can count those who've actually fought the Spaniards on the fingers of one hand."

His father glared from under his bushy gray eyebrows. "I won't rest till there's nought but republics in the Americas."

"I know that," Robert said gently.

"And you shouldn't, either."

"That's your dream. Mine is different."

Michael stood stiffly for a minute. Then his face softened. "Well, I suppose I can't be holding you to my dreams. *My* father's dream was to put a Stuart back on the English throne." He snorted, and shook his head. "Will you sup with me tonight?"

"Tonight is for Louise," Robert answered with a smile. "But tomorrow, if I may." He put down his glass and got up.

"Of course you may." Suddenly he gripped Robert's arm and pulled him close. Robert had the feeling he was looking at himself thirty years from now, two deep lines coming down from the hooked nose to the mouth, but the chin still firm and the blue eyes still sharp. "Lad, whatever those dreams of yours are, stick to them. Don't let anyone, not even me, be diverting you from them. Now get on with you to Louise."

As Robert left he could hear him, rustling the papers on his desk, muttering about Caracas.

When Robert arrived at the house on Queen Street, Louise's carriage and horses were standing in the street, with Japheth, who doubled as groom, waiting at the reins. The freedman tipped his hat. "Morning, Captain Fallon! Welcome home." But his eyes strayed worriedly to the house.

"Good morning, good to be back." Robert hurried up the steps to the long side veranda. At that moment the door opened, and Louise came out on Martin Caine's arm.

Her face lit in a huge smile. "La, Robert. You are home. I had no word."

"So I see," he said drily. The two men stared at each other stiffly. Spots of color appeared in Louise's cheeks.

"Mr. Caine has most graciously consented to escort me on a drive."

Robert said nothing.

"Glad to be of service," Caine said levelly. "Since you were away."

"I'm back, now."

Caine's face tightened. "So you are." He turned to Louise with a formal bow. "Ma'am, it's been my pleasure. But since Captain Fallon is here, I think I'd best be going."

The overseer straightened and walked down the steps to the street. As he passed Robert, the two men stared at each other coldly. Robert had half a mind to go after him.

"That was most ill done," Louise said heatedly.

He looked at her in astonishment. "Ill done! I find you lolling on that fellow's arm, and you expect me to act as if I was meeting him at an assembly?"

"I was not lolling. He was merely going to take me for a drive in the carriage. There was not the slightest impropriety in his manner or—"

"And there is in mine? Damn it, I expect faithfulness from a mistress! Not men who 'just want to take you for drives.'"

"*Parbleu!* You are so *juste,* so righteous. I know your

appetite, and your eye for women. How many did you bed while you were away? Five? Ten? More?"

"What? What are you talking about? It's different for a man!"

"*Eh!* A man! You are that!" she laughed bitterly. "I am to sit quietly, while you chase every *putain* you see?"

He caught her chin in a fierce grip, and held her face up against her struggles. "As long as you're my mistress, you'll sit quietly when I tell you to sit quietly, or I'll tan your creamy hide till you can't sit quietly at all."

"Am I interrupting anything?"

Robert released Louise and turned toward the street, an angry reply ready. It died on his lips. Catherine stood at the foot of the steps.

She had a happy, almost satisfied, look on her face as she walked up to them. She darted a mocking little smile at Louise, but it was to Robert she spoke. "If this is inconvenient, I can always come back later."

"Actually," Robert said, "it is inconvenient." Catherine looked faintly surprised, and Louise glared at him again. "What I mean is, Louise and I were having a private talk."

"Yes," Catherine said smugly. She threw an amused glance at Louise, and the Frenchwoman colored.

Robert cursed to himself, wondering how much she'd heard. "What is it you want?" he said curtly.

For the first time she seemed unsure of herself. She hesitated, looking from him to Louise, then took a deep breath. "Karl . . . Karl is at Seven Pines, and I detest dining alone. I . . . would you dine with me this evening?" She waited, wide eyed, for his answer.

He stared in disbelief. "This is my first night home," he said slowly. "I'll be dining with Louise."

Catherine's eyes flared, but whether with anger or some other emotion he couldn't tell. "I understand," she said quickly.

Thinking to avoid another stricture from Louise on boorish behavior, he added, "Of course, I'll be all too happy to come some other night."

"Some other night," Catherine echoed. She was definitely flustered. "Of course. I . . . I'll have to let you know when. I mean, if . . . . '' She took another breath. "I really must go now. It . . . it's good to have you home, Robert." With a cool nod to Louise, she left.

Robert stared after her. What was the matter with her? Her invitation, her coming to the house he shared with Louise, her parting words . . . none of it was like her.

"You must stay away from that woman," Louise said softly.

He looked at her, but she refused to meet his gaze. "What do you mean?"

"I am sorry." She sighed. "I have no right to speak so."

"No. I'm the one who has no right. There's nothing wrong with you having an escort for a ride. I just let my jealousy run away with me."

"Are you indeed jealous?" A secret smile played on her lips.

"I am. I *do* expect you to be as faithful as a wife."

She stepped into his arms and put her head against his chest. "I will be faithful to you, Robert, as long as you live."

XV

Murad Reis could never look at the *Asad* without pride. Lion she was, indeed. Before him, the pirates of the Barbary states had sailed only the xebecs and polaccas their fathers and grandfathers had. It was he who had insisted for years on something different. Now, with the help of Justin Fourrier, he had it. Three masts, thirty-two gun, a sleek English copy of a captured French design. She knifed through the blue waters of the Mediterranean like a dolphin, and with only a slight quartering wind out of the hot, cloudless sky. There was nothing he would not dare with such a ship. Fourrier had done him well.

The thought of the gaunt man in Jamaica reminded him of the rambling letter he had picked up that morning off Sicily from a Fourrier ship. He took the folded sheets from under his white robes and moves to the quarterdeck rail to peruse it again. The crew were not yet proficient in handling the *Asad* but they could do without his eye for a few minutes. He quickly found the part that interested him most.

> I have received information about the man Robert Fallon through my agent, W, in St. Louis, on the Mississippi River. W's information is always reliable.

He knew who was concealed behind that initial. James Wilkinson, the senior general in the American Army. Reliable? Murad snorted. An agent in the pay of the Spanish! He wondered if Fourrier knew that. Probably. It would make no difference to Fourrier, but to Murad it made the man twice a traitor, and that was once too many for him.

Fallon has been in New Orleans. He fled there under a charge of rape, which does not surprise me. Reports come so slowly that he was gone before I knew he was there. I will have him yet, though, and his father. *That* whoreson dog survived two pistol balls in the chest, I discover. The devil cares for his own. But I will have them. I will have them both. And that bastard pederast Trask. That hellborn scum burned a good ship to save his worthless hide, and disappeared with the gold from the sale of the slaves. But I know where he is. Every shilling will come out of his hide. It will be sweet rehearsal for the Fallons. Oh, to have them here, under the knife—

Murad grimaced. The man was becoming madder by the day. The way he drooled over the tortures he wanted to inflict on the Fallons was disquieting. He cared nothing for what Fourrier did to them, so long as *he* had his revenge on Robert Fallon, but if insanity claimed Fourrier too completely, more than one plan would go glimmering. He skipped ahead, to a saner portion.

The news is confirmed. New Orleans returns to France. It is being talked in every coffee house, here and in America, though they think it is only rumor. I have invested the money you left with me according to the shifts this will make in the sugar trade and marine insurance rates. The increased trade from the Caribbean to France will provide many targets for you, ironically raising the rates further, and making you even greater profits.

That brought a smile to Murad. The thought of gold always did. There was only one other part of the letter he wanted to reread, and that because it, too, made him smile.

I think, from your last letter, that you take this war with the Americans too lightly. I have lived among them. They are a dirty, ignorant, loutish people, and as such deserving of contempt. If they wish to be your friends, they will accept any insult and grovel with apology for forcing you to make it. This makes many hold them in further contempt. But, once roused, they are madmen. Against one they hold as a true enemy, they will go to any lengths, even if it means their own destruction. I have seen it happen. I have seen the great armies of England ground away. Beware of them.

"*Sidi?*" Mousad, his first mate, bowed low at his side. "A thousand pardons, *effendi,* but the American captain begs to speak with you."

Murad put the letter away. Amidships, twenty Americans, crew of a vessel taken only hours before, huddled under the muskets of Tripolitan guards. The captain stood apart from the rest, glaring at the quarterdeck.

"He begged, you say?"

Mousad ducked his swarthy head. "It was his intent, *sidi,* if not his words."

"Intent?" Murad asked drily. "Well, this is my intent. Strip them all naked. Do not touch the captain, but give every second man of the rest thirty lashes. And beforehand, let them know it is their captain who has earned it for them."

"It shall be done, *sidi.*"

Murad grinned. Beware of Americans, indeed. *This* was the way to treat Americans.

In Charleston, Robert, listening to the November rains drumming on the roof tiles, was glad to be inside in front of the fire. A glass of brandy, a pipe, and a stack of London newspapers and periodicals completed his comfort. Catherine had twitted him more than once about the way he could be enthralled by news two months old.

Louise was somewhere round the house, doing something or other. She'd been preoccupied for the last two days. At first he'd thought it was temper, but when he confronted her, she said, "Do not be silly," and scurried to the attic with a maid in tow. Until she decided to tell him what the matter was, he intended to made do with the pipe and papers for company.

He was engrossed in the *Times* when there was a knock on the study door.

He put down the paper. "Come."

Simon, the butler, entered deferentially. "I'm sorry, sir. I know you didn't want to be disturbed, but Mr. Holtz is here."

"Karl? Show him in. All that doesn't apply to him."

"Very good, sir." The butler bowed and disappeared. He was replaced in a few minutes by Karl.

Robert got to his feet with a smile. He liked the young Saxon. "On a day like this, Karl, a man needs a drink inside him. Wine, or brandy?" He freshened his own glass as he spoke.

"Nothing, thank you."

"Nothing? I can send Simon for a pot of coffee."

"No. On second thought, I will have a brandy. A large one."

"Done," Robert said, and went on as he poured. "Tell me, Karl, did you ever think of powering that mill of yours with steam?"

"Steam?"

"Yes, steam. As from a kettle. They have engines in England powered by it." He got his first close look at Karl as he handed him his brandy. "Good God, man! You're soaked. Get that coat off and sit in front of the fire."

"I was walking when the rain began," Karl explained as he got out of the sodden garment. Robert settled him in a chair and sent for Simon to have the coat pressed.

With all that done, Robert sat back in his own chair and returned to his enthusiasm. "I've been reading an article in one of these London papers. Man says he thinks steam power might be a useful adjunct to horses on the canals. A man of small vision, that, and his own article shows why. Did you know a man named John Fitch had a boat powered by steam in this country, on the Delaware River, fifteen years ago? And James Rumsey one on the Potomac the same year? Fifteen years ago! If there were more men with vision around, there'd be steamboats on every river."

Karl nodded. "But my mill is on a river with a reliable flow of water. I have no need of a steam engine."

"Yes, but with steam power, a mill doesn't have to be by a river. You could build anywhere. Well, I'll leave the mills to you. It's the ships interest me. I've a mind to buy one of these engines. He names some manufacturers. Boulton and Watt. Think of a ship that isn't slave to wind and tide."

"It would be very interesting, I am sure," Karl said politely.

Slowly it dawned on Robert that the other man wasn't sharing his enthusiasm. "Karl, you didn't get that wet in a few minutes. You must have walked quite a distance. Is there something wrong?"

Karl shrugged, and stared into the fire. "I was thinking. I often walk to think." He gulped the rest of his brandy and breathed heavily. "What I was thinking about is not easy to speak of. And yet I must speak of it to someone. You are her brother, so . . . . '' He shrugged again.

"Catherine?" Robert said. "It's about Catherine?"

"A man does not speak of troubles with his wife," the Saxon said heavily. "He works them out himself. But no matter how I think, I cannot see the way." For a time Karl sat looking into the fire. "I do not know where to begin," he said at last. "We have had the problems that I think all married people have. She is a woman of strong will. Such women often like to meddle in things that are the provinces of men. Business and the like. So it has been with Catherine, and we have had the arguments over it. In the last month, though, this has stopped.'

"That doesn't sound like something to worry about," Robert said lightly.

"*Bitte*. There is more. The arguments have stopped, but she has become a woman of *das Gefulslages,* the moods. At times she is happy, more than happy, ecstatic. An hour later she is in a rage, and in both cases there is no reason. At all times, though, she seems nervous, starting when I speak to her as if she did not know I was there, even if I have spoken to her only a moment before. She weeps without reason, or laughs the same way."

"Karl," Robert said carefully, "some women react strangely to their time of the month."

Holtz' mouth tightened primly. "Such things do not last so long."

"Well, frankly, I've seen her more in the last month than I have in the year before. At my father's house, and even here, though she'd never come before. At any rate, she's been bright the times we were together, even friendly. Friendlier than in the past. And she hasn't seemed moody at all."

"You will forgive me, but since you have mentioned it, there has been some, ah, animosity between you in the past, yet? Are you certain there have been no disagreements? Her blackest times have been after she returned from meeting you. Forgive me."

Robert suppressed a grimace. If there'd been any strain in those meetings, it had been on him. "No, Karl. We haven't had a single disagreement." And that, he realized suddenly, was as strange as any of the rest. But he didn't say anything.

"This morning," Karl said, "Catherine told me I am going to be a father."

"Congratulations! Well, there you have it. Of course she's been acting strange, and there's your reason for it." He felt a strange flood of relief, and a twinge of something else. She was bound to Karl now, more safely than ever.

"I wish I was so certain, Robert. She has acted this way before she could have known of the child, and this morning . . . this morning she told me that she does not want the child. She said she hated it, then ran to her bedchamber. I could hear her crying."

"Well, that's proof, then, isn't it? Of course she doesn't hate the child. How could she? It's just the way women are when they're expecting."

"Perhaps," Karl said flatly.

"Why don't you sleep on this? Have a few drinks and go to bed. There's nothing serious to this. After you get some rest and look at it fresh, you'll think so, too."

He rang for Simon to bring the pressed coat, then saw Karl to the door and on his way. The rain had stopped, and the Saxon refused his carriage. After he shut the door, though, Robert stood with one hand still resting on the door handle. Catherine pregnant. Her moods worst after she'd seen him. *Could* they have anything to do with him? Impossible. It had to be the child. There was nothing else. There *could* be nothing else.

"Are you all right, Robert?" Louise looked down worriedly from the stair. "Are you all right? You stand there so still."

"I'm fine," he said slowly. "Karl just told me he and Catherine are going to have a baby."

"And a baby is something to make you stand like a poleaxed ox?" she said tightly.

Before he could answer she disappeared toward the kitchens in back. She'd sounded almost angry, he thought. He hurried after her and caught her at the end of the hall.

"Wait a minute, Louise. I'm tired of you saying two sentences and running away. What's the matter? Why are you mad?"

"Let go of my arm," she said. "I am not a horse. You are hurting me."

He released his hold and she made a great show of rubbing

where he'd gripped her. She turned to the door, but he blocked her way. "I want to know what the matter is, Louise."

She stood staring at his chest. "You do not like *les enfants,* children?"

"Of course I like children. What does that have to do with anything?"

"You do not act so. You seem most distressed at the child of your sister."

"For Christ's sake! I'm put out because Catherine's got the wim-wams over her baby, and Karl's taking it to heart! Now what in hell is bothering you?"

"I'm am going to have your baby," she whispered. Wide-eyed and pale-faced, she stared up at him. "Do not be angry with me."

"Angry? Why would I be angry?" A grin blossomed on his face, and he swept her up and around in a circle. "I'm delighted!"

She took a deep breath and put a hand to her hair as he set her back on her feet. "You disarray me. You are certain that you are not angry?"

"For the love of . . . no, I'm not angry." All thoughts of Karl and Catherine were swept from his head. "I'll have to hire another maid. You shouldn't be doing so much work. And a mauma for the baby. And—"

"*C'est assez!* Your son has not been born, yet. It will be many months before there is any need for any of that."

"You seem mighty certain it's going to be a boy."

She smiled mischievously. "I think me, you are a man who will make sons."

He laughed out loud. "We'll find out after I get back from Washington City."

"Do you still intend to go?"

He looked at her with a slight frown. "I promised my father," he said slowly. "I'll return months before the child is due. There's not some reason I should stay, is there? You're not worried about the baby?"

"Of course not. It is just that I wish you to be with me always."

"I wish the same. It'll be a short trip, though. And a boring one, I've no doubt."

XVI

When he climbed from *Osprey*'s launch onto Lear's Wharf, in February of 1802, Robert was sure his prediction was going to be confirmed. From the Potomac the shore had seemed to be the purest countryside, except for the wharf. Ashore, he found a steady stream of two-wheeled carts creaking away into what seemed to be woodland. They were the sole means of conveyance to the city.

Robert quickly struck a deal with a lanky carter, hoisted his bag and himself into the cart and settled among the bales and boxes as it lurched off into the woods. When the trees at last gave out, he wished briefly that they hadn't. The hamlet before him was dreary beyond expectation. Perhaps three or four hundred houses, mainly wood and for the most part looking hastily built, were scattered widely over a depressing landscape. There had been an obvious need to cut trees in order to build the city, but surely they had gone overboard. Stumps outnumbered the standing trees.

Snow was on the ground, giving an illusion of cleanliness, and there was ice on the few ponds he could see, but the roadways were chopped into a muddy quagmire by the constant flow of carts and wagons. People picked their way along the side of the so-called streets, searching for shallow places to ford the bog.

As they passed a large house of white stone with fields of corn stubble stretching almost to the door, the carter spoke. "President's Palace."

Robert spared it a glance, and wondered how Jefferson liked living there, after the grace of Monticello. A dozen pits scarred the earth among the corn stubble, and half that many rickety workman's shacks stood seemingly abandoned.

"How much further to the Congress House?" he asked.

The carter gestured over the back of his plodding horse toward the only other structure of note, a square stone building. "About a mile and a half," he said. He cast a sidelong glance at Robert, slipping a finger under his cap to scratch his scalp. Finally he said, "You going to see them Congress men?"

"Yes," Robert said.

The carter nodded and mumbled to himself, swinging the cart wide where the marshy bank of Tiber Creek encroached on the road. "Call this Pennsylvania Avenue."

"I see."

"Don't look like much, do it?"

"No."

The carter frowned over his shoulder. "Don't talk much, do you?"

"No," Robert said, and grinned when the man grunted sourly and turned back to driving.

At last the cart stopped in front of the Congress House, three impressive stories of white stone with a modest door at one corner. It was eventually supposed to be but one wing of the completed building, and it looked it. Knots of well-dressed men stood about outside, holding their cloaks tight against the cold wind as they talked. They, Robert supposed, were Congressmen.

He paid off his driver, tossed his single piece of luggage off the cart, and followed it to the muddy street. As he scooped up the bag he found himself facing a tall, lean man with exasperated pale blue eyes. The man's trousers were splattered with mud, obviously from Robert's leap.

"Your pardon, sir," Robert said before the other could speak. "I should have looked where I was throwing my bag. I'm afraid I don't have a servant with me, or I'd offer to let him clean them for you."

The exasperation faded, to be replaced by a somewhat studied smile. "I thank you for the spirit," he said in a soft drawl, "if not the actuality. In fact, no one has room to keep a servant here. It makes for ragged living, I fear."

"In that case, let me send them out to my ship. My boatswain does a fair imitation of a valet." He offered his hand.

"I'm Robert Fallon, captain of the *Osprey*.

"Fallon?" the man, who seemed some ten years Robert's senior, said as he shook hands. "I met a Fallon, once. Michael Fallon, of Charleston. It was back in '89, during the Constitution brawl. I'm James Monroe. Governor of Virginia," he added with a flicker of genuine smile.

"Michael Fallon is my father, governor."

"A good man, your father. Now, do you have letters of introduction?"

"Why, yes, sir. To the Vice-President."

"Burr!" Monroe seemed surprised. He puffed his cheeks out, and shook his head pompously. "Precious little help he'll be, Captain Fallon. He is hated by the Federalists, and anathema to the republicans." His eyebrows arched suddenly. "Speak of the devil."

Robert turned to see. A woman was leaving the Congress House, escorted by two men. Pretty, if stout, with a merry smile, she was tall for a woman, and seemed taller next to her companions. Neither of them was more than five and a half feet tall, one of them a good two inches shorter. The taller of the two had a head too large for his slight body, a receding hairline and a prominent nose, but his strong chin and deep-set electric eyes gave him an air of power. The other was pale, almost sickly, with full lips and a weak chin. He had a frown on his face, but as if he were perpetually serious rather than angry.

"One of those men is Burr?" Robert said.

"Yes, the man with the eyes." Monroe stared at the trio frowning, and seemed to begin thinking out loud. "They should not be seen together. Even Jemmy's presence won't stop the rumors."

"Rumors? Jemmy?"

Monroe looked back at Robert, his pale eyes suddenly wary. "James Madison. The shorter man. He's Secretary of State. That's his wife, Dolley. I expect he can get by being seen with Burr," he added with sudden bitterness. "The rest of us can't."

"I take it this isn't a good time for me to present my letter of introduction," Robert said.

"No. No." Monroe eyed Robert in a calculating fashion. "I

suppose I'd better let you know what I meant about rumors."

"Oh, no need at all," Robert said hastily.

"But there is. In this place, innocently saying the wrong thing can destroy you as quickly as a pistol shot."

"I prefer not to. I'll simply say nothing. That will take care of it."

"Here everyone listens to the silence, wondering what you really mean. A chance word connected with a rumor you never even heard can send you packing, preferment gone, hopes of advancement shattered."

"My only hope is to be sailing back to Charleston in two or three days."

"But you want something," Monroe said flatly. "Everyone in this wretched village wants something. Oh, very well. I would help you for your father's sake, but if you don't want it . . . ."

Robert shrugged. "You're right, of course, governor. I'd be grateful for any information you can give me."

"Good, then." The studied smile returned. "Do you have rooms, yet? I should say, 'a room.'"

"No, sir."

"Come along, then." Monroe took him by the arm and started picking through the quagmire toward some disreputable-looking buildings clustered nearby. "There aren't really enough boarding houses to go around. Some congressmen are sleeping two to a room. But a room has come open this very morning at Mrs. McQuade's, where I'm staying. If we hurry, you may get it before it's snapped up."

By noon Robert had his clothes unpacked in a garret room. Mrs. McQuade, a fierce-looking harridan, had demanded her money in advance, announcing with an ominous glare toward the Congress House that the city was full of grifters and confidence men. By evening he had also had his ear filled by Monroe, and a dirtier mess of gossip he'd never heard. The relish with which the Virginian had related it all disconcerted him.

The rumors about Burr and the Madisons had been as bad as any. Burr had introduced Jemmy Madison to Dolley, and the talk was that she and Burr had been lovers. Some even said she was still unfaithful. Not that there was anything to it, Monroe had hastened to add. But on no account must Burr and Dolley Madison be mentioned in the same conversation.

There had been numerous other disreputable tales. Jefferson supposedly had a mistress, a woman of color, the Virginian termed her, hidden away at Monticello. Robert Smith, the Secretary of the Navy, was corrupt to the point of larceny, too stupid to hide it, and too well connected to be touched. A dozen more scandals were told, each enough to spark a duel in Charleston, and each freely passed about in the Federal City.

He spent a restless night, hating the sort of town he was in, and presented himself at the Congress House early the next morning. A doorman took his letter of introduction off to the Vice-President. He waited with several score petitioners beneath the portraits of Louis XVI and Marie Antoinette. Strange hangings, he thought, for a government that had welcomed the French Revolution.

For two hours he cooled his heels, and just as he was preparing to give up, Burr appeared accompanied by the doorman. As he made his way through the crowd of petitioners, not one approached him. The doorman pointed Robert out, and Burr fastened his dark eyes on him.

"Captain Fallon?" he said with a raised eyebrow. His voice had a deep timber, surprising for a man his size. "You risk your reputation in this city being seen speaking to me." His thin mouth was wryly twisted, as if the thought of being outcast amused him.

"My father thinks well of you, sir," Robert said. "That's good enough for me."

Burr chuckled. "It is not enough for many folk. I am the next thing to the devil, you know." He paused to gauge the effect of his remark. "However, if you're willing to risk it, let us step outside, away from sharp eyes and curious ears. The cold is preferable to prying."

The wind from the Potomac had grown sharper, and the sky was gray with a new snow coming. They had the rubble strewn expanse to themselves.

"Now," Burr said when they had walked a dozen paces from the building, "what is it you want? I only know your father slightly, but he did try to help me in my late—unpleasantness.'' His mouth tightened for an instant. "He must be desperate, indeed, to call on my aid now.''

"I must get to see President Jefferson. I have proof that the French Army is interested in New Orleans.'' For a time Burr stared at him, with eyes colder than the wind.

"The French Army,'' he said at last. "That *is* interesting. And not too likely to be welcome news for our friend in the white house.''

"White house?''

"It's what some people are calling the President's Palace. The other's too grand for a republic, you see, especially for that half-finished pile. No, Jefferson won't like that. He's said publicly a dozen times that whomever controls New Orleans is our natural enemy, but he's willing to excuse anything the French do. Anything else would be betraying the revolutionary ideal, as he sees it.''

"Then you don't think he'll be interested?''

"Oh, he'll be interested. He's no fool, our Long Tom. He won't like it, but he'll be interested. But how to get you to him? That's the question.''

"I thought that you, as vice-president . . . . '' Robert let his words trail off as Burr's mouth twisted again.

"Captain Fallon, I'm the last man to be able to give you a decent introduction to Tom Jefferson. In some ways he's like a crotchety old woman, getting his fingers into the smallest details of the government and never changing a notion once it's fixed in his head. Do you know anyone else in the city?''

"I've met Governor Monroe, of Virginia. He helped me get a room.''

Burr shook his head. "Some devils you can trust, a little. Me, for instance. I seldom slit a friend's throat unless there's great cause. Others, though . . . . ''

"You're saying I shouldn't trust Governor Monroe?''

"He was a Patrick Henry man until he saw Jefferson was the rising star. Then, overnight, he became an ardent Jefferson man, and no matter that he had to change his politics a hundred and eighty degrees to do it. That is a touch rank, even for this town. There are times I near regret not letting Hamilton shoot him.''

"Shoot him? Alexander Hamilton?"

"His would-be Majesty himself. It was back in '96 before I knew as much of Monroe as I do now. Between Hamilton's big careless mouth and Monroe's nitpicking, they went round and round until they found themselves committed to a duel. I managed to talk them out of it, got each man to write a note the other could take as an apology. Neither one's forgiven me, since they found out. I'd meddled in affairs touching their honor," he finished sarcastically.

"I don't know Governor Monroe very well," Robert said slowly. "But I know no one else at all, excepting yourself, sir. If you say you can't help, there's no other for me to go to."

"He's a gossip," Burr grimaced. "We all gossip in Washington. Except myself." He grinned. "But James, now. Whose opinion would you believe? What about General Washington's?"

"If General Washington were alive, I'd trust his opinion, of course. Since he's not, however—"

"It's the manner of his dying that will tell you," Burr broke in. "The General came in from riding, wet with a cold rain, and met news of Monroe's election as governor of Virginia. Instead of changing and getting in front of a fire, he spent hours stalking up and down in his wet clothes, cursing the mutton-headed voters and Monroe as well. That was how he caught the chill that killed him. That was his opinion of James Monroe, gentleman and governor of Virginia. You needn't take my word. The story's well enough known."

"On my arrival in the city yesterday you were pointed out to me, sir. There was a man with you, James Madison. Perhaps, if you could introduce me to him . . . . "

Burr eyed him sharply. "Madison." His voice was flat. After a moment, though, he nodded. "Yes, Jemmy could do it, and I think he will." A genuine smile appeared on his face. "He's a capital fellow, you know. Something of a poet. He spent most of his time at Princeton writing obscene verse with Philip Freneau and Hugh Henry Brackenridge. Come back inside. He's here today."

As they turned back to the Congress House, the first flakes of the long-threatening snow fell. The sky darkened quickly. As Burr and Fallon began to hurry, a coach appeared. The galloping horses were pulled to a plunging halt before the door.

"I wonder what the hurry is?" Robert said.

"People always hurry in Washington," Burr said. "Otherwise, how could they be busy, and important?" But he stopped in the doorway with Robert to watch.

The driver opened the door of the coach. Three very diverse men got out and hurried for the door. One was as short as Burr, with a blunt chin and a prominent, sloping nose. He held his walking stick like a weapon, and surveyed his surroundings with a piercing gaze as he strode. His eyes froze on the two men. He stopped in the snow, rigid in almost a dueler's stance.

Beside him came a large man gone to fat, his curly hair surrounding a broad, large-featured face. His air of aristocratic ease shattered at the sight of Burr and Robert. He stiffened; his eyes darted from them to the man beside him. Then, clearing his throat loudly, he darted past them into the building with surprising speed.

The third, who had followed at the other man's heels, was nondescript, of medium height and uncertain features that seemed to fade from memory as soon as you looked away. His mouth fell open, and with a strangled shout he scrambled back into the coach.

Burr bowed coolly, a courtesy the man in the snow did not return, and turned to push through the crowded entrance. "Come along, Fallon. We'd best get your introduction done." He sounded grim.

Robert followed. "Who were those men?"

"The one who pushed past us was DeWitt Clinton, a State Senator from New York. He hates me for my influence in the state, and he wants my position as Vice-President. He's been attacking me lately for being too close to the Federalists. He's supposedly a republican, too, you see. But the man he was riding with is Hamilton, himself. My first chance to prove they've been meeting, and no one there to see it. My pardon, Captain Fallon. I meant, no one of the government."

"Granted. But which one was Hamilton? I've never seen him before."

"The one with the nose," Burr said drily. "And here we are." He pushed through a door into an office little larger than a closet.

The diminutive James Madison was bent over a desk that took up most of the space, spectacles sitting low on his nose. Without looking up he said, "What rhymes with 'fine'?"

"I'm here on business, Jemmy," Burr said. "I don't have time for your versifying today."

"Oh, hello, Aaron." Madison looked up and flashed a grin at Burr, a curious glance at Robert. "I will be with you as soon as I get my rhyme. It's the easiest ones that evade you longest, you know."

"What about 'line,' sir?" Robert said.

Madison nodded and bent back to his paper. "Very good, sir. Goes to show you what I said about the easy ones. Listen. 'Her dress was cut from muslin fine, cut, indeed, on the sheerest line, and when I—'"

"Jemmy," Burr broke in. "I truly do need to be on the floor. This is Captain Robert Fallon, of the *Osprey*, I believe it is, out of Charleston, in South Carolina. He could use some small help, and I believe you can trust him." And with that he disappeared, leaving Robert and Madison staring at each other.

"You don't happen to know a rhyme for orange?" Madison said suddenly.

Robert managed to suppress a sigh. "No, sir."

"I don't think there is one, actually. At least, I've never heard of one. Still, Captain. Fallon was it? Captain Fallon, you've chosen a bad time to ask for favors. Even small ones. I am waist deep in work that should have been done months ago."

"Mr. Madison—"

"Even this bit of doggerel is brought on by work," Madison went on. "I call it 'To Georgia.' You see, our government, in its infinite wisdom and mercy, has turned me into a procurer."

Robert forgot what he was going to say next. "I beg your pardon?" he managed.

"Yes, Captain Fallon," Madison laughed bitterly. "A procurer. Some might say a fitting job for the Secretary of State. You see, it seems that Mellimelli, the Ambassador from Tunis, insisted that one of his perquisites was to be provided with a concubine. Mr. Jefferson confronted the issue by passing it on to me, along with instructions to acquiesce."

"An uncomfortable position," Robert said, fighting a smile.

"To say the least. Well, I did it. Through machinations too involved to go into, I got the fat bastard a Greek girl, the Georgia of my verse. But do you think I'm allowed to wash my hands of it now? Not at all. I find I'm required to account for the money. How in hell do I list it? Purchase of slave? God, I can hear the Congress howling for my head now."

"What about 'promotion of foreign intercourse'?"

Madison stared, then burst into a bray of laughter. "By God, I'll do it!" He tossed his spectacles on the table and rubbed his eyes. "Sir, a rhymester, and a punster as well, deserves whatever help I can give. What can I do for you, Captain Fallon? Wait a minute. Fallon. Charleston. Do you have any, ah, connection with Spanish America?"

"My father and I have some trade with the Spanish colonies," Robert said carefully.

"There's no need to worry, Captain. I do know about the, shall we say, special items, your family trades to the south, but only because I have a personal interest in Spanish America. No one else does. And I, for one, approve. Now, how can I help you?"

First sketchily, then, under probing questions, in detail, Robert told Madison about what had happened in New Orleans, and what he had brought back. "The French Army," he finished, "has an interest in New Orleans. Remember that forts are marked on those maps. The President should know about it."

"You're correct," Madison said. "I'll arrange a meeting for you as quickly as I can. Perhaps tomorrow. Where are you staying? And can you hold yourself ready?"

"Mrs. McQuade's boarding house, and yes, I can."

"Until tomorrow, then, Captain.

Mrs. McQuade, pounding on his door, wakened him the next morning. "Mr. Falcon! Wake up! There's a man here! From the President hisself! Wake up! Mr. Falcon!"

"I'm awake!" he called. "I'm awake, Mrs. McQuade." The pounding continued. He fumbled for his pocket watch on the nightstand. Half-past five. He lurche to his feet with the quilt around him and crackled the door.

Mrs. McQuade's hatchet-face glared at him from a distance of six inches. "There's a man from the President, Mr. Falcon. Are you in trouble? I don't allow troublemakers in my place. You'll have to get out if you're in trouble."

"Fallon, Mrs. McQuade. Not Falcon. And I'm in no trouble. Where's the man?"

"Downstairs. I don't like his looks. I left him—"

He shut the door on her, and after a minute her mutters moved away. With another disbelieving look at his watch, he hurried into his clothes and snatched up his packet from New Orleans. Why on earth was Jefferson sending for him so early? Something must have convinced him Robert's visit was important after all.

The messenger from the President's Palace was slouched uneasily in the entry hall under Mrs. McQuade's auger eye. A few years younger than Robert, with a sharp nose and chin, he straightened at the sight of someone else.

"Captain Fallon?" he said eagerly.

"You're from the President?" Robert replied.

"I'm his secretary, sir. Meriwether Lewis. You *are* Captain Robert Fallon?"

Robert nodded. "Yes. Yes. Why am I being summoned so early?"

"The President keeps long hours, compared to the rest of us. He's been at work an hour or more already." Lewis glanced again at Mrs. McQuade. "Are you ready to go now, sir?"

Outside, a coach and driver waited in the dim light. It lurched away over frozen ruts in the mud as soon as they were in.

Lewis, glancing back at the boarding house, shook his head. "I've served on the frontier, Captain Fallon, on the Ohio. I've fought Indians more than once. But I vow I've never been fixed by a beadier eye."

Robert chuckled. "She has that. How is it she manages to keep an inn?"

"The devil himself could run a boarding house in this city. There's simply no place else to stay. I'm grateful for my room at the Palace, believe me."

"Do you know why I'm seeing the President, Mr. Lewis?"

"I'm his secretary, sir. Secretary Madison spoke to me before he spoke to President Jefferson."

"And he's interested in New Orleans?"

"The President has always been interested in the western lands," Lewis said cautiously. He seemed to feel that courtesy called for a fuller answer, for after a pause he went on. "More than fifteen years ago the President—he was then Minister to France—encouraged John Ledyard, a Connecticutter who wanted to cross the continent from west to east. And back in '93 he got the American Philosophical Society to finance an attempt by André Michaux, a French botanist, to find the shortest and most convenient route between the United States and the Pacific Ocean. I wanted to go along, myself, but Mr. Jefferson thought I was too young."

"Yes, my father knew Michaux. He made a great botanical garden in Charleston. His expedition turned back in Kentucky, didn't it?"

"He was recalled," Lewis said tightly. "Recalled. He didn't turn back. He could have made it."

Robert sighed. Everyone in Washington had a bone to pick. "I'm certain he could have," he murmured.

"It was politics, pure and simple. He was a friend of Genet."

"The Frenchman? The one they called 'Citizen' Genet?"

"The same. Rumors grew up that Michaux was involved with his intrigues, trying to stir up the settlers, perhaps trying to bring their French version of revolution here. Rumors breed in this city like flies in a dung heap."

"Yes, indeed they do."

"He was right," Lewis said fervently. "It can be done. It will be done. Someday, by someone." He sighed and looked out the window as the coach drew to a halt. "We are there, Captain Fallon. The President will be waiting."

The two-story house of white sandstone, with its low peaked roof and four columns flat against the front wall, seemed gray in the dim light against the night's snow. The dark shapes of the workmen's shacks seemed vague mushroom growths.

Inside was a hodgepodge of furnishings left by the Adamses,

combined with cheap pieces Jefferson had bought in a wave of republicanism. Gloom pervaded the entry hall. Three candles struggled to light the entire expanse. A single servant, unliveried, met them there. Lewis waved him away and led Robert to a side corridor, to a door at the foot of a flight of stairs. He tapped, and entered to a murmured, "Come." Almost immediately he reappeared, motioning Robert in.

The room he'd been shown to was a study. A tall, lean man in a long dressing robe and run-down slippers stood by the fire. His bony nose and faintly red hair corresponded to what Robert knew of Jefferson, but he couldn't believe the President would meet a stranger attired for the night.

"Sit down, Captain Fallon." The voice was high and thin.

Robert realized that Lewis had disappeared. "Pardon me, but you *are* President Jefferson?"

The other man, who had been turning to his desk, looked back in surprise. "Of course I am. Who else would I be?"

"I'm sorry, Your Excellency."

"Not Excellency." Jefferson's face darkened. "I'll leave that sort of European nonsense to Mr. Adams and his Federalists. If you must have a title for me, a simple Mr. President will do. I will not have that royal codswollop draped about me. This is the President's House, not a palace. But even my closest associates persist."

"I've heard it called 'the white house,'" Robert said.

"Another title. Let it be used ten years, or 'President's House,' for that matter, and they'll be giving it all the reverence of the Court of St. James." Jefferson looked at his robe and laughed. "I am a country gentleman, captain. No more. And I have a love of country simplicity. There's none of it here, though, even among those who profess the belief."

Robert itched to get on with his business, but he kept silent. It didn't seem proper to interrupt the President. Jefferson turned to the window and seemed to forget his presence.

"None of them truly believe," the President said softly. "I came here hoping to put my beliefs, the beliefs I thought others shared, into action. The Congress should be the power, the representatives of the people, not a Godlike president. But the ones I can trust don't have brains enough to run their own households, let alone a country. And those with brains have ambition embedded in them. I find I must sneak and intrigue like any European Prime Minister. If I want to see a thing done well, I must involve myself in it, no matter how petty it might seem." Suddenly snatching a handful of papers from his desk, he shook them at Robert. "Do you know what these are?"

"No, sir," Robert said, but Jefferson wasn't listening.

"Detailed instructions for the Postmaster on which streams must be bridged to facilitate mail delivery, and on how to select a ford. The route for reports from consular officials to the Secretary of State, and guidelines for which are to come to me. Plans for a force of coastal gunboats. Those fools in the Navy want to build frigates, and even ships-of-the-line. They'll involve us in foreign wars yet."

"Mr. President."

Jefferson stopped with the papers in mid-brandish. He looked at Robert as if he did not remember him. He dropped the sheaf back on the desk. "I'm told you have information about New Orleans. What is it?"

"The French are taking over the colony from Spain," Robert began.

"That much is talked in every coffee house from Boston to Charleston."

"But not that the French Army's involved." Hastily Robert unwrapped his packet while he explained. Jefferson brushed past the maps and the orders to pick up the surveying instrument. He studied it closely, nodding as Robert spoke.

"A beautiful piece of workmanship," he mused when Robert had finished. "The French always seem to make the most utilitarian things objects of beauty."

Robert stared.

Jefferson looked up sharply. "I heard you, Captain Fallon. It's simply difficult for me to contemplate the French threatening us, here. I once hoped . . . " He sighed. "I'll have Mr. Madison in to discuss this. You've jelled certain thoughts of mine, though I'm sure you'll understand that I cannot tell you more."

Robert nodded. Understand or no, there was little he could do about it. "In that case, sir, I'll be going."

"I've been remiss, Captain." Jefferson was once again

frowning at the surveying instrument. "I haven't offered you a drink."

"No, thank you, Mr. President. I wish to return home as soon as possible, and I may make the afternoon tide if I hurry."

"Very well." Jefferson, now immersed in the French maps, gestured vaguely toward the door. "You can find your own way?"

"Of course, Mr. President." Jefferson didn't look up. After a moment Robert let himself out.

The carriage that had brought him was gone. He pulled his collar up and cast an eye at the sky. The clouds were heavy with snow. It'd likely begin before he got back to the boarding house, but he was damned if he'd go back to ask Jefferson for a coach. He had just started down the front steps when another coach pulled up, and a woman got out.

He recognized Dolley Madison immediately, despite her heavy, hooded cloak. "Mrs. Madison," he said with a bow, and found himself answering a ready smile. She wasn't particularly pretty, looking more a comfortable housekeeper than the wife of the Secretary of State, but in some fashion she was very attractive.

"I remember you, sir, but I cannot recall where—I have it! I saw you yesterday with Mr. Monroe, when I went to see my husband at the Congress House. Mr.—?"

"Fallon, ma'am. Robert Fallon."

"Mr. Fallon. Have you come to see President Jefferson?"

"I've seen him already. And if I might say so, Mrs. Madison, if *you're* here to see him, this might not be a good time. He's preoccupied, right now."

"Thomas is always preoccupied," she laughed. "You mustn't let that put you, Mr. Fallon."

"I didn't, ma'am."

"Because if it did, you must let me take you back to him and make him listen to you. I act as his hostess, you see."

Robert knew now why she seemed attractive. She seemed genuinely interested in him and in whatever his problems might be. He already felt as if he'd known her for years. "There's no need, truly, ma'am. I assure you President Jefferson listened to me. And you must forgive me for sticking my oar in. I didn't know you were an intimate of the house."

"Tush, Mr. Fallon! There's nothing to forgive. There is no earthly reason you should know. Tom is a widower, you see, and I do love parties. Speaking of which, there's to be a gathering tonight. Not precisely a party, but a supper. Any number of amusing people will be there. Do say you will come."

"You make me regret very much having to refuse, ma'am. I'm afraid I sail for home this afternoon."

"Oh, that *is* too bad," she said regretfully. "But you must promise me if you return to Washington City, you will accept my invitation then."

"Gladly, ma'am." A glance at the sky reminded him of the impending snow. "But if you'll excuse me now, I must hurry to get back to my room. We South Carolinians aren't used to being snowed on."

"You're walking? That Tom Jefferson. It's certain you didn't come to talk of new methods of fertilizing, or some such, or he'd keep you here for days, with a carriage at your beck and call. For everyone else, though, he seems to forget the meanest courtesies. You must take my rig."

"Oh, no, Mrs. Madison," he hastened to say. "I can walk, I assure you."

"Nonsense. I won't need it for hours. Abraham, take Mr. Fallon wherever he wishes to go, then return here. And Mr. Fallon," she added with a twinkle in her eyes, "my friends call me Dolley."

He found himself bowing over her hand. "And I am Robert, Dolley." She laughed amusedly. "I thank you for the use of your carriage."

"Robert." She smiled again, and disappeared inside.

He stood looking after her. A lady worthy of the house, he thought. Then he gave directions to the driver and climbed in.

There were several coaches outside Mrs. McQuade's when he hurried in. The landlady was in the entry hall, glowering at a sweeping maid. Her face went blank when she saw him.

"I'll be leaving," he told her. "Make out my reckoning."

She nodded tightly, and silently. He wondered as he trotted up the stairs if the pleasure of losing him as a tenant had overwhelmed her. When he reached his room, he knew the reason for her silence. There was a visitor in his room. Alexander Hamilton.

The short man sat the one good chair in Robert's room like a throne. "I," he announced, "am Alexander Hamilton."

"I know," Robert said shortly.

Hamilton seemed to take it as a matter of course that he was known. "Have a seat, Captain Fallon." He gestured vaguely toward Robert's bed.

"I'll stand, thank you," Robert said drily.

"If you wish." Hamilton tipped his head back. He seemed almost to be looking down at Robert. "I've had my eye on you."

"Why?" He wasn't certain whether to be amused or angry, and he made no effort to keep his feelings out of his voice.

Hamilton tilted his chin up a touch more, and smiled coldly. "I have heard things about you."

"From whom?"

"Do not be so curt with me, Captain Fallon," Hamilton barked. "Your height will avail you nothing here." He made an effort to control himself, and sat back in the chair. "In two short days you have managed to meet Madison, Burr, Monroe, even Jefferson. Four men who hold considerable strings of power in their fingers, and you, a simple ship captain. But then, you're not so simple, are you? Your family trades all over the world, doesn't it? Offices in London and Stockholm. And of course we mustn't forget the plantations in the Carolinas."

This was no casual skein of gossip, picked up in a day or two. Robert doubted there was a man in the city outside his crew who knew as much about him, and they were under orders to talk to no one.

"I wonder why you show such an interest in me," he said finally, "and for that matter, how you found out so much."

Hamilton shrugged. "I asked questions here and there; there are always people willing to talk. I have an interest in everything that happens here, and I have a feeling that your reasons for being here will be of great interest to me. What are they?"

Robert stared, outraged. "Mr. Hamilton, it is time for you to leave."

"Come, Fallon. Don't be a fool. From the men you choose to visit, I know we have no politics in common, but in this town the cat and the rat often bed down together. Think, man. Your reasons may indeed be something you wish kept from me. In which case it will take me a week, a fortnight at most, to ferret them out. But if you don't need to keep them from me, if I can help you gain the ends you seek, what matter it if we be brothers of blood or deadly enemies? Consider, sir, and tell me."

Robert thought quickly. In their first minute of meeting he had known he would never have any liking for Hamilton, but he could see no way his news could be used against his father's goals. "I brought proof to Mr. Jefferson that the French Army is mapping the area about New Orleans. For what reason I could not discover."

Hamilton grimaced; after a moment Robert realized that it was a smile. "This will goad that Jacobin bastard," Hamilton muttered. "This will prod that towering son of a bitch into action." His face grew composed. "It does not matter what it means, Captain Fallon. It means what we wish it to mean. For me it means that we must move against New Orleans before we discover a French Army on our doorstep, marching to spread Jacobinism and the Terror across America."

"There's no evidence of any of that," Robert protested.

"I said it means what we wish it to mean, and that is what I wish it to mean." He chuckled, a thin sound. "You are surprised? You should not be. How else does a man gain what he wants other than by using information, manipulating events?"

"You said 'move against New Orleans.' What did you mean?"

"Exactly what it sounded like. I've said it often enough. And with what you've just told me . . . well, this is our final chance. While there's only a miniscule Spanish garrison to face. Before Bonaparte ships in his divisions."

"Invasion? You speak very casually of sending us to war, Mr. Hamilton, especially when we are to be the cause."

"It is the way of nations, captain, to grow by conquest. You obviously do not object to our acquiring New Orleans. How else, then, if not by force of arms? If we must go to war, and to get New Orleans we must, then better with Spain than with

France and its armies.''

"It could be bought. War isn't something to be stepped into lightly, no matter with who.''

"Bought!'' Hamilton laughed. "And why on earth would they sell? Even if they did, how could we afford to buy? Oh, you do sound like one of Long Tom's Jacobins, all right. No, it must be war. This country needs a war, a real war. Not this foofaraw with the African pirates.''

"Needs a war, Mr. Hamilton? In God's name, why?''

Hamilton let out his breath slowly, studying Robert. "You are indeed one of Mr. Jefferson's creatures, captain. He will avoid war at any cost, if he has to crawl on his hands and knees to do it. No matter, it will be seen to, despite him and his damned republican Congress.'' He rose to his feet, settled his cloak about him regally, and picked up his hat.

"You haven't answered my question, Mr. Hamilton. Why are you so eager for war?''

"You may rest assured, Captain Fallon, that the information you have given me will be used for the purpose you wish. The acquisition of New Orleans.'' And with a fractional bow, he was gone.

Furiously, Robert pulled out his bag and began throwing his clothes into it. If he hadn't just witnessed the insanity of Washington, he never wanted to. And if he couldn't sail with the afternoon tide, he'd stay on *Osprey* until he could. There was a rap at the door. With a muttered oath he threw it open.

"I'll pay my nick when I come down, Mrs.—''

The lean man standing in the doorway tugged at his bushy black whiskers nervously. "Begging your pardon, Captain Fallon—''

"Trask,'' Robert breathed. The next instant found his hands locked around the slaver's throat.

Trask struggled for footing, clawing at Robert's hands, but Robert forced him back against the wall. The man's face darkened through red toward purple, and his eyes stood out. He beat at Robert with flapping hands. "Talk,'' he managed to squawk. "Let. Me. Talk.''

Robert stared. Talk, he wanted, did he? Bodily he hurled the slaver into his room, slamming the door behind them. "Talk, then, damn you! See if you can talk me out of slitting your throat.''

Trask, on the floor, gasped for breath and cast a truckling look up at Robert. "You got no call," he whined, massaging his throat. "I wasn't the one as shot your father, and he's alive anyway, ain't he?" He hurried on as Robert took a step toward him. "I got information! I can tell y ou things as you don't know, things you'd like to know, else I miss my guess."

"Such as?" Robert grated.

"I . . . I come on hard times, captain. Since I lost my ship, I mean. That hell-spawn Fourrier's been hounding me." His eyes shifted. "He thinks I done it. Man tried to knife me in Savannah. Said Fourrier sent him. I bashed his head, and went to New York, but another one turned up. I just got away with the clothes on my back."

"I don't care about your troubles, Trask. You'll rot in hell, if I have my way."

Trask hunched as if to study the floor. "I was thinking, captain, sir, that you might be giving me a bit to help me on my way. In return for my information, so to speak."

"Why, you—"

"Love of God, sir! I got to have some money. One of Fourrier's men is in town. He'll kill me sure, if he sees me."

"A Fourrier man? Who? Where?"

Trask looked at him with glittering desperation. "Some money. Just a few dollars. I seen a man skinned alive once, on his order. Alive! I got to get away."

Robert returned the gaze dispassionately. Killing Trask would give him great satisfaction. "I'll give you what I think your information's worth, Trask. But don't think this ends anything. If I ever see you again, I may kill you anyway."

"Thank you, captain. Thank you, sir."

"I don't want your thanks. Who's this Fourrier man?"

"His name's Jemmy Carde. Fourrier sends him where there's money to be talked. Man's got a mind like an account book. But he's not soft, for all that. I seen him slice him a nigger from crotch to gullet, once, in Cormantine, and he never blinked an eye."

"What's this Carde look like?"

"Like nothing much of anything, I guess. I don't reckon he's got any looks to speak of. Just looks like anybody else."

"There's a Fourrier man about, but you can't tell me anything about what he looks like? What is he? Tall? Short?

Fat? Thin? There's no such man, is there, Trask? You just took a chance. Thought you could euchre me out of some money if you prated about Fourrier.''

"Ask your friend," Trask snarled. "If you think I'm lying, ask your muckety-muck friend. I near froze me cods hiding outside till he'd gone, for fear Carde was with him again. Waiting outside, I was, when he drove up. That frowzy old bat as keeps this place wouldn't let me wait inside.''

"Hamilton?" Robert said softly. "You saw Hamilton with this Carde?''

Trask shrugged. "Whatever his name is, I seen him with Jemmy Carde, all right. Twice.''

A man with no particular sort of features, Robert thought, and he remembered Hamilton arriving at the Congress House. "What about Clinton? Does that name mean anything to you?''

Reluctantly Trask shook his head. "Rich folk up to New York is all. I did see somebody else with Carde and the other fellow, though. Big man, fat, with curly hair. He was with them both times.''

Robert was silent. A Fourrier man in company with Alexander Hamilton and DeWitt Clinton. The possibilities were so fantastic he didn't even want to consider them.

"That's the lot of it?" he said. "A man named Carde who works for Justin Fourrier?''

"Ain't it enough? Fourrier's going to kill you," he added maliciously, then cringed when Robert looked at him.

"It's enough." He tossed a handful of milled Spanish dollars on the floor. "Take that and get out." Trask scrabbled the coins into his pockets and darted to the door. "Trask!" The slaver halted at his name like a beast at a whipcrack. He looked back fearfully. "Remember what I told you," Robert said quietly. "The next time I see you, I'll hang you with my own hands. Now get out.''

For a time after the slaver was gone Robert sat thinking. Fourrier, Hamilton, and Clinton. How could they be linked? However it was, it could spell no good. He had best get on his way, and let his father know.

With greater urgency he resumed his packing.

XVII

Charleston sweltered in the summer of 1802. Heat rose in waves from the paving stones. Songbirds kept to the cool of the forests outside the city. Only the men on the docks, struggling with the baled cotton and casked rice, hurried. Everything else moved langorously, like the vultures tilting in the sky over the meat market.

Martin Caine wiped the sweat from his forehead as his wagon drew up in front of Thomas Millward's cabinet shop. Replacing his broad-brimmed hat, he climbed down from the high seat. "Come on inside out of the sun, Enos," he told the driver, a slave from Seven Pines.

When the bell on the door rang, Millward himself appeared from the back of the shop. His ready smile faded when he saw the overseer. "I suppose you've come for those things Mr. Holtz ordered. Well, the boy isn't here." His voice was tinged with satisfaction.

"Jeremiah's not here?" Caine was surprised. He'd have thought pride alone would make the lad show up to watch his first commissioned work go to its new owner. "I reckon it doesn't matter. He's done his part of the work. You can do what's left."

He was pleased to see the bolt go home. The boy had an eye for wood, that was a fact; he was going to be a better cabinet-maker than Millward, far better. The bluff man didn't like to be reminded of that.

"You'll be pleased to load the goods and go, Mr. Caine. I'm a busy man."

"Your lads will do the loading, of course," Caine said as the other turned away. Millward nodded sourly and disappeared into the rear of the shop.

Soon four apprentices emerged and silently took a cypress and mahogany chest-on-chest out to the wagon. They kept their eyes down; they weren't inclined to make themselves targets of Millward's mood. Caine snorted. That would be like the man, taking his anger out on those who couldn't fight back. Enos helped them, and it wasn't long before the rest of the order, a mahogany sideboard, a table with six chairs to match, was in the wagon.

Fancy pieces, Caine thought, French-looking. He followed them out. With one foot on the wheel hub, he stopped. In a passing carriage Louise de Chardonnay sat with a parasol on her shoulder.

Then Caine saw Robert Fallon riding beside the carriage. He frowned and quickly swung up beside the driver.

"Drive on, Enos," he said, and the wagon rumbled off down the street.

It wasn't right, he thought. Fallon shouldn't treat her that way. She was going to have his child. A man should marry a woman carrying his child; that was the proper thing. She was near her time, unless he missed his guess, yet she showed not the slightest bit of shame. She acted as if it was the proudest time of her life, bearing Fallon's bastard.

Scowling, he barked at Enos for more speed. Enos looked at him sideways, but said nothing. Caine fell back into his ruminations.

Women were strange, that was a fact. There was no understanding them. Catherine Holtz was with child, too, and she was behaving worse than Louise. Women were supposed to be delicate, to stay at home when they were that way, especially when ready to give birth at any moment. Catherine wasn't showing any delicacy at all. There wasn't a ball or assembly of any kind she didn't go to. She flaunted her pregnancy like a banner.

It hadn't always been that way. Back in November, last year, she'd screamed loud enough for half the parish to hear. She'd hated the baby, and her husband, too. Then, just about the time Louise's pregnancy became known, Catherine's attitude changed completely. Without rhyme or reason. Women!

Caine stared blindly at the passing wagons.

Jeremiah stumbled into Vesey's shop, sniffing back his tears. Vesey came running from the back.

"What's the matter, boy? Are you hurt?"

"Millward," he said through tight lips. "He beat me this morning."

"Christ, boy. What happened?"

"Some white man saw that sideboard I made for Mr. Holtz. He told Millward he liked it, and could Millward make one for him just like it. Millward said he could, said it was one of his new designs."

"Trying to steal your work," Vesey muttered. "Whites'll steal anything you got, cheat you any way they can."

Jeremiah shook his head irritably. He wasn't in the mood for one for Denmark's speeches. "That was when he saw me standing there. He got puffed up till he was like to burst. Started shouting, yelling I was a lazy nigger, and why wasn't I working. He grabbed me by the collar, snatched up a lathe and started beating me. I wanted to fight him, Denmark. I wanted to. But I was scared." Tears began to pour down his face. "I was scared of hanging for hitting a white man, so I let him beat me. God help me. I was too scared to do anything else." Sobs swallowed up his words, and tears ran down his cheeks.

Vesey's head swung from side to side, and his powerful shoulders hunched like a bull's. "Too scared to fight? Boy, you need a chance before you can fight, else it's the same as cutting your own throat. You have to wait, bide your time, and don't trust anybody white. You trust the whites, you'll get what L'Ouverture got. But you don't even know about that yet, do you?"

"Denmark—"

"Even the whites here don't know yet."

"Denmark—"

"Toussaint L'Ouverture. The great general. He trusted the French. He went on one of their ships for a parley, and they put him in chains and sailed away."

"Denmark, I don't care!" Jeremiah shouted. "They can hang him, if they want. They can hang every black in Haiti. I don't care. I care about me."

Vesey jerked him close by his shirt. "You have to care," he growled. His eyes burned.

"I care about me!" Jeremiah insisted. "How can I walk down the street? How can I hold my head up? Any white man I pass can beat me if he wants, and the thing I can do is—maybe—get another white man to sue him. If I can't do that, I've got to pull wool and take it. What kind of man can I be? No man lays down and lets another man beat him."

"Our day will come, boy. It will come."

"When?" He searched Vesey's eyes. "When, Denmark?"

"Someday, boy." Vesey released him. "Someday."

Catherine spurned help as she climbed from her coach in front of Karl's house in the city. That was the way she thought of it. Karl's house. Not hers. He didn't know that, of course, nor did any of the smiling black servants who convoyed her inside. They all thought her marriage was perfect, just as they thought she was overjoyed about the baby inside her.

She thrust her belly out even more. It made her back ache to walk that way, but it made everyone beam at her. Such fools. She hoped it was a girl. Karl did so want a boy.

Ezekiel opened the door to let her in, her abigail at her heels, and bowed low. "Good afternoon, ma'am. A little cooler than it was."

Catherine handed her parasol to Mary and took off her gloves. "Is my husband home?"

"Yes, ma'am. He's in the upstairs drawing room. I'll tell him you're back, ma'am."

"I'll tell him," she said. "No, Ezekiel, I am perfectly capable of climbing the stairs," she added firmly.

Karl was propping a series of sketches on a sofa in the drawing room. He smiled when she entered, a slightly worried smile, and took her hand. "My dear, you should have had Ezekiel tell me you were here. Sit down, sit down."

She took pleasure in stepping away from him, and stood in front of the sketches, studying views of a grand house. "What's this, Karl?"

"It is for you." He wore an almost bashful smile. "The work will begin next month, at the foot of East Bay, with a grand view of the harbor." He chuckled fondly, a sound that made her roil inside. "It is barely grand enough for my wife and my child."

She studied the drawings. A tall house of brick, it had a hugely columned portico across the front, and wide, sweeping stairs. Her house? Yes, it would be, and more so than Karl thought. There would be no detail of it that was not as she wished. "It will do," she said languidly, and turned away.

"You are all right?" he said worriedly. He put his arm around her. "You seem pale. So close to your time you should not—"

"I'm all right," she snapped, twisting out of his embrace. Her flesh crawled when he held her, of late. But it was none of her plan to let him know that. It was her revenge that he think she loved him, think she loved the child he had put in her, like the fool he was, never knowing the depths of hatred that lurked behind her eyes. She put on a smile. "It's just the heat. For some reason I just cannot bear to be touched in this heat."

"Of course," he said awkwardly. "I understand."

His plaintiveness made her smile. She had managed to refuse him her bed ever since she'd discovered she was pregnant.

"Robert is coming this afternoon," he went on. "I wish him to see the drawings of the house, and the plans."

Robert was as hateful as Karl, more so. She had tried to befriend him—just that, no more—and he had repaid her by putting his baby in that slut's belly! It was meet that the bastard's son should be a bastard in turn. It was just. Her face twisted. God, why did she have to cry whenever she thought of it?

Karl stepped toward her again and hesitated with his arms halfraised to her shoulders. "*Liebchen,* you are right about the heat. It has made you overwrought. You must lie down and let Mary sponge you with cool water."

"I don't want to be sponged. There's nothing the matter with me. I'm going back out. What I need is a carriage drive above the city."

"In this heat? You are going about too much, my dear. Your time—"

"The drive will at least stir the air. It'll be cooler than staying here."

"But the jouncing . . . . *Ach!* Besides, your brother is coming."

"ror Heaven's sake, Karl! I don't need to be here just so you two can look over plans, and I don't intend to be." Her face grew taut as he opened his mouth again.

Ezekiel tapped on the door, and coughed discreetly in the doorway. He was grinning. "Pardon, Mr. Holtz. Mrs. Holtz. But there's a message from Mr. Robert."

Karl spoke impatiently. "Yes? What is the message?"

"Mr. Robert—his lady done had her baby." His face cracked wider. "He say it be a boy."

Catherine staggered, not hearing Karl's exclamation of delight. Damn the French slut! Damn her. Damn him. Damn the boy. Damn all of them.

She grunted as a sudden pain darted through her. Numbly she stared at her swollen body. Another pain ripped at her. Too quickly, she thought. They weren't supposed to come so quickly. A third jolted her, and she dropped to the floor with a cry.

Karl dropped his knees beside her, his mouth working, but she couldn't hear a word. She bit her lip to stifle a groan. Balefully her eyes fixed him, venom riding on her gaze. God curse him. He had done this to her. She didn't want his baby. She wanted—her scream drowned the thought.

Dimly she was aware of Mary holding her hand, mouthing what must be comforting sounds; dimly she was aware of being lifted.

Let it be a girl. Please, God, let it be a girl.

Karl was drinking his fourth brandy by the time Michael arrived, but he felt none of them. He put a hand to his undone stock. "Your pardon, sir. I am somewhat disarrayed. You will take a brandy, *ja*?"

Both men froze in the middle of the study floor as a scream tore through the house. "I will that," Michael said as it faded away. He looked upward. "Is all going well up there?"

"I do not know," Karl replied. He knew his voice trembled; he tried for calm. "The midwife will not let me in. Mary is with her, but she will tell me nothing. *Gott in Himmel!* I am the husband, the father. Have I no right to know anything?" He gulped the rest of his brandy and poured another.

"Easy, man," Michael said. "You must be letting them

have the rule of it. It always comes out right in the end.''

Karl sighed. "I suppose you are right. It will be right. *Ach!* I have forgotten your brandy." He poured another glass. "I understand you are doubly to be congratulated, sir. You are twice today a grandfather."

Michael laughed, and raised his glass in a toast. "I am that, Karl, lad. A fine, big boy, Robert's son is, with the Fallon beak stuck in the middle of his face. Catherine escaped that, thank God, so your child may escape it, too."

"I do not care what sort of nose he has," Karl smiled. At the sound of running feet overhead he took a step toward the door. "I must go to her."

"Indeed you must not, man. Sit you down. Tell me how your crop is coming."

He looked at Michael miserably. "I cannot bear to hear her, knowing she is in pain, and I can do nothing."

"Now that's the right of it. You can do nothing. Sit you down and tell me about your mill. You're not shipping much for export. At least, not on my ships."

"No. No, I have not." He took an uneasy seat on the edge of a chair and watched the door warily. "There is much trouble in Europe, and it spills onto the sea. Every day the English take more American ships, claiming they are trading with the French. Insurance rates climb, freight rates climb, and many ships will not clear except for an English port. I cannot sell my goods in England. There are laws to protect their mills. But you know all of this."

"Aye, I know it. I know more than you. For instance, I know it's going to get worse. Fewer ships will clear for anywhere in Europe. Have you ever heard the word 'impressment'?"

"No, I—"

"More water," Mary shouted above. "And boiling hot. Hustle your feet."

Karl leaped up, then stopped and swallowed. "No," he said hoarsely, "I do not know the word."

"Something ugly's happening. The British have stopped ships at sea and taken seamen off. American ships and American seamen."

"I do not understand you," Karl said.

"They claim some poor sod's a Royal Navy deserter and haul him off to serve in a British man-o'-war. They're taking more than a few who've never had a smell of the British Navy, or England, either."

"That is not what I mean. I mean that I do not understand you. You." His voice was rising, but he couldn't stop it. He hurled his glass at the wall. Broken glass fell to the rug and brandy splattered the plaster. "Your own daughter lies upstairs, and you sit talking of ships and seamen and the British Navy. She may die. Women die. Women *do* die sometimes in giving birth."

Michael didn't speak for a time. "I'm not calm," he said finally. "I'm not calm at all. But I know I must act it, as you must. You'll do no good if you walk about with your fears on your face."

"But—"

"But nothing. When you go in to see her, after the baby's come, you must be in control of yourself, not coming apart at the seams. You must tell her everything will be all right, and make her believe that, when you know that she, or the baby, or both, might die from childbed fever or a dozen other causes before the week is out. You must do it because it's the only damned way you can help her, now. And you can't do a bit of it when you've let panic strap a saddle on your back."

"I . . . I understand." Karl straightened. "I will try."

"Good, then. Now. Have you ever thought of shipping to the Spanish Americas?"

"Spanish Americas?" Karl felt thick-witted and slow. "No, never. My thoughts have all been directed at Europe."

"Try redirecting them. The Spaniards and the Indians down there use a lot of cotton. It's not hard to get the licenses to sell it. Boston folk have been shipping there for a long time."

"Charleston is much closer. My freight costs would be less, so I could undersell them." He felt quite proud; he could discuss business coolly.

"There's a small group of men here who're interested in Spanish America," Michael said. "The main requirement for sitting down with us is a dislike of colonies. Perhaps you'd care to attend a meeting."

A baby's cry echoed through the house.

"*Gott in Himmel!* The child has come." Karl dashed out of

the room, with Michael close behind.

Mary met them on the third-floor landing, a mewling bundle in her arms. "Here she be, Mr. Holtz. Your daughter. Your granddaughter, Mr. Fallon."

"A daughter?" Karl exclaimed, fingering aside the swaddlings. The wizened red face that peered up at him took him aback. "She is beautiful," he said stoutly. "She will be as beautiful as her mother."

"Don't worry," Michael said smiling. "They all look like that to start."

"She is beautiful," he repeated. Awkwardly he took the child in his arms, beaming down at her, then suddenly fearful, handed her back to Mary. "I might drop her. We will name her Helen. What is the matter?"

Mary had drawn a deep breath, then snapped her mouth shut. Now she spoke diffidently. "Miss Catherine, she say she want her named Charlotte. She kept on saying that, most particular."

"But we agreed," Karl said. "A girl child would be named after my mother. A boy—" He stopped suddenly, embarrassed. "A boy was to have been named Michael. We spoke of the names weeks ago."

"You'd best talk to her again, then," Michael said, "and consider letting her have her way."

"I will talk with her," Karl agreed. "And now I must go to her. She will be wondering where I am."

Mary put up a hesitant hand. "Mr. Holtz. Sir. She don't want to see nobody right now. I mean, she can't. That midwife, that Mrs. Bates, she say Miss Catherine ought not to have no visitors. She need rest." She watched Karl blandly.

"I cannot see her?" Karl said. He looked at Michael as if he expected to find a different answer there. But Michael nodded slowly. "Very well," Karl said. "I . . . I will see her when she is rested."

Catherine heard the footsteps moving away from her door, and relaxed. The midwife continued washing her face. Dimly she was aware of the dark face bent over her, the cool, damp cloth on her forehead. She had won. She had given Karl Holtz a daughter. And yearn as he might for a son, he'd never got one from her. She had won.

XVIII

As 1802 drew to a close, calm reigned over the Holtz and Fallon households. Robert forsook his friends and the coffee houses for the company of Louise and James Christopher. He took on a fatuous grin at the very mention of the boy, and maintained he already had a grip like iron. Michael divided his time between his grandchildren, dandling the boy on his knee, bringing yet another doll to Charlotte. Catherine had remained firm on the name, and Karl was too enthralled with the little girl to resist. They turned inward, all their troubles seemingly left behind. In the outside world it was different.

From Haiti came rumors that General LeCler was taking as many casualties from the fever as from the blacks, and fears, of slave uprisings were voiced aloud. In Europe the Peace of Amiens limped along. The French Navy freed of the British, once more seized American ships for carrying unspecified "contraband." Although they were no longer fighting the French, the British had taken to impressing American sailors within sight of American ports.

In their studies, men spoke of free trade and national honor; other men spoke of the weakness of America, the foolishness of being provocative toward anyone. After all, the United States Navy had been unable to put down so small a foe as the Barbary pirates; how would they fare against the Navy of England or of France?

A blustery wind blew out of the harbor as Robert pulled rein in front of his father's house on the first of March in 1803. He looped the reins around the cast-iron hitching post and strode to the door. Caesar let him in.

"Good afternoon, Mr. Robert. And how is young Mr. James Christopher today, sir?"

"Fine, Caesar. I vow he'll walk any day now. Where's my father? He sent for me."

"In the study, sir, with the others. He said for me to show you right in."

Once in the study, Robert paused. Michael sat in a wing chair beside the fireplace, a brandy in hand, with Karl seated on the other side. Langdon Cheves, his face lighting at the sight of Robert, sat slender and erect at one end of the sofa, while Louis Middleton slouched at the other, idly flicking his quirt against his riding boots. Henry McKeig, dour as always, sat frowning against the wall, while Joseph Alston, his black side-whiskers almost meeting at his chin, stood by the windows, pipe in hand. And seated nervously on the edge of his chair, his cigar and brandy held awkwardly, was young Oliver Daniels.

It was a strangely mixed group, Robert thought. At twenty-five, Daniels was captain of one of Michael's schooners, the *Wampanaw*. Michael might well have him for brandy and cigars, but it wasn't likely he would be socializing with the others. Joseph, still fresh from his marriage to Aaron Burr's daughter, Theodosia, was one of the state's wealthiest planters, and a member of the State Lesiglature. Langdon had taken his seat there at the same time. Louis cared for little beyond horseracing, cockfighting, and women, while McKeig cared for nothing but his cotton crop. He could think of nothing to have brought all of them together.

"Gentlemen," Robert said with an all-inclusive bow. "Oliver, you look anxious. Trouble?"

Daniels flickered a grin at him, and a questioning look at his father. "No, Robert. Everything's all right. I hope."

"Captain," Michael said, "why don't you tell him what you've told us. Briefly."

"Well," Daniels began. "I was in Port-au-Prince, down to Haiti, trying to pick up a cargo of cane sugar and molasses. I'd gone down in rice, cotton goods, and cutlery. I'd been there near two weeks, because the French were being slow about papers, and—"

"Michael," McKeig broke in. "Do we have to listen to the whole damned thing again?"

"It is a bit long," Alston said.

Michael nodded to Daniels. "Go on, Captain. Briefly."

Daniels hesitated, then took a deep breath. "The French are just waiting till they've got this Christophe fellow put down, then LeClerc is sailing for New Orleans with his whole army. They're going to attack the United States."

"Rumors," McKeig growled. "As I said before, innuendos and suppositions."

"Oliver," Robert said, "what makes you think they'll attack us?"

"They told me," Daniels replied. "There wasn't a tavern or a coffee house without soldiers talking about how eager they were to get to New Orleans, and about how easy Americans would be to beat." He flushed angrily. "They don't account us more than rabble!"

"Tavern talk!" McKeig cried, throwing up his hands. "Whiskey talk. I'll wager a thousand dollars they're not sending more than a handful to garrison New Orleans."

"The maps showed forts," Robert said quietly.

"Maps?" Joseph asked.

"What are you talking about?" McKeig said.

Michael studied the toe of his book. Robert stared at him. "For the love of . . . . Father, you didn't tell them about the maps?"

"All things in time," Michael said. "It's best not to tell everything at once." He looked at the tense faces around him and nodded with a slight smile. "I think this might be the time, though. Gentlemen, my son came into possession of some French Army maps of New Orleans. They had locations marked for building naval facilities to handle a fleet and forts that'd take ten thousand to man. Aye, they're sending an army, all right."

McKeig was on his feet. "By damn, why didn't you tell us this before?"

"You must forgive me, sir," Middleton said, "but if we are all in this enterprise together, we deserve to know everything about it."

"Gentlemen," Robert said as McKeig opened his mouth again, "the important point is that the maps do exist. I can testify to that."

Alston nodded thoughtfully, tugging at his whiskers. "It

would not be pleasant having a French army so close at hand. But common soldiers in Haiti could not possibly know—''

"It wasn't just common soldiers," Daniels broke in. "LeClerc had a sort of ball, and invited all the American ship captains in port. I guess he just wanted to look at us close. His officers had a big laugh with us, kept saying things that'd cause a duel anyplace else. I suppose they didn't think any of us was smart enough to know French, or maybe they didn't care. Anyway, I heard one, a colonel on LeClerc's own staff, say, 'These Americans will roll over like dead dogs. We will be in their capital in three months.'"

"You didn't tell us that before," Louis said quietly.

"None of you gave me a chance!" Daniels exploded. "Every time I tried, one of you'd start in about how I didn't know what I was talking about." The young captain glared at McKeig.

"That doesn't matter, now," Robert said quickly. "The important thing is the French interest."

"But what are we to do?" Louis asked.

"If we acquired New Orleans before the French army got there," Langdon mused.

"Acquired?" Karl said. "How?"

"Some in Washington City already went to send troops to New Orleans," Langdon replied. "Mr. Hamilton has just made another speech proposing just that."

"Hamilton!" McKeig exploded. "I'd sooner support the devil!"

Louis shook his head. "Seems to me it means war with France just the same."

"By God," McKeig said gloomily, "it seems we're to have this war whether we will or no. Free trade or New Orleans—whatever we do, it's war."

"Perhaps not," Michael said. Robert looked at him sharply. He knew that silky tone of voice. His father drew a letter from his pocket. "A reply to inquiries of mine, from the Vice-President."

"Burr's as bad as Hamilton," McKeig said.

"Have you ever met Mr. Burr?" Michael asked before Alston could speak.

"No," McKeig said shortly. Alston still watched him, unappeased.

"I *have* met him. And I believe he's a man of honor. So, if you'll listen . . . . " Michael opened the letter with a snap. "Here's the part. 'It is known to all that Robert Livingston has this past year been the Ambassador to France. What is known to few, and, if our Tom had his way, would be known least of all to me, is that Mr. Livingston has instructions to buy New Orleans.'"

"Impossible!" McKeig thundered.

Alston shook his head. "Mr. Jefferson has not the authority."

"That hasn't seemed to stop him," Michael said drily. "For the rest, Burr says Jefferson is worried that there's been no progress after a year. He's sending James Monroe over to speed things up."

"Monroe!" Robert said.

"Yes. Do you know him?"

"I only met him once. But I don't think he's the man for this."

"All the more reason for us to do something," Michael said. He seemed to gather intensity. "First we must get this information to Washington City. Captain Daniels, can you sail on the morning tide with a letter for President Jefferson?"

"I can, sir."

"Good, then. But we can't trust to Jefferson alone. He's a sluggard."

Karl appeared shocked. "He is the President."

"Yes," Michael said, "and he hasn't changed since he was Governor of Virginia during the Revolution. He neglected his defenses then, and nearly let the entire state government, himself included, be captured by the British under Benedict Arnold. Three times he promised troops to aid us in South Carolina, but the one time they came, they came too late to do any good. No, Karl, he may be President, but he's still a sluggard." Michael turned toward his son. "You, Robert, must go to Paris."

"Me!"

"You," Michael repeated. "You're the only one of us who's met either Livingston or Monroe. That will be the extra ounce to make them believe."

"But what good will that do, father? The French won't sell if they've plans for New Orleans."

Michael nodded. "Still, perhaps we can light a fire under Livingston and Monroe. The only other thing we can do is try the bog the French down in Haiti. I suggest we divert our next few shipments of guns."

"What!" McKeig's face went purple. "Put guns in the hands of blacks!" He cut off abruptly, his angry gaze resting suspiciously on Robert and Daniels. "We shouldn't be talking this with them here."

Robert saw the stormclouds gathering on his father's face and spoke quickly. "Captain Daniels and I should be leaving in any case, if we're to sail in the morning. Oliver?"

Daniels nodded.

Michael escorted them to the door. "They really will feel easier with you not here, Robert," he said quietly.

"Can't say I blame them," Robert said. "I have to ready *Osprey* anyway. The sooner I get to France the better."

Michael gripped his hand hard. "Godspeed, then. Over and back home fast."

Robert found Louise dandling young James Christopher on her knee. His chubby hands clapped at the sight of his father. His little nose already had a hook to it. Louise's features hadn't softened that, Robert reflected. Childbirth had changed her, though. It wasn't just that she was fuller of breast. Something had been overlaid on the gamin to make her seem regal.

"There was a messenger," she said, smiling at the infant. "A steam *génie* has arrived for you. It is at your papa's warehouse."

"The steam engine? Damn!" he said. "It'll have to wait till I get back."

Her smile froze. "Get back?"

He cursed to himself. He had meant to bring it up in a roundabout way. "I have to go to France. I'll be perfectly safe, though. The fighting's over, remember. Perhaps I can see your *advocat,* Villemassant. I can check on your inheritance."

Her dark eyes searched his face worriedly. "You must leave soon?"

He nodded. "In the morning. Crane's with *Osprey.* The sooner I sail, the sooner I'm back."

"I do not trust that man, Robert. He is demented."

"I'll admit he's grown a bit crazy about religion, but he's a fine seaman. I'd not have kept him, or given him *Osprey*, if he wasn't. But he's had her for two voyages, now, and I've not heard a word against him from the crew."

"I do not care what his crew thinks of him. *Pardieu!* The way he holds that Bible to his chest, the way he looks at me, they frighten me. His eyes burn me." She held the baby close, as if to protect him.

"There's no need for you to worry about Crane. He's harmless. Look you, now. There's something that's been in my mind for a time." He knelt beside her and put an arm around her. "Louise, when I come back, will you marry me?" He felt her stiffen.

"No!" She didn't even look at him. "You do not have to marry me."

"I know I don't *have* to. I *want* to."

"You wish perhaps to give you son a legal right to his name?"

"Legal right be damned! If that was what I wanted, I'd have married you before he was born!" He realized he was shouting, but he couldn't seem to lower his voice. "He'll make his name, or nor, as I did! I want you! I love you, damn it!"

Her eyes were moist, but a mischievous smile played on her lips. "You have a very gentle way of telling me so."

"Perhaps I do," he growled. "But you haven't said yes or no."

"Yes, yes, yes, yes! Ten thousand times yes!" Tears were running down her face, and she was laughing at the same time.

"Do you think you might give the baby to his mauma? I *do* sail first thing in the morning."

"You think only of your appetites," she said, but she laughed as she said it. "Sally!" she called. "Come take James Christopher."

Osprey crossed the bar shortly after first light, her rigging humming as she ran before the wind. The pale green of coastal waters became the deep blue of open sea, the misty gray-green of land sank behind them, and Robert wandered forward.

The crew moved with a neat economy of motion. They were as good as any he'd ever sailed with, Robert thought. Not a bad one in the lot.

He found Miller on the forecastle deck, keeping a wary eye on the men aloft. "Still the mother hen, eh, Miller?"

The big, balding man knuckled his forehead. "They need it, captain. Too many new ones for my liking."

"I'm not the captain any longer. Mr. Crane's that. The captain has new men in the crew?"

Miller shifted the wad of tobacco in his cheek and looked as if he wanted to spit. "He don't much favor ungodly men. Those as are too ungodly finds it better to sign on some other ship."

"I see," Robert said thoughtfully. "Thompson? I haven't seen him."

"He were right ungodly, sir, what with his cussing and all." This time he did spit over the rail. "I'd better go, captain. Some folks hold talking too much ungodly, too." The big man scrambled into the rigging like an ape.

Robert looked back toward the quarterdeck. Crane stood watching him. Dressed in unrelieved black, his Bible clasped to his chest with one hand, he looked more the New England preacher than he did a sea captain. And Robert realized for the first time what Louise had meant about Crane's eyes. They looked accusing and fanatical. It had been a mistake giving him *Osprey*. It would be rectified once they were back in Charleston.

XIX

"Mr. Livingston is not at home," the liveried butler said, keeping a good grip on the door.

"He wasn't home yesterday, either," Robert's voice was flat.

"No, sir."

"And he wasn't here the day before."

"No, sir."

"Nor was he here the day before that, the day before that, or the day before that. I've been coming here for nearly two weeks, and he hasn't been here once."

"Ambassadors are often busy men, sir. If you will pardon me, I think I am being summoned." There hadn't been a sound, but Robert found himself staring at a closed door. With a muttered curse he left the large, square house with its encircling gardens.

Osprey had made a fast crossing, and he had hired the swiftest horse in St. Nazaire for his ride to Paris. Now, after twelve days in the city, he was no nearer his goal than he had been on the first.

Damn the butler! On the first of April a letter of introduction had gone in, "to await Mr. Livingston's return." A note of his own had been accepted on the fourth, to be brought to Livingston's attention "as soon as he is back." The man lied like a lawyer. Robert had twice seen a carriage he was certain contained Livingston. The second time he'd run after it, shouting, but it never slowed. His note of the eighth had brought no response, either. If he wasn't given entrance tomorrow, he would push in and—

He stepped dead in the street. A sedan chair had to swerve suddenly to avoid him. He paid no mind. Lie like a lawyer.

There was one man in Paris he might get in to see. André Villemassant, Louise's *advocat.*

Since the revolution in France had given way to the Consulate, the bureaucracy had become so well organized that it took him a mere hour to find the proper clerk. Money passed from one hand to another, for some things never change, and he was in possession of the addresses of Villemassant's home and office. The office was easy to find, but there was no one there, and it took until early evening to discover the house, tucked away on the pastoral outskirts of the city.

"Oui?" The man who opened the door was obviously no servant. He lounged in his shirtsleeves, stock undone and wineglass in hand.

"Monsieur Villemassant?" Robert said.

The man raised an eyebrow. *"Anglais?"*

"Non. Americain."

"Ah, Americain. I speak the English most well. Come you in. *Vite. Vite."* He clutched Robert by the arm and began drawing him down the hall.

"You are *Monsieur* Villemassant?" he asked.

"Mais non. I am not the good Villemassant. I have the honor to be Paul Honoré Courbet." He stopped long enough to bow shakily, and Robert realized he was drunk. *"Le bon* Villemassant is watching the—how you say?—the little plays, the . . . it does not matter. We are here." He pulled open a door and led Robert into a darkened room.

"Paul?" came a man's voice. *"Taisons! Elles commencent."*

"Asseyez-vous, Paul," someone else said. A chair was thrust into Robert's hands—by Courbet, he thought—and he sat without speaking.

After a moment a curtain at one end of the room opened, revealing a small stage, decorated as a bedchamber. In the light from the stage, Robert could barely make out that there were eight or ten other men in the room.

At that instant a beautiful young blonde woman appeared on the stage, attired as if for the street. She touched a bell pull, and a maid entered from the opposite side of the stage. The two women talked softly, of inconsequential things, as the maid began helping her mistress off with her outer garments.

But when gloves and hat and pelisse were gone, the skirt joined them. Robert sat up straight. Petticoats came off, and the chemise. The blonde wore only her high-heeled slippers and stockings, with red lace garters indenting her thighs. The wisp at their juncture was so pale as to be almost invisible. Her breasts, round and tipped with brown aureoles as large as a Spanish milled dollar, swayed gently as she paraded about the stage, displaying herself from every angle.

Robert looked around in amusement. The others sat absolutely still, their breathing heavier. God, he knew what to do with a naked woman, and it wasn't put her on a stage to stare at. He swallowed his laughter.

On the stage the maid turned to go, and her mistress caught her sleeve. As they murmured to each other his smile faded, and then his face went red. The maid's clothes began to join her mistress's. Robert picked a spot on a dark wall and stared at it rigidly as the two women moved toward the bed.

What in the name of hell had he found his way into? The sounds from the stage filtered into his head. The sighs and murmurs, the—he refused to think of it. He thought he had seen the worst a waterfront bar could offer, and that meant the worst there was, but he had never even imagined anything like this. As what was happening started to impinge on him again, he forced himself to concentrate on the steam engine waiting in his father's warehouse in Charleston. The boiler would be located amidships. He made himself imagine every detail of its installation. He visualized the two pistons the boiler would power, and now they would be constructed. The pistons would turn an eccentric shaft, and that would turn a pair of paddle wheels, one on either side of the ship. He had heard talk of something called a screw propeller, and claims that it was more efficient than paddles, but he knew little of it. He was planning the storage of wood for fuel when the lights came up.

Robert looked around. Courbet was up on the stage and had an arm around each of the naked actresses. Everyone else was staring at Robert.

"Excuse me, *Messieurs*," he said. "I came to see *Monsieur* Villemassant. I ask you to pardon my sudden appearance."

"You are English?" a sallow, long-faced man asked with a heavy accent. He was shorter than Robert, but heavier.

"American." The man seemed suddenly wary. "I explained to *Monsieur* Courbet when he let me in. If you please, which one of you is *Monsieur* Villemassant?"

The sallow man rubbed the side of his sharp nose, then nodded once. "It is I. But why does *un Americain* come to my house in the night? Who are you?"

"My name is Robert Fallon, of Charleston, South Carolina. I'm betrothed to Louise de Chardonnay. It is on the strength of that I come to you."

The *advocat*'s nose twitched, like a fox sniffing the wind, and he licked his lips repeatedly. "*Eh bien.* Let us go to my *cabinet,* my study." Loud and laughing conversation, centered around the women, sprang up behind them as they left.

Villemassant's study was a cramped room, its walls covered with shelves of books that showed little sign of being disturbed. It was ill lit, and seemed too orderly, as if the *advocat* were seldom there, and then only in full light.

"*L'eau-de-vie, monsieur?*" The Frenchman asked. "Brandy? Or perhaps you would prefer wine?"

"Brandy, thank you," Robert replied. The other did the offices.

"You have been long in this country, *monsieur?*"

"About two weeks."

"It is a beautiful time of the year." He paused politely.

"Yes," Robert said. "If you don't mind, *monsieur,* I'm anxious to get to the point."

"Why such haste, *monsieur?*"

"I've been trying to see Mr. Robert Livingston."

Villemassant stood for a moment with his mouth half open. "Your ambassador?" he said finally. "You wish to see your ambassador?"

"I do. I was hoping you could help me."

"But why me? Why do you come to see me?"

"Because I hope you can arrange an introduction for me to Mr. Livingston, or to someone who can introduce me to him."

"*Une introduction.*" Villemassant muttered to himself. "Very well, *Monsieur,* Fallon did you say? I will arrange you your introduction."

"To Livingston?" Robert asked eagerly.

"I do not know your *Monsieur* Livingston. I will give you

the introduction to Barbé-Marbois."

"Who?"

"The Minister of Finance." The *advocat* began writing hurriedly, with frequent dippings of his pen. "If there is anyone who can introduce you to an ambassador, it must be he. I will put his address on the outside. So."

Robert examined the missive before putting it in his pocket. It was as Villemassant had said. "I thank you, *monsieur*. And now, if you will excuse me."

"*Mais non,*" Villemassant said, suddenly expansive. "You must stay. There are more of the entertainments."

"I'm sorry, *monsieur*, but I must rise early tomorrow." He touched the introduction in his pocket. "*Adieu, monsieur.*"

"*Pardon,*" the *advocat* said as Robert reached the door. His face was wary once more. "You are indeed betrothed to *Mademoiselle* de Chardonnay?"

"I am," Robert said, and smiled at the sweat that popped out on the other's forehead. Whatever part of Louise's inheritance the man had stolen, there would be time to recover it later. And for now it had served a good purpose. "Again, *monsieur, adieu.*" And he left.

The enormous house of Barbé-Marbois was sheathed in granite and white marble and glinted in the early morning sun. The door was answered by a bewigged and liveried butler.

"Captain Robert Fallon to see Minister Barbé-Marbois. I have a letter from *Monsieur* Villemassant."

The butler opened the door wider, bowing him in without a word. Inside was a vast, marble-floored entry hall, where at least fifty men already sat or paced. At the far end of the hall, broad stairs swept up to the balcony that overlooked the hall. At their foot one man sat officiously behind a table, obviously a secretary. Robert presented his letter.

The man was bored. "You will be called when the Minister can see you."

The chairs were taken; Robert joined those pacing the hall. It was fifty-two paces across, he discovered. When he grew bored with that he paced the long way. It was eighty paces in that direction.

From time to time a man would appear at the head of the

stairs and intone a name.

"Monsieur Charles Henri LaFon."

"Capitaine d'infanterie Louis Masson."

"Monsieur Phillippe Marie Grouchy."

After an hour or two, Robert was able to seize a chair. Midday came and went, and evening came closer. His stomach began to grumble. He had been in such a hurry that breakfast had been a single roll, and he'd had nothing since then. He couldn't leave to eat, though, his name might be called. He'd see the cursed minister, and then a *paté* of goose liver, a carafe of wine—

"Capitaine Robert Fallon."

—roast duck, with white truffles and—

"Capitaine Robert Fallon."

With a start Robert leaped to his feet. "Here!" he shouted, then colored sheepishly. Summoning as much dignity as he could, he walked slowly up the stairs, and followed a lackey to a large room. There, behind a desk, a man sat facing the door.

He was tall, with a high forehead and a slender, finely chiseled face. He was frowning at Villemassant's letter of introduction as Robert came in.

"An American ship captain," he said. His English was almost without accent. "You will forgive me for wondering why an American ship captain would wish to see me."

"Actually, sir," Robert said, "I hope that you can introduce me to Mr. Robert Livingston, the American Ambassador."

Barbé-Marbois arched an eyebrow. "You wish me to introduce you to your own ambassador?"

"Yes, sir. I realize he must be busy, as you are, but my business is important. At least to me," he added with sudden caution. It wouldn't do to have the man asking what that business was.

"Sit down," Barbé-Marbois said. "I will explain to you why it is ironic that you should come to me for assistance. I, too, have important business with *Monsieur* Livingston. I have been trying for three days to sell to him, and to your country, *le Territoire du Louisiane.* I know he is hard of hearing, but he does not seem to wish to listen to me at all."

Robert was still on the edge of his chair. "Louisiana, sir?

You mean New Orleans? You wish to sell us New Orleans?''

"*Non*. I am ordered to sell—" He frowned suddenly. "Is your visit official? Is this in fact some form of overture from *Monsieur* Livingston?"

"I only wish it was, sir. But please go on. I would like nothing better than to see New Orleans American."

"And I, *monsieur*. I have an affection for your country. I served there during your revolution. But no matter. To begin at the beginning. This Sunday past, de Talleyrand-Périgord and I were summoned by the First Consul. He received us sitting in his bath," he lifted an eyebrow wryly, "and told us that we were to arrange the sale of the Territory of Louisiana as soon as possible."

"That's almost unbelievable," Robert said. "If you'll forgive me, sir, it's no secret in America that the next target of the French army in Haiti is New Orleans."

"Oh? It is a secret here, monsieur. The good Bonaparte likes to do what is unexpected, sometimes even by the good Bonaparte himself," Barbé-Marbois said drily. "But events march on, and if such was his intention, it is no longer."

"I must say it's a relief, sir. But—to sell Louisiana?"

"France needs money, for the wars begin again soon."

"You seem certain of that, sir."

The Minister shook his head sadly. "I only wish that I were not. Bonaparte has insulted Lord Whitworth, the English Ambassador, in public only one month ago, and the English cry loudly of it. They complain that we do not return Malta, as agreed, though it is no secret they wish to make of it a naval fortress, securing a stranglehold on the Mediterranean. They claim that the encampment of *l'Armée de la République* at Boulogne is intended for an invasion of England, and Bonaparte being Bonaparte, he will neither confirm nor deny. And all the while they build their navy stronger. Against whom else can it be aimed but France? No, the English fear Napoleon Bonaparte, as they fear that our revolution will spread to their own lower classes. They will not rest while he rules France."

Robert was taken aback by his intensity, but he made an effort to get back to the main subject. "Louisiana, sir—if you want to sell it, what is the problem?"

"Monsieur Livingston is the problem, *Capitaine* Fallon. My

efforts to meet with him have been thwarted time after time, while he speaks with de Talleyrand-Périgord. And that man, *capitaine,* bears no love at all for your country.''

''Sir, how determined are you to sell to the United States?''

''Very, *monsieur.* Very determined, indeed.''

''Then if I might suggest a plan. It's what I intended if all else failed. I am certain that Mr. Livingston is at home . . . . ''

It was pitch black when Robert and Barbé-Marbois entered the grounds of Livingston's house. Thick clouds covered the moon, and the only light from the house came from one room at the rear.

''This is madness,'' the Frenchman muttered, stumbling over a coping. He extricated himself from a bush with an oath. ''I am a Minister of France, not a *brigand à pied.*''

''If you can't arrange a meeting,'' Robert said, ''you must make one. Here's a path.''

He led the way along the path to the rear of the house, into the pool of light spilling from the rear of the house. He saw a face looking out of the window, surprise on its thin lips, and then it was gone.

''That was Livingston,'' the Minister said drily. ''If he does as before, he will no doubt leave the house to avoid me.''

Before Robert could answer, though, Livingston appeared in the garden. A man of medium height, thin but with the beginning of a paunch, he hurried to them. He had a manner of canting one side of his head toward whomever he faced. Robert remembered what Barbé-Marbois had said about his being hard of hearing.

''*Monsieur le Ministre,*'' Livingston said with a precise bow. ''I . . . am a trifle surprised to see you.''

''I was out walking. the Frenchman said smoothly, ''and I felt an intense desire to see your garden.''

''I don't recognize your companion, sir,'' Livingston said.

Robert made a slight bow. ''Captain Robert Fallon, sir, of the brig *Osprey.*''

''Fallon,'' Livingston said flatly. ''It is a name some associate with that of Aaron Burr. You choose a strange, ah, confidant, *monsieur.*''

''I would choose *le diable*, himself, if necessary,'' Barbé-

Marbois retorted. "Why have you avoided me, *Monsieur?*"

"De Talleyrand-Périgord—" Livingston began weakly, and stopped.

"Mr. Ambassador," Robert said, "I know you have orders to buy New Orleans—"

"How do you know that? No one is supposed to know!"

"—and I know all of Louisiana is available instead. You must speak to the Minister."

"Delicate, delicate," Livingston muttered. "*Monsier* de Talleyrand-Périgord feels it best if, ah, if all negotiations are carried out through him."

Barbé-Marbois barked a laugh. "The Minister of State does not wish you to acquire *Louisiane, Monsieur* Livingston, nor even New Orleans, alone."

Livingston eyed them quizzically. "That's the second time you've mentioned all of Louisiana. He *has* hinted at something like that."

"And he will continue to hint," the Minister said, "until it is too late for you to do anything."

"For the love of God," Robert said. "Do you mean you didn't even know it was all being offered? Move now, sir, and assure your place in history."

"I have no authority," Livingston said stiffly. "I am authorized to attempt the purchase of New Orleans. Nothing more."

"Perhaps a *douceur*," Barbé-Marbois murmured.

Robert waited for the explosion at the offer of a bribe, but Livingston leaned closer. "A *douceur?* Perhaps we should move out of the light. I'm dining with a newly arrived colleague, Mr. Monroe, and he might not understand the, ah, finer details of diplomacy. Now. The *douceur* . . . . "

The two moved away into the fragrant shadows; Robert hurried after them.

"Yes," Livingston was saying, "one per cent sounds eminently fair."

"It is done, then," Barbé-Marbois answered. "You will come to my offices in the morning, yes?"

"I will, *Monsieur le Ministre*." And he was gone.

The Minister of Finance looked wryly about the dark garden. "And I think we, too, should be going, *capitaine*. You may expect a packet from me on the morrow.''

"Yes, sir," Robert replied. It wasn't until they had parted in the street that it struck him. He had just seen the United States doubled in size, at midnight in a Parisian garden.

The packet came at dawn, containing the necessary clearances for *Osprey* to sail, and a license enjoining any French ship from interfering with her. A half-hour later Robert was in the saddle. That night he spent in St. Nazaire, rounding up his crew, and with the first light of the following morning, *Osprey* stood out to sea.

Land had barely begun to fade behind when a cry came from the masthead.

"Sail ho!"

Off the port bow a frigate was already in sight, her closeness testifying to the lookout's slackness. Crane, his Bible under one arm, held a spyglass up with the other.

"French," he said after a moment's study. "The lines are clear.'

Robert nodded. "Yes. Take us two points to starboard, Captain Crane, and we may outrun her."

"Outrun her?" Crane sounded surprised. "I would think now is the time to put those papers of yours to work."

"If need be. If need be. But I don't like being boarded, even by friends." He frowned at the closing warship. "And I don't like that ship appearing just as we lose sight of land."

"Come now," Crane said scoffingly. "'The wicked flee where no man pursueth.' If we run, they'll think we have cause. No, we'll not risk taking cannonshot, when we've papers to clear our way."

The man was captain, after all; grudgingly Robert agreed.

The two ships closed, until there was no need of spyglass to make out the frigate's French lines or the Tricolor fluttering at her stern. Of perhaps thirty guns, she was sleek, and looked near as fast as *Osprey*.

"Them in the rigging," Miller called suddenly from amidships. "Look at their breeches."

Robert picked out the men; they did look odd. Those baggy trousers surely weren't French. "Captain Crane," he began.

At that moment the frigate crossed *Osprey*'s bow. All her

gunports slammed open, and a cloud of smoke hid her as her broadside roared.

Osprey leaped and staggered in the water. Yards and rigging fell. Blood running down his face, Robert crawled to his feet; a falling block had struck him. Where the wheel had been, jagged stump jutted from the deck. Crane stood with his mouth open and his eyes wide, his Bible for once dropped unnoticed to the deck.

"Crane," Robert shouted against the ringing in his ears. "The guns, Crane." But Crane remained frozen.

Once more the frigate crossed *Osprey*'s bow, and once more the brig rocked from a hammer blow. Robert caught the rail to keep from falling again. With a mammoth crack the foremast pitched over the side.

"Captain, why don't we fight?" Miller cried.

Robert looked around him helplessly. "With what?" Amidships only two cannon still remained upright. The screams echoing across the deck, the still shapes and those writhing in widening pools of red, told the impossibility.

Miller looked at him in disbelief. "We surrender, sir?"

"We surrender." Robert looked to Crane, but the captain still stood, staring. Robert stalked to the sternrail and hauled down the American colors. His eyes closed as a cheer went up from the other vessel, and his fists knotted in the flag.

"They ain't French," Miller shouted.

Robert turned just as the frigate grated alongside. Over the rail, in baggy pantaloons and turbans, poured a wave of swarthy Barbary pirates. Numbly Robert let himself be bound and pulled aboard the frigate. He was thrown down against the quarterdeck ladder, and when he attempted to rise, a bayonet beween his shoulders kept him there.

"I never let a man best me and get away," someone said. He stared up past the pirate's boots to the frigate's captain. It was Murad Reis.

"Betrayed," Robert spat. "Which one of them took Fourrier gold? Livingston? Talleyrand? Barbé-Marbois? Which one, damn you?"

Murad threw back his head and laughed. "It wasna' Fourrier gold at all that nestled you in my hands, though we spread enough coin about between the two of us. But we didna' anticipate the rarified circles you'd frequent. No, it was a weasel of a French lawyer, looking for men to bash your head in.''

''Villemassant!''

''Aye. That's his name. The ruffians he tried to hire had already taken my gold, and they recognized the name. It wasna' hard for my agent to convince the man you'd disappear for good if he got me the time of your sailing. He broke his back getting to St. Nazaire ahead of you, and a fast launch did the rest.'' He laughed again. ''The fool was afraid you'd discover he'd looted some woman's inheritance.''

Then Murad's boot caught him in the mouth, and the next instant the pirate was kneeling beside him with a fistful of hair, forcing his head back. He could taste the blood filling his mouth.

''Fourrier wants you dead,'' Murad grated. His laughter was gone. ''He thinks the way to deal with you is a knife, or a bullet to the head. But, then, he's never spent time in Africa.'' His tone made Robert's skin crawl. ''I condemn you to the living death, Fallon. You'll sweat away the rest of your life under the lash, slaving to quarry stone for the mole in Tripoli harbor. Was the woman worth it, Fallon? Was she?'' He slammed Robert's head to the deck, then turned to snarl an order.

Immediately Robert was grabbed and hustled away to an open hatch. The last sight he had before they hauled him below was *Osprey*, lying on her side, the water beginning to wash over her masts. Then the hatch was slammed shut, and he was in darkness.

BOOK TWO

XX

Michael paused, as he had so many times, by the chalk board in the warehouse where ships were posted. Across the top of the board it said, OSPREY-ROBERT FALLON-ST. NAZAIRE. Nine months had passed since *Osprey* was due, seven since news had reached Charleston that Louisiana had been purchased, but he had refused to rub the posting off. When the chalk became worn, he ordered it freshened.

He shook his head sadly and went out into the street. Why did he refuse to admit that Robert was dead? Perhaps he was just losing his grip on things. He had let himself be talked out of sending guns to the blacks in Haiti, and out of whatever slender control of events that might have given him. And now, in early February of 1804, word had come that Desaline had ordered a massacre of all whites left on the island. Even at home he felt adrift. There was something wrong between Karl and Catherine, he was sure, and he hadn't been to see Louise in a month. The energy to act simply would not come.

"Mr. Fallon?"

He started; Jeremiah was in front of him, hat in hand. The lad had grown! He was an inch taller than Michael, a slender greyhound of a man.

"Good morning, Jeremiah. Are you keeping busy?"

"Yes, sir." He was twisting the hat against his leather apron, and his mouth was tight.

"What's the matter, lad? Are you in trouble?"

"No, sir. Yes, sir. I want to get married."

"Married! Well, why not, then? How old are you, lad?"

"Seventeen, sir."

"Then there's no reason at all not to. Go to it, man. You've my blessing, and a gift of money to help you get started. There's never enough money when you're just beginning."

Jeremiah's face twisted with rage. "It's not money," he choked out. "I got money. But Sarah belongs to Mr. McKeig, sir. He said he wouldn't sell her to no . . . no nigger. He said, go ahead and marry her, he'd give . . . oh, God, help me . . . he'd give the litter a good home."

Michael stared at him, dumbfounded. It was true enough that if a slave woman married a free man, their children were still slave. It was a law he'd tried to get changed more than once. He'd never have thought that McKeig would make use of it, and so cruelly.

"Come with me," he said, starting off down East Bay.

Jeremiah followed, stumbling a little. "Where we going, sir?"

"Henry McKeig. He'll damned well sell the girl to me. Her freedom will be my wedding gift to you."

"It shouldn't have to be this way," Jeremiah said.

"Things are the way they are," Michael replied. You have to get used to that." And he had to get used to it, too. Robert was dead. There was no changing it. All that was left, now, was to live the last years of his life as if he was just starting out.

He lengthened his stride, so that Jeremiah had to hurry to catch up, and moved purposefully down the Bay.

The heat was unbelievable for a February night, Catherine thought. She lay naked on her bed at Seven Pines. The ceiling fan, a drowsy slave pulling the cords in a closet beside the bedroom, stirred the air, but gave no coolness.

"Damn," she muttered. Shrugging into a batiste robe, she strolled down the dark hall to Charlotte's room. Clotilde, the child's mauma, opened her dark eyes as the door opened. Catherine ignored her.

Almost two, the child slept with a slight smile on her lips. She had Karl's blonde hair, though Catherine prayed every day for it to darken. There would be no more tow-headed children for him, though he tried hard enough. She had used every old wives' tale, folk remedy, and witch woman's cure to make sure. He would have no more children. If only Charlotte's hair would darken, it would be as if he had no part of her, either.

Restlessly she left the nursery, wandered downstairs and out onto the front veranda. She leaned against one of the columns, and found herself clutching it for support. There was more to her sleeplessness than the heat, and she knew it. The solace she found with her own hands was no longer enough. She wanted to hold a man in her arms while the fantasies of those lonely times came true. She wished that Karl were there, instead of at Riding Green.

No, she thought bitterly, there were no dreams to be realized in his arms. He was as clumsy a lover as he had ever been. And if he hadn't been, she still would not want pleasure at his hands.

A glimmer through the trees caught her eye. It seemed to come from the overseer's house. But what could he be doing awake? It was almost midnight.

She started down the drive, wincing as pebbles and cracked oyster shells bruised her feet. But her curiosity pulled her on. Anything to take her mind away from why she could not sleep.

She stopped at the edge of the pool of light spilling from the window. Martin Caine, stripped to the waist, had just finished washing. The muscles of his arms and shoulders were smooth and sleek, and his chest was covered with a mat of dark hair. His hands looked strong, and gentle. It was hands like those that could bring her fantasies true.

She realized she had stopped breathing. She had never thought of Caine as a man before. He was Karl's overseer, no more. A stubborn man, who took delight in thwarting her. Karl's. She would make him hers. She moved to the door.

At her third tap he opened the door. She slipped in past him.

"Mrs. Holtz!" he said in surprise. He looked at her oddly, and then at the door.

"I . . . want to talk to you, Mr. Caine. Martin. And call me Catherine." She stopped uneasily. It was easier to think of seducing a man than it was to do it.

"What is it, Mrs. Holtz?" He frowned. "Is there trouble?"

"Martin, I . . . . " She couldn't go on. Her fingers fumbled with the ties of her robe, and it drifted to the floor. Firelight gleamed on her skin, highlighting her slender thighs, the curve of hips and breast. Without realizing it, she struck a pose, shoulders back, head erect. Her face colored; there didn't seem to be anything else in the world except his eyes. But now, surely, he would know what to do.

Picking up her robe, he laid it gently around her shoulders. "You'll be getting cold on the way back to the house, ma'am."

Dumbfounded, she said, "Do you know what I'm offering you?"

"Mrs. Holtz, I reckon you should go back up to the main house."

"Damn you," she spat. "You're refusing me? What would you do if I cried rape, Mr. Caine?"

He jerked, and she thought she'd scored a hit, but the words that poured out of him were driven by rage. "Rape! You're the sort who *would* use that, aren't you? Fine lady on the outside, and gully trash inside. Well, shout it, and be damned. Shout it! How'd you like explaining what you're doing in my quarters in nothing but a flimsy bit of lawn? By God, if I'm going to have the name, I reckon I'll have the game." He took a step toward her, and she took three steps back, clutching her robe to her. "No. Get yourself out of here, Mrs. Holtz. Get yourself out before I throw you out."

For a moment she was too petrified to move. Then she edged around him as if he were a wild beast, and ran. He slammed the door behind her.

She had never suspected he was capable of such anger. Or such violence. He had been on the point of it, she was sure. If she hadn't left when he'd ordered her out, he would have hurt her in some way. Ordered out! Ordered out of a house her husband owned, by an overseer. How dare he? She'd go right back, order him off Seven Pines! She turned to see a carriage pull off the drive and halt in front of Caine's house.

Catherine moved deeper into the shadows. A woman got down, a small portmanteau in her hands, and started for the house. So that was why he refused her! "I didn't know whores' hours were so late," she called mockingly. The woman stepped into a patch of moonlight. It was Louise de Chardonnay.

"*Madame* Holtz?" Louise said. "I did not expect to find you about at this hour. "Or," she peered into the shadow, "dressed so."

"You're quite the little strumpet, aren't you?" Catherine

laughed softly. "You come prepared, complete with bag. Robert doesn't seem to have had very good luck with his . . . bits of fluff—isn't that what your sort is called? You can't be faithful to his memory, even when his banker's still paying your bills."

"Robert has been dead for a year," Louise said quietly. "I do not remember hearing that your husband was dead."

"Why, you little—"

"Mrs. Holtz," Caine said behind her, and she jumped. She hadn't even heard the door open. "Shouldn't you be up at the main house?" he said. His voice seemed to hold its usual calmness, but she watched him warily.

"Don't think you've heard the last of this," she spat. And she ran for the house.

From her bedroom window she watched until the light in Caine's house went out, and then she cried herself to sleep.

*   *   *

Michael pushed himself as if he were Robert's age. Or at least, not his own. He saw Jeremiah married to his Sarah by a Methodist minister, and uneasy truce in force between Catherine and Karl. He could get neither to admit that anything had been wrong, but at least they no longer seemed on the brink of disaster.

With the domestic situation seemingly in hand, he turned his mind to business. Since December, when the United States had taken control of New Orleans, there had been more problems for American traders than under the Spanish. There was twice as much paperwork, and where it had taken a week to get a permit, it now took four. He decided the answer lay in Washington City. Accordingly, he booked passage on one of his own coasters, the *Sprite,* and arrived in late June of 1804.

The city was still a scattered hamlet of mud streets and open country, although the second wing of the Congress House had been completed. Before noon Michael presented himself there, asking for Burr. He was directed to a farm house on the outskirts of the city.

When Michael was shown in, Burr sat in his shirtsleeves at the dining-room table, which was covered with papers. He took off his spectacles with a tired smile. "Mr. Fallon. It's been too long since we met, sir.'' He gestured at the papers. "You've not caught me at a good time, I fear. I must see that my affairs are in order, in case the devil and I have to see who really rules hell.''

"Are you ill?'' Michael asked.

"Tired, sir. That is all. But come. What brings you to this pesthole of a city?''

"I came to find out what's happening with New Orleans. It's harder now to get a pelt through the city than it was when the Spaniards ruled. But I'll not pile my problems on top of your own. If you could give me an introduction to someone who knows what's happening there . . . . ''

"William Claiborne has a fine situation in New Orleans, Mr. Fallon. He's making the most of it, too. Do you know the Bill of Rights has no force there? Nor even the Constitution. It's not properly part of the United States, you see. By God, it's a place made for Hamilton. Yes,'' he went on thoughtfully. "Hamilton.'' He put his spectacles back on and peered through them, then over the tops. With a sigh he tossed them on the table. "The eyes go so slowly we never realize it. I'd gladly give twenty years off my life if everything simply functioned to the end. But I'm forgetting my hospitality. Sit down, sir. Mrs. Beames can fetch you a drink. This is her house, and I and my manservant merely lodgers.''

"Nothing, thank you, sir.'' Michael said as he sank into a chair. "If you will excuse me, there *is* something troubling you. Let me earn my seat by offering what help I can.''

"It's beyond help, Mr. Fallon. Before the end of this day, I expect to be engaged to kill Alexander Hamilton.''

"Good God! A duel? But surely there's some way around it. You're both too highly connected for there not to be scandal, sir, even if no one's hurt.''

"For ten days now I've tried to find that way,'' Burr half shouted. There was a noise from the kitchen, and he moderated his tone. "At least, I was trying. No longer, though. Some things a man can ignore because the source is beneath notice. Or for advantage. But not this. No longer.''

"Mr. Burr, what has Hamilton done?''

Burr rubbed the heels of his hands into his deep-set eyes. "There were letters in the Albany *Register* from some country clergyman. He quoted Hamilton as saying I was despicable. Despicable, sir. A dangerous man who ought not to be trusted."

"You've challenged him on the strength of that?"

"I've challenged no one." Burr motioned to forestall Michael. "I asked for an explanation, a retraction. I was reasonable. But Hamilton has dithered and twaddled about. He's insulted me more than once since, and insulted Mr. Van Ness, who has carried my notes. If there was not cause for a challenge in the beginning, there is one now. But I still have not offered it."

"But you said—"

"—That I expect a challenge, Mr. Fallon. His notes have grown more abusive by the day. Today's can be no less than a challenge."

"Perhaps if *I* could speak to Mr. Hamilton?"

"You know him, sir?"

"We've never met," Michael admitted, "but this must be stopped. You're not two private gentlemen. You are the Vice-President of the United States, and a republican. He's the leader of the Federalist Party. We're not so old a country we can't be torn apart; this could pit Federalist against republican in a civil war."

Burr sat back, studying Michael. Finally he nodded. "Very well, Mr. Fallon. If you can arrange something suitable with Mr. Hamilton, I will accept it. My man will give you his direction."

"I'll go now, then," Michael said.

Butt's voice stopped him at the door. "A retraction, Mr. Fallon. I demand that, at least."

At Hamilton's boarding house, the landlady, a broad woman with a round, red face, informed him that Mr. Hamilton was in his suite. "But I don't think the gentleman will see you, sir," she added. "He gave word not half an hour ago that he wasn't to be disturbed."

"Please," Michael insisted. "Tell him it's urgent I see him."

"I'll try, sir," she said doubtfully, and disappeared up the stairs. In two minutes she was back. "He cannot see you, sir." She closed the door.

Michael hurried back to the farm. In the dining room, Burr was staring out the window. A tidy man, almost as short as he, stood by his elbow. Burr looked over his shoulder as Michael entered.

"He's asked for two weeks to get his affairs in order," he said simply.

"God help us," Michael breathed.

"God or the devil," Burr said with a sardonic grin. "We'll find out who looks out for whom at Weehawk, on the Jersey shore, at seven of the morning, the eleventh of July. But I haven't made any introductions. This is Mr. William Van Ness. Mr. Van Ness, Mr. Michael Fallon. Mr. Van Ness had consented to act for me. I should appreciate it if you would accompany us, Mr. Fallon."

Michael nodded numbly.

The day of July 11 dawned warm and clear, but Van Ness carried an umbrella. What he intended it for Michael could not say. The northern handling of duels was odd in any case. Only the day after arrangements were made they had left for New York, and Burr's estate of Richmond Hill, for the duel would be just over the border from the two men's home state. The site needs must be reached by boat, which had necessitated their setting out before Wednesday's first light had dawned. Such things were done in a more civilized fashion in South Carolina.

As the boatman turned in to shore, another craft rounded a point ahead and came toward them. Hamilton scrambled up the slope to them, followed by two men, one with a pistol case under his arm.

"The one with the case is Judge Pendleton," Burr murmured to Michael, "his second. The other is Dr. Hosack." He laughed suddenly. "I could wish the surgeon weren't Hamilton's brother-in-law."

Hamilton spoke to no one in particular. "Is this where the killing's to be done?" He startled Michael by jogging a few steps in place, as if to limber up.

"Killing?" Burr said. "Well, very well, if there's killing to be done, let us get on with it. Hell grows hotter for awaiting one of us."

With a sharp nod Hamilton started up a path through the bushes. Pendleton, Van Ness, and Michael followed with Burr. Hosack stayed behind.

"The surgeon's not coming to the field?" Michael said. "What if he's needed?"

"He didn't want to watch," Pendleton said apologetically, then, perhaps regretting speaking to a member of the other party, he hurried forward to join his principal.

The field of honor was a small, grassy clearing surrounded by cedar trees. Michael stood with Burr, a little apart from where the seconds were loading the pistols Hamilton disdained to watch.

"The Church pistols," Pendleton said.

"They've done this duty often enough," Van Ness replied. That was all either of them said.

With the pistols loaded, the field was arranged, Hamilton at one end, Burr at the other. Pendleton and Van Ness took their positions midway between and out of the line of fire. Michael stood behind them. Hamilton made another bouncing step. Burr turned up the lapels of his coat to give no white for a target.

"Gentlemen," Van Ness said, "Judge Pendleton and I have chosen lots. He will make the call. He will call, one, two, three. At one you will get ready. At two you may present. At three you may fire."

"And now, gentlemen," Pendleton said, "duty requires me to ask a question. Is there no way in which this may be avoided?"

"A retraction?" Burr called.

"I will see you in hell first," Hamilton shouted.

"Very well," Pendleton said. And immediately, with no pause between numbers, he began counting. "One two thr—"

Both pistols exploded. Burr held his rigidly level, a bead of sweat on his forehead. Hamilton's was only half lowered. He took a stumbling step forward and fell on his left side.

"It went off too soon," Burr said disbelievingly.

"You fired before I said three," Pendleton shouted.

Burr didn't seem to hear him. "I barely touched the trigger." He dropped the pistol and started for Hamilton.

Van Ness darted forward to grab him. "It is not proper,

sir," he hissed. "Judge Pendleton, your principal."

Pendleton, face slack, hurried to the still figure. Michael picked up Burr's fallen pistol. As he did, his finger struck the trigger, pushing it forward with a tiny click. "Oh, my God," he whispered. Almost hesitantly he cocked the hammer, then pulled the trigger. The hammer fell at the first touch. A set trigger that would be of use only to the man who knew of it. But these were not Burr's pistols. Supposedly, neither man had ever seen them before.

"Mr. Fallon," Burr said, "Mr. Van Ness suggests that we leave now. If you are ready, sir."

Michael nodded, and laid the pistol in its case. Hamilton made no sound except for a groan.

At the top of the downward slope they came on Dr. Hosack, making his way slowly up from the boats. Van Ness quickly opened his umbrella and held it in front of Burr, so that no one could swear to seeing him leave the field. Hosack caught a glimpse, though, and the effect was electric. His mouth fell open, his eyes goggled, and with a strangled shout he ran off toward the clearing. Burr and the others continued down to the boats.

"Mr. Van Ness," Michael said once they were out on the river, "I heard you call them the Church pistols. Who owns them, sir?"

"Why, John Barker Church, Dr. Hosack's brother-in-law. He is a duelist of some repute."

"And Hosack is Hamilton's brother-in-law," Michael growled. "Mr. Burr, it might be best if you come away for a time. In South Carolina you could visit your daughter, Theodosia. I understand she and my own daughter, Catherine, are acquainted."

"Go away?" Burr said. "Certainly not, Mr. Fallon. I will not run and hide. I will visit my friends. Commodore Truxton, I think, and perhaps Charles Biddle in Philadelphia."

"Mr. Burr, murder was intended back there. This will end worse than we can imagine."

"Nonsense," Burr replied wearily. "It's regrettable, sir, but it was just another duel."

XXI

There was no shade in the North African sun. When a quarry guard's harsh cry signaled the day's work was done, each chain of men dropped where they were, panting in their sweat and rock dust. In a short time, slaves from the kitchens would bring kettles of watery mush. Quarry slaves never left the quarry alive.

Robert lay with his eyes closed, breathing deeply. His skin had darkened except where his breechclout covered him and where he had been whipped; the scars on his back refused to turn. His beard was grown wild and tangled.

"Must be time for Race Week, captain," Miller said. Chained beside Robert, he was little changed by the quarry, save for the dirt. Beyond him were Kemal, a huge Turk with no tongue, and Barak, a wizened Arab. At the end of the chain huddled Crane. "It's February," Miller went on, "unless I miss my reckoning."

"You don't," Robert said. "February, 1805." He sat up straight and looked around the quarry, his prison for almost two years. A thousand men huddled on the floor, surrounded on all sides by fifty-foot cliffs. At one end of the pit was a packed earth ramp. There the guards came in and the stone went out.

"They sinned the sins of Kings," Crane said suddenly, "and they were brought low with the punishment of Kings." None of them paid any attention. Crane hadn't spoken a sensible word for months.

"Two years, captain?" Miller shook his bald head. "And a lifetime of hell to come."

It had been two years of despair. Perhaps the low point had been a year gone, when the city erupted with celebration. The news had filtered down to the wretches in the quarry that the American frigate *Philadelphia* had run aground in the harbor, had surrendered without firing a shot, without even being called on to surrender. Even the burning of the ship a few weeks later in a daring American raid had buoyed no one. But now despair was almost at an end.

"Are you ready to think about escape, then?"

"Suffer thy punishments gladly," Crane chattered. "Take joy in the bite of whips and the sting of scorpions."

Miller shook his head. "Escape, captain? We can't cut these chains, and we ain't going nowhere linked together like six sausages."

"We can't cut them," Robert said, "but we can break them. Tonight. This is what we'll do . . . ."

"The sinners must burn for their sins," Crane chanted. "Draw their flesh with pincers, pluck out their eyes with hooks."

The night was black as pitch. Heavy clouds hid the moon, and thunder rumbled on the horizon. Robert led his chain to the quarry wall, where he had hidden the broken pieces of n iron prybar.

Without a word Robert set to. The two pieces were forced through the chain between Miller and him. They each grasped an end of one length, while Kemal took the other in his huge hands. Arms the size of a normal man's leg knotted and twisted. They twisted the other way, and with a loud snap the chain broke.

For a moment they froze. "I never believed it'd work," Miller breathed. Thunder rolled again, closer.

Robert quickly ripped a strip from his breechclout to tie the end of chain to his leg iron. "Help Kemal with the next section."

One by one the sections were broken, and each man seemed to breathe differently once it was done. Crane alone did not help break himself free. He stared at Kemal and Miller as though at lunatics. When the chain snapped, he started and stumbled backwards. "No!" He screamed.

"For the love of . . . be quiet, Crane!" Robert hissed.

"Sinners!" Crane shrieked. Miller dove for him, a

lumbering bear. Crane faded into the darkness.

Warily they looked at each other. They couldn't leave him, Robert thought. Wandering loose and babbling, he'd have the guards on them before they'd gone a mile. Lightning flashed overhead, illuminating Crane on top of a boulder, an accusing finger leveled at them.

"Don't you understand?" he said, and his voice was the epitome of reason. "We have all committed sins of the flesh. Sins of the spirit. We have gambled and fornicated, consorted with loose women. You, captain, have kept a whore, and given her your bastard."

"Come down, Crane," Robert said. He peered into the dark, but Crane was no longer visible. "We . . . we must go back to Charleston, to speak against the sinning there."

"We cannot leave, captain. This is the punishment given us on earth. It is God's mercy! We must open ourselves to our punishment, gash ourselves with rocks, and—" His voice cut off abruptly.

Robert hurried toward the boulder. The massive shape of Kemal bent over something on the ground.

"Not to be angry," Barak said in his thin voice. "Must be done if we are to escape."

Another lightning flash lit the quarry. Crane lay on his back, his head twisted unnaturally.

"God grant him peace," Robert said softly, straightening up. "All right. If his shouting didn't give us away, this lightning may. Are you ready, Barak?"

"Death is always close," the shriveled Arab said cryptically, but he moved swiftly to the quarry wall. Clinging to cracks with fingers and toes, he disappeared upward.

"What about Mr. Crane?" Miller whispered.

"What about him? You want to chip a grave in the rock?" He took a deep breath. "If you want to pray over him, Miller, go ahead." A rope clattered down the rock face, and he felt the first lessening of tension. He'd feared there might be a guard on the stores. Or that Barak would not come back. "No more time. Up you go."

One by one they climbed the quarry wall. The wind blew harder, and a swirling rain began to fall. When Robert reached the top he was soaked, and he was laughing. His slavery was being washed away.

Like wraiths, they stole to the stores hut, one dirt-floored stone room with no door.

"Remember," Robert whispered. "Waterskins, bags, knives. Don't waste time."

A lightning flash lit the room. A crust of bread and a cheese rind lay in the dirt. Robert could barely restrain himself. The other three dove for it.

"Back off," he hissed. "Back off there, damn it."

Hesitantly, sheepishly, the three got to their feet. Miller handed the crust and the rind to Robert. He trembled when he held them.

"Ain't much, captain," Miller said.

"A bite apiece, Miller." He passed it around, and closed his eyes to savor his share. It was exquisite.

They put themselves to searching for what they needed. There were plenty of sacks, for food if and when they found it, but no knives, no clothes, and only one waterskin.

Barak began to pull at things already searched. "Must be more."

"Perhaps there are," Robert replied, "but we've no time to look further. The hook is waiting."

There were no guards between the quarry and the desert, for no one was expected to try an overland escape. Robert and the others stopped at a fountain on the edge of the city and filled the skin.

"The harbor," Barak said wistfully. "Is so close."

"No good," Robert replied. "That's what they expect. We'd never get past the harbor watch."

"Might be worth the try, captain," Miller mused. "We could be sitting on an American ship, swilling grog, before tomorrow night."

" Think, man. The last we heard of an American ship was the bombardments. How long ago was that?"

"Maybe five months," Miller said reluctantly.

"Aye. Five months. The whole damned war could be over for all we know. We're going down the coast, and that's that." He shouldered the waterskin and started away from the city. One by one the others followed.

In Charleston, Race Week was over; nonstop gaiety had

given way to full-time work. Which to Charlestonians, Caine thought drily, meant no more than two balls a week, and formal horseracing only on weekends. But there was work done, he had to admit. The new planting of rice and cotton were getting under way. The tail ends of last year's crop were being sold off. It was that brought him to the city, seeing the last of the green-seed from Riding Green swayed aboard a ship at Carver's Bridge. The black-seed, the long-staple cotton from Seven Pines, had gone as soon as it was baled.

After he and the factor's agent agreed as the weight and number of bales, he left with a jaunty step. He had time yet to take Louise and young James for a carriage ride up the Neck.

Outside the warehouse a young man stood leaning against the wall. Caine slowed at the sight of him. His leather leggings, his fringed hunting shirt, and the long rifle he cradled with seeming carelessness, all brought memories of Tennessee. The young man straightened and swept off a broad-brimmed hat with a coontail pinned to it.

"I be looking for Martin Caine," the Westerner said. "By your walk, I'd say you were him."

"Who is it asking?" Caine asked.

"Crockett's the name. David, rightly, though most folks call me Davey. Now, do you be Martin Caine, or don't you?"

"I'm Caine," Martin said. He'd heard of the family, though he didn't know it, and they had nothing to do with the Applegates. "You got business to do with me?"

"Just to talk a spell. I had me a hankering to see one of these eastern cities, and somebody allowed as how if I came this way maybe a fellow named Martin Caine might like to hear about the Martin family back in Tennessee."

Caine nodded, and his eyes burned with sudden emotion. It had been a long time. "I reckon I'd like that, Davey. My friends call me Martin. Step over the way with me. We'll have us a drop of something smooth."

Crockett rubbed his chin with a laugh. "My pa don't hold with me touching strong spirits, but I don't reckon he'd hold with me refusing a man's hospitality, neither."

"Done, then," Caine laughed in reply.

He quickly led the way to the tavern just down East Bay Street, and they took a corner table where their talk would be undisturbed. When the brandies came, Crockett eyed his, then took a long pull.

"Now that is smoother than corn squeezings any day," he breathed.

"A mite," Caine said. "You said you had bad news of the Martins."

"That I do. Mr. and Mrs. Martin are fine. She had a spell with the chilblains about two years ago, and he broke his arm last year when he fell out the loft in the barn, but they're both all right, now. He bought him a couple blacks to work the crop with him, and—"

"Pa, I mean, he bought slaves?"

"That's right. When the Applegate place was sold off."

"The Applegate place was sold?"

"Are you going to let me tell you this, or aren't you?"

"I'm sorry. Go ahead."

"Like I said, he bought these two blacks. He's getting a good enough crop, but it's hard shakes competing with the big plantations. Anyhow, Sary Martin married Lemuel Johnson about three years ago, now."

"I remember him," Martin said, but subsided at Crockett's glare.

"They had them a young one, a boy they named Thomas. About a year ago Lem bought a whole quarter section up to Ohio, and they moved up that way. Then there's the Applegate thing. Some folks said Tom Martin killed Ben Applegate and a couple others before he went off. Some folks said that, anyway."

"Said?"

"A few folks have been asking some questions about that whole thing. Right after her husband was killed, Mrs. Applegate sold off the plantation, lock, stock and barrel, then disappeared. Some folks say she run off to meet Tom Martin. Some folks say they planned killing her husband together."

"It seems some folks do a heap of talking," Martin said heatedly.

"Don't it?" Crockett grinned. "Andy by-God Jackson ain't some folks, though. He got a grand jury to sit on the Applegate killing just as soon as Mrs. Applegate took off. Then he asked them a lot of questions, like where was anybody who saw Tom Martin kill anybody? And where was anybody who'd seen Tom Martin do anything except walk into the Applegate house, then walk back out again just as cool as anything? By the time he got done, they said there wasn't no evidence against Tom Martin at all, and they surely couldn't bring no indictment against him. Matter of fact," he finished solemnly, "if Tom Martin was to want to go back to Tennessee, there wouldn't be nothing in his way at all."

"That's always supposing he was wanting to go back," Martin said.

"You don't reckon to?"

He shook his head. "A heap of things change in five years. A man finds out he wanted something he didn't even know about."

"What do I tell your ma and pa?"

"Tell them I'm alive. Tell them I'm healthy and happy. Tell them I'll try to come visit, but I won't be coming to stay."

"I guess a man's got to make his choices."

"I guess so," he said, getting to his feet. "You drink what you want, Davey. I've got an account here. But I've got to see somebody important."

"Girl?" Crockett said with a smile. He looked absurdly young.

"Lady," Caine corrected, and with a nod he left.

Louise herself answered the door when he reached the house on Queen Street. He stood looking at her silently.

"What is it, Martin? Why are you staring so?"

"I've got to tell you something, Louise, and I can figure no easy way."

"*Eh Bien*. Come into the drawing room. You can tell me as we sit." Once she had him ensconced, and was herself seated with her hands folded on her knee, she said, "Now what is it that you must tell me?"

"My name isn't Martin Caine," he began, and went forward from there. Always he kept a careful eye on her face, trying to judge her reaction, but she sat as though carved from alabaster. ". . . So I left him and came here," he finished, and waited for her to speak.

"Your poor sister," she murmured. "I am glad that she found *un bon mari*. But why have you told me all of this?"

"It's behind me, now. Don't you see? I can look for a real

future, now. These past two years I've come to love you, and before that, too, I expect. Well, hang it all, what I'm trying to say is, will you marry me?''

"*Oui*," she said simply. "I will marry you."

XXII

Robert Fallon rolled down the sand hill and lay without moving. He could hear the sea nearby, and the cries of seabirds. He knew he would have to go back, but for the moment he couldn't find the strength. How long had they been on the move, he wondered. A month? More. It had to be. They had kept to the shore, going wide around villages, eating sea birds and their eggs, digging pits among the dunes and drinking the brackish seep. Once they had found a turtle, dead, and fought off the gulls and crabs that had claimed it. Thirst cracked their lips and blackened their tongues. The sun cracked their skins. One morning, he did not know how long ago, dawn had found Barak staring lifeless at the sky. They had pushed sand over him and gone on, wondering which would be the last man left. Who would go unburied, even by a scraping of sand? Two days ago the seep hole had remained empty. And yesterday. One more and they'd be reduced to trying seawater, though he knew it would rot their brains.

A shadow fell on his face. He struggled to rise. He would not be taken again. The man above him moved, and he found himself staring into a sunburned face above a dark blue uniform tunic.

"Hey, sergeant!" the man called. "This one's got blue eyes."

"Button up that tunic," a rough voice called. "You're a Marine, not a damned sailor. And put on your hat before you fry away the little brains you've got." Another shadow fell across Robert, but he couldn't see the second man. "Well, I'll be damned. You did find something. All right, then. Hoist him up and get him back to the castle."

Robert struggled weakly. "Others," he croaked. "Get . . . others."

"Some of you get up that dune and bring back any men on the other side," the rough voice shouted, and a knot of men, some in tunics like the first, scrambled up.

Robert waited until he saw them coming back, four men to carry Kemal, two for Miller, before let himself be helped up. They sounded American, he thought, but who in God's name were they?

"Lieutenant Presley Neville O'Bannion," the tall officer said, "of Virginia and the United States Marines. And this," he indicated a stocky, graying man with a pink face, "is William Eaton. He holds a commission as captain in the United States Army."

Robert sat in a cool room in the ruined fortress of Massouah, and poured some more water. He couldn't seem to get enough.

Eaton thrust his chin toward O'Bannion, and his pale blue eyes seemed to blaze. "General, lieutenant. I'm General of the Army that's going to put Prince Hamet on the throne. Or are your Irish brains too limited to comprehend that?"

O'Bannion gripped the hilt of his scimitar-like sword tighter. He looked as if he had endured this tirade often.

"Prince Hamet?" Robert asked. "What throne are you going to put him on?"

"Tripoli," Eaton snapped, and Robert almost dropped his cup.

"Tripoli! You'll need more than I've seen so far to take it. Or perhaps you have more troops, that I haven't seen."

"We are a mixed bag, indeed, Mr. Fallon." O'Bannion said. "I've a sergeant and six privates. Then there's Lieutenant Constantine and his thirty-eight Greek mercenaries. And a score or so of mongrel cannoneers, with one brass piece among them."

"I don't think you should be saying so much," Eaton said stiffly.

O'Bannion shrugged. "What harm can it do?" When Eaton didn't answer, he went on. "Oh, yes, we are a jumbled lot. There's Eugene Leitensderfer, of uncertain nationality. Calls himself a colonel. Claims to have been a Capuchin monk in Messina. And you know, I believe him. Then there's Selim

Comb, our Turkish gentleman, and the English brothers
Farquhar, Reginald and Richard, and Vincenti, and Roco, and
—you should have the picture by now."

"Always complaining, Lt. O'Bannion," Eaton said.
"There's never enough, is there, Lt. O'Bannion?"

"I'm a United States Marine," O'Bannion said calmly,
"and that means if I'm ordered to take Tripoli with six men
and a sergeant, I will damned well take Tripoli with six men
and a sergeant."

"Take an Irishman," Eagon snorted, "and make him a
Marine, and—"

"By God, *General* Eaton," O'Bannion exploded. "I swore
to obey orders, and obey them I will. Sneer if you want. But
we must make do with what we have. We were supposed to
have three hundred Marines. *And* a full field battery. It was
the penny-pinching bureaucrats brought us to this. And it was
you, sir, who dealt with those bureaucrats, who let them chip
and slash till there was nothing left of the original plan."

"And if I hadn't," Eaton shouted back, "there'd have been
no attempt at all. Do you think any of them think we can
succeed? Do you think any of them care?"

Robert stepped into the breach. "Gentlemen, if you don't
mind, my friends and I would like to rest here a day or two
before leaving for Alexandria. I can pay for whatever supplies
you can spare with a promissory note on the firm of Fallon &
Son, of Charleston, South Carolina."

Both men looked suddenly embarrassed.

"What's wrong?" Robert asked. "The note—"

"It isn't the note, Mr. Fallon," Eaton said. "It's that we
can't spare so much as a water skin. We may be on no rations
at all before we reach Bomba. We'll be met there by a supply
ship."

"Perhaps you could help me arrange with the Bedouins
here—"

"There won't be a one left once we march," O'Bannion
said.

Robert looked from one to the other. "Then what do you
suggest?"

Eaton shrugged, and O'Bannion hesitated. At last the
Marine spoke. "I'm afraid you've no choice but to join us,

Mr. Fallon. You must be ready to give a blow back to the Tripolitans.''

"Perhaps," Robert answered slowly.

"Yourself and the others," Eaton said. "We've neither food nor water nor horses to spare. There's no choice for any of you."

"I'll have to speak to them."

Miller and Kemal were housed in a room overlooking what had once been a garden. The two were wolfing dried meat when he stepped in.

"Captain!" Miller cried, "where you been? Taste this. Best goat I ever ate."

Kemal continued to eat, his eyes following Robert's every move.

"It's lush compared to what we've had the last two years," Robert agreed, "but it's hardly what you'd expect for an Army."

Miller looked at Robert doubtfully. "I don't understand, captain."

"They don't have any supplies to spare. Not so much as a waterskin, I was told. We can go back to what we've been doing the past month, or . . . . ''

"Or?"

"Or we can join this lot. They intend to take Tripoli and put some Prince named Hamet on the throne."

Miller laughed. "This lot, captain? Take Tripoli?"

"Nonetheless," Robert said, "that's our choice."

"Starving's better than going back to Tripoli," Miller insisted.

Kemal suddenly touched himself on the chest, then gestured to Robert and nodded. "I expect he's saying he'll go where you go, captain," Miller said. Kemal nodded again.

"All right, Miller. I'll try to get you a waterskin or two, despite what Mr. Eaton says, and some of that goat."

Miller shook his head. "If the Turk's going with you, captain, then I will, too. I wouldn't get very far by myself."

"I'll tell Eaton, then." He hoped it was the right decision.

Michael examined himself in the mirror on the wall of his bedchamber. Most men would be wearing trousers, he knew, instead of breeches, although a wedding was a formal event. He would give the occasion its due, though. He could do no less for Louise and Martin Caine.

It should have been Robert and Louise. He grimaced at the thought and shook his head. Time didn't stand still for anyone. And there would be other days for Robert; there had to be. He almost believed it. In soft gray silk, snowy lawn, and pitch-black superfine he went down to his carriage.

At Louise's house he was admitted by Simon, and found his way to the garden in back. More than fifty people crowded among the flowers. The rector of St. Michael's entertained a small coterie in one corner. Karl and Catherine were standing under the boughs of a spreading oak.

"Mr. Fallon," Karl said, smiling and bowing stiffly. "I am glad to see you."

"Many people have not arrived," Catherine said too sweetly.

"There were no more than half a dozen regrets," Karl said. "Even if some do not think it proper . . . . " He coughed and cleared his throat. "I thought that your presence, and mine, would . . . . would . . . . "

Michael shook his head; Karl trailed off. "We're in trade," Michael said drily.

"But you are a rice planter, at Tir Alainn. And I a planter of cotton!"

"You own a mill, and you gin and card other men's cotton for money. I own ships and warehouses. It didn't used to be so. I had nothing when I came to this country, but when hard work and luck brought me up in the world, men of the finest families in South Carolina were ready to shake my hand. Rutledge. Pinckney. Middleton. Izard. Of course, they were most of them in trade then, too."

"But they aren't now, father," Catherine said. Her tone was so sugary again that Michael looked at her sharply. Her eyes were drawn, and her mouth was tight. Karl had taken on a look of discomfort when she opened her mouth. Michael wondered suddenly if all was indeed well between them. "They got rid of their warehouses and ships," she went on, "and they never thought to do another man's milling. Now they've forgotten they ever did it, and so has everyone else."

"I haven't forgotten it, daughter, and neither have they. It's the Johnny new-comes, the men who've become planters since the Revolution, who talk this nonsense. They'd do better in England. You'll find the true men of worth in the state here in this garden, men who value a man for the sort of man he is, not whether he's a planter or not."

Catherine sniffed. "You always date everything that way. Before the Revolution, during the Revolution, or since the Revolution. Father, no one cares about the Revolution anymore, except on the Fourth of July!" She colored suddenly. "I overheard two young men at a dance. They . . . dismissed me as a tradesman's daughter who'd married another."

"You never told me," Karl sounded outraged.

Michael's eyes and voice were cold. "Tell me who they were, and there'll be two fewer loose tongues in South Carolina."

Catherine suddenly threw her arms around him and laid her head against his chest. It was a thing she hadn't done since she was sixteen. "No, papa," she said against his coat. "I won't let you get hurt."

"Child, I'm the best shot in the Carolinas, and there's no man in the country I wouldn't face with a sword."

"You're sixty-four, papa," she said softly. "You're too old to fight duels."

"Old!" he shouted. People turned to look, and he lowered his voice. "Girl—"

The portable organ, its bellows pumped by two small black boys, burst into music. Martin Caine took his place beside the minister, and Karl walked forward to stand beside him. Michael hurried inside. Louise's maids of honor clustered about her, checking for the hundredth time that all was ready.

"I was beginning to think I'd have to make the walk alone," Louise laughed.

"Don't be silly," Michael said. He tucked her arm in his, and patted her hand absently. "Do I seem *old* to you, child?"

She glanced at him, smiling. "Of course not. If I were not marrying T—Martin, I would set my cap for you."

He smiled, and escorted her out at the proper point in the music, but he heard little of the ceremony. He'd asked the question before, when he was tired or pressed, but never seriously, never meaning it. He meant it now. Was he old? In years, perhaps, God knew. But he didn't feel old. Absently he handed Louise over, and stepped back. He could think as quickly and as clearly, shoot as straight, navigate as sharply as any man. If he couldn't run twenty miles and be ready to fight at the end of it, well, it had been more than twenty years since he had needed to. Vaguely he heard the minister speak: "Those whom God hath joined together"; vaguely he saw Martin kiss Louise. He shook himself. Other things counted besides years, and in those he was still young. As food and wine were brought from the house, the guests clustered around the bride and groom. Michael found a place alone with his thoughts near the garden wall. It was there, after a while, that Caine found him.

"Mr. Fallon," the overseer drawled, "I want to thank you again. For Louise and the boy. She wouldn't rightly like leaving him."

"What? Oh. Yes. James Christopher." Michael looked toward the upper bedroom, where the boy's mauma was readying him for the morning's journey. Resolutely he pushed the thought of Robert aside. "He needs a father to raise him, not a grandfather. And I never did believe in taking children away from their mothers."

"Still," Caine insisted, "I thank you. Aren't many men would give up the chance to have a grandson around while they grow old."

"I'm not old," Michael said sharply.

Caine seemed take back. "No, sir. I didn't rightly mean you were."

"No matter," Michael muttered. "I'm just on edge today. But the boy, Caine—I want your oath on him. You'll raise him as your own, never throwing it up to him that he's another man's son."

"I promised that already," Caine said. "I'll treat him same as any other son of mine. One thing I haven't said, Mr. Fallon. He'll be raised as James Christopher Fallon. I figure he ought to keep his rightful name."

"I thank you for that, Mr. Caine." Michael's eyes burned. He put a hand to them, then quickly jerked it down again; what was this womanish weakness? "And if you ever need help out there in Louisiana, send word to Esteban Lopes in New Orleans. I've written him to help Martin Caine as if he was helping me.''

Caine opened his mouth, then simply nodded. He took Michael's arm and led him toward the house. "Mr. Holtz—Karl—gave me some brandy. Something called cognac. I was hoping you and Karl would take a drink with me to a new beginning in Louisiana.''

"I will that," Michael said. "This land Louise inherited—you intend to grow sugar cane there?'' He listened with only half an ear to Caine's reply. Louisiana. Half the continent away, it was. The Fallon name he'd hoped to make large in South Carolina was done there. Catherine had the blood, but not the name. That would go with young James Christopher to the wilds of Louisiana. "Carry it proud, lad," he whispered to his small grandson upstairs. "You're the last.''

XXIII

On the morning after leaving Massouah, O'Bannion poked his head into the tent where Robert slept with Miller and Kemal.

"Have you any money?" the Marine said without preamble.

Robert lifted himself on one elbow and brushed the night's sand from his hair. "What are you talking about?" he asked irritably.

Miller spoke from his blanket. "Money, Mr. O'Bannion? Even our clothes are borrowed."

O'Bannion seemed embarrassed. And well he might, Robert thought. In between an Arab headdress and a pair of cavalry boots gotten from a Greek mercenary, Robert himself was wearing O'Bannion's second-best uniform tunic and trousers. His pistols came from Eaton and his sword from a Bedouin.

"Sorry," the lieutenant mumbled, and ducked out of the tent.

Robert hurried out after him. The sun was no more than half above the horizon. Some of the night's coolness still clung to the air, though to the east moisture shinnered as it baked away.

"A moment, Lieutenant O'Bannion," Robert called. "Why this need for money?"

"There's nothing to worry about, Mr. Fallon. We have the situation well in hand."

"O'Bannion," Eaton shouted. He galloped his horse up, hardly seeming to notice Robert. "El Tayel and Mahamet have agreed to make the camel drivers go on. I gave them six hundred seventy-three dollars and fifty cents." He seemed to take bitter satisfaction in naming the exact sum. "And I'll tell you, I don't think there's so much as a clipped Greek drachma left among us."

"The camel drivers?" Robert said.

"Oh, hello, Fallon," Eaton said. "There's no trouble now. It's all been sorted out."

"But there was trouble. What was it?"

"Oh, bloody hell," O'Bannion broke in. "It's no great secret. Fallon, the camel drivers announced this morning they wouldn't go on until they'd been paid. Or rather, until the sheiks were given their money."

"You had to take up a collection?" Robert said incredulously.

"They agreed to be paid at Bomba," Eaton snapped.

"We're to be met there," O'Bannion explained. "Captain Isaac Hull in the *Argus*, with supplies and money."

"We've no time for talking," Eaton said, scowling. "I want to be on the march before the first real heat of the day. Let's get cracking."

Thirty minutes later the column was winding its way toward the west. In the lead, as always, was O'Bannion with his seven Marines, with Eaton riding as if they were his honor guard. The Greek mercenaries, tough men, as swarthy and unkempt as the Bedouins, marched behind, and to their rear came the cannoneers, their single brass field piece broken down for transport on a mule. Behind them were the volunteers, including Robert.

Then came the Arabs, streaming behind. Like vultures, Miller spat, waiting to pick their bones.

By the third day they were eating little more than rice, wild fennel, and sorrel gathered at water holes. Eaton insisted that the Arabs were stealing food and giving it to the Bedouins, who seemed to find them in the middle of nowhere, spend a night, then disappear. Prince Hamet took sick and kept to his cot. The Europeans and the Arabs took to camping apart.

On the sixteenth morning after leaving Massouah, Robert was jerked out of sleep by a trumpet. Immediately he rolled out of his blankets and buckled on his curved Bedouin scimitar.

"What's the matter, captain?" Miller asked. Kemal took one look at Robert and began to arm himself.

"Trouble," Robert said succinctly, and dashed out of the tent as the trumpet sounded again. Miller and Kemal followed at his heels.

O'Bannion and his Marines were drawn up in a line, bayonets fixed and muskets at port arms, flanked to the left by the Greeks. Lieutenant Constantine stood to their front, occasionally preening his fierce mustache. Facing them were the Bedouins, most mounted and all armed. Midway between, Eaton was gesticulating at the two shieks. The rest of the volunteers, Leitensderfer, Selim Comb and the others, were forming to O'Bannion's right. Robert ran to join them.

"What in hell, captain?" Miller asked. Somewhere he had found an ancient musket; he began to load it.

Leitensderfer, a mild-looking, middle-aged man with an incipient paunch, smiled. While the others were unshaven, he had kept his gray-streaked beard trimmed to a near point. "You had better ask the good Lieutenant O'Bannion." His English was cultured and without accent.

Robert went to O'Bannion, at the end of his line of Marines. "Another mutiny, O'Bannion? Don't they know there's no more money to be had till we get to Bomba?"

The lieutenant stared at Robert, then over at the volunteers' formation. Robert stood waiting. Finally, O'Bannion shook his head. "It's not a mutiny."

"It by damn looks like one. You and Mr. Eaton had best look sharp, or we'll wake one morning to find they've all run off."

"This isn't the sea, Mr. Fallon," O'Bannion said wryly. "At this minute they're trying to decide on one of two courses. Either they ride off and leave us—taking all the horses and supplies, or course—or they kill us and then take all the horses and supplies."

O'Bannion's sunburned face seemed in earnest. Robert glanced at the Arabs. The sheiks were riding back to the Bedouins; Eaton rode toward O'Bannion.

"It'll be a hell of a fight," Robert said. "Where are the cannoneers? They're a scruffy lot, but anything would be a help."

"They're behind a dune to the left of us and forward, assembling their fieldplace." He sighed. "If they're doing what they've been told. Wish I could be sure for once."

Eaton reined in by O'Bannion and thrust his chin at Robert. "What the hell are you doing here, Fallon? Your place is with the volunteers."

"Mr. Eaton," O'Bannion broke in, "what are their grievances?"

"Cowardice," Eaton snapped, then took a deep breath. "They say that Yusuf Karamanli has taken hostages from any family that might support Hamet, and that we'll find ourselves with no aid from the countryside. They also claim Hassen Bey is marching against us with an army."

O'Bannion whistled between his teeth. "They say Hassen Bey is the best general Tripoli has."

"It's all the fault of those damn Bedouins sneaking in at night," Eaton growled. "Steal food and spread rumors, that's what they do."

There was a sudden stir in the Arab ranks. "Gentlemen," Robert said warningly. Perhaps a hundred horsemen broke away from the main body of Bedouins and disappeared to the south.

"What in hell!" Eaton roared. Slashing his quirt at his horse, he galloped back to the sheiks, shouting in Arabic as he rode.

"Where *is* Hamet?" Robert muttered. "He could stop this with a half-dozen words."

O'Bannion shook his head. "This lot want pay and loot. Hamet's Tripolitan, and they couldn't care less what he wants."

"Who is he? Hamet, I mean."

"You don't know? He's Yusuf Karamanli's brother. Hamet Karamanli."

The sun was now above the horizon, and Robert had to shade his eyes to watch the sheiks and Eaton. The glare would be in their eyes, he thought, when the Arabs attacked. Aloud, he said, "I've no love for any Karamanli. Still, I've not objection to pulling Yusuf down, either, no matter who we put in his place. If we *do* reach Tripoli, though, the man I want is Murad Reis."

"You aim high," O'Bannion said, eyeing him oddly. "The United States has first claim. Yusuf and Murad are both to be turned over to us."

"I'll believe it when I see it."

"You have my word that it's in the agreement with Hamet."

"That I believe," Robert laughed. "But the United States

government will find some way to bollox things up. The President, the Congress, and the whole damned population of Washington City put together don't have the brains to run a pig sty, much less a country. With a few exceptions," he added, remembering Burr and the Madisons.

"The Sedition Act," O'Bannion said coldly, "prohibits such speaking. Your words are treason, Mr. Fallon."

"But they're true, none the less."

O'Bannion was prevented from replying by Eaton's return. He sawed his horse around in a tight circle, staring angrily down the line from the Greek mercenaries to the volunteers. "We'll be moving out immediately," he said abruptly.

"The ones who left," O'Bannion said, "where are they going?"

"Siwa oasis. To gather dates. El Tayel says they'll rejoin at Bomba." He pulled his horse around in another circle. "Myself, I doubt if we'll ever see them again. Prepare your men to march. Leitensderfer! Ready the volunteers." He rode off shouting for the cannoneers to assemble.

"We'll need those men," O'Bannion said worriedly. "At Derna as well as Tripoli."

On they marched toward the Bomba. The rice dwindled, and on the thirteenth of April the first camel was killed. The Arabs, who ate most of it, demanded that its price be repaid at Bomba. One morning soon after, forty of them turned back. Hamet, a thin, bookish-looking man wasted by his sickness, managed to talk them into returning. The rest of the army wondered why; they would not be able to depend on the Arabs.

As the food gave out, so did the water dwindle. Water holes were dry, or could not be found. The sun burned men to the bone, dried them to the marrow. Arab and Christian alike had glazed eyes and cracked lips, faltering as they walked or clung to a saddle.

On the eighteenth of April, twenty-six days out of Massouah, a Bedouin topped a rise ahead, then whirled, swaying in his saddle. "Bomba!" he yelled.

Robert lashed his staggering horse into a semblance of a run. There was food ahead. And water. He kicked his mount over the dunes and around the headland. There were the sun-baked, deserted mud houses of Bomba, and there was the sea. The sea was empty.

The Marines, sun-blackened scarecrows all, pounded to where he sat his horse and stopped in disbelief.

O'Bannion swayed in the saddle as he peered at the empty sea. "Where's Hull?" His voice began to rise angrily. "Where's *Argus*? Hull said he'd be here! *You* said he'd be here!" he shouted at Eaton.

"He swore," Eaton mumbled. He stared numbly at the bare sea. "He swore."

Suddenly from down the beach came a wordless howl. The Arabs were waving muskets and scimitars overhead, shouting at each other and at the Christians. Some pointed to the sea; others rode a pace or two toward the men around Robert, shaking their weapons fiercely.

"To the high ground," Eaton shouted. "Lieutenant Constantine, have your bugler blow assembly. To the high ground, damn it! For your lives."

Desperately they ran for the hill overlooking the village and formed a ragged circle. The cannoneers assembled their brass three-pounder.

And then they waited.

Through the rest of the afternoon and evening the Arabs watched, and the Christians stood to their guns. At nightfall Eaton ordered a beacon fire; the flames lit the circle of men throughout the night. The Arabs' campfires twinkled among the village houses.

Robert found himself between Miller and Eugene Leitensderfer, Kemal close behind him.

"Kemal keeps an eye on you," the Austrian said with a nod toward the big man. "He watches your back like a faithful hound."

Robert didn't take his eyes from the Bedouin encampment. "Kemal escaped with me from Tripoli. I suppose I'm the only face he knows here, except for Miller."

"He don't watch *my* back, captain," Miller said. He, too, kept his eyes on the campfires below.

"I see," Leitensderfer said. "You helped him escape from slavery. He owes his freedom to you. In his eyes, his freedom belongs to you. Literally. And his life. They are terrible enemies, the Turks, but faithful servants.''

"I'm more interested in the Bedouins down there," Robert said irritably. "If a few hundred of them come sneaking up the hill in the dark, they'll be on us before we know it."

The Austrian yawned and stretched. "Oh, they will not attack for two or three days. It will take them that long to be certain the ship is not coming and then argue over who will command the attack."

"You seem to know an awful lot about these Muslims," Miller said.

"I should. I was one. I even made the pilgrimage to Mecca."

"I thought you were a monk," Robert said drily. "What was it? A Capuchin?"

"I have been many things, Mr. Fallon. I am many things. A dervish. An engineer in four armies. A monk and a pilgrim. Other things in other places, at other times."

"Sounds like too much for one man," Robert laughed.

"But I am more than one man. I am Leitensderfer, and Gervasio, and Santuari, and Hassando, and a dozen others. I have seen mountains so high a man turns blue and dies before he reaches the top, and seas so salt a fish cannot live. I have seen golden idols worshiped by thousands, birds that cannot fly, and giant islands of ice floating in the ocean. I have fought for kings and peasant villagers, against maharajahs and slavers."

"I've heard of them ice islands myself," Miller said. "From whalers. They're down around the Horn, and the Cape of Good Hope."

"I've heard of them, too," Robert said. "Tell me, Leitensderfer, while you were fighting the slavers, did you ever hear the name Fourrier?"

"Which one?" Leitensderfer asked. "Justin? Or his son, Gerard?"

Robert felt as if he'd been hit in the stomach. The question had been idle. "Gerard?" he said finally. "Gerard is in the trade, too?"

"He was. But then his father bought him a commission in the British Army. He has made quite a name since the war with

France resumed.''

"So that's started up again? Barbé-Marbois told me it would." He shook his head. It seemed as if he were speaking of another world. "So much has happened that I don't know about.''

Leitensderfer watched him closely. "You are interested in the Fourriers?''

Robert stared back. The Austrian said he had fought slavers, but . . . . He made up his mind. "Justin Fourrier has tried at least twenty times to hire me dead, and twice that many for my father. He hates my family, and we feel no love for him. In fact, I intend to see him dead. Or, at the least, pulled down.''

"I do not know a great deal of the Fourrier," Leitensderfer said slowly, "but I will tell you what I know. I do not like slavers.''

"Look," Miller interrupted, pointing out to sea. The sun limned an arc of brightness on the horizon. A moving line of light glided across the sea from the east.

"I've seen the dawn," Robert said. "About their slave dealings, Colonel Leitensderfer. What—''

"Not the dawn, captain." Miller was beginning to laugh. "Out there. To sea. Look out there. It's the ship. By God, we're saved!''

By mid-morning the *Argus*'s boats were ferrying supplies ashore. Rice, peas, flour, bread. There was even a hogshead of brandy and two of wine.

Robert found Eaton hurrying through the village, his arms wrapped around a large satchel. "Mr. Eaton, I want to talk with you. Just how far is it to this Derna? These supplies won't take us far.''

"No time now, Mr. Fallon," Eaton said. "I have seven thousand Spanish milled dollars here. I can pay those damned sheiks what they're owed." He scurried on toward the Arab tents.

"I can tell you," O'Bannion said behind Robert, as he whirled. The Marine sat in a small patch of shade beside a hut, sharpening his Mameluke sword.

"How far is it, then?" Robert sat down next to the Marine.
O'Bannion sketched a curving coastline in the sand with his

sword and added two circles. "We had to get this final resupply close to Derna. We must be fresh when we reach there, for we'll have to fight for sure." He rested the sword point on one circle. "We'll rest here in Bomba. One day or ten, whatever it takes to recover. Then, one day's march, and—" he drove the sword into the second circle—"Derna."

XXIV

Where Bomba had been mud, Derna was stone, built around a central fortress-palace, with a battery of guns on a narrow spit to the northeast. Running north and south to the east of the city was a wide, shallow gulley. The Wadi Derna, Leitensderfer called it. Beyond it was a stone breastwork, spouting cannon mouths and swarming with men. West and south of the city the plain stretched level and barren to the low hills that ringed the city, with only low barricades, sparsely manned and without artillery.

Before the column had been in sight of the city, Eaton had sent in a long-winded, flowery demand for surrender. The reply had been simple: "Your head or mine. Mustifa."

Robert rode forward to look at the city they had to take, Miller, Kemal, and Leitensderfer with him. Atop a hill to the south of the city he pulled his Bedouin headdress lower against the noonday sun and studied the city through a glass. The *Argus* floated offshore; inside the barricaded city the Arabs swarmed.

"They expected us to continue down the coast," Leitensderfer said, "instead of curving inland. Mustifa is a fool."

"Even a fool can cost us," Robert said quietly. He lowered his glass to study the Austrian. Every day for the past five days they had talked of Fourrier. The man certainly knew enough of Justin's operations, and Gerard's. Robert had tested him with questions whose answers he knew, and Leitensderfer's information had always been correct.

And yet, for all the knowledge he was given, he had little to use against Justin. Fourrier had bribed unnamed Congressmen to prevent the reopening of the foreign slave trade in the

United States, for he could make greater profits from the illegal trade. Fourrier had lost a great deal of money when the United States bought Louisiana; he had taken large loans from the Clintons and Livingstons of New York. Robert remembered seeing DeWitt Clinton with a Fourrier hireling in Washington City; now he wondered at the real cause of Robert Livingston's reluctance to buy Louisiana.

Fourrier had in his pay a high official of the United States government in St. Louis—Wilkinson, Leitensderfer thought his name was. And Fourrier had obtained British Army supply contracts by paying a general named Ross, and an admiral named Montfort and at least one Cabinet Minister were partners with him in the slave trade. Robert shuffled the pieces once again; there was no pattern he could use or even prove.

"Captain," Miller said. The bulky seaman pointed to the low headland to the east. Two more brigs were creeping round it, gunports open. They dropped anchor within a hundred yards of the city. The furious activity of the Arabs in Derna redoubled.

"The *Nautilus*," Leitsensderfer said, collapsing his glass, "and the *Hornet*. We may have a chance."

From behind the hill came the jingle of harness and the grunting of camels. Eaton and O'Bannion galloped up, reining in beside Robert and the others.

Eaton surveyed the city below. "Good," he said. "There's no use wasting time, now the ships are in place."

"Where did they come from?" Robert asked.

O'Bannion answered. "From the squadron blockading Tripoli. They showed up a few hours ago. I went out with Mr. Eaton to see if I could get a few more Marines, or even a naval landing party. I was lucky to get off without being dragooned for a sharpshooter."

"If you're finished, Lieutenant O'Bannion," Eaton growled, "I want to deploy the army." Leitensderfer snorted, but Eaton affected not to notice. "The Arabs, under Prince Hamet, will attack from the west. They can use their horses best on the flat there. You will take the Christian contingents and attack from the east."

O'Bannion took one look at the stone gun emplacement and the wadi, and shook his head. "We have to take that breastwork, all right. If we get into the town they can shell us to flinders from it, and the Navy can't bring its guns to bear. But we'll need the Arabs and their horses to outflank the position while we pin them to the front with our infantry.''

"Very good,'' Leitensderfer murmured.

Eaton's face had reddened as the Marine spoke. "Perhaps you weren't listening. Or perhaps you've forgotten who is general of this army. I've given my orders, Lieutenant O'Bannion. Now I want to see some of that Marine obedience you're always prating of. I've given orders for the ships to commence firing at two sharp.''

"Yes, sir,'' O'Bannion spat. Eaton jerked a nod and galloped back toward the column.

"He must be mad,'' Robert said. "We can't afford casualties this close to Tripoli.''

"He is not mad,'' Leitensderfer said. "He is a politician.''

O'Bannion nodded. "He is that,'' he said angrily. "He's afraid if the Arabs get chopped up too badly here, they'll desert before we reach Tripoli.''

Slowly the miniscule army arranged itself according to Eaton's commands. Prince Hamet, still sick and swaying in his saddle, led the Bedouins to the plain west of the city. The Arabs at the breastworks raised a howl at the sight of the banner-dotted mass sweeping to the south. The Bedouins screamed back, waving their muskets in the air and loosing useless shots. Eaton watched from the hill.

O'Bannion formed his men out of sight of the city, then marched them around the hill to confront the stone gun emplacement. His seven Marines formed the center of the line, with the Greeks under Constantine to the left and the volunteers to the right. The motley cannoneers straggled behind, dragging their brass three-pounder. Robert, marching with the volunteers, checked his pistol primings again. Kemal followed, carrying a huge two-handed sword acquired from the Bedouins.

Precisely at two in the afternoon smoke blossomed down the sides of the Navy brigs, and they opened fire on the gun battery on the spit of land.

O'Bannion drew his curved Mameluke sword. "Formation will advance at my command.'' The blade went up, sliced down. "Forward!''

As Robert took his first step, an erratic booming began. The Arabs returning the Navy's fire, he realized. The stones in the wall ahead were massive, but it wasn't high. A man could climb it from another man's hands, or even leap and catch an edge. But screaming Arabs lined the top of the wall; it would be as hard as any boarding at sea.

He drew his sword, and ran an eye down the line. The Marines advanced as if on parade, backs erect and bayonet-tipped muskets slanted precisely. Lieutenant Constantine waved his sword overhead, exhorting his men with shouts. The mercenaries' advance was ragged, but no less purposeful than the Marines'. Now Leitensderfer unslung a carbine, his coat shifting to reveal half-a-dozen pistols stuck in his belt.

The stone breastworks grew closer. Eight hundred yards. Seven hundred. A cannon on the emplacement roared and belched smoke, then another. The balls whistled low overhead to lift gouts of earth behind the advancing men. Six hundred yards. Five hundred yards. More guns began to fire, individually rather than on one command. The gunners corrected desperately for the last fall, but always the shot fell behind the advance. Four hundred yards. Three hundred. Two hundred. Suddenly hundreds of smaller smoke clouds appeared along the parapet. Musket balls began to chew the sand around them.

A marine abruptly grunted and fell, the front of his coat stained red. A greek mercenary went down, and another. Then a second Marine, and Captain Vincente of the volunteers fell. Robert cursed. Men halted in the teeth of that leaden gale. The Marines were at a standstill; a handful of the Greeks began to retreat.

Without warning Eaton was before them, sawing his horse about, waving his sword violently. "Charge, damn you!" he shouted. "Attack, you God-rotted cowards!" And still shouting he spurred toward the wall.

"Come back here you bastard!" O'Bannion screamed after him. "This is my attack!" With a final shout of, "Marines, follow me!" he set out after Eaton at a dead run. The five Marines followed, and Robert pounded after. From the corner of his eye he saw Constantine, his howling mercenaries close behind. Leitensderfer was beside him, he realized, and Miller, and all the rest. Even the cannoneers were sweeping along.

And then they were at the wall. Someone offered cupped hands, and Robert let himself be vaulted up. Sword in hand, he readied himself to face the Arabs. And found there was no one there, except the others of the charge. The defenders were streaming back toward the city. They had broken before the charge reached their emplacement.

"The cannon!" O'Bannion howled. He wrestled with one of the Arab's carriage guns, and his Marines ran to lend a hand. "They're still loaded," he shouted. "Come on, damn it!"

Robert ran to a cannon with Kemal and Miller. Throwing their shoulders to the gun, they horsed it around towards the fleeing Arabs. Robert bent to lay it. Miller handed him a slow match, and he set it to the touch hole. With a roar the gun leaped back. They hadn't set the gun tackle. The carriage slammed into the outer wall of the redount and overturned.

All down the parapet the act was repeated. Cannon after cannon, left loaded by the Arabs, fired after them and toppled over.

"After them!" O'Bannion yelled. "Don't let them regroup!"

Robert leaped to the sand, and in a wave the rest rolled after him, over the wadi to the barricades on the edge of the city.

A musket fired at Robert at point-blank range. In another step he was close enough to grab the hot barrel with his free hand. The rat-faced Arab clung to his gun; Robert pulled him half over the pile of rubble and spitted him on his sword. Then Robert was atop the barricade, kicking one Arab in the face, sabering another. Leaping down on the inside, he saw that, once more, the enemy had broken. Musket fire began to pepper them from the rooftops and windows. He dashed for cover towards the first buildings of the city itself.

Miller, crouching near him, peered around a corner. Kemal had taken shelter in a doorway, his long sword was bloody for half its length. Leitensderfer hunkered down on his heels, back to a wall, as if he intended to wait there forever. O'Bannion searched for a way to go forward.

Robert could hear nothing but musket fire—the enemy's and their own. "What happened to the Navy?" he called to O'Bannion. "And Hamet's attack?"

"The Navy did what they were supposed to," O'Bannion answered tersely. He didn't look back. "The battery on the spit was silenced before we reached the city."

"Yes," Leitensderfer said. "And the gunners made it safely back to the city. More for us to face."

"I suppose Hamet was beated back," Robert said. "There's not a sound from that side of the city."

"Who knows what's happening there," O'Bannion said. "It's us we have to worry about. Come on, before we're shot to pieces where we stand." He darted around the corner and up the street.

The day became one long confusion, a fight that never ended. From street to street they fought, from building to building, from room to room. Robert fought his way through two score houses, across two dozen streets with musket fire chipping the stone around his feet. Time and again he tried to dig a hole to hide in while the ground around him was torn by a leaden rain.

Then he was in a building with marble walls and silken hangings, creeping down a wide corridor with mosaics in the floor, sword extended before him, cocked pistol in his left hand. His belt held four more pistols. He wasn't sure where he had gotten them.

A turbaned Arab, bayoneted musket gripped like a spear, lunged out of a side corridor with a scream. The scream became a shriek as Miller, trailing behind Robert, spitted the man on his bayonet.

For an instant they froze, Robert in the lead, Miller standing over the dead Arab, and Kemal bringing up the rear with his sword. There was no sound but the echo of the scream. Robert started forward again.

His mind wandered. How long had it been since they had entered this city? This building? His sense of time was gone. It couldn't be long, he thought. An hour, perhaps. Maybe a bit more.

He came to a door and pushed it open carelessly with his sword. An axe swung down and severed the blade just in front of his hand.

The man who loomed in the door was taller than Robert by a head, and half again as heavy. He was lifting the axe for

another stroke. Robert fired from the hip and threw himself
forward.

Together they went to the floor, but the giant threw him
over, scrambling to regain his axe. Robert slid toward the far
wall, helpless on the smooth marble. The axe was raised once
more when Kemal hurtled into the room. His great two-
handed sword fell, and the giant's head rolled on the floor.

Then seven more Arabs rushed through a draped doorway,
before the first's head had stopped rolling. Robert pulled a
pistol, cocking it as he leveled. There was a dry snap. He threw
the thing at the nearest Arab and rolled desperately away. He
was below a rack of swords, gleaming with silver and ivory.
Flinging himself upward, he seized the bottom sword, and
unsheathed it just as the first Arab fell upon him. He beat
aside the man's blade, ran him through, slashed at another.
Kemal's huge blade rose and fell, and then Miller was in the
room with his bayonet. The Arabs, caught from both sides,
fell like grain.

Robert drew breath. Kemal had blood running down his
face, and Miller's sleeve was torn and bloodied.

"I'd have been in quicker, captain," Miller panted with a
nod toward the Turk, "but he pushed me out of the way to get
to that fellow with the axe."

"It's all right," Robert said. "All right. We best keep
moving."

"We've won," O'Bannion said from the door, as Robert
whirled to face him. "Constantine and Rocco found Mustifa
hiding in his harem. The city's ours. We're about to put the
flag up. Come along if you like."

On the tower above the palace the light was strange; the sun
was sinking in the west. Robert's hour and a bit had actually
been closer to five. He felt his weariness creeping on him.

A Marine approached the flagpole with a folded American
flag. "We'll take it back down before sunset," O'Bannion
said, "but the flag will fly over Derna today." The Marine
undid the line.

"Hold on there," Eaton called from the stair. He led three
Bedouins and two of Hamet's retinue out onto the platform.
"This isn't an American conquest, O'Bannon. This victory
has been won for Prince Hamet, and his banner will fly over
Derna."

"Be damned to Hamet and his banner," O'Bannion said.

The Arab's faces turned ugly.

"Easy, man!" Eaton said quickly. "Some English they can understand. Their flag goes up, and there's an end to it."

O'Bannion stared, turned, and growled, "Stand away, private." The Arab from Hamet's retinue took the Marine's place, and the Prince's green-bordered banner rose.

"It's the way it has to be," Eaton said to no one in particular. "It's the way it has to be." He followed the Arabs from the parapet.

The men remaining stared up at the Muslim flag. "Have you heard what happened?" O'Bannion asked without lowering his gaze.

"No," Robert said.

"They were supposed to attack when we did. Hamet and the sheiks, I mean. They had the easiest part of it, and they were supposed to attack when we did." He fell silent.

"Didn't they?" Robert prodded.

"They did not. After we were in the city, after most of the western barricades had been abandoned, that's when they charged. They didn't join in the house-to-house, either. They set up court down where the defenders had run away."

"Court!" Miller gasped.

O'Bannion didn't seem to notice. "While the rest of us were taking the city one square foot at a time, the three of them tried a few townsmen for not acknowledging Hamet's authority quickly enough. Cut their heads off in a courtyard for not forcing Mustifa to surrender when he was called on."

Everyone's eyes went to the flag.

"We could take it down easily enough," Robert suggested. "Put up the one that should be there."

O'Bannion hesitated. "No. No, we still need the bastards. Hassen Bey is still out there, somewhere, and, God help us, we need this miserable lot. It's late, gentlemen. I suggest we get some sleep."

The Marine left, and slowly the others followed, leaving the Moslem flag flying over a city won by Christian blood.

XXV

In Charleston the heavy rain came to an end, but it had already made the April night as cool as February. Jeremiah, sitting at the back of the church, was relieved. At least he wouldn't get wet walking home. The meeting was almost over. He wasn't certain if the white minister had said anything yet that was worthwhile. But he was a southerner, and that was a thing in itself. There seemed to be more southern abolitionists, of late.

The minister raised his arms to the hundred blacks who sat before him. Despite the coolness of the night air sweat ran down his long, pale face. "Brothers," he said in a soft Virginia drawl. "My brothers and sisters, I know that you suffer. I know that you know pain. but your pain and your suffering are stored up in heaven."

"White men never say much when they talk, do they?"

Jeremiah looked up at the stocky black man who had slipped into the pew next to him. It was Peter Poyas, a ship's carpenter, a friend from Vesey's shop.

"What you doing here?" Poyas asked. "I never heard of you going to meeting before."

"I wanted to hear him. His society has been trying to get laws passed for black people. Ease the curfews. Make manumission easier. Maybe . . . ."

"Maybe . . . freedom?" Poyas sneered.

Jeremiah looked at him sharply. "I've never heard of you going to meeting, either."

"Sarah told me where to find you. The constables going to be here any minute. The sheriff, he raiding this meeting."

Jeremiah nodded. "Let's go," he said.

The air outside had been freshened by the rain.

"That Sarah," Poyas said suddenly, "she a good wife. And that Leonie is one fine baby girl."

"What are they calling it this time, Peter? Disturbing the peace again?"

Poyas laughed harshly. "Can't expect them white folks to take kindly to men talking abolition. Especially no white man."

"And that's good enough for you? You don't mind being chivied out of church like a pig out of a pen, as long as it only happens once in a while?"

"If you can't make the way things is," Poyas answered sharply, "you takes what you get like a man." He took a deep breath, and his next words were softer. "Hell, you know what I believes. It was you read me that first bit."

"I know, Peter," Jeremiah said wearily. "Sometimes I feel so tired."

"Then you get on home to your wife. And that sound like good advice for me, too." He snorted. "Old Master James, he expect his nigger to be at the shipyard bright and early. You get on home, Jeremiah. I see you tomorrow."

Poyas didn't understand, Jeremiah thought as the other man turned down an alley. It wasn't physical tiredness. He was weary of nothing ever changing.

As he started across King Street, a galloping horseman rounded the corner almost on top of him. The horse reared and whinnied, the rider struggled for control.

"Damn it!" the rider bawled. "Watch where the hell you're going!"

Jeremiah started on down the street. A northerner, by the accent. A Yorker, probably. He wanted no truck with any whites that night.

"Wait!" the rider called. "Do you know where Michael Fallon's house is? Speak sharp, damn you! I can't fathom this mush-mouth you southern niggers talk. Well, do you know where it is?"

Jeremiah deliberately broadened his speech. "Yassuh. I know."

"Well, where is it? You're not simple-minded, are you?"

"No, sir. It six blocks down that way," Jeremiah said, pointing. "You turns left at a big white house, and goes seven more blocks. Mr. Fallon, he in a big brick house on the corner.''

"See? Not so hard, was it?" The rider tossed a coin that hit Jeremiah in the chest, and spurred off in the direction he had pointed.

After a moment Jeremiah picked up the coin, insults or no. With a wife and baby, every penny was needed. As he walked on his way, though, he laughed out loud. That white man was going to play hell finding Michael Fallon's house by those directions. Mush-mouth, indeed.

Michael had fallen asleep in front of the fireplace again, a half-drunk brandy on the table, his clay pipe gone out on his chest. Someone was shouting downstairs; that must have wakened him. He went to see what was happening.

In the entry hall below, Caesar, gray-haired and stooped, was staring at a noisy young man in muddy riding clothes. "Damn you, can't you understand English? Do any of you niggers have brains? I want to see Michael Fallon. Michael Fallon! Can you get that through your thick head?"

"Whoever you are," Michael said coldly from the stairs, "I expect decent treatment of my servants."

The young man started. "I am Thomas Stuyvesant, Mr. Fallon, of New York." He paused. Michael showed no reaction. "The New York Stuyvesants."

"You rode all the way from New York to tell me that?"

Stuyvesant stiffened. "I have a letter for you." He produced a packet from under his coat. "From Vice-President Burr. I am to return with your reply."

Michael eyed the man's mud-streaked clothes; the packet looked fresh. "What happened to you? Caught in the rain earlier?"

"That damned nigger!" Stuyvesant said. "I followed his directions to get here, and rode right into the damned marsh for my trouble. He had your house somewhere out in the river."

"You probably didn't hear him right." Michael opened the letter and began to read.

Dear Mr. Fallon,

I have written before to tell you how much I enjoyed our conversations during my week in South Carolina last year, but I do so again. And again I will admit that you were correct in your evaluation of the Hamilton affair. Still I find myself condemned wherever I turn. Ardent republicans now remember Hamilton as the best of men. The indictments for murder—murder, in the name of God!—still are in force in New Jersey and New York. Livingston and Clinton are missing no chance. Almost I could think to retire to South Carolina, to Hagley and the Oaks, watching young Aaron Burr Alston grow up. I cannot do that.

There are stirrings in the wind. If I have, as some claim, sold my soul to the devil, then the adage is proven. The devil gives his own no rest. As I am condemned and censured in public, others seek me by the back door. The idle conversation of Gallatin has become less idle. I have had letters from General Wilkinson, hinting at things I dare not put down here. And Merry, the English Ambassador, has himself approached me on the same matter, though I do not trust him. If aught goes badly, he will forget me, or remember what is convenient. No matter. I am embarked on a tour of the West, my old friend. I must see with my own eyes if what I have been told is true. I remember your opposition to the Dons. You must join me. I need to have at hand a man I trust, and you may find your interests engaged. I have attached an intinerary, with the approximate dates I will be at each place. Join me at any of them. Give my love to Theodosia and young Aaron. Godspeed.

I remain, your humble and obedient,

Aaron Burr

Michael tapped the letter thoughtfully on his palm. This smacked of some kind of adventuring. An expedition against the Dons? Some foolhardy attempt to take a Spanish colony?

"No," he said. "Mr. Stuyvesant, did you say? No, I'm afraid you'll have to tell Mr. Burr I must decline."

"God damn it," Stuyvesant breathed heavily.

"I beg your pardon?" Michael said coldly.

Stuyvesant didn't seem to notice. "I rode all the way from New York," he growled half to himself. "I was nearly drowned in Virginia; the best inn in North Carolina had bedbugs the size of saucers; and when I finally reach this God-forsaken city some idiot black gets me dumped in the marsh. Now some old man who ought to be drinking warm milk tells me . . . . '' He became aware of Michael's icy stare.

"Would you be caring to repeat that?" Michael asked quietly.

"Mr. Fallon, I've had a long journey, and I'm—"

"'An old man drinking warm milk'?"

"You must excuse me, sir."

"Are you a gentleman, Mr. Stuyvesant? My friends may not act for me if not. They set great store by such things."

"A duel?" Stuyvesant took a deep breath. "Mr. Fallon, any insult was purely unintentional, and I retract anything you found offensive. I'll return to New York and tell Mr. Burr you won't be coming. A good night to you, sir." He bowed and turned for the door.

"No."

"Sir, I do apologize—"

"You tell him I'm coming," Michael snapped. "You hear that? Tell him I'm coming." He studied the itinerary and grimaced; he could barely read it without his spectacles. "Tell Burr I'll meet him in Tennessee. In Nashville."

After Stuyvesant was gone, Caesar turned from the door with a worried frown. "Mr. Fallon," the old black man said, "you too old to gallivant around like this."

"Hush, Caesar," Michael said. He squinted at the itinerary, and frowned when it didn't come clearer. "I'm not in my dotage yet."

"No, sir. And you ain't no cockerel, neither."

"You go on to bed, Caesar. It's late. I'm going up to my room."

"You ain't no spring rooster, Mr. Fallon," the butler called after him up the stairs.

In his room, Michael closed the door, then stared at the mirror over the washstand. The face in the mirror was lined. It looked like a piece of granite that had been out in centuries of storms. And there was as much white in his hair as black, now. Angrily he pulled his eyes away. He had as much in him as any man half his age. Whatever Burr was planning, he'd be ready.

North Africa didn't really have a May, Robert thought as his horse plodded over the dunes. It didn't have months, or seasons. Just heat and sand, unchanging and without end. Even the patrols were the same. Leitensderfer commanded this one, riding in front, with Robert, Miller, Kemal, and a half-dozen Bedouins, but that made it no different.

For weeks they had waited at Derna for Hassen Bey and the Tripolitan Army, and for weeks there had been no word of him. Nothing had moved on the sands except Bedouin nomads, and every time a band of them came near, the number of Arabs remaining at Derna had shrunk. Those still there claimed that the way to Tripoli was open, and they should march to take the city now. Eaton himself was coming to believe it. Only O'Bannion and Leitensderfer, hammering home the fate of their column if caught in the open by a real army, convinced Eaton to keep them at Derna. But even they were beginning to doubt.

Robert moved forward to the Austrian's side.

"You've told me much about Fourrier in England. And in France. Why not more about Fourrier in America?"

Leitensderfer didn't look around. "Have I told you of my pilgrimage to Mecca? Of course I have. But have I told you of the Ka'aba?"

"Why don't you tell me some names, some times and amounts? How much has Fourrier paid to whom in Washington City? When, and for what?"

"They say it is the stone Jacob used for his pillow. I have seen the Ka'aba, Fallon, for I was of the faithful, then, and I tell you they may be right. It is just a black stone, just that, but it is not of this world. The strangeness reaches out to you like fingers as you look at it. It is of some alien place."

"For the love of Christ, Leitensderfer! Will you stop talking about this heathen shrine?"

Leitensderfer reined in, and the rest of the patrol stopped too. He looked at Robert. "But what if they are right? If the stone is indeed the pillow of Jacob, perhaps they are the true religion. And it is not of this world." He sighed abruptly. "Always you want what may be used against Justin Fourrier. You try to forge what I say into a weapon against him. I can only tell you what I know, not what you want to know. Of America I know little. Now let us turn back. We have ranged as far as our orders take us.''

Robert turned his horse to follow, and stopped as a camel grunted beyond the next dunes. ''More nomads,'' he said simply. Eaton wants them all brought in.''

''Eaton wants many things,'' Leitensderfer retorted, but he turned back toward the dunes. ''I wonder how many of our Arabs will leave with this lot when they go?''

At the foot of the dune the Austrian motioned Robert to follow as he dismounted. Climbing up, their feet slid backwards at every step. Near the top they dropped to their bellies, wriggling forward the last few yards. Robert peered cautiously over the top. For a few seconds he forgot to breathe.

Little more than half a mile away was the first of an army. Thousands of pale-robed men on horses and camels rode in a thick column beneath hundreds of bright banners and pennons. Like the hordes of Saladin, they stretched toward the horizon.

''Hassen Bey,'' Robert said softly.

Leitensderfer nodded.

Suddenly, behind them, the Bedouins of the patrol spurred their horses forward to scramble up the dune. Frantically Leitensderfer waved them back, but they came on, breaking into wavering cries as they topped the mound. Defiantly they waved their weapons in the air. First one, then another shouldered his musket and fired. From the advancing army came a howl, and at least three hundred men peeled off toward the patrol.

''Let's get the hell out of here!'' Robert shouted, and he and Leitensderfer scrambled down the dune to the horses.

''What's happening, captain?'' Miller asked, as Robert swung into the saddle. ''What do the gyppos be shooting at?''

''Hassen's army!'' Robert answered. ''Ride like hell!'' And they put spurs to their horses.

Minutes later Robert, low on his horse's neck, realized that their Bedouins had joined them. From behind came the howls of the pursuers. Robert risked a glance over his shoulder. A wave of pale robes and banners crested a dune a bare half-mile behind. He faced forward grimly.

For an hour the chase continued, until they were out of the dunes and onto the coastal plain, a flat stretch of windblown sand broken by expanses of hardpacked clay. Derna lay just on the other side of the hills ahead. He took another look back and cursed. The lead had been cut by half. Still, there were only a few more miles to go.

Suddenly there was a roar of musket shot, and something tugged at Robert's cloak. Startled, he looked around. The pursuing Arabs were too far behind.

He caught a movement from one of the patrol's Bedouins. The Arab was sliding his musket down on the far side of his horse as if to hide it. Then he grinned, and quickly pantomimed with his hands—his musket had gone off accidentally. But his black eyes looked hate.

Kemal rode up behind the Arab. One huge hand grabbed the man's burnoose and plucked him from the saddle to drop on the sand. With a wail the Bedouin rolled to his feet. Frantically he looked behind, at the onrushing pursuers, then began to run after the patrol. None of the other Bedouins looked back.

Robert didn't slow. That the man had intended murder, to go over to Hassen, he did not doubt. The pursuing Arabs would see only a member of the patrol unhorsed by mischance; they would settle with him for his treachery.

As the patrol topped the last hills and galloped down on Derna, a trumpeter began to blow assembly. The barricades were manned with a rush, and Eaton and O'Bannion raced into the street as they rode in.

"What is it?" O'Bannion shouted, struggling into his leather-collared tunic.

Eaton, red-faced and sweating, shouted simultaneously, "Who gave the order for assembly? Stop that bugling!"

"Hassen and the army!" Leitensderfer shouted.

"They're right behind us!" Robert yelled.

Everyone's eyes went to the hills. They were bare except for a few sun-parched bushes.

"Perhaps you just saw a large party of nomads," O'Bannion said doubtfully.

"It was the army," Leitensderfer grated. "There are not that many God-damned nomads within a thousand miles of here."

Once more everyone looked at the empty hills.

"I think the Bedouins are right," Eaton said. "Hassen isn't coming at all. I've half a mind to give the order to march while we can still get some distance before dark."

"Look at your Bedouins," Leitensderfer said.

The five surviving Bedouins had joined the other Arabs a hundred yards away. Their wild gesticulations toward the hills were being taken up by the rest. A high-pitched babble rose from the crowd.

"Eaton," Robert said, bending low in the saddle so his voice wouldn't carry, "if you give any order except to man the barricades, I'm taking a boat and trying my luck with the Navy. If they won't have me, I'll damned well row to Alexandria."

"And after I get through talking to them," Leitensderfer said, "the Greeks and the volunteers will join him. We are here to fight, not to be slaughtered like sheep."

Eaton glared at the Bedouins, his chin thrust out angrily, then at Leitensderfer, Robert, and O'Bannion in turn.

"There must be *something* out there," the Marine said quietly.

"Then man the barricades and be damned," Eaton growled. Hands clasped behind him, he stalked off toward his headquarters in the Governor's Palace.

For the rest of the morning they stood to the barricades, sweating under the blazing sun, and the hills stayed barren of man or horse. Then, shortly after noon, a single rider appeared. He paused, then headed for the city at a dead gallop, his robes whipping about him. Bedouin muskets began to pepper the ground around him. The christians held their fire. Twenty yards short of the barricades the man stopped, whirled a sack above his head, and hurled it into the city. In the same instant he wheeled back toward the hills, but his pause had given the Bedouins their chance. The rider jerked in the saddle, and the horse went down. Both lay motionless.

"A brave man," Leitensderfer murmured.

"Leitensderfer!" O'Bannion shouted as he ran to the sack. He upended it, and a severed head rolled out onto the packed dirt of the street, its eyes wide with terror and the mouth drawn in a rictus. Robert recognized the Bedouin who had tried to shoot him.

There was a paper in the head's clenchéd teeth. O'Bannion ripped it free and after one glance passed it to Leitensderfer. The Austrian perused the scrawled Arabic.

Eaton came puffing down the street from the palace, belting on his sword. "What's the shooting about? Are we under attack?"

"Not yet," Leitensderfer said. He flashed a sardonic grin at Eaton. "Hassen Bey is offering a reward for you. Six thousand Spanish dollars for your head, twelve thousand for the whole of you, alive. It seems a very good price."

"Let me see that!" Eaton grabbed the paper and frowned. "Well, I'll give him an answer. I'll offer twice as much for him, dead or alive."

Down out of the surrounding hills, first from one voice, then from thousands, echoed a shrill, ululating cry. Every eye in Derna jerked to the hills. Silence fell upon the city.

Massed along the hilltops and ridges was the army of Hassen, poised like a tidal wave ready to break over Derna. Muskets shook above the wave, and banners waved in the air. And the echoing cry rolled from the hills.

"Holy Mother of God," Leitensderfer breathed.

Robert nodded slowly. "I think shooting the messenger was answer enough for Hassen."

With a roar the wave broke; thousands of Arab cavalry streamed down toward Derna.

"To the barricades!" O'Bannion shouted. The mercenaries and volunteers scattered to their posts; the Bedouins went reluctantly. The Marines had never left. "On my command only! No one fires till my command!"

Robert hurried to his two nine-pounders. Miller was in one guncrew, and Kemal as always, shadowed Robert. He felt unnaturally calm as he watched the horsemen hurtling toward him. A certainty that he would return to Louise filled him. He checked his musket, eased his sword in its scabbard. The roar was louder. The charge was less than five hundred yards away, on the flat of the plain. He settled his cloak on his shoulders, adjusted his Arab headdress. Miller hunched over his gun, a slowmatch in his fist and sweat running down his face. The charge was at three hundred yards. Two hundred. One hundred.

"Fire!" O'Bannion shouted.

Miller slammed his match to the touch-hole before Robert could repeat the command. All along the line cannon roared, hurling langrage, solid shot, anything that could be found. From the harbor *Nautilus* and *Hornet* added the weight of their small broadsides. A pall of smoke drifted over the city. Gouts of dirt fountained among the charging cavalry; men and horse pinwheeled into the air. But on they came. Hurriedly Robert's guncrews reloaded and fired. The line in front of them wavered.

"Quick!" Robert shouted. "Again!"

As Miller touched his match down, an Arab horseman appeared from the left, his horse leaping cleanly over the barricade to knock Robert sprawling. As he rolled on the ground he heard the roar of Miller's gun, the truncated scream of an Albanian gunner. He managed to bring up his musket. The Arab whirled his horse toward Robert, his scimitar sweeping up at the instant Robert fired. The bullet took the rider in the chest, throwing him spread-eagled off the back of the horse.

Then another Arab horseman was inside the barricade, and another. Kemal's great sword clove one at the waist, and Miller transfixed the second on a boarding pike. Robert pried the slowmatch from the dead Albanian's hand and scrambled to the still-loaded cannon. A dozen riders were less than ten yards from the muzzle when he fired. Eighteen pounds of nails, broken glass, and rocks sprayed from the gun, and the charging Arabs were swept away as if by a flood.

Behind him came a cry, "They're in the city!"

Robert leaped to his feet and looked down the line. O'Bannion was forming his small contingent of Marines. As they started into the city, Robert called, "Follow me," and hurried after. Miller and Kemal obeyed. The rest hesitated, then sank back beside the two cannon.

O'Bannion frowned when he saw them, but Robert spoke quickly. "They're in the city? You'll need help. Where are they? How many?"

O'Bannion shook his head as if exasperated. "I don't know. To any of your questions."

"Two to three hundred of them," Leitensderfer said, appearing suddenly from a side street. His face was streaked with dirt, and there was a bloody bandage around his head.

"They broke through on the east, where El Tayel commands. They are between us and the harbor. We are going to need more men than this, Lieutenant O'Bannion."

"We can't spare any more," O'Bannion said irritably. "Weaken the outer defense too much, and Hassen will ride us into the ground."

"And if these take us in the rear?" The Austrian threw up his hands. "We cannot fight on two fronts at once. We must have more force to deal with them."

"A cannon," Robert said.

O'Bannion shook his head. "We had enough trouble getting those garrison carriages to the barricade. We could never manhandle one through the streets quickly enough."

"The three-pounder," Robert and Leitensderfer said together. O'Bannion suddenly smiled.

The brass three-pounder was sitting on its high-wheeled carriage fifty yards inside the barricade, its limber piled high with shot-boxes and powder bags. It was still unfired; larger guns already in the city had been more suitable for the defense.

Miller and Kemal hefted the limber end; Robert and Leitensderfer pushed. O'Bannion led the way, the Marines spread in a fan across the street. Slowly they rumbled along between houses of adobe and stone, pausing at each corner to search the empty cross streets. Then, as they started across a broad street that ran nearly the width of the city, a mass of Arab cavalry was suddenly at the far end.

"Action front!" O'Bannion shouted. "Prepare to receive a mounted charge! Independent rapid fire! Commence!"

The Marines formed a line facing the Arabs and dropped to one knee. Their muskets began to sound. O'Bannion had a musket, too, and was kneeling at the center of the line. With blood-curdling screams the Arabs charged.

Into the open middle of the street Robert and the others manhandled the brass three-pounder. As if they had practiced often, Kemal held a powder bag to the muzzle for Leitensderfer to ram home, Miller slipped in two bags of langrage, and Robert lay the gun on the center of the charging men and horses. A cloud of smoke filled the street as he fired; the screams told of its effect.

Before the gun had settled from its leap, they were swarming over it again. The smoke blinded Robert's eyes and choked his throat; he fired as quickly as they could reload. Load after load of langrage sounded its deadly whistle down the street, joining the constant bark of Marine muskets. Then, through the solid wall of smoke, the Arabs loomed, dying men and horses falling to roll into the line, living men plunging in with swinging scimitars.

Robert flung the slow-match at an Arab who leaped his horse over the cannon, ducked under the man's blade, tugged a pistol from his belt and fired. There wasn't time to see if he had hit, for another mounted man was in front of him. He heaved the rider from the saddle by his leg. The horse ran from between them, and he ran the man through before he could rise. At the ready he whirled expecting new opponents, but there were only his compatriots and a handful of horses running loose.

Slowly the smoke thinned, revealing the scene. Robert gasped. From the end of the street to the cannon stretched a carpet of flesh, men and horses in a tangled jumble. Here and there a man moaned, and someone screamed shrilly and continuously. Halfway down the street a horse kicked once.

Miller began to mutter; with surprise Robert realized that the burly seaman was praying. "Holy Mary, Mother of God, blessed art thou and the fruit of thy womb, Jesus . . . ''

"Did any of them get away?" O'Bannion asked after a moment.

Robert shook his head. "No," he said, and it was a croak. He looked at the others. There were new wounds, but everyone was still standing. "I think we got all of them."

Leitensderfer was staring up at the hills.

Robert followed his gaze and groaned. Once more the ridges were covered with horsemen, their numbers seemingly undiminished.

"Back to the barricades," O'Bannion said. "At the double."

XXVI

Michael frowned again at John Cranford's back. The sallow, leather-shirted man with the broad-brimmed hat had appeared in Nashville saying General Jackson had sent him for Michael Fallon. He hadn't said much else, then or since they'd ridden out of town.

"How much further, Cranford?" he asked suddenly.

"About two hundred yards," the man said, pointing through the trees to a farmhouse, part of which seemed to have once been a log cabin.

Michael let his thoughts go unspoken as they rode up to the house and dismounted.

He followed Cranford inside, then almost ran into him as he stopped abruptly. A pretty woman of middle years stood beyond him, hands on hips.

"Wipe your feet, John Cranford," she said sharply. "And take your hat off in the house."

"Yes, Miss Rachel," Cranford mumbled, managing to jerk off his hat, duck his head, and scuffle his boots all at the same time.

The woman shook her head, then turned to smile at Michael. "Mr. Fallon? I'm Rachel Jackson. I know my husband is expecting you. He's in the parlor. Would you care to freshen before you see him? I know it's been a long ride, and no doubt a silent one if I know John Cranford."

Michael smiled and bowed. "It's pleased I am, Mrs. Jackson, to make your acquaintance. If you don't mind, I'd just as soon see your husband now."

She smiled at Michael once more, disappeared through a side door, and reappeared almost at once. "You may go in, Mr. Fallon."

There were two men in the room, a tall, lanky, hawk-faced man with a head of gray-streaked hair, who must be Jackson, and next to him Aaron Burr. The two of them stood by the fireplace, where logs blazed despite the mild May weather. Their poses were identical, feet apart, chins thrust forward, hands clasped behind their backs. Despite their difference in size, there was something else alike about them. Both had the air of electricity about them, the feel of great personal will.

As Michael stepped into the room, Burr strode forward with a smile and an outstretched hand. "Fallon. I knew you'd come. Come, meet General Jackson."

Jackson shook Michael's hand, but his face remained grim. "Mr. Fallon. Mr. Burr has told me much of you, but I would like to ask you one thing myself. Why are you a part of this?"

"Come now, Jackson," Burr said.

Michael returned Jackson's look levelly. "I'm not sure what 'this' is. From Mr. Burr's letter, I assume it's some move against the Spanish Americans. If it is, well, I hate colonies. Especially colonies in the Americas."

"You assumed that from this letter," Jackson said flatly. "Mr. Vice-President, I've said it before. You're a sight too open. Secrecy is paramount. If your friends don't know what you're going to do, your enemies can't."

"I'll use a cipher from now on," Burr said carelessly.

"Then it is a move against the Spanish?" Michael asked.

Jackson nodded tightly, but Burr waxed enthusiastic. "Not *a* move, Fallon. *The* move. We're going to seize all of Spanish Mexico. We'll found a nation, an empire such as the world has not seen in modern times."

"Then it won't be taken in the name of the United States?" Michael said with a sharp glance at Jackson.

The general grunted, and began to pace in front of the fire. "The United States is run from the East," he said. "From New York and New England and Virginia. The West has no power, and it gets nothing. Why should I help give the East more land?" He rounded suddenly on Michael. "Why should I, Mr. Fallon?"

"No reason," Michael answered. "The United States has no need to go on expanding forever. Why, most of this Louisiana is useless, or so I'm told by men who've been there."

"It's settled, then," Burr said, briskly rubbing his hands together.

"Nothing's settled," Michael said. Both men stared at him; he stared back. "It's a grand-sounding plan. But grand-sounding plans have a way of collapsing like a pricked bubble. I'd like a few details. Men. Guns. Supplies. Things like that."

Jackson unbent a little. "It's good to meet a man with his feet on the ground. Despite Mr. Burr's fervor, little if anything is set. We're still feeling our way. For may part, I can bring five thousand Tennesseans, good riflemen all, if this does indeed come to pass."

"If?" Burr exclaimed. "If, General Jackson? General Wilkinson has agreed to give such orders to Army posts on the frontier as will assist our passage, and he himself will march with us with a contingent of the United States Army. I have letters to Clark and others in New Orleans, men who call themselves the Mexico Association. With us to give them the impetus, they will supply food, medicines, clothing, and, most important, information about Mexico. And finally, I have assurances from Ambassador Merry of England, himself, that three British frigates will assist us."

"I don't like dealings with the British," Michael said.

"Nor I," agreed Jackson. "I don't trust them."

Burr seemed taken aback, but only for a moment. "It's not as if they were to be partners, gentlemen. Their part is the ships. Nothing more. And it's good to have a Navy. Even one of only three ships."

Jackson turned to a sideboard, "Gentlemen, I want some good corn whiskey. What about the rest of you? There's brandy if the whiskey's not good enough."

"Besides General Jackson's Tennesseans," Burr said, "there will be a great number of men in need of muskets. You deal in shipments of thousands of muskets at a time, so—"

Michael took his whiskey and settled in to listen.

The next morning, in Jackson's boat, Burr and Michael drifted down the Cumberland River. At the Ohio they boarded a sixty-foot barge Burr had purchased and continued downriver to Fort Massac, near the village of Cincinnati.

At the gate of the fort, a large log stockade, a blue-coated lieutenant met them.

"Mr. Burr? I'm Lieutenant Warbeck, General Wilkinson's aide. He's waiting in his quarters, sir."

Burr looked surprised. "Where is Lieutenant Pike?"

"On an expedition up the Mississippi, sir. There was an order from the President to explore it to the source. If you'll follow me, sir."

The general's quarters were very grand—a large, white, two-story house that would have fit into any eatern city, looking incongruous near the dusty parade ground. Wilkinson was waiting in the study.

"Mr. Vice-President," the general said with a ponderous bow. He was a pendulous man, curly white hair framing bags beneath bulbous eyes, slack, heavy lips, and jowly, sagging chins. A heavy paunch completed the picture. "You may go, Lieutenant. Would you care for brandy, Mr. Vice-President?"

Burr waited until the door closed behind Warbeck. "So, Wilkinson. What's this about sending Pike up the Mississippi?"

"Orders from President Jefferson," Wilkinson said smoothly. He finished pouring the brandy and offered them each a glass. "I don't believe I've had the honor of your acquaintance," he said to Michael.

"Michael Fallon," Michael said with a short bow, "of Charleston, South Carolina."

"Mr. Fallon," Wilkinson said, with too much oil for Michael's taste.

"General," Burr said tightly, "I'm still awaiting a clear answer. Why send your right-hand man to the end of creation, just when we need him?"

Wilkinson spread his pudgy hands. "My right-hand man, yes. And just the right sort for it. Ambitious and not too bright. But, in this case, perhaps too ambitious. If he were to go over my head to Washington City, I might be ordered not to take part in this, ah, venture. You know how averse Mr. Jefferson is to military force."

"You actually think this Pike might try to stop you?" Michael asked.

"Zebulon has been loyal to me so far," Wilkinson replied, "because attaching himself to the Army's ranking general was to his advantage. If he thought bringing himself to the notice of Washington City would make him rise faster, who can say?"

Michael shook his head. "When is he to return? From what I've been told, we can't move till some time next year."

"It doesn't matter. He can always be sent off again. There are endless miles of nothing out there to be explored."

"Pike isn't important," Burr broke in. "I want to know when you're moving to St. Louis. You were supposed to go last month. If the Army is changing your orders, it will affect everything."

Wilkinson waved him away. "There's been no change in orders. I merely thought we should confer before I left this post. It will be better for me to take supplies with me when I shift my command rather than send for them later."

"I suppose," Burr said grudgingly. "But I don't like unexpected changes. We can't afford any mistakes, Wilkinson."

"Of course," Wilkinson said, then added carelessly, "I suppose Jackson has committed himself?"

"He has," Burr replied. "He will meet us with five thousand men."

"Five thousand," Wilkinson murmured. "Of course, they won't be regular Army troops. And Jackson himself is merely a militia general. Good enough for fighting Indians, I suppose. He's a crude man, too," he added, looking around at the Sheraton furniture, the gilt chandelier. "He's been known to attack men with his walking stick, or even his fists. A brawler, rather than a general."

"I found him very much the gentleman," Michael said coolly.

"Certainly," Wilkinson said hastily. "I didn't mean to imply otherwise, I'm sure."

An amused smile played on Burr's lips. "There will be no problem," he said diplomatically. "We'll all defer to your advice, general." Wilkinson gave a self-satisfied smile and bowed preeningly to Burr.

"I think I'll take a turn outside," Michael said suddenly. Both men looked at him in surprise.

"But we're going to talk over supplies," Burr said.

"You don't need me for that," Michael said, "and I've

never seen a frontier fort before. If you'll excuse me, gentlemen.''

He took his leave, refusing Wilkinson's offer of a guide. He wanted no guide to report back to the general.

Ohio's summer heat was drier than Charleston's. Squads of soldiers drilling on the parade ground raised clouds of dust; the flag barely stirred in the light breeze.

He spoke to a man here and there, and watched a score of fresh cavalry recruits learning how to mount. Bit by bit he approached the stables. A single private, bare to the waist, his galluses hanging loose, was mucking out the stalls.

"Afternoon, son," Michael said; the private jumped. "What's your name?"

"Bergman, sir," the private said nervously.

"Hard work, that. I did a sight of it when I was a lad."

"You, sir?" Bergman said. He stared at Michael's coat of blue superfine, and his tall beaver hat.

"Aye, me. A man doesn't need to end up where he starts out." Bergman nodded and smiled. "Do you go into Cincinnati much, lad? I expect they cater to the soldiers' custom."

"A bit, sir. Ain't but maybe a thousand people there, and most of them get their money from trappers, or the farmers coming in." He leaned on his fork. "Besides, a private don't get much money."

"Seems a shame. A man rides over half of hell and creation, he deserves to buy a drink now and again."

"Oh, we don't ride all that far, sir. Except when the general goes down to Mexico, of course."

Michael felt his scalp tighten. "Mexico? That is a long way. I didn't realize you patrolled that far."

"Not regular, sir. Just sometimes the general has to go down to confer with the Dons."

Someone cleared his throat. Michael looked over his shoulder to find Lieutenant Warbeck standing in the door. Bergman snapped to attention.

"Mr. Fallon," Warbeck said, "the general asks you to come back to his quarters, sir. Bergman," he went on, not looking at the private, "that fork's not to lean on."

"Yes, sir," Bergman shouted, and began furiously forking manure.

Warbeck gave no sign of anything but correct military punctilio. In front of the house he sketched a salute and disappeared. Michael frowned after him.

Burr came out of the house, alone. "Ah, Fallon. There you are. Wilkinson insists on marching his soldiers about for us to look at this afternoon."

Michael looked around. They were alone. "Do you know Wilkinson goes to Mexico? To confer with the Spanish?"

"No," Burr said slowly, then continued more briskly, "but it should be no surprise. He *is* military governor of the Louisiana Territory. Matters of the common border, and so on."

"I've looked over his troops. None of them are equipped for an expedition like we're discussing. Most are little better than recruits."

"He's only bringing a small contingent, to leaven and train the rest of our men. What are you getting at, Fallon?"

"I don't trust him. His manner smells like a week-old fish. What if he sent Pike off, not because he fears the man will betray us to the government, but because he fears Pike will betray him to us?"

"God, man, the next thing you'll be seeing footpads under the bed!"

"I tell you, he's not to be trusted."

Burr laughed. "He can be trusted. He wants to be Commander-in-Chief of the Army in our new nation too much to betray us. Now come along. We've just time to clean up before this parade."

XXVII

As the sun rose over the North African horizon, Robert inspected his two nine-pounders. It was the tenth of June, the forty-first day of siege. Forty-one days of mass cavalry attacks, of sniping and night-time harrassments, but the garrison was holding up. His cannon crews, an Albanian, a Bulgarian, a Pole, a Russian, and a Swede, slept beside their guns. It had dawned on them, slowly, that if the Arabs won, their heads would end up on pikes.

He had been given five of the Greek mercenaries for his part of the barricade. They seemed to keep their good humor no matter what. When he left the guns to check on them, one was playing a mandolin and the other four were dancing, each with an arm about the next man's shoulder. The end man motioned for him to join, and he did.

Miller shook his head and went on changing the load in his musket. Kemal, who seemed suspicious of the Greeks, watched closely.

Robert had thought it strange the first time he had seen the men dancing together, and he'd had too much wine the first time he joined in, but now he enjoyed it. It broke the monotony, and filled him with the joy at being alive the Greeks had.

"They're comingggg!"

At the echoing cry the dancers broke like a covey of quail, darting for the barricade. Over the far hills rolled the wave of Hassen's horsemen.

"Just as before," Robert said quietly. "Solid shot till they reach five hundred yards, then langrage and grape. Steady. Steady, now." The Arab charge swept on, multicolored banners whipping in the wind. From thousands of throats came a wavering cry. "Steady," Robert said. "Wait. Wait. Fire!"

Down the length of the barricade the command was echoed, by O'Bannion, and Eaton, and Constantine, and Leitensderfer. With a roar that momentarily drowned the Arabs' battle shouts, Derna erupted in fire and smoke.

A thousand yards out, gouts of earth lifted to the sky. Men and horse tumbled, but the charge sped on.

Robert had labored over his guncrews, and they were the first to get off their second shots. Their third followed close on the heels of the other guns' second. Gaps were torn in the oncoming line, but it never wavered.

"Grape!" Robert ordered as the attack closed to five hundred yards. Suddenly his eye caught something odd about the oncoming riders. He began to shout. "They're riding double! O'Bannion! They're riding double!"

Down the line the Marine waved his sword. "I understand!" he shouted back, and ducked as wild shots from the charging horsemen chipped the stones around him.

"Be ready," Robert told the Greeks. "They'll be coming in on foot."

"Good by damn," bushily mustached Spiros said. A blond boy the others called Demetrios spat on his thumb and ran it along his bayonet with a grin.

"Put your bloody backs into it!" Miller shouted at the gunners. "They'll be boarding any time now!"

Acrid smoke wreathed the barricades. Three hundred yards. Two hundred. One hundred. Fifty. Suddenly, the charge appeared through the smoke, closing on the barricades, the second riders afoot, now, with muskets, running among the charging horses.

"Allah akbar!"

From the city muskets rattle fiercely, and the cannon continued their roar, but the charge reached the barricades. Men began to scramble over.

"Allah akbar!" screamed a swarthy Arab as he thrust a bayonet at Miller.

"Stow your gab!" Miller howled back, and hacked him down with a cutlass.

Robert slashed at the burnooses around him. There was no

time to draw or cock a pistol. In the space of ten seconds he ran a man through, kicked another in the stomach, and ripped open a third's throat to fountain blood over his robes. Ominously, the cannon had all fallen silent. Their deafening roar had been replaced by the grunting and screaming of fighting and dying men.

Then, suddenly there were no more Arabs inside Robert's position. Men were streaming back across the plain toward the hills.

"We got them!" Miller shouted. "We got them, captain!"

"Back to the guns!" Robert ordered, and the men sent nine-pound shot whistling after the retreating Arabs.

"Theos!" Demetrios shouted suddenly, pointing.

On the hills fresh masses of Hassen's cavalry were forming. The fleeing men were rallying, merging into the formations above the city.

"Fallon!" O'Bannion called from behind him. The Marine was mounted, with Hamet, Lietensderfer, Constantine, a dozen of the Greeks, and a hundred Bedouins. There were three horses with empty saddles. "Tell off two of the Greeks and come on. If they come at us like that again, they're getting a surprise on the flank."

From the hills echoed a lone voice. *"Allah ill'Allah!"*

Five thousand answered. *"Allah akbar!"* And the juggernaut rolled toward the city once more.

"Spiros!" Robert snapped. "Demetrios! Mount up!"

He swung into a saddle, and Spiros likewise, but Kemal pushed Demetrios aside. The big Turk scrambled up on the horse.

"Allah akbar!"

"Follow me," O'Bannion yelled, and they galloped down the dusty streets to the east side of the city. Then they waited while the attack flowed nearer. Robert's mount stamped and shook its head, rattling the bridle. He drew his sword.

"Allah akbar!"

The charge came on, swifter and swifter, banners of green and silver, gold and scarlet whipping in the wind, swords and lances glinting in the still-rising sun.

"Steady," O'Bannion said. "Wait the moment."

Hamet murmured something under his breath.

"Allah akbar!"

The Arab onslaught pounded nearer and nearer. Half a mile. A quarter mile. O'Bannion's Mameluke sword swung up, then down. "Charge!" he shouted.

The small knot of them swept forward toward the Arab left flank. From the Europeans came a wordless roar, a howl of battle fury. The Bedouins erupted with *"Allah akbar!"*

Robert felt the hair on his neck rise at hearing the cry from front and rear at the same time. Were some of the men behind taking this chance to go over? Even as the thought came, the small counterattack knifed into the flank of the charge. There was no time to think.

The Arabs, intent on the city, had not noticed the tiny contingent moving out to meet them. Robert cut down astonished men and slashed deeper into the Arab army before they could fall. An Arab turned to face him, and froze, eyes wide, as Robert beheaded him. The next screamed before Robert's sword ever touched his flesh.

Fear was doing part of their work for them. The Arabs knew the infidel lay within the city. Yet here they were, by magic. And Arabs—Bedouins—were attacking their fellows. It had to be the work of an evil *djinn*. One, then another of them, slipped away. The few became many, the many a rout as infectious panic raced through them. The mass that had roared toward Derna now streamed back to the hills.

"Form up!" O'Bannion shouted. "Back to the city!"

Kemal, swinging his bloody sword with a grin, started after the retreat, but Robert caught his arm. A handful of the Bedouins raced toward the hills, hacking at fleeing Arabs. Hamet rode a few paces after them, shouting, but they paid him no heed.

"Back to the city!" O'Bannion called again.

Robert motioned Kemal and Spiros to follow, and fell in behind the Marine. All along the barricades men climbed into the open, shouting and cheering, as they rode in.

Inside the city, Eaton came running up to O'Bannion before he had dismounted.

"Magnificent!" the bluff man shouted, reaching up to pump O'Bannion's hand. "A hundred against five thousand. There's never been a charge like it. You've saved the city."

"Good God damn!" Constantine suddenly spat. He was looking back at the ochre hills. *"Merde! Scheisse!* Shit!"

Robert followed the Greek's gaze. Horsemen were pouring down the slopes.

"It's impossible," Eaton mumbled. He still held O'Bannion's hand in both of his as if he had forgottten it.

"It's possible," O'Bannion growled. "Back to your posts! Everyone back to his post!"

"Allah akbar!"

The evening shadows stretched long, giving the once-more retreating Arab army the look of a fever dream.

"How many times they come so far, captain?" Miller croaked, throat dry with powder smoke and dust.

Robert only shook his head. He had lost count after the fourth—or was it the fifth—attack. Charleston seemed impossibly far away. For the first time since he had been taken by Murad, he was beginning to doubt that he would ever see it again.

"Think they'll come in the night, captain?"

"They have not so far," Lietensderfer said, dropping down beside them. Robert didn't look around.

"They haven't fought all day before, either," Robert said. He looked over his shoulder at the grimy Austrian. "We can't take another day like today. Christ, I didn't think we could take today."

Leitensderfer lifted up enough to peer at the sun, a dull, red ball touching the horizon. "Help may be coming. Eaton sent a messenger off by small boat two weeks ago, demanding one hundred additional Marines."

"He's asked for help before and never got it."

"I know, Fallon, but this time he has said we cannot hold Derna without them."

"He may be right," Robert muttered. "How did you find out about this? Eaton barely lets O'Bannion know what he's doing."

"He does not notice his valet, a Syrian with whom I have lately begun having a drink each evening." He looked to the west again.

"What are you looking for?" Robert asked. "They

retreated south.''

"I look for darkness. Another twenty minutes, I think. I want to find out what they are up to.''

"You're going out there?'' Robert said incredulously. Miller crossed himself, and Lietensderfer smiled.

"Exactly. I do not relish it, but it must be done.''

Robert shook his head. "I can't believe Eaton ordered this. It's crazy.''

"Eaton most certainly did not order it,'' the Austrian replied. "I am ordered to remain in the city. He is afraid I will be captured and tell how weak the city is under torture. But we must know if Hassen is ready to attack us again tomorrow.''

"I suppose,'' Robert said slowly. "You'll need some company.''

"Thank you, I will be safer alone. I have no wish to discover whether Eaton is right about my resistance to torture. If you please, I shall meditate now before I go.''

Gathering his cloak about him, Lietensderfer closed his eyes. His breathing deepened. Robert and Miller looked at each other. Robert shrugged and returned to his study of the hills.

Just as gray dusk became blackness, the Austrian opened his eyes. "I will return by dawn,'' he said. "If I am returning.'' And he slipped over the barricade. Robert peered after him. Not so much as a shifting shadow marked his passage.

The night passed slowly. Robert tried to sleep, but only intermittent naps would come, less restful than being awake. They were punctuated with terrifying dreams, distorted images of Louise, of Catherine, of his father Between times he paced his section of the barricade. The gun crews tossed and snored beside their cannon. As the night flowed into the dead hours of morning, he began searching the moonless black for movement.

About four o'clock O'Bannion appeared. He held a steaming pottery beaker that filled the air with the smell of coffee. "Those Navy bastards have been holding this out,'' he said, passing the beaker to Robert. "Is he back, yet?''

Robert paused in the act of drinking. "You know?''

"Of course I know. You think I've got my head in the sand like Eaton?''

"He said he'd be back by dawn," Robert said. Both men looked to the still-dark east.

Robert and O'Bannion sat in silence against a wall. Somewhere in the city a dog barked viciously. A curse floated in the pre-dawn, and the barking turned to retreating yelps. Fingers of light poked above the horizon, and a distant brightness lined it.

"Sta'sis!" the sentry yelled suddenly. "Halt!" He fired; a shape tumbled down inside the barricade.

Men woke, shouting, firing their muskets wildly. Robert's Greeks closed in on the intruder with their bayonets.

"It is Leitensderfer!" the man shouted, clutching his shoulder. "Put those damned bayonets up! It is me!"

Robert and O'Bannion rushed to the Austrian.

"How badly are you hit?" Robert asked.

"I think it went through the muscle cleanly. I will survive. I will tell you, for the first time I am glad those Greeks are not marksmen."

"Why didn't you call out?" Robert said. "Why try to sneak in?"

"What did you find out?" O'Bannion asked insistently.

"I was afraid if I made a sudden noise, the sentries might shoot at me," Leitensderfer said drily. He looked at O'Bannion. "I will tell my news once. Help me up and let us go to Eaton."

Lietensderfer was able to walk, and they followed him, O'Bannion growling impatiently, to the Governor's Palace. There Ali, Eaton's serving man, bowed regretfully.

"I am begging pardon, *effendis*. The General Eaton is not yet waking."

"Eaton!" O'Bannion bellowed suddenly. "Eaton, get out here!"

Ali practically danced in front of the Marine, flapping his hands frantically. "Please, *effendi*. No! Please!"

"Eaton! Wake up, Eaton!"

The door to the bedchamber slammed open, and Eaton appeared barefoot and belting on a robe. "What is it? An attack? Oh, it's you." His jaundiced gaze took in O'Bannion, Robert, and Leitensderfer in turn. Suddenly he frowned. "There's blood on you, man! Damn it, did you go out after I ordered you not to? Didn't I tell you the risk? Now look at you."

"For God's sake," Robert broke in. "He got back safely, and one of our sentries nicked him. Now are you going to listen to what he has to say?"

Eaton thrust his chin forward angrily. "Now you listen here, Fallon—"

"I think," Lietensderfer said suddenly, "I have bled more than—" He swayed. Robert and O'Bannion caught him.

"Don't just stand there!" Robert shouted at Eaton. "Send for the doctor!"

Ali was dispatched for Doctor Mendrici, and the slender, dark-eyed surgeon appeared quickly with his bag. He uncovered the Austrian's wound, swabbing, probing, and bandaging while muttering to himself in Italian. *"Ebbene!"* he said at last, wiping his hands. "He must have *riposo*. Rest. A day, at least."

"First my report," Lietensderfer said faintly.

"Yes," O'Bannion said quickly.

Eaton nodded. "Will you leave us, Doctor Mendrici? You may go too, Ali." He waited till they were gone, then rounded on Lietensderfer. "Well? It had better be good, I'll tell you."

"God damn it," O'Bannion said, "let's hear the report first. How soon will Hassen be able to attack us again?"

"A year," Lietensderfer said. "Perhaps two. If he keeps his head. I think perhaps Yusuf will have his head, though. It is very bad for a general to be defeated by so small a force."

O'Bannion began to grin.

"What are you talking about?" Eaton asked.

"A retreating army. An army that lost a score of men to desertion last night, and will lose a score tonight, and the next, and the next. An army that is entirely lacking in will and spirit. If we attack tommorrow, it will disappear like sand in the wind."

"We've done it?" Eaton asked. "By God, we've done it!" He began to chuckle, then to laugh. "We've done it!" he howled, and the others laughed as if he'd said the funniest thing in the world. There was a knock at the door and Eaton flung it open. "We've done it!" he yelled.

The blue-coated young naval lieutenant standing in the door

pulled a linen handkerchief from his sleeve and dabbed delicately at his nostrils. "I'm sure you have," he said, superciliously.

"*Our* Navy?" Robert murmured. O'Bannion smiled.

"I don't recognize you," Eaton said. "You aren't from *Nautilus,* are you?"

"Certainly not." The lieutenant seemed offended at the idea. "I am on Commodore Barron's staff." He made a short bow. "Lieutenant John Standish Cabot, of Massachusetts."

"The commodore!" Eaton said eagerly. "Is he sending the Marines I asked for?"

"I came on *Constellation*, which dropped anchor within the half hour," Cabot began, then stopped as Eaton whirled to the others.

"*Constellation!* Barron didn't send a frigate just to tell me no. He's sent the Marines!"

"And the way's open," O'Bannion said. "to Benghazi, and then Tripoli."

"We'll make Yusuf himself hoist the American flag!" Robert roared.

Lietensderfer nodded, grinning broadly.

"Mr. Eaton." Cabot tugged an oilskin packet from under his tunic. "I think you'd better read this. Orders from Commodore Barron."

Eaton froze at the lieutenant's tone, then ripped open the packet. As he read, his frown grew; then, face empty, he sank into a chair. The orders fell from his hand.

"We're not getting the Marines?" Robert said.

"We don't need them," O'Bannion said. "With Hassen broken, we can take Tripoli with what we have."

Eaton spoke. "We've been ordered to withdraw."

"Withdraw!" Robert and O'Bannion shouted together.

"Within twenty-four hours," Eaton said tiredly.

"To hell with the orders!" Robert said. "We can take Tripoli with what we have."

Lietensderfer let out a long breath. "I have been in many armies, Fallon. The first thing I learned to do was read the wind. Suddenly it is against us."

"O'Bannion?" Robert said slowly.

The Marine jerked his head. He seemed on the point of

tears. "I want to go on, Fallon. You know I do. but the orders—I have to obey the orders, damn it. I have to." He turned away.

Robert faced Cabot, and the Navy man took a step back. "Why?" Robert said grimly. "In the name of God, why? We won here!"

Cabot jumped at Robert's final shout. "We've signed a treaty with the Bashaw. The war's over."

"A *treaty?*" Eaton said. "What about our prisoners in Tripoli? What about Prince Hamet?"

"He wasn't mentioned," Cabot said. "The prisoners will be released—"

"There's more, isn't there?" Robert broke in. "Why did Yusuf give up? We get the prisoners. What does he get?"

Cabot hesitated. "Sixty thousand dollars."

"Christ!" O'Bannion snapped, whirling to face them. "You mean after all this we're back to paying tribute? I can't believe Commodore Barron agreed to that."

"Actually," Cabot said, "it was Tobias Lear did the negotiating."

Robert snarled, "Who is this Lear? Another Washington City man? Another bureaucrat? God, they'll sell you every time."

"I do not think we will be remembered," Leitensderfer said suddenly. "If history speaks of this at all, it will be changed beyond recognition to hide the shame. But I do not think we will be remembered."

That night they abandoned their Bedouin allies. With muffled oars, Eaton, O'Bannion, the Marines, the mercenaries, the volunteers, and the cannoneers were rowed out to the ships. Before dawn they had sailed for Gibraltar.

XXVIII

Wilkinson fitted Burr and Michael out with a boat and Army rowers when they left Fort Massac, a boat with purple sails and canopy. Hardly the vehicle for men who wanted secrecy, Michael thought, but Burr accepted it as due the Vice-President. In Natchez they were wined and dined by the people on the bluff, the Bingmans, the Surgets, the Minors, the Burneys, the Duncans, people who lived the fine life while ignoring the brothels and gambling hells at the foot of the bluff called Natchez-under-the-Hill. There were offers of support from some of those families, sons and cousins who wanted to join the grand adventure. Burr welcomed them all.

New Orleans was even warmer in its welcome. Creoles, both French and Spanish, fell over themselves with eagerness once they discovered what Burr was up to—which didn't take long, Michael thought sourly. Still, he could not deny that the Creoles who had discovered that Jefferson's ideas of democracy did not extend to Louisiana were more than ready to follow Burr. A Creole had lent them the house they were staying in, one of the largest in the city. The party this July night of 1805 was to repay the hospitality Burr had received, and to cover the meeting to be held later that night in the study.

Michael lifted his chin before the mirror to tie his stock.

"Yes?" he said to a knock on the door.

Lopes stuck his head in. "May I come in, *Señor* Fallon?"

"Certainly." He turned into the mirror. "Well?"

"Nothing, *señor*."

"Damn it, I'm leaving for Charleston tomorrow. There's not much time left."

"I cannot discover what is not there. I have spoken to every

288

member of the Association except *Señor* Clark, and none of them thinks less than the highest of General Wilkinson.''

Michael sighed grimly and shrugged into his coat. "Well, come along. Let's go down to the ball.''

The ballroom was packed with color when they entered. A rainbow of women showed expanses of shoulder and bosom; their necks and wrists glittered with diamonds, emeralds, and rubies. Few of the men failed to wear the sash and medallion of some European order. When Michael entered, the conversations gave way to applause, and the string quartet struck up a heroic strain.

Michael bowed to the gathering, whispering to Lopes as he did. "Stay close to me, tonight. I don't know most of these people. Lopes?''

Lopes was intent on a woman, a redhead in a daring green silk dress. "I am surprised to see her here, *señor*.''

"Why? Is her husband not likely to support us?''

"Not exactly. It is the best-kept secret in New Orleans—perhaps the only secret—that she is William Claiborne's mistress. I do not think that Governor Claiborne would, as you say, support us.''

Michael smiled. "Then she must be here for a purpose. Introduce me.''

Lopes hesitated, and seemed about to say something, but then he led the way across the crowded floor. "*Señora* Applegate?'' The redhead turned, smiling, her glorious hair a coronet of elaborate braids. "*Señora* Applegate, may I present *Señor* Michael Fallon. *Señor* Fallon, *Señora* Cordelia Applegate.''

"*Señora*,'' Michael murmured, and kissed her hand with his courtliest bow. He had the odd feeling that there was recognition in her eyes. But he was sure he had never seen her before.

"Mr. Fallon,'' she replied, and made a deep curtsey, looking up under her lashes with a seductive smile. She held the pose long enough for him to make a study of her cleavage.

Lopes raised an eyebrow questioningly at Michael, then drifted away with a smile.

"May I offer you some ratafia?'' Michael asked.

"I'd prefer wine,'' she said with so significant a look that

Michael started. If the idea weren't insane, he'd think she was trying to seduce him.

Applause started up again. Burr was entering the room, preening like a bantam cock. "Would you like me to introduce you to the Vice-President?"

"I prefer you," she said in the same throaty tone, and put her arm through his in a way that pressed her breast tightly against him.

"I'm old enough to be your father," he said quietly. What was her purpose?

"Surely not, Michael. I may call you Michael, mayn't I? Besides, I would much rather have a man of experience."

His last doubts disappeared. When he was twenty he had believed women who claimed to be overcome with desire for him on sight. At thirty he had been a little wiser. Now he was twice that, and more. Cordelia Applegate wanted something else from him. He decided to see how high a price she was willing to pay.

"Shall we walk in the garden?" he suggested. "It's quite beautiful out there."

She hesitated only a second. "I'd love to."

The brick paths beneath moss-draped oaks were cool in the moonlight. A light breeze carried scents like perfumes. The ball faded behind them as they strolled down to a gazebo of close latticework.

Once inside, he swept her into his arms. She made one muffled sound of protest as his mouth came down on hers, then sank against him. When he released her, he could make out an amused smile in the dim light.

"You're impetuous," she laughed softly.

"I'm more than that. I intend to have you."

Her smile widened briefly. "I like a man who goes directly after what he wants." His hands went to the fastenings of her dress, but she stepped back. "No. Let me."

The green silk swirled to the floor, followed by a froth of lace, and she stood in her stockings and high-heeled slippers.

"Take me."

Without another word he bore her down on the floor. She squealed when he thrust into her, and he stopped her mouth with his. He lost himself in the sensations of her, the soft breasts crushed beneath his chest, the satin skin rubbing against him, the long silken legs that wrapped around him. The moans that began to issue from her throat made him smile. When he had gasped out his own release, he rolled off her and lay breathing heavily. His left arm ached; he rubbed at it and laughed to himself. At his age this sort of thing left him as full of aches as pleasures.

"You're very vigorous," she panted, "for—"

"For a man my age?"

She rolled over to lay her head on his chest. "Oh, no. You're magnificent. Besides, I told you, I like men with experience."

He couldn't resist a smile.

"I'll wager you're very experienced," she went on, "and not just with women. You must have had many adventures."

"A few," he said.

"Why, just look at your trip down the Mississippi, through the wilderness. If that wasn't an adventure, I don't know what is."

"I'm afraid it wasn't very exciting."

"But just the people you met must have been an adventure. At least, they would be for me. We women never get to go anywhere, or do anything."

He smiled in the darkness. "I want to make love to you again."

"Again?" she said in evident surprise. "But of course. After you rest. For now, tell me about—"

"I don't need to rest," he said, and taking her head in both hands he began to urge her slowly down his body.

"What? I don't under— Oh, no! I've never—"

Her words ended abruptly. For a moment her hands pushed futilely against his thighs, but then he relaxed to her liquid caress. If she wanted information, he thought, let her earn it. And again he lost himself in the pleasure of her.

After, she lay panting against his legs. "I . . . I've never done that before," she said angrily.

"Then you did well for a first try."

"Damn you," she said, then controlled her anger. Her voice took on a pout. "Why do you treat me like this? I want you to be gentle with me."

"Gentle? Then ask your questions, instead of trying to pump me."

"I don't understand," she said weakly.

"My trip down the Mississippi. Who did I meet? What did we talk about? You've asked that much already. Who sent you? Claiborne? I know you're not a whore off the streets."

"God damn you!" She scrambled up, slapping and clawing. With difficulty he trapped her wrists behind her and secured her wildly kicking legs with one of his.

"Quiet down, woman! Quiet down or I'll blister your hide and deliver you back to Claiborne in your natural state. Naked."

"He'll kill you," she hissed. "He'll shoot you like a dog."

"It would be my pleasure," he said grimly, "to shoot any man who'd send a women to do a thing like this. Or was it somebody else? Do you whore for the highest bidder?"

She convulsed in anger again. "You're up to something! You and Burr and whoever you've been meeting with. But William will find out. He'll hang all of you. All of you, damn your soul to hell!"

"Claiborne," Michael said thoughtfully. Releasing her, he rolled quickly to his feet and began to dress but she didn't move. "Once you get dressed, it would be best for you to be going back to Claiborne. I don't think this ball is the place for you."

"I don't want to go to your damned ball," she snarled. "I hope you rot in hell. You and your son both."

"Robert? You knew Robert?"

"Yes, I knew him, and . . . knew? You mean he's dead? Well, I'm glad. It's one less of you Fallon bas—"

With one step he was lifting her off the floor, his hands round her throat. Her nails dug at his wrists; her feet scrabbled at the door. Coldly he watched her face darkening, her open mouth straining for air that would not come. Abruptly he hurled her back to the floor. He was panting as if he'd run for miles. His chest felt leaden. She looked up at him in terror, sucking in deep, long breaths.

"If I ever hear you mention him again," he said finally, "I'll kill you."

She was lying there naked, staring after him, when he left.

His mind was a welter. Claiborne. The Governor of New Orleans could be a powerful enemy. It would take time to collect and ship the number of guns needed and they would have to be stored in New Orleans.

The ache in his left arm suddenly ripped across his chest. With a strangled groan he sagged to his knees. Oh, God, Robert! He fumbled for something to hang onto, but his hands no longer worked. He fell, and felt his cheek split on the bricks. The terrible pain jolted him again and again, forcing him down into unconsciousness.

When he woke, to pain and weakness, there was a deeper feel to the night. Every muscle in his body ached. His chest felt as if he had been beaten with hammers; his left arm was numb.

He got to his feet and staggered to the house. Music still floated from the ballroom; he made his way by a back stair to the second floor. Clark, Livingston, and Burr should be meeting in the study. When he opened the door and lurched through, they surged to their feet. Burr rushed to his side.

"Fallon!" he cried. "Are you all right?"

"Lopes told us you were with, um, a lady," said Daniel Clark, a husky, dark-haired merchant.

"It is true," Lopes said, "or we would have looked for you. What happened, *señor*?"

"I fell," Michael said, dropping into the chair held by Ned Livingston, Burr's slender friend from New York. "Missed my footing in the dark."

"Some women," Burr said gently, "should be left to the foolish young bucks. Clark, we need some brandy here." He and Livingston began chafing Michael's wrists.

Michael pulled loose irritably. "I'm all right," he said sharply. He took the glass Clark offered, drank, and sat back. "What have you decided so far?"

"A year from next January," Burr said, a worried eye on him. "Everything is to be in New Orleans and ready to go then."

Michael nodded. "Eighteen months. We'll need that. But we may need to change our plans. That, ah, lady was sent by William Claiborne to pump me. She claims he's out to stop us."

"In God's name, why?" Clark exclaimed. "If he hated Mr.

Burr—I beg your pardon, sir, but it's no secret that's where most of our opposition arises—if he did, it might make sense, but I know of no reason for it otherwise."

"He's ambitious," Livingston said. "He sees himself as a senator. Perhaps even President. If he could make splash enough out of stopping us—"

Burr interrupted. "What if he charged that we aimed, not at Mexico, but at the United States? A massive insurrection! Defeating that would put his name on everyone's lips!"

Into the horrified silence, Michael spoke, "What made you think of that?"

"Some of the Association—Hawkins, Sauvinet, others—have been whispering that maybe we shouldn't be satisfied with Mexico, that New Orleans should naturally go along with Mexico, and maybe even a large part of Louisiana. If those fools have been doing their talking where Claiborne could hear . . . ." He clasped his hands behind his back and bounced up and down on his toes, scowling into space.

"If they have," Livingston said, "we're done."

"Yes," Burr said. "Those whispers must be quieted. You know who to talk to, Ned. And now, I think we had better call this meeting to a close. The hour is late."

"A moment," Michael said. "Mr. Clark, I'd like your evaluation of General Wilkinson. Is he to be trusted?" Burr's eyes narrowed; inwardly Michael shrugged. He had to know, and there was no time for subtlety.

Clark looked at him curiously. "I trust him implicitly, Mr. Fallon. In fact, I propose asking him how to counter Claiborne."

Michael nodded. God, he felt weak. He had no strength to argue. He struggled to his feet and let Lopes help him to his room.

Catherine touched the bodice of her lavender muslin. It was just the right compromise, she thought, between seeming wifely and seductive. Everything was perfect. First, she would rouse Karl's desire—an easy task considering the number of times she had denied him her bed of late. Then, all wifely eagerness to help, she would let him know how many thousands of dollars she had cost him. She fanned herself against the early August heat. Everything was ready. If only he would come.

She took another look out of the drawing-room window. This far down East Bay, there was a good view of the brilliant blue harbor, but she was intent on the street. For over an hour she had waited there, watching the carriages pass. Now, at last, one swung into the drive, and Karl stepped down, a short, round man after him. She checked her dress again, patted her hair, and fixed a smile on her face as she hurried out into the hall.

At the head of the stairs she stopped, put one hand on the rail, and posed to await his entrance. Below, Ezekiel, the butler, opened the door.

"I do not understand," Karl was saying over his shoulder as he strode in. "My wife does not take any hand in business."

"That's as might be, sir," said the rolypoly man trotting after him. "But she come into my place and signed to deliver the entire crop from Seven Pines and Riding Green, a guarantee of twelve thousand bales, at eight and a half cents."

"Mr. Hudson, that is four cents a pound under the market at this moment, and the price rises by the day." Karl stopped, looking sharply at Hudson. "Come into my study. We must talk."

Catherine bit her lip in vexation as the men disappeared into Karl's study. This wasn't the way she had planned for Karl to find out. She scurried down the stairs and, with a quick look for the servants, pressed her ear against the door to the study.

"You say, Mr. Hudson," came Karl's muffled voice, "that my wife signed this agreement. Are you certain it was my wife?"

"Yes, sir. I am that. Mrs. Holtz is well known in the city, sir, if you'll pardon my saying it."

"Of course, of course. I simply cannot believe that she could do this. Why, with the drought, I do not believe I will even make twelve thousand bales. Perhaps as little as half that."

"Maybe so, sir. But I got a guarantee of twelve thousand."

Catherine frowned. Karl seemed entirely too bewildered. She swung open the door and stepped in. Karl and the cotton factor were standing by the windows.

"Good afternoon," she said with a smile. "Why, Mr. Hudson, how nice to see you again."

Hudson bowed to her, giving Karl a triumphant look. Karl shook his head.

"Catherine," he said. "Catherine, you have actually signed this paper? Twelve thousand bales at eight and a half cents a pound?"

"Why, yes," she said with her sweetest smile. "I thought I should help you. Isn't that what a wife is for?"

"Help me?" Karl sounded strangled. "Not only will I make no profit on this crop, but to deliver the guarantee I must buy cotton at half again what I will sell it for. I will lose thousands of dollars."

"That's awful," she said. "Next year you'll have to raise your prices to make up for it."

"Mr. Hudson," Karl said, "I will talk to my wife alone." Suddenly he seemed very calm.

"I'll come back later, then, Mr. Holtz," Hudson said.

Karl shook his head. "Remain, please. We will go upstairs for a moment."

He clamped an iron grip on Catherine's wrist and pulled her out of the room after him. "Karl, stop this. Karl, let go of me! You're hurting my wrist."

He didn't answer, drawing her up the stairs and into their bedchamber, slamming the door behind them. He released her, then, and she stood rubbing her wrist.

"You should remember you're supposed to be a gentleman, Karl. Not just a German miller."

"Why, Catherine? You still have not told me why."

"I told you, Karl. I was just trying—"

"*Gott Verdamnt!* Do not play the games with me." He began pacing back and forth, all the while glaring at her. "You are not the simple fool of a woman you are suddenly pretending to be. What you did, you did deliberately. I want to know why."

His anger fueled her own, and swept away her caution. "Not the simple woman? But I must be, Karl. You give me no say in running Seven Pines or Riding Green. Oh, yes, I can run the house, order the house servants. But you won't listen to me about the planting, or the lazy field hands, or anything to do with the real work of the plantation.''

"I listen to you," he said slowly, "but your ideas will produce less work, not— *Gott in Himmel!* Do you mean that you have done this because I would not let you work the slaves until they drop? For revenge?''

She turned to the mirror, patting the tight curls of her hair. "I don't know what you're talking about," she said brightly. "I'm just a simple woman.''

She shrieked as he suddenly grabbed her wrist and jerked her across the room. He dropped into a chair, still pulling her, and then, unbelieving, she realized she was across his knees.

"What are you doing?" she gasped.

Her skirts and petticoats tumbled over her back and around her head.

"Since you act like a little child," he growled. His hand exploded against her bottom.

She screamed in shock. "Stop! Stop this instant." She looked around wildly, and found the strange tableau in a mirror. Herself looking out from a welter of petticoat lace, her pale buttocks elevated by his knee, his hand raised high. "No," she shrieked, then howled again as his hand landed.

Wildly she struggled, long legs kicking in all directions, trying to claw through his trousers. She writhed and twisted, but all to no avail. His hand rose and fell inexorably.

Tears of rage and frustration rolled down her face, and the fact that she was weeping made her cry all the harder. She might as well have been the child he called her, for all the good her struggles did.

Suddenly he rolled her off his knee. She hit the floor with a thump, arched up with a cry, and rolled onto her face. Sobs of fury wracked her as she gingerly felt her no-longer-pale bottom.

"I am sorry," Karl said suddenly. "But you have provoked me severely. You should not have done what you did. I am sorry, though.''

The door closed. She looked around; he was gone. She struggled to her feet and hurried after him. On the broad landing above the entry hall she stopped in confusion. Ezekiel, Mary, all the house servants, were gathered down there, staring up at her. Karl was halfway down the stairs, and

Hudson stood in front of the study door, hat in hand. The loathsome little man had a broad grin on his face.

"I am sorry I took so long," Karl said. "Our discussion grew . . . heated."

Hudson's grin widened. "Yes. I heard." Catherine felt the scarlet flood her face and breasts.

"You may return to your tasks," Karl told the servants. "Go on." They scattered busily, Mary turned a last worried look at Catherine before she went. "Mr. Hudson," he went on, "I will honor the conditions my wife agreed to."

"Well," Hudson said, "as to that, sir, I can see you have a little domestic problem. Though I'm sure it's well in hand now." His grin flickered in Catherine's direction. She turned away, her color deepening. "I don't see any reason why we shouldn't negotiate a new deal. One without any women poking in."

As Karl showed Hudson out, Catherine stood stunned. After all her planning and work, after being spanked almost publicly, it was all going to go for nothing. The men were going to stick together against a common enemy. Her.

She glared at Karl as he started back up the steps. "I hate you," she breathed. "I hate all of you. I wish you were dead." With as much dignity as she could muster she marched back into her room, slammed the door behind her, and collapsed crying onto the bed.

Michael started up the broad marble steps of Karl's house, leaning heavily on his walking stick. Since the spell in New Orleans, the stick had become a necessity, especially on stairs. "Ah, Mr. Hudson. Calling at home to buy cotton now?"

"Good afternoon, Mr. Fallon," Hudson said. "In a way, sir. In a way." He glanced over his shoulder at the large, white-columned house. "If you'll excuse me, Mr. Fallon, I must be on my way. Business. Yes, business." As he hurried off down the street, Michael went on up the steps and grasped the heavy brass knocker.

Karl was in the study, staring into a large brandy.

Michael went to the sideboard and poured one for himself. "I met Hudson on the steps," he said.

Karl nodded vaguely. "Does a marriage ever settle down, sir?"

Michael sighed. "Some never do. I was married for over twenty years, and to the day she died Gabrielle and I had disagreements. It's a thing you must live with."

Karl gulped his brandy, then let out a long breath. "You wished to see me about something in particular, sir?"

"Yes. I want to use your lighter, the *Santee,* to load the first shipment of guns at the Bridge. The *Carolina Queen* can't cross the bar till tomorrow to load, so I thought I'd use the *Santee* to carry them out."

"Why is there such a hurry?" Karl asked. "You told me there was no action planned for over a year."

"We can't be waiting till the last minute. Ten thousand stands of muskets can't be shipped in a day. Besides, this first shipment is a symbol, man. It means we're actually under way."

Karl nodded. "*Ja,* I understand. Use the *Santee* by all means. You know, it is funny. When you first brought me into this, shipping guns to Spanish American revolutionaries, I never dreamed that we might actually become part of a revolution ourselves."

"A man's not complete till he's taken part in a revolution. Look you, why don't you come out with me? We'll see the guns safe aboard the *Carolina Queen* ourselves. There's nothing clears the head like time on the water."

"*Ja. Ja,* I need that."

It was coming on dusk when the *Santee,* forty feet long and with a single, fore-and-aft rig, stood away from Carver's Bridge. Decks piled high with crated muskets, hold crammed full, she sat low in the gray-green water, and a brisk wind sent a constant spray along her deck. A single lookout at the masthead made certain they didn't run down any late-returning shrimper.

At the stern Michael and Karl clung to the rail as the sloop breasted the chop, watching the city sink into gray mist.

Finally Michael spoke. "These troubles of yours, lad. Do you think they're serious?"

"It is possible." He hesitated. "She made me very angry. I gave her *eine Prugelstrafe.*"

"A what?"

Karl gestured vividly. "I used only my hand." Michael

looked away to hide his amusement. Karl continued. "You must pardon me, but she made me very angry. I do not know if she will ever forgive me."

"Women generally do. She'll likely make you pay for it, but she'll forgive you."

"You truly think so?"

"Certainly. But perhaps you'd better go away for a while."

"Go away?"

"That's right," Michael said. "She'll soon stop thinking about having her bottom smacked and start thinking about you not being there. You'll still pay for it in the long run, but it'll lower the price. Go out to New Orleans, see to storing the guns."

"*Ja*," Karl said slowly. "To leave quickly would be good. I do not relish facing her—"

"Snag!" the lookout screamed. "Snag dead ahead!"

Suddenly the sloop staggered, then ran on, heeling slightly.

"*Mein Gott!*" Karl said. "What happened?"

Crewmen ran to the side, while one stuck his head up from below. "She's taking water fast!" he yelled.

"We hit something floating just under the surface," Michael said. "Damn! It must have been a whole cypress tree. Cut the ropes on the deck cargo!" he shouted. "Get it over the side before it pulls us over."

A man struggled across the slanted deck to the piled crates, opening his clasp knife as he went. He reached to cut the first rope.

"Not there!" Michael yelled. "From above! Above!"

It was too late. The man's knife slashed the rope. A two-hundred pound crate slid off the pile, slammmed into him, and carried him over the side. The stacked crates shifted, and slid after him. Then the sloop was heeling over more rapidly, and the starboard rail was touching the water. From the hold came the crash of crated muskets breaking free.

"Jump for it!" Michael shouted, and went into the water in a flat dive. It was cool; he surfaced, and swam directly away as fast as he could. When he stopped and looked back, he gasped.

The *Santee* was gone.

A few heads bobbed in the water—far too few, Michael saw.

There wasn't as much as a hatch cover to cling to. And full darkness was almost there, he realized. The sinking might not even have been seen from shore. There'd be no boats putting out.

He swam back to the others. There was Karl; the Saxon seemed barely conscious. Blood streamed down his face.

Michael cursed. He'd seen twelve-foot sharks taken in that harbor. "Karl! Karl, can you swim?"

"Head," Karl said groggily. "Something—hit head." His eyes didn't seem to focus.

"All right, lad. It's all right." As well as he could tell in the fading light, the current was going to carry them out to sea. With luck, they might make a landing on the tip of Sullivan's Island, just at the harbor mouth. "Swim for it, lads!" he shouted, pointing to the island. "Swim!"

The rest nodded and splashed off. Michael locked a hand in Karl's collar and began to follow. The Saxon tried to help, but his splashes were feeble.

Michael thought of the first time he had swum the harbor. He'd been barely thirty, then, escaping H.M.S. *Tamar*. The Royal Governor had been aboard, impatient to resume governing the colony. Michael laughed to himself. Sir William hadn't realized a revolution was upon him. There were so many memories tied up in that harbor, that city. Himself arriving at twenty-four, with a few pounds in the bottom of his bag, and Christopher Byrne scrambling over the rail. "Which one of you is Michael Fallon?" Christopher again, years later, dying in the fight with the British frigate *Apollyon* off the coast of France. Elizabeth Carver, with her lavender lynx-eyes in an angel's face. "I'm not a child, Michael. I'm a woman." Till she danced away to marry Justin Fourrier. Fourrier, with his sword in hand. "You Irish bastard!" Gabrielle Fourrier, smiling at him. "Yes, I'll marry you, Michael." Thomas Carver, sitting in his dark study on the edge of a pool of light. "A tidal wave is coming, and we shall all be swept away."

Pain stabbed up his left arm into his chest. He grunted, missed his stroke, then regained it with an effort. The pain was still there, dull now. He lifted his head for a look around and was startled to see the pool of light that he thought had been just in his mind. All else was dark, save one patch of golden light ahead. And Gabrielle was standing there, looking as she had the first time he saw her, when she was only sixteen, looking so much like Catherine. She held out a hand toward him.

He shook his head. "No, Brielle," he whispered. "Not yet. Got to get him back to Catherine." The pain was building again. Desperately he put his head down and swam into the darkness.

"Miss Catherine?"

Catherine rolled over in bed and blinked at the ceiling. Karl wasn't beside her, she realized, furious memory sweeping over her. Good! She'd keep him out of her bed for a long time—a very long time. "What time is it, Mary?"

"Six o'clock, ma'am. Some gentlemen be in the drawing room to see you."

"Six! Good Lord, Mary!"

"Ma'am, they say it most urgent." The abigail began rocking back and forth anxiously. "It about Mr. Holtz, Miss Catherine."

"Karl? At this hour?" She sat up slowly and looked at the black woman. "He's dead, isn't he? That's the only reason they'd come like this."

"Yes, ma'am." Mary gulped back tears. "I wasn't supposed to let you know, ma'am. I'm powerful sorry."

Catherine swallowed her sudden smile; she was free at last. "Oh, hush up, Mary. Now help me dress. The black silk. Hurry, girl. These gentlemen have come to tell me I'm a widow. It would be impolite to keep them waiting."

In the drawing room Langdon Cheves, Louis Middleton, and young John Calhoun were arrayed in front of the fireplace like a row of owls.

"Mrs. Holtz," Cheves began awkwardly, then stopped. "It seems you've already heard. I'm sorry."

Catherine let her eyes close and reached out to a chair back as if for support. "Yes. Mary couldn't help but tell me."

"They were found on Sullivan's Island," Louis said. "Their, I mean they will be brought back by boat. Be here in no time. I mean . . . . " He let his words trail off uneasily.

"A terrible loss, ma'am," Calhoun said. He was a lanky,

angular man. "Please accept my deepest condolences."

"Thank you, Mr. Calhoun." She managed a wan smile. "How did it happen, Mr. Cheves?"

"Mr. Petrie said they were lightering something to a ship beyond the bar. They must have sunk, somehow. Ma'am, are you sure you want to hear all this?"

She lifted her head in what she thought was a pretty picture of womanly bravery. "Of course, Mr. Cheves." She touched dry eyes with her handkerchief. "I must know."

"Yes," Cheves said uncertainly. "They were washed ashore on Sullivan's Island. Mr. Holtz had a deep gash in his head, as if he had been struck when the ship sank. It must have been peaceful for him, like going in his sleep. Your father had his hand locked on your husband's collar."

Her mouth silently formed the word, father, and the chair she was gripping suddenly became a very necessary support.

"It looked as if he was trying to save your husband," Cheves went on. "We couldn't get his hand loose. I knew your father, Mrs. Holtz. I would guess he had no intention of reaching shore without your husband."

"Exactly, ma'am," Calhoun said. "Your father was of a hardier breed than we modern men. There is some comfort in the fact that he died as he could have wished, fighting for the good."

She looked from man to man vaguely. Their faces seemed distorted, their mouths moved too slowly. But every word was like a blow. Her legs were rubbery; she managed to sit on the chair. "DeSaussure," she said weakly. "I need Thomas DeSaussure."

"DeSaussure!" Louis said. "Old Tom?"

"Her father's lawyer," Cheves said shortly. "And her husband's."

Louis nodded suddenly. "Oh. Of course. I see. Is there anything else, Mrs. Holtz? Can we do anything else?"

"I need Thomas DeSaussure," she repeated tightly.

She would say nothing else. After a while the men left. Mary came, and was sent away with a shake of the head. Catherine sat, staring at the wall, concentrating on not allowing herself to think. Ezekiel appeared in the door.

"Ma'am? Ma'am, it's Mr. DeSaussure."

"What? Show him in."

DeSaussure was a wizened, bent little man with a big nose, clutching his leather paper-case in both arms. "My deepest condolences, Mrs. Holtz." His voice was high pitched and rusty. "May I offer, both on behalf of myself and my—"

"The will," Catherine said. She still hadn't looked at him. "You must know about Karl's . . . about Karl's will."

"I drew it up," he said simply. "Both your husband's and your father's."

Catherine flinched, then regained control. "My husband's will. What are the bequests? And the conditions?"

"Your husband left everything to you, Mrs. Holtz. With no conditions. You're a young woman yet. What? Twenty-four? Five? You look younger. You'll have no trouble finding another husband."

"Another husband?" she flared. "Why should I commit myself to slavery again, when I'm free at last? I can give the orders now."

"Ah, yes, ma'am." He seemed shaken; he hurriedly began to rummage in his paper-case. "Your father's will is quite different, of course. He never would credit that your brother Robert was deceased, so a considerable portion of the estate devolves upon him—Tir Alainn, Fallon & Son—but the transfer to your name will not take an unreasonable period. A good portion of land is left to you outright. Over fifteen thousand acres adjoining your husband's, pardon me, your plantation of Riding Green. And further upcountry—"

"Mr. DeSaussure," Catherine broke in. "The cotton mill is to be shut down immediately."

"But, Mrs. Holtz, the mill is very profitable. I'm sure—"

"No, Mr. DeSaussure, *I* am sure. Milling is trade, even cotton milling, and I will have nothing to do with trade."

"But at least it could be sold, Mrs. Holtz. Not just shut down."

"Whatever, Mr. DeSaussure. But I want it disposed of. Also Fallon & Son, and the Bridge, as soon as they come into my hands. And you will send riders to Seven Pines and Riding Green with this message. Beginning immediately, all field hands will work a full day on Saturday and a half day on Sunday. Dancing is forbidden, and so is any religious meeting except the Baptist meeting on Sunday morning. Do you understand that?''.

"Ah, yes, ma'am."

Catherine rose. "There will be more later," she said, and left him sitting there with his mouth open.

She went up the stairs with cold, queenly erectness, and shut the door to her bedchamber behind her. She didn't feel like one of the richest, most powerful women—no, one of the richest, most powerful people—in South Carolina, in the entire South. But so she was. A fluttering curtain caught her eye; beyond it, through the window, was the wide harbor, glittering in the new day's sun.

It was out there it had happened. Out there that Karl had died. Out there that—a wail ripped from her throat. Sobs wracked her, and she collapsed to the floor. "Papa!"

XXIX

The *Yorkshire Lass*, a British merchantman out of Gibraltar, made port in Charleston on the fifteenth of August, 1805. Her cargo of oranges and lemons was welcome, but the three men who disembarked drew curious glances.

Sun-darkened and hard, the first man down the gangplank was dressed in unrelieved black. A bearded fellow, looking like a bear in a suit, followed at his heels. And the third, head and shoulders taller than either of the other two, had a shaved head. Not at all a usual trio, even on the Bay.

"See to the bags, Miller," the man in black tossed over his shoulder. "I'm going to the Queen Street house. Bring the luggage there. Come along, Kemal."

Robert Fallon looked neither right nor left until he stood before the house he had rented for Louise. The butler who answered the door was a stranger.

"Yes, sir?" The man's mask of politeness fell away as he peered up, astonished, at Kemal.

"Where's Simon?" Robert asked. "Who are you?"

The butler managed to pull his eyes away from the huge Turk. "Sir? I be Moses, sir. I don't know no Simon."

Robert frowned. "Well, let me in and tell Miss de Chardonnay that . . . that there's a gentlemen to see her."

"I don't know the lady, sir," Moses said. He eyed Kemal again, and closed the door a little. "This be the Chamberlain residence."

"Chamberlain! Where did Louise de Chardonnay go? Let me speak to Mr. Chamberlain. Or Mrs. Chamberlain."

"Sorry, sir, but they not to home. If you'll pardon me, sir." And he firmly shut the door.

Robert glared at the closed door. Kemal gestured to himself,

306

then to the door, but Robert shook his head. "No, Kemal. My father will know where she is. I should have gone there in the first place."

But the Tradd Street house was closed. Weeds were beginning to poke through the bricks of the front walk, and through the windows Robert could see furniture covered with dust-cloths, and empty spaces where some pieces had been removed. His father must have moved. The weeds in the yard hadn't had more than a month's growth. It was possible Louise had moved, too. But a panic he never thought he'd feel again was growing in him.

He ran down to Back Street, Kemal at his heels, to Karl's house. Another strange butler answered the door. Robert took a deep breath and made an effort to regain his calm.

"Does Mr. Holtz still take this house?" he asked.

The butler looked at Robert oddly. "No, sir," he said finally.

"Where is Mr. Holtz' residence now?"

"Down to the end of East Bay, sir. Got four big white columns on the front piazza. Anybody can tell you which one it be."

People in the street could indeed point out the way to the house, often with a sudden disbelieving dawn of recognition as he hurried on. When Ezekiel opened the door, Robert felt a surge of relief. He realized he had been expecting to find a stranger there, too.

"Yes, sir?" the butler said politely.

"It's me, Ezekiel! Robert Fallon. Don't you recognize me?"

Ezekiel's face slowly went back. "Oh, my God. It *is* you. Mr. Robert, we done thought you was dead these two years and more. Come on in, sir! Come on in! Miss Catherine! Miss Catherine!" He had half turned toward the stairs, but paused, eyes widening, as Kemal followed Robert into the house.

Robert asked, "Where's my father, Ezekiel? I went by Tradd Street, and it was closed up."

Ezekiel's mouth worked. "I'll get Miss Catherine," he said, and trotted up the stairs.

Robert went on into the study; Kemal took up a position where he could observe the study door.

Robert poured a brandy and drank half of it. Then

Catherine was suddenly in the doorway.

"When Ezekiel . . . . " she said faintly. "I didn't believe . . . That, that behemoth in the entry hall is yours?"

He nodded. "Kemal. He's my friend."

"Your friend," she said blankly. "Where have you been? You dropped off the edge of the world! It's been three years!"

"I was in Tripoli."

"Tripoli!"

"That's right. I was a prisoner for two years, then . . . but never mind that now. It seems a lot of things have changed here. I went by the Queen Street house, and Louise was gone. Where is she?"

Catherine smiled. "She married Martin Caine. You remember—the overseer. They went off to Louisiana or some such place. And they took your little boy with them."

"Can't ask a woman to wait forever," he said slowly. He had expected something like that, he realized. After all, Louise was a young and vital woman. But expecting it didn't make it hurt any less. His hand shook as he raised his glass to his lips. "Where's papa? I went by the house, and it was closed up."

She turned away. "Papa's dead. Him and Karl both."

"Christ!" he breathed. He gulped the rest of the brandy and poured another glass. It tasted like water. He poured a third. "How?"

"Doing work you should have done," she spat. "They were out on the harbor, and they both drowned. Papa pushed himself after you disappeared. He was always trying to do his work and yours, too."

"Damn it, Catherine, I didn't just disappear. I was in a North African prison. So don't try to blame me for papa, or for Karl. God damn it all!" He hurled the almost empty glass into the fireplace.

"That's it. Break things. You probably think it's all yours anyway. You probably think he left everything to you."

"What are you talking about?"

"The will, dear brother. Papa's will."

"Oh, Christ!" He filled another glass, and kept the decanter in his hand. He had the feeling he'd need most of it to make it through this meeting. "He's buried up at Tir Alainn? I'll go up there tomorrow."

"That's right. Next to *my* mother. Bastard!"

He took a threatening step toward her. "Damn it, Catherine. Do you have to start with this the minute I get back? I've been gone for nearly three years, for Christ's sake. At least give me time to understand that my father's dead!"

"A North African prison—hah!" she sneered. "You knew he was dead. You just came back to see what you could scavenge. Go away again! Go away and don't come back!"

"I don't care about his will, damn you! I don't care if he left every cent to the pesthouse. Or to you."

"No? Write it out, then. There's paper and pen in the secretary. Write it out and sign it. Then go away. You're not wanted here!"

He set the decanter down and in one step had caught her chin in a powerful grip, lifting her till only the toes of her slippers touched the ground. She gripped his wrist angrily, dug her nails in like claws. He sipped the brandy and regarded her coolly.

"You sound eager, Catherine. Why is it? Why do you want me to go? Why do you want this trumpery bit of paper? Why, Catherine?"

"I suppose you'll find out sooner or later," she said. "Damn you! Papa left you Tir Alainn. And the shipping company. There! Are you satisfied?"

He set her back on her feet with a disgusted noise, and filled his glass again. "I told you. I don't care . . . . Oh, the hell with it. Well, if Tir Alainn's mine, I'll have to see to freeing its people."

"Free—are you insane, Robert? How are you going to make a rice crop with no slaves? You'll ruin yourself. Though God knows why I should care."

"You let me worry about that." He dropped into a chair. It took two tries to refill his glass. "You were provided for?"

"Why should you care?" she snorted.

"You're a bitch, Catherine." He laughed at the shock on her face. "A lovely, beautiful, delectable—bitch. Right to the core. But you're my sister. My sister, and I have to take care of you. If the factor's got liens on Karl's estate, if Papa forgot about you because your husband could take care of you, I'll settle an income on you. Get you a house."

She looked at him oddly, one hand to her throat. "You're really worried about me," she said incredulously.

"My sister," he said. "Oh, a bitch, too. Pretty bitch. Beautiful bitch. Luscious." He shook his head and emptied his glass again. "You're my sister. If they didn't look after you, I will. Settle it on you. It'll be yours. Won't have to ask for it. Not even me."

"The factors have been most kind," she said quietly. "Especially since papa left me a large parcel adjoining Riding Green. And we anticipate the sale of the cotton mill will pay off all outstanding debts."

"You're selling the mill? Why? Karl worked so hard for it."

"It's trade," she said primly.

He laughed and had some more brandy. "Then I'll buy it. I'm not afraid of trade. God, freeing the Tir Alainn people will tar me for some kind of abolitionist in most people's eyes. Why not trade?"

"You're insane," she said. "And you're drunk."

He looked up with a ready answer to find Catherine had somehow been replaced by Louise. "I knew it was a lie," he said. "I knew you wouldn't leave me."

"What are you talking about?" she said.

Catching her arm, he pulled her to him. At first she resisted, then with a sob she melted against him, her lips becoming soft under his. Abruptly she pulled away.

Struggling to his feet, he looked for Louise, but she was gone. Only Catherine was there, standing in the middle of the room drawing great gulping breaths. "Where is she?" he said. "Where's Louise?"

"She's not—" Catherine began, then stopped abruptly. Her eyes closed, and she let out one sob. "She's upstairs," she whispered. "Louise is upstairs. Let . . . let me take you to her."

He leaned on her as she led him, staggering, out of the study. Kemal got to his feet, but Robert waved him back with a laugh. The Turk watched as Catherine half-supported Robert up to the turn in the stairs.

She helped him into a bedroom, and left him standing— swaying—as she moved to close the curtains. "Where is she?" he asked.

"In a moment," she said nervously.

The room was almost dark. There was the rustle of a woman's clothing dropping to the floor, and then there was naked flesh beneath his hands.

"Louise?" he said, and there was a murmur of assent. He scooped her up and carried her to the bed. "My darling," he murmured, and she cried out as he entered her. For three years of nights he had been away from her. Now he tried to make up for all of them.

When Robert awakened his head felt like the bottom of a discarded brandy barrel. He turned it gently. Across the pillow from him was Catherine, lying in naked perfection.

"Oh, God," he murmured. "Oh, God, no." It was a dream. A nightmare born in the bottom of a bottle. It had to be.

Catherine opened her eyes and smiled at him, and he wished he had never been born. "Good morning," she said brightly. "Did you sleep well?" Her stretch was that of a totally satisfied woman. He wondered if he were going insane.

"Good morning? My God, Catherine. Do you realize that . . . do you know . . . oh, my God." He buried his head in his hands.

She stroked his back, and he flinched. "Yes, I know what happened. A man and a woman made love."

"For the love of God, Catherine!"

"No one was killed. No one was robbed. No one was even hurt. All that happened was a man and a woman made love."

"Incest, Catherine. Does that word sound familiar to you? Sweet God have mercy. We're brother and sister! Doesn't that mean anything to you?"

"All I know is I want you. For years I thought I hated you; it was because I wanted you and thought I couldn't have you."

"That's right. You can't have me. For the love of God, Catherine, isn't there any decency in you? It doesn't matter. I'm going away. I'll leave Charleston." He began to get out of bed, but she grabbed him.

She pressed herself against him, and he flinched at the feel of her silken naked breasts. And even more at the pleasure he derived from the feeling.

"I *have* had you, Robert. And I intend to have you again. I intend to have you for a long time. If you leave me, I . . . I'll say you raped me. Damn you, you want me, too. I know it."

"No." She began to rain kisses around his mouth.

"You *do* want me," she whispered along his cheek. "You said I was beautiful. Desirable. I *know* you want me."

"God help me," he whispered, and fell on her.

XXX

June of 1806 was a sweltering month in Jamaica. The heat in Justin Fourrier's study was unrelieved by the large wooden-bladed fan revolving on the ceiling. The blonde girl in the center of the room sweated from more than the heat, though. She was naked, sweat dripping down her pale curves, and she balanced desperately on a plank laid across a triangular block of wood. Every time she let one end of the plank touch the Oriental carpet, she received a stroke of the cane. There were four red welts across her plump buttocks already. She had given up covering herself with her hands after the second. Balance was more important.

Fourrier watched her through thinned eyes, flexing a length of rattan in his hands. His gaunt face was expressionless.

"How much longer?" the girl gasped suddenly.

A slight smile flickered on his lips as she bobbled on the plank and caught herself with a shriek. "Until I say, my dear," he said in a fatherly tone, and smiled again at the look of pure terror she gave him.

There was a knock at the door. The girl looked around with a gasp, and one end of the plank thumped to the carpet. Fourrier gave a satisfied smile. "And that's one more, my dear."

"But the door," she protested. "It's not fair!"

"Come," he called, and she scuttled to the corner with a squeal, covering herself as best she could with her hands.

A nondescript man appeared in the doorway, hesitating at the sight of the girl.

"Well, Carde," Fourrier said. "Do you have a reason to bother me, or did you just want to look at the girl?" From the corner she made a small noise.

Carde cleared his throat and came to Fourrier, his eye straying to the girl. "I have the latest reports, sir." He produced a sheaf of papers. In a lower voice, he added, "Sir, that girl. She . . . she looks remarkably like Melissa Somerset."

"She *is* Melissa Somerset," Fourrier said without looking up from the reports.

Carde made a strangled noise. " But, sir . . . Jonathan Somerset . . . I mean . . . sir."

Fourrier chuckled thinly and glanced at the huddling girl. "Jonathan Somerset has had terrible business reverses lately. He's almost bankrupt. And his darling daughter heard him say I'm out to ruin him. She came to me, to plead for him. Said she'd do anything to save him." His face twisted with mirth. "She didn't quite realize I'd take her at her word. Of course, she thinks our little game is the end of it. Once she's properly broken, though . . . . "

"But, sir, Somerset isn't without friends. Do you think it's safe—"

"Somerset will be a pauper by the end of the month, and paupers have no friends." He returned to the papers. "What's this item? The Americans are going to outlaw slave importation again?"

"Yes, sir. It seems certain."

"No matter. There's more profit from smuggled slaves anyway."

Carde cleared his throat discreetly. "I'm afraid there's worse, sir. The Wainwright letter. About four pages on."

Fourrier ruffled quickly to the letter from Jeremy Wainwright, a senior clerk in the Foreign Office, and his best source of information on the inner workings of the British government. He scanned it, and the pertinent lines seemed to leap out at him.

It is therefore, sir, certain beyond any question or doubt that the slavery question will be decided once and for all in this term of Parliament. The least that is expected is the prohibition of slavery in Jamaica or any vessel flying the British flag. Actual cessation of trade with nations still allowing slavery is not, however, contemplated.

"Not contemplated," Fourrier growled. "Not contemplated!" He suddenly slashed a vase to the floor with the rattan. Both Carde and the girl jumped. "Where are Montfort and Ross? Where are Baxford and Manton? What in hell is the good of owning Members of Parliament if they let the bastards cut my throat?"

"There's a good deal of sentiment in England, sir."

Fourrier jerked the cane up, and Carde took a step back. "Sentiment?" Fourrier hissed. "Sentiment! A lot of damned mill owners in the north of England are afraid someone will start mills here in Jamaica, with slave labor. Even the starvation wages they pay would be undercut. That's the source of all this sudden hue and cry against slavery in Jamaica."

"Yes, sir," Carde said simply.

"Mill owners and a damned lot of namby-pamby lords. That's a fine mix for you. Those noble asses would turn up their noses at being in the same room with someone who owns a mill, but they'll side with them because slavery isn't clean. It isn't refined enough for them." He spat on the rug. "They can watch a beggar starve to death without turning a hair, or see him hang for stealing a potato, but slavery's not clean enough for them."

"No, sir," Carde said. His eyes rolled as Fourrier hurled the papers at his desk. Some scattered across the desk top; the rest fell to the floor.

"Is there anything else?" Justin asked. "Well?"

"No, sir. Unless . . . well . . . your agent W, sir."

"Wilkinson?" Fourrier growled. "What about him?"

"He seems to be involved in something, sir. Possibly some sort of expedition against Spanish America. It's not really certain."

"Not certain," Justin sighed. "No matter. Wilkinson could use being taken down a peg. He's still taking money from the Spanish, too, isn't he? Arrange to inform the Spanish military commander in Mexico that—let me see. I want Wilkinson scared a bit, not killed out of hand." He smiled suddenly. "Tell them he is being asked to lead an American invasion of Mexico. Wilkinson will be made to sweat. And there will be some sort of trouble for the Americans as a result. God, it's almost amusing enough to make me forget the other. Enough of this. I'll talk to you later, Carde. Get out." He held up the rattan to examine it minutely. "And now, Melissa . . . ."

XXXI

As Christmas approached in 1806, Americans were still agog at Meriwether Lewis and William Clark. They had returned in September from their expedition to the western lands. The strange tribes they had seen, the severe trials they had undergone, were the topic in every Charleston drawing room. In other Charleston rooms, the talk was often different.

Jeremiah stopped in the street outside Vesey's carpenter shop and took another look at his brother Billy. Four years younger than his own twenty, Billy already had most of his man's growth. He was six feet tall and handsome, and his shoulders were filling out, but his swagger disturbed Jeremiah, as did his taste for showing off and taking dares. Jeremiah wished Billy were not with him; he would never have let Billy near one of Vesey's meetings if Danmark hadn't insisted.

"All right, Billy," he said now, hunching his shoulders against the cold. "You keep your mouth shut. And don't repeat a word of what you hear. Not a word."

Billy pursed his lips scornfully. "What are you talking about? You acts like this some kind of big secret. Everybody know Vesey always talking against slavery." He snorted. "Like he going to do something about it."

"Not everybody knows. And if too many people find out, if the whites find out, there could be bad trouble."

"White folks don't never find out nothing. Look. You don't want me here, I go on some place else. I got friends waiting. Won me two dollars yesterday."

"Damn it, Billy, I told you . . . " Jeremiah got a grip on his anger. He'd gambled a little when he was Billy's age, too. He'd grow out of it, settle down. "Come on inside."

In the shop, there was a fire in the crude fireplace, and three men warming their hands stiffened and looked around at the door opening. "Oh, it's you," Vesey said. "Come on in. And close the door behind you."

"People traipsing in," grumbled Ned Bennett, "we ought to be some place where can't anybody just walk in." He was a valet to Thomas Bennett, Jeremiah knew, and terrified that his master would discover his association with Vesey.

Peter Poyas, the third man, made room on his bench. "Sit yourself down, Jeremiah. Get up to the fire and get warm. This the boy?"

"My brother Billy," Jeremiah said. Each man nodded and shook Billy's hand.

Bennett eyed the boy up and down, and chuckled. "You do grow to height, you Carpenters. That what you call yourself, ain't it? Carpenter? Like your brother?"

"I guess," Billy said slowly. "Yes. Billy Carpenter. That's it."

"You have any more brothers, Jeremiah?" Vesey asked.

Jeremiah shook his head. "No. There's just me, Billy, and my sister Esther."

"Esther!" Bennett cackled. "Well, bring her in. Bring her in."

"Ned," Poyas said warningly, but Bennett didn't seem to notice.

"Denmark, he like to recruit some females. Specially one with big, round—"

"Damn it, Ned!" Jeremiah broke in, but Billy jumped for Bennett, screaming, "That my sister! You talking about my sister, old man! I'll cut your throat seven ways from Sunday!"

From somewhere Billy produced a knife. Poyas and Vesey grabbed him as Bennett rolled over the back of his stool.

Jeremiah snatched the knife out of his brother's hand. "What are you doing with this?" he shouted. "You going to stab one of those fine gambling friends of yours? Get yourself hung?"

"I ain't got no fine furniture shop," Billy said sullenly. "Maybe if my brother as gots one gave me a dollar now and then I wouldn't have to gamble with them folks he don't like so much."

Jeremiah made a noise as if he wanted to spit. "I've given

you money, Billy. And seen it spent on rum, gambling, and whores. If papa knew the way you carry on, he'd have you up at Tir Alainn slopping hogs."

Vesey experimentally let go of Billy's arm. The boy shrugged and jerked his other arm free from Poyas, but he made no other move.

"Why don't you learn a trade, Billy?" Vesey said. "I can use an apprentice here."

"That what Jeremiah want," Billy said peevishly. "Always after me to work in his shop. I can make ten times as much ten times as easy with dice or cards."

Bennett, who had been huddling against the wall, suddenly piped up. "He don't need no trade. What that boy needs is a strap! Pulling knives on decent folk. Where do he think he is?"

Jeremiah rounded on him angrily. "Why don't you keep your mouth shut, Ned? I swear, I don't know which is worse! Denmark chasing every woman he sees, or you talking about every woman you see."

Bennett opened his mouth, but Vesey stepped in smoothly. "Easy, now. Easy. Ned, you *do* talk a good bit. And it surely wasn't right, talking about somebody's sister that way. And you, Jeremiah. There's no call for you to be so sanctified. You're not telling me you've never stepped out on Sarah. I know she's a fine wife, but a man needs a little change. Right?"

Jeremiah sighed. "Denmark, I thought we were going to talk about the curfew, and about permits to travel. I have plenty of work back at the shop."

"The shop," Billy sneered. "That's right. You go on back to the shop, and leave these old men to say how they going to stop the curfew." He laughed. "Shit."

"Why don't you go on to your gambling friends?" Jeremiah said sharply. "You're not interested in this. Go drink and gamble, and pull wool and scratch gravel the rest of your life."

"Fine one to talk," Billy snapped back. "Spend all your time building furniture for that Fallon. You can talk all this abolish talk you want to, but you just a Fallon nigger!"

"Is this true?" Vesey asked. "Are you spending time with

this white man?"

"He's different," Jeremiah said. "You know he's freeing all the slaves he inherited from his father. And the rest of the whites aren't too happy with what he's doing. He's had to fight to get the magistrate and three witnesses he needs for each manumission."

"Has he spoken out against slavery?" Vesey said. His words began softly, but rose in power as he went on. "Has he used any of the wealth accumulated by the sweat of slaves to buy slaves and free them? And the people he's *given* freedom—something that should have been theirs by right—how much gratitude does he demand? Has he given them the plantation their labor built, the plantation they earned with their blood?"

"He isn't throwing them out," Jeremiah said stubbornly.

"Then what is he giving them? What? Tell me!"

"Fifty acres of land for every man, woman, and child. One hundred dollars cash to every family. New clothes and household goods. A mule, a wagon, a plow. Tools of a trade, if they've got one."

"So generous," Vesey sneered. "All the wealth that was flogged out of black hides, and he gives them fifty acres and a mule. He's white, Jeremiah. White! That's all you need to know. He's white, and he's just like any other white. He's going to gouge the black man for everything he can."

"Old man," Billy said suddenly. "I likes the way you talk."

"Boy," Vesey replied, "you call me 'old man' again, and I'll nut you like a pig. Now. This new city ordinance. It's going to hamper us some, getting word to the people out on the plantations, but this is what I plan."

Jeremiah took a seat, scarcely listening to Vesey. He kept watching Billy's face, and the hero worship that was suddenly there. It disturbed him. And he wondered why.

Robert slid out of bed, and Catherine stirred in her sleep. The noonday sun peeked through the curtains and laid bright bars across the rug. She resumed the deep breathing of sleep, and he gave a sigh of relief. He dresed briskly and hurried down to the study. Karl's study it had been, and he still thought of it that way, even though Catherine insisted on calling it his. She had had his things brought there, and all of their father's papers and journals. Karl's papers had disappeared. But it was still Karl's study to Robert.

For the thousandth time he wished that he had taken rooms instead of moving into the East Bay house. Catherine always seemed to appear when he was busiest, leaning against him, filling his nostrils with her scent, nibbling at his neck, driving him mad, half with desire and half with fear that someone would walk in. Her visits always ended upstairs, in her bed. For some reason he'd kept them from his. But her bed was always there, sometimes three and four times in a day, cutting into the work he was trying to do, putting him further behind, filling him with a rage that he tried to extinguish by throwing himself even harder into his work. At least he had managed to avoid the bottle so far. But he was beginning to think about it. He definitely needed rooms apart. But then, if he could control himself enough to take rooms, he could control himself enough to break free of her, and that was something he was beginning to fear he would never do.

He had just settled in at the desk when Ezekiel appeared. "Sir, Mr. Louis Middleton is here. And Mr. Calhoun."

Robert tossed his pen on the desk. Not much work was going to get done that day, he could see. "Show them in, Ezekiel."

Louis burst in with a laugh. "Not business again, Robert. I'll say it straight. You may have come back from the dead, but there are more than a few in the city who don't know it yet, the way you stay cooped up here. Or at the Bridge. Or the mill."

"Hello, Louis," Robert said. "Hello, John. Whiskey, brandy, or wine?"

John Calhoun, who had hung back near the door, grinned. "Brandy, sir. It's colder than a Yankee merchant's heart out there."

"Whiskey," Louis said. "Dreadful stuff. I've acquired a taste for it."

Robert rose to do the office. "If this is another try at pulling me away from my work, you can forget it. I'm a month behind, and I'm waiting for a new ship to be delivered. It's a variation on the Baltimore clipper design, but larger. A hundred and thirty feet long, with three masts. Where's

Langdon? He's usually along when you try to lure me to low pursuits."

"In Columbia, Mr. Fallon," Calhoun said. "Legislature business. He rode up this morning with the latest word from Europe. Napoleon has declared a blockade of Britain, and closed Continental ports to British ships, or ships that trade with Britain."

"Damn!" Robert muttered. "That's all I need."

"You believe his blockade will be effective, then, sir?" Calhoun asked.

"No. The French Navy couldn't blockade its own home-ports. But the British will likely retaliate, just the same. There's enough trouble trading with Europe now, without this."

"I suppose we are at the mercy of the European powers," Calhoun said.

"We don't have to be," Robert snapped. "If we had a few men with gumption in Washington City, we could stop being Europe's bootscraper."

Calhoun nodded slowly. "No one likes having to take turns being kicked by the French and the British. But what can we do about it?"

"First, build fifty more frigates like the *Constitution*. Then use them to make certain our shipping is left alone by the big powers. Oh, I know we can't match them ship for ship, but we have to be strong enough to gain their respect. At present they ignore us even when they're stepping on us. We have to be belligerent to get their attention. We must resent every insult."

"Resent every insult," Calhoun said. "Yes, sir. I like that."

Louis, who had been drinking quietly, suddenly laughed. "He's filing it away, Robert. It'll end up in a speech. You watch. He means to run for office, you know."

"I do," Calhoun said. "Once I've entered the bar, I hope to run for the State Legislature."

"I've no doubt you'll do a fine job," Robert said. "Now if the two of you will excuse me, I have a job to do."

"Work," Louis snorted. "You're always working. The mill, or ships, or the warehouse. I tell you, it's no thing for a gentleman, Robert. Give it up. Stop freeing your slaves before you ruin yourself, and go back to being a planter. That's what you were meant for, not all this trade."

Robert sighed. "We've been over this a hundred times, Louis. I don't want to own slaves. If that shocks or offends you, it's too bad."

"Doesn't offend *me*," Louis said quickly. "Doesn't offend me at all. I can't say the same for some others, though. If you want to know the truth of it, you're making a lot of people uncomfortable."

"Uncomfortable!"

"That's right. There are others who worry about the rightness of owning slaves, you know. But they aren't prepared to bankrupt themselves to get rid of them. It makes people damned uncomfortable to see you doing just that. Some of them are more than uncomfortable. Some of them are angry."

"Christ!" Robert muttered. "I'm not bankrupting myself. I'm just getting rid of my slaves. And I'll keep on till they're all free, no matter how often the magistrates try to hide or how many men refuse to stand as witness. To hell with them. To hell with all of them!"

"Come, Robert. Don't tell me it isn't costing you a packet. I know for a fact you've given some of the larger families as much as four hundred acres."

"Mr. Fallon," Calhoun said, "how is the south to survive without ctton, and rice, and tobaco? And how can they be grown without slaves?"

"I don't know," Robert said. "I don't know, but there has to be something better. There's shipping. And I've plans to open a foundry up the Neck. We could try manufacturing."

"I've seen New England mill towns, sir, while I was a student at New Haven. The workers are little better off than slaves, and their health is generally worse."

"You see?" Louis said. "Now, why don't you give it up? You know, your father had some strange ideas. He probably gave his slaves less work and easier treatment than any planter I know of. But even he didn't try to free them all."

Robert smiled sadly. "I found one of his old journals, Louis, and that's exactly what he wanted to do."

"What?"

"Yes. When he bought them, he intended to free his slaves

after seven years' service. But the Revolution came. And debts. And children. He was afraid he'd give away his children's birthright if he did it. Well, the mill and Fallon & Son will be enough legacy for my children.''

"Oh, enough of this drivel," Louis said. "Robert, are you coming with us or not?"

"I'm afraid not, Louis."

Middleton gathered himself up. "All right, then. Come along, John. The cards are waiting." He paused at the door. "Look, Robert, don't let all this work drown you. If you can make it to the Carolina Coffee House tonight, there'll be a place at the table for you."

Robert threw himself into the work piled in front of him. Reports from Lopes in New Orleans and Tom Jarvis, who ran the London office. Price quotations on rice and cotton. There was competition from Egypt on one and China on the other. Costs on the foundry were running higher than expected. The men building it had never seen one before, and the builder, a Scot named McGregor, said he was beginning to doubt they'd see this one. *Stagehound,* the new ship, was three days late arriving from the Chesapeake. Likely the weather had been against her, but he worried all the same.

There were a hundred items, worrisome at best and potentially disastrous at worst, and all had to be pulled together if anything was to be left after the Tir Alainn slaves were freed.

Robert found himself staring at his father's papers, at the leather-bound journals and the packets of letters, the bills and orders and recordings of Michael Fallon's private life. Robert had tried reading them. He had begun with the first, a cheap copybook, now in the attic, that told of a young bondsman's first year in America. He had followed Michael through his rise to planter, through the Revolution, but when he reached the 1790s, the point where Michael's wife, Gabrielle, and son, James, had died, and he himself had appeared in Charleston, it had suddenly seemed too much like prying. But now he couldn't get the journals out of his mind.

With a sigh he put his pen down and reached for the packets of letters. He hesitated before untying the first bundle, then quickly ripped open the top letter.

It had come after his father's death—an invitation to a hunt. Next in the stack were notes about bloodstock, invoices from tailors and bootmakers. Then came one that seemed to make no sense.

> General W wants a written confirmation that you will come to the French city before the end of January 1807 with the needed implements in the required numbers. Please write to him, taking great care to guard your words.
>
> B.

A peculiar letter. Who was B? What French city? What implements? What required numbers? He put it aside thoughtfully.

As he worked his way to the bottom of the stack, other strange letters appeared. General J was mentioned as well as General W; from being kept out of the way, ZP seemed likely to become a national hero; because he could not go back to New York, B was having trouble raising money; the Association claimed that all was in readiness.

A letter referred to the powder Michael would supply. That seemed to indicate the implements were guns; logical enough, Robert thought, considering the numbers of guns Michael had shipped to Spanish America. But what French city? Michael had returned from New Orleans shortly before his death. Was that the clue? If so, his father had been supposed to deliver guns to New Orleans before the end of next month. He felt a momentary flash of satisfaction. But for what?

He poured a glass of brandy, then went to the window. The harbor had a chill gray look, and so did the sky. Three schooners followed each other up the Cooper River like ducks, but the other ships in harbor seemed lifeless. The cryptic letters were all in the same hand, a hand he thought he'd seen before. But where?

Quickly, he pulled out all the letters to his father or to himself that he could find. One by one he compared them with the notes. In five minutes he was smiling at a letter written to him by the same man. Aaron Burr.

Burr had appeared in Charleston the preceding January. He hadn't known of Michael's death, and the news had shaken him more than Robert had thought it would. Burr had retreated to Hagley, Joseph Alston's plantation on the Waccamaw, as soon as he discovered Michael was dead. After a few days with Theodosia, his daughter, and his grandson Aaron Burr Alston, he had returned north as suddenly as he had come. Now Robert saw that none of the cryptic messages were dated after that visit.

Suddenly Robert gathered up the letters from Burr and stuffed them in his coat pocket.

"Ezekiel!" he called as he strode into the hall. "Bring my hat!" He pulled his walking stick from the blue porcelain stand by the door.

Ezekiel appeared with the tall beaver and a caped outer coat as well. "Here, Mr. Robert. It's too cold out there for you to go traipsing around without no coat. And the carriage is—"

He shrugged into the coat and was already out in the cold. He was in no mind to wait; he turned briskly up East Bay.

At the long warehouse with the Fallon & Son sign, he slowed. He found Petrie in what had been Michael Fallon's office, bent over a ledger.

The one-armed man was nearly bald, and what hair he did have was white. He pulled off his spectacles and rubbed at his eyes as he rose. "Good morning, Mr. Fallon. I was about to send a messenger to you. The semaphore from Sullivan's Island reports *Staghound* is in sight. She should be at anchor before nightfall."

Robert brushed that aside. The ship's arrival no longer seemed important. "Mr. Petrie, tell me of my father's business with Aaron Burr."

"Burr? Why, there was none, sir. To be sure, they were friends. Of a sort, at any rate."

"Of a sort? What do you mean?"

"Did you know that your father was there at the duel? The one where Hamilton was killed?"

"No, I didn't."

"Not many did. Why, I'll wager there's not another in the city besides myself who knows that his trip west—the one just before he died—was with Burr. They went down the Mississippi together."

"They did? Do you remember who they visited? Try hard. It's important."

Petrie laughed softly. "That's one thing I don't have to try hard for. It seems the older I get, the easier I remember names. I can't say the same for faces, but names, now . . . . Let's see. There was General Wilkinson at Cincinnati, on the Ohio."

"Wilkinson," Robert muttered. W.

"General Jackson in Tennessee. And at Natchez, on the Mississippi, Bingman, Surget, Minor, Burney, and Duncan. He never mentioned Christian names. From New Orleans, he only mentioned three names. Daniel Clark, Ned Livingston, and Joseph Sauvinet. And Lopes, of course. Does that help any?"

"Some," Robert replied. General W and General J. Wilkinson and Jackson. "Do you know what my father was up to when he died? Was there a new revolution he was supporting?"

Petrie shook his head. "Not that I know of. But," he added slowly, "the night he . . . the night he died, he was lightering a cargo of muskets out to the *Carolina Queen*. Bound for New Orleans."

For a time the two men stared at each other in silence. Finally Robert spoke. "What chance is there," he said slowly, "that he was involved in something aimed against the United States?"

"None," Petrie replied promptly. "Your father loved this country, Mr. Fallon. He bled to make it. He'd never have done anything to harm it."

"How many muskets do we have on hand?"

Petrie smiled. "About two thousand stand. And another thousand I can get to the warehouse today if I take the carts from other hauling."

"And our fastest ship?"

"*Staghound,* if she lives up to her design."

"As soon as she makes port, start loading the muskets into her. And all the powder and lead you can find."

"You're going to go through with it, then? Not knowing what it is that's planned?"

"I'll go slow. If I don't like the look of things, the muskets can always be sold."

"You sound as if you're going yourself, sir."

Robert frowned. It was the only way. And perhaps it was his

only chance. If he could get away from Catherine now, break free of her . . . . "Yes. I'm going."

On his return to the East Bay house, he found Catherine in the drawing room. She sipped her wine and gave him barely a glance. For once she didn't demand a kiss.

"I'm afraid I have business in New Orleans," he said finally.

She gave a surprised twitch, and muttered a curse as she spilled wine over her hand. All she said was, "You'll be going yourself?"

"Yes. Yes, I have to go myself." He poured himself a brandy.

"How long will you be gone?"

"I can't say. A few weeks. A few months." Out of the corner of his eye he watched her. She frowned at her wine.

"I suppose I might go away myself for a while, then," she said.

"This trip is business," he said cautiously. "I don't think . . . I don't think I'll have any time to be with—"

"I was thinking of Newport."

"In the winter!" he said incredulously, then cursed himself. If she wanted to go away, without him, he shouldn't care if she went to the Arctic regions. "Well, I suppose it will be quite different."

"Yes," she said drily. She looked at him strangely, half uncertain and half defiant. "You'll never be free of me, Robert."

"It's disgusting," he growled. "Why can't you realize that?"

"You don't want to be free of me. And that's good, because you can't."

"I could walk out that door this minute," he lied. "Walk out and never come back."

"Then do it," she said softly. Standing up, she began to undo the laces of her dress.

"For the love of God," he said. "Anyone could walk in. The servants. Anyone."

"Then go," she said. Her breasts, round and white and heavy-nippled, sprang free of the dress. She began to push her skirts down over her hips.

Quickly he moved to the door, but when his hand was on it, he found himself shutting it. Catherine laughed throatily, and he whirled. She stood naked in front of the blazing fire, holding her arms out to him. With a curse for his own weakness, he went to her.

XXXII

Catherine paused on the step of the carriage drawn up at Chisholm's Wharf and peered toward the harbor mouth. She thought she could still dimly see the sails of the *Staghound*. At any rate, Robert was gone. And that, she thought, was most fortuitous.

"Are you getting out?" Theodosia Alston asked from inside the carriage. "Or do you intend to stand there all day?"

"Oh, don't fuss so," Catherine said, but she climbed on down to the cobblestones.

Aaron Burr's daughter, a pretty, pale-skinned brunette, stepped down after her, tugging at her dress. "I declare, these streets are so rough you might as well be dragged in a sack as drive over them."

"And I declare," Catherine said with a smile, "that you become more southern the longer you're here. Another year or two and no one will ever believe you were born in New York."

"I'm sure I don't know what you mean." She turned toward the carriage. "Ezra! Jacob! You hurry up there! And mind you have a care with those trunks, or I'll have your hides."

"Softly in public, Theo," Catherine murmured.

"Catherine, what *are* you talking about?"

"Nothing is all, Theodosia. Just talking to myself. Come along. The flag is up." A green flag had been hoisted to the forepeak of the *Sally J.*, indicating that the ship would be leaving within the hour.

"Hurry with that luggage!" Theodosia called once more, then hurried after Catherine. "I swear," she muttered, "they are bone lazy. All of them. And thieves to boot. You have to watch them every minute."

Catherine was intent on threading her way through the bustle on the dock. Roustabouts horsed bales of cotton across the rough planks; other bales were being swayed aboard a ship opposite the *Sally J.* Pushcarts laden with crates rumbled back toward the warehouse. At the foot of the gangplank, a bearded man looked up forbiddingly.

"I'm sorry, ladies," he rumbled. "We sail shortly. No visitors allowed aboard."

"I'm Mrs. Karl Holtz," Catherine said coolly. "And I have a cabin paid for."

He looked at the manifest again, and nodded sourly. "Yes, I see. Mrs. Karl Holtz. One cabin. No maid or companion." His look told what he thought of women who traveled alone.

Catherine's voice dropped another twenty degrees. "What is your name?"

"Melville," he said shortly. "Israel Melville. First mate."

"Well, Mr. Melville," she went on in the same frigid tone, "I do not usually explain myself, but I will make an exception this time. I know the way you New Englanders act toward slave holders, despite the fact that you sell us most of the slaves and buy most of the cotton the slaves grow. Therefore, I intend to hire a maid in Boston for my stay. Now, if that satisfies you, or even if it doesn't, get out of my way. I'm going aboard, and my friend is going with me."

She glided regally up the gangplank with Theodosia at her heels while Melville stood there with his mouth working. Theodosia maintained a dignified silence until they were in Catherine's cabin. Then she clapped her hands delightedly.

"That was wonderful, Catherine! The way you put that awful man in his place."

Catherine looked around the tiny, dark cabin, with its narrow bed and its featureless walls. The thought of spending a trip to Boston in such quarters was depressing. But the alternative was worse. With a sigh she sank to the bed. There was no chair.

"Why, you must be exhausted," Theodosia said. "You poor dear. I'll get a damp cloth for your forehead."

"No," Catherine said sharply. She managed to moderate her tone. "I'm sorry, Theo, but what I really want is just to lie here quietly. I'm sure you understand."

"Of course, Catherine." A bell rang on deck, and a man began bellowing, his words indistinguishable in the cabin. "I believe visitors are being put off now, anyway. You take care, now, Catherine. And write me often."

When Theodosia was gone, Catherine sighed and sank back on the narrow bunk. She *did* feel exhausted, but she didn't want to close her eyes. Not until she was certain the ship was safely at sea, safely away from Charleston.

Slowly she brought up her hands and rested them on her abdomen. It was there. The reason she had refused all Theodosia's offers to accompany. The reason she hadn't brought a servant from Charleston. The reason she was leaving Charleston at all. No one must ever discover her secret— that life was pulsing beneath her hands, the life of her brother's child.

XXXIII

Even as the launch carried him from *Staghound* to shore, Robert could see that something was wrong in New Orleans. There were soldiers along the Rue de la Levee, and almost no civilians. He wrapped his cloak tighter against the chill January wind and spoke over his shoulder. "Miller, you and Kemal will come with me. Kurian, take the launch back as soon as we're ashore. Tell Mr. Carlyle he's to allow no one ashore till he hears from me."

The boat bumped against the levee, and Robert leaped out and scrambled up the grassy mound. Miller and Kemal dogging his heels. By the time they reached the street on the other side, a squad of soldiers was waiting for them.

"One moment," a brisk young lieutenant said. "Your names?"

"Why?" Robert said quietly.

"Government business," the lieutenant said officiously. "Don't you know martial law's in effect here? Now, what's your name, and what's your business here?"

"Robert Fallon," he replied slowly. "I just arrived on the *Staghound* for the purpose of trade."

"Sergeant?" the lieutenant said. Behind him, a blue-coated sergeant consulted a ledger, running his finger down the pages and moving his lips as he read.

"Fallon's not here, sir," he said finally.

"And who are you here to trade with?" the lieutenant asked.

Robert hesitated, averting his eyes from the ledger. "I don't really know. I thought I could find the best men once I was here."

"You won't find many now," the sergeant snickered, then

333

subsided under the lieutenant's glare.

"Lieutenant," Robert said, "what's happened here? I mean, if there's trouble, perhaps it's best I take my trading elsewhere."

"You and the other civilians just obey instructions and rest assured that General Wilkinson has the situation well in hand."

Robert's heart leaped. If Wilkinson was commanding this force, perhaps his father's dream wasn't dead yet. And perhaps, he told himself grimly, the soldiers being there meant it should be dead. "Where is General Wilkinson's headquarters? I expect if I'm to trade under martial law, I'll need special permits and such."

The lieutenant pointed to a two-story building with a steeply pitched roof. "In the *Gouvernement,*" he said.

The Governor's house was just down the levee, beyond the Place d'Armes. Inside the front doors a table had been set athwart the hall, with another young lieutenant behind it. Robert approached the table at the same time as a roughly dressed, unshaven man with a strongly hooked nose.

"I'd like," Robert began, but the lieutenant ignored him for the other man.

"You're to go right up, Captain Vance," he said. A captain? The unshaven man nodded and hurried on by the table. *That* man was a captain? Robert thought. The lieutenant's voice dropped into practiced boredom as he turned back to Robert. "Yes?"

"I want to see General Wilkinson," Robert said.

The lieutenant sneered. "You do, do you? And who are you? The Cham of Tartary?"

"I'm Robert Fallon, of Charleston, South Carolina," he said levelly. "And I'm making a civil request to see the general. I expect a civil reply."

"You can expect to get thrown in jail if you don't get out of here. We don't much like civilians coming in here demanding things. Now get out."

Robert took a deep breath. "If you'll let me send my name in?"

"I said get out. Sergeant Beroman! Escort this man to the street."

A burly sergeant appeared at Robert's side, two privates with bayonet-tipped muskets at his heels. Robert, exasperated, turned to go.

In the street Kemal and Miller gathered to him. "We'll go to Lopes," he said. Lopes would know the next step.

But the big warehouse with the sign ESTBAN LOPES had its doors shut and padlocked. And an Army private with a musket walked guard in front.

Robert approached the guard alone. "Hello, son. What's your name?"

At the sound of his voice the private whirled, bayonet dropping to the ready and mouth dropping open. He was a round-faced boy, no more than seventeen. "Private Benjamin, sir. Ain't nobody supposed to come here, sir. This here property is under U. S. Army control."

"I thought this warehouse belonged to Eastern Lopes. I came to do some trading."

"Lopes is in jail, and he ain't going to be doing no trading till the general lets him out."

Robert had halfway expected it since he'd seen the Army guard, but it still took his breath away. He managed to keep his voice steady. "In jail? What did he do?"

Benjamin grinned. "I don't know. He's just one of them the general had locked up. You must have just got to town. Most folks don't ask questions any more about what the Army's doing."

"Yes, I just arrived this morning," Robert said.

"Well, the most important thing is, no civilians are allowed on the streets after dark. That, and no gatherings of more than three people not in the same family."

"Hardly sounds American."

"Martial law, sir. General tells me to lock them up, I lock them up. General tells me to guard something, I guard it. And sir, I been told there ain't supposed to be no civilians around this warehouse. So I guess you'd better move on."

Robert nodded and retreated. Benjamin watched him go.

Kemal and Miller followed him around the corner, the huge Turk frowning back at the guard. "Captain," Miller said, "back when you asked if we'd come along, I said I'd go anywhere you wanted. But captain, I got to say I think it's coming time to get out.''

Robert nodded. "First I have to see what I can do for Lopes. There are people up on Rue de Bourgogne that might be able to tell me, if they haven't been arrested, too. Once I've seen them, we'll be back to *Staghound* and downriver before dark.''

Though it was hours yet till the forbidden hour of sunset, there were few men in civilian dress on the streets, and no women. The men walked quickly and looked neither to left nor right. There were no peddlers, no hawkers; the markets were empty. What was very apparent were soldiers. There were never more than eight or ten at a time, but it seemed impossible to look down a street without seeing one such group.

As Robert and his friends started down Rue St. Louis, the first carriage he had seen suddenly raced around the corner of Rue L'Dauphin. He leaped back; the heavily curtained carriage was reined to a halt. The driver backed the carriage to him.

The door swung open, and from the dark interior a vaguely familiar voice spoke, "Get in, Robert.''

Robert stepped closer, peering into the dim carriage. When he saw the woman sitting there, smiling at him like a self-satisfied cat, he muttered under his breath. It was Cordelia Applegate.

"Get in, Robert. Or would you rather me shout who you are, and who your father is, and who his friends are?'' Her smile deepened.

Could he reach the ship if he simply ran? There'd still be the problem of taking the ship downriver. "Go back to the ship,'' he said to Miller and Kemal, and climbed into the carriage.

Cordelia tapped on the roof. "Finisterre! And quickly!'' The carriage rocketed ahead at its former breakneck speed. "Well, Robert, how pleasant to see you again.''

"Why play games, Cordelia?'' he said quietly. "I'm sorry for what happened the last time we were together. Somehow I don't see that an apology is enough to make you all forgiveness and light.''

"No. You're right. It isn't. And your father . . . . '' Her nostrils flared angrily.

"My father?''

"We met a year or so ago. Briefly. He told me you were dead."

"He thought I was." He paused. "He died before he found out differently."

"Aaah." It was a small sound, with just a touch of satisfaction that made him frown.

"No condolences, Cordelia?"

"As you said, Robert, why play games? I had no love for him."

"What did my father ever do to you?"

He was astonished to see that she colored.

"Nothing," she said quickly. "It's enough that he was mixed in this conspiracy. And that gives me a hold over you."

"What conspiracy?" he asked. A hold?

"No games, remember," she said angrily. "You think I'm a brainless fool, just as William does. Well, I know that your precious Mr. Burr intends to break off the Western half of the United States. Or at least, he did. But General Wilkinson found him out, and now he's moved to scotch the whole thing."

"My father would never have been party to anything that would harm the United States," Robert growled.

"Then why are all his friends arrested as fast as the Army can find them? General Wilkinson's already sent a letter to the President, detailing the plot as he uncovered it. There's no use in denying it exists."

The rest of the ride was silent, Cordelia satisfied, Robert glowering. This fool woman might get him hung, if her story was believed by those in power. Where *did* Wilkinson stand? If this was the first move of his father's plan with Burr, why was Lopes, his father's friend, arrested? And what kind of move against the Spaniards required this kind of hold on New Orleans? Why violate the rights of an entire city? And if it was a government attempt to stop his father's plan with Burr, why was Wilkinson in charge? He was convinced the general was a part of the plan.

As the speeding carriage was reined to a halt, Cordelia smiled coolly and motioned him to get out.

His boots crunched on a crushed-shell drive in front of a large stucco two-story house that had the look of having been unoccupied for some time. In an overgrown garden to the left of the house, moss-draped oaks had put out limbs that were scraping scabs of plaster from the house. He wondered how far from the city they'd come.

"His name is Robert Fallon, Rafael," Cordelia said to the coal-black driver. "Robert Fallon." Rafael turned equally dark eyes on Robert before he gathered the reins and drove around behind the house. "Inside, Mr. Fallon," Cordelia said.

Inside the house, open doors to either side of the entry hall revealed furnishings covered with dusty gray dropcloths, cobwebs festooning the ceilings. But the floor in the entry hall had only a light coating of dust, as if it were often used, and the stairs grew cleaner as they climbed. The second-floor landing was polished brightly, and the room she led him into was a neat and tidy study.

He shook his head. "Now this, I confess, is beyond me. Why a house that looks abandoned from the outside, and has one usable room inside? Surely not to just keep me prisoner."

"Two rooms, Robert. There is also a bedchamber." She smiled suggestively. "I like a place that no one else knows of."

"That the man who's keeping you doesn't know of, you mean."

Her face went pale, and she raised her fists toward him. "I ought to kill you out of hand. I should have killed your father, too. He's the one told you, wasn't he? All right, then. I'm William Claiborne's mistress." She spat the final word. "To him that means the same as chattel. Well, he doesn't know about his place. You're right."

She was as beautiful as Robert remembered, certainly, with her emerald eyes, her flaming hair, her creamy skin.

"Why don't you charge him with rape?" he said maliciously.

"You bastard!" she hissed, then suddenly laughed. "I don't have to, Robert. You're going to take care of William for me."

"I am?"

"You're going to kill him for me. Him and General Wilkinson, both."

Robert whistled softly. "I'll just walk out of here now."

"I wouldn't," she said as he started for the door. "Rafael is watching the house, and he's mounted." He stopped. "Before you get close to town, the alarm will be sounded. How you stopped my carriage in the city, forced your way in at gunpoint, and brought me here. Rafael, of course, managed to escape with one of the carriage horses." She laughed at him. "Why don't you realize you're beaten, and do what I want?"

"You've brought strange men here before, haven't you?" he said quietly.

She colored. "Damn you! You might as well make up your mind, Robert Fallon. You're going to kill Wilkinson and Claiborne."

"Why me? Kill them? For God's sake."

"I'm not asking you to do it, Robert. I'm telling you. Damn it, Robert, when I saw you, it was a gift from heaven. I've been trying to find the right man for six months, and then there you were. I remember you, you see. All that violence in you. You could have killed me. I could tell. And you've killed men since."

"Only for cause, Cordelia."

"I'll give you cause. If you don't do it, I'll see you hang." He took a step toward her. "Remember Rafael," she said quickly. She clasped her arms in front of her so that her round breasts were lifted and pressed together. The fingers of her left hand gently stroked the pale slope of her right breast. "It could be as it was with us. Remember how good it was?" Her breath began to come faster.

"Why, Cordelia? I can't kill a man without knowing why."

"You know as much as you need to know. Or at least, as much as I'm going to tell you. Now come here."

The door banged open suddenly, and Lopes stepped into the room, a pistol in his hand. "Perhaps I can tell you why, *Señor* Fallon." Behind him crowded Miller and Kemal. Then came three more men. Robert recognized two of them immediately.

"Beluche! Dom! Where on God's earth did you spring from? Lopes, I thought you were in prison."

Dominique You still had the thin mustaches, though he had grown heavier with the years. He shrugged. "We extracted *Monsieur* Lopes from the embraces of *le bon Général*, may he rot in hell."

Lopes nodded. "Two weeks in a filthy cell, without light or bedding. I was on my way to . . . friends when I saw you get into that carriage. I recognized it, and I recognized your man Miller. So, we are here." He eyed Robert curiously, though his gun never wavered from Cordelia. "I wonder, señor, why you have come at this particular time."

So Miller had been discreet. Robert said, "I came to complete what my father started."

Lopes sighed heavily. "I fear it is too late, señor."

Then the stranger spoke for the first time. "I think," he said with a strong French accent, "that we should leave as quickly as possible. There will be time for talk later."

Beluche snorted. "Always cautious, Jean. I think me you are even suspicious of your own shadow. Eh, Fallon. This is mon cousin, Jean. Dom's brother."

The slender young man bowed. "Jean Lafitte, Monsieur Fallon, at your service. For whatever reason you were brought here, I think we should leave now."

"As soon as I find out why she wanted me to kill James Wilkinson and William Claiborne," Robert said.

Beluche whistled, and gave Cordelia an appreciative ogle. Lopes said, "Claiborne set her to sleeping with Wilkinson to spy on him. Wilkinson promptly started using her for the same thing. My information says both men have altered their wills, leaving her two tidy sums. Of course, when their interest in her fades, so will the money. Therefore, she must see that these men die promptly."

"Sacré bleu!" Jean breathed. "It is to be expected among the women of the streets, but this . . . . " He shook his head.

Robert drew Lopes aside and spoke softly. "What in hell is going on? I thought Wilkinson was in this thing with my father. And you, I assumed."

"He was," Lopes sighed. "I am the only one of the Association who knows it, and only because your father told me. It is well I did not reveal this, or I would be dead by now. There was most particular questioning on who I knew outside of New Orleans."

"So Wilkinson is betraying the whole adventure?"

"Exactly, señor. We must get word upriver to Señor Burr. The Lafittes managed to get me out of jail, but they will not undertake to carry a message upriver.''

''We are your friends, *Monsieur* Lopes,'' Dom said suddenly, behind them. Both Robert and Lopes started, surprised that he was so close. ''That, by damn, is why we break you out of the jail. This other, though . . . perhaps—''

''*Non*, Dom,'' Jean broke in. ''It is the politics, remember? We are smugglers, and privateers. We are safe on Grand Terre because we bring much money and we do not interfere in the politics. If we do, even the one we support will remember only that we interfered. Next time we might be against him. Our safety will be gone. I am sorry, *Monsieur* Fallon, *Monsieur* Lopes, but we can involve ourselves no further.''

''I understand,'' Robert said. ''But if you get me a horse, I'll— Damn it! Her driver's out there with a horse now. He's probably halfway back to . . . . '' Beluche was shaking his head and grinning.

''The black fellow on the horse?'' the old smuggler said. ''He is now well trussed and lying in the carriage behind the house. He watch this house so good, he don't even see us coming. You can use his horse, *non*?''

Robert nodded. ''I can. And that leaves just one problem.'' They all turned to look at Cordelia.

She blanched and took a step back, then raised her chin. ''You can't frighten me. You don't have the courage to kill me.''

''There is a man,'' Lopes said, ''named Thomas Martin, a sugar planter. I know him only slightly, but he is trustworthy. He has no connection with the Association, but I believe he knows the Lafittes. He might let us, shall we say, store her at his plantation.''

''This Martin can be trusted,'' Dom said.

Robert shook his head. ''We'll bring no more people into this than we must.''

''She should be killed,'' Jean said quietly.

Cordelia flinched.

''She's not to be hurt,'' Robert said quickly.

''*Señor*, are you forgetting that she tried today to blackmail you into killing two men? That she tried to have you hung as a rapist for the crime of leaving her bed before she wished you to? She cannot be turned loose. She is not to be trusted.''

"Yes, she has to be kept somewhere secure for a day or two," Robert said. "Long enough for us to get out of the city and my ship downriver."

"I can put a pilot on your ship," Dom said, "who knows this damned river like he knows his own woman."

Beluche took off his coat and tossed it on a chair. "I guard me this little vixen. Right here." He settled into another chair with a comfortable sigh.

Cordelia looked at him contemptuously. "You'll all hang. You, Robert. This fat old fool. All of you!"

"I just make a rule," Beluche said. "You call me 'fat old fool' again, and I cut me a switch for your *fesses*." She grimaced and looked away, he seemed satisfied. "She is right, this vixen, about one thing. If you waste time here, we *will* hang. Go. *Vite. Vite.*"

Leaving Beluche and Cordelia, the others hurried down to the front door and the horses. As Robert swung into the saddle, a thought struck him.

"Dom, you'd better warn your uncle. She'll likely try to offer her body for her freedom, if I know her."

Dom and Jean both laughed. "*Mon oncle* is no doubt hoping she will," Dom said. "For two or three days he will accept it. He enjoys greatly shocking young women who think them he is too old to have the vigor left in him."

The others chuckled, but Robert frowned. Twice now he had run into Cordelia, and both times she had been humiliated. What would happen the third time they met? Suddenly he was sure there would be a third time. She would get get her own back.

He shook off the fancy. Five minutes later he was pounding north along the Mississippi, Kemal and Miller close behind him.

XXXIV

In Natchez people Robert questioned for Burr's whereabouts had shifted and squirmed in their eagerness to be away. One had blurted simply "Bayou Pierre," and darted off. It was clear the rumors, whatever they were, had spread.

The Bayou Pierre was a straggling stream of dark water. A fit place, Robert thought as he rode down it, for Burr's camp. Abruptly Robert rounded a twist in the bank, and there was the camp, a small tidy grouping of tents with a dozen or so stout Schenectady boats drawn up in front of them.

A cleanshaven young man in gentleman's hunting garb stepped out of the bushes, holding a musket nervously. "If you please, gentlemen."

One of Burr's New York younger sons, Robert thought. He sighed and shifted tiredly in his saddle. "I'm Robert Fallon. These are my men, Miller and Kemal. Tell him I'm tired and hungry, and I've bad news."

"There's been more than enough of that," the young man said. "I, for one, can't wait till we join General Wilkinson." He raised his voice. "Peter! Go tell Mr. Burr what this gentleman said." Another young man in hunting clothes darted out of the bushes and back toward the camp.

In a few minutes Peter was back. "Mr. Burr says to send them on, Henry."

The sentry lowered his musket. "The big wall-tent," he said. "And I hope your news is better than what we've been hearing."

Robert rode past without answering.

Outside the wall-tent he motioned Miller and Kemal to wait, and went in alone. Burr, his spectacles pushed up on his forehead, wore a look of weary cynicism.

"Mr. Fallon," he said without rising from his camp table. He sounded tired. "I have to say I'm surprised to see you. When I saw you last year, you gave no sign of knowing anything of my plans."

"I discovered some of my father's correspondence," Robert said. "I brought three thousand muskets to New Orleans because I had an insane idea about . . . I don't know . . . fulfilling his dream, carrying out his wishes, something like that."

"Muskets!" Burr bounded out of the chair as if the word had electrified him. He began to pace the narrow confines of the tent. "Yes," he said half to himself. "They might still be put to good use. To tell the truth, Fallon, I can't tell you how good it is to have some news that isn't bad. Harman Blennerhasset, one of my men in Ohio, wrote editorials for a newspaper under a transparent pseudonym calling for separation of the western states and territories from the Union. Got his island raided and his house ransacked by the local militia. Then, when I got to Jackson, I'll be damned if I didn't find the same rumor there ahead of me. Every other man in the Tennessee militia believes it. Even Jackson was more than half convinced. It took me hours to make him believe the truth, and even so there's no hope in hell of the Tennessee militia marching to help us until they're sure we're really going against Mexico. I even had to face treason charges at Lexington. God! With those muskets of yours, perhaps we can recruit enough men more to take a few towns in Texas. That ought to convince the Tennesseans."

"Mr. Burr, I'm afraid the muskets aren't going to be any use."

Burr stopped in his tracks. "So you've brought bad news after all," he said quietly.

"Perhaps the worst. General Wilkinson has moved into New Orleans and declared martial law."

"Wilkinson!" Burr turned, hope lighting his eyes.

"He's arrested members of the Association. It isn't safe to mention the name Burr anywhere in the city. He is saying you intend to seize the western United States, and he is going to prevent you and save the country."

"That bastard. That bastard!" The light in Burr's eyes was

anger, now. "He's betrayed me. Betrayed all of us, and lied in the bargain. But why? Damn it, why?"

"What matters now is that it's happened. What are you going to do?"

Burr sighed heavily and ran a hand through his thinning hair, muttering a curse when he tangled his fingers in his spectacles. "There's nothing left *to* do. I suppose there'll be charges against me. Yes, there would be. Treason again, most likely." He thrust his head out of the tent and shouted, "Seabrook!"

Another of the clean-shaven young men appeared, dressed apparently for a New England hunt. "Yes, Mr. Burr?"

"Assemble the men in front of my tent. I want to speak to them."

Seabrook withdrew, and Robert said, "What are you going to tell them?"

"The truth," Burr said grimly.

Robert was surprised by the small number of men. No more than seventy or eighty, none with the look of veterans, either of war of anything else. Burr regarded them sadly for a time before speaking.

"Gentlemen," he began, and his voice broke. He cleared his throat and began again. "Gentlemen, it is over. Our grand adventure is done. We have been betrayed by General Wilkinson." A growl went up from the assembled men, but Burr ignored it. "The stories we have had to struggle against since coming west, the tales that we intended to dismember the United States, have been spread by the General and used to further his own ends, whatever they may be. I regret that I cannot give you the money I promised you, but you may keep the weapons, equipment, and supplies that you were issued. Further, you may sell the boats and divide the proceeds among you. Finally, you will remember the lands I own in the territory. The Bastrop Grant. Any of you who reach the Grant are free to settle there. And that, I fear, is the last I have to give you. Godspeed, gentlemen, and be wary of sheriffs."

A half-hearted cheer went up as he ducked back into his tent, but most of the men stood looking at one another as if stunned. Slowly they began to leave. Robert followed Burr into the tent.

"What do you intend to do?" he asked. "Try for those Bastrop lands yourself?"

Burr was stuffing clothes into a small portmanteau. "I'll ride down to Natchez and turn myself in to a magistrate. If anyone's going to prove treason against me, they'll have a hard fight. I certainly don't intend to give them ammunition by running." He finished buckling the portmanteau and straightened up. He touched Robert's shoulder with his free hand. His elvish face was drawn to a gnome's with suffering. "If your father had lived; if Wilkinson had kept faith . . . . It was a grand adventure." He ducked out of the tent.

Robert followed; Burr was already in the saddle, Seabrook handing up his case. He trotted away to the south without a look back.

Miller and Kemal came to Robert with their horses. "Captain," Miller said, "what do we do now? I'm eager to get back to the ship, sir, but my backside ain't ready for another ride like that last without it gets a rest."

"We all need a rest," Robert said, pulling himself into the saddle. "We'll follow Burr down to Natchez and spend a day or so there. Then we'll start back to the ship."

"Don't look like there's much come of this," Miller said as they rode out.

Robert didn't look back. "Nothing came of it, Miller. It's all over."

That night Robert sat at Corgan's, a tavern near the bottom of the bluff. The place was dirty, and the whiskey was rotgut, but Cogan's was a mite safer than most under the hill. A man who drank too much didn't run much risk of having his throat cut for his last coins.

While Robert sat at his corner table, Kemal and Miller standing at the long bar where they could keep an eye on him, the sentry from the encampment came in and took a table. Seeing Robert he started, then slowly settled into his chair. He sat nervously, though, with an awkward eye on Robert, as if afraid Robert would come over.

They had already learned the first lesson of survival, Robert thought. Their safety lay in not associating with anyone who might be associated with Burr. Burr's grand adventure was most certainly over.

It was time to go to bed in his room upstairs. As Robert got up, a roughly dressed, unshaven man paused by the ex-sentry's table. He took one good look, then walked on out of the tavern. No one else had taken any interest in the fellow at all. But Robert had a vague impression of having seen the unshaven man somewhere before. Somewhere important.

He had settled into the room's lone bed when suddenly it hit him. He sat up in the dark. "Captain Vance," he said half to himself. "That's who he was."

"What, captain?" Miller asked from his pallet on the floor. Kemal got up and checked the wedges he had placed under the door.

Robert rolled out of bed and began dressing in the dark. "That fellow who was interested in the sentry—he's an Army captain named Vance. I saw him at Wilkinson's headquarters in New Orleans."

"You think he's come to arrest Mr. Burr, captain?"

"In civilian clothes? Wilkinson was part of Burr's plan, Miller. His pose as savior of New Orleans won't last long if that leaks out. The best way to keep the secret is to keep Burr from coming to trial."

"Mother of God," Miller breathed. "We'd best find Mr. Burr, captain, and warn him." He began scrambling into his clothes. Kemal, who slept in his, disposed of various pistols and daggers about his person.

Where to begin the search? The fine gentlemen atop the bluff, who had received Burr with open arms on his first visit, were denying they knew him, now. He would not be there. He did not have the money for the best inns, but he was too smart to venture into Natchez-under-the-Hill, where men could be killed for their boots. That left the kind of tavern that Robert was staying at, cheap, with a bare respectability.

They hurried through the night, down dusty, packed-dirt streets. Slatternly blowzes hung on the street corners, blaring their raucous invitations. Men from the flatboats rubbed elbows with buckskinned men from the Western mountains, and occasionally they rolled in the dirt, kneeing and gouging. The crowds always split around the fights, few even seeming to notice as they headed for whatever pleasure had caught their fancy.

There were dozens of bars, taverns, and inns that met his

criteria, Robert discovered, and they visited all of them. Tyler's. The Catfish Club. An endless stream of places filling with unruly laughter; the night was warming up. The Keelboat. The Golden Cock. At the American Eagle they found Burr, sitting alone in a corner, sipping whiskey and ignoring the merriment around him. He looked up in surprise when Robert dropped into the chair across from him.

"Again you surprised me, Mr. Fallon. The denials have already begun, you know. 'Who is this Burr? I know him not.'" He laughed bitterly. "In a month they'll be howling for my blood, just to prove they were never my friends."

"Someone may be after your blood sooner than that," Robert said. "I believe General Wilkinson has sent someone to Natchez to kill you.

"In New Orleans, before I knew what was happening, I went to Wilkinson's headquarters. A man there was addressed as Captain Vance. I saw him last night, unshaven and in civilian clothes. He took an interest in one of your men at Corgan's."

Burr swallowed the rest of his whiskey and grimaced. "Probably sent to spy on me."

"Sir, I think it's more than that. Esteban Lopes was one of those arrested. And he says that Wilkinson was particularly interested in finding out whether anyone knew he was a party to the plot. It's my advice that you leave Natchez. Go back East where you have friends, where it won't be so easy for an 'accident' to be arranged."

Burr made a disgusted noise. "I gave my bond to a magistrate today, Mr. Fallon. I swore I'd remain available for trial. I don't break my word, certainly not to run from a chimera." He scrapped back his chair and got to his feet. "No, Mr. Fallon. I must seek lodging for the night. If you will excuse me." He bowed and made his way unsteadily out of the bar.

Robert sat for only a moment before motioning to Miller and Kemal and hurrying after Burr. If the man wouldn't believe, he would have to be protected. In the street he caught sight of the diminutive man weaving his way through the throng. He followed at a discreet distance, keeping an eye on Burr.

Slowly Burr made his way out of the crowds, toward the

darkened main part of the city, where the boarding houses were. In the emptier streets Robert was forced to hang back still further to avoid being seen. At his whispered command Miller and Kemal dropped back twenty more paces. The songs and laughter from the bars had been left behind. There was no sound except the padding of their feet.

Robert began to think Burr would reach his destination unharmed. They were no longer in the part of town where street violence was common. At that moment he realized Burr could no longer be seen. Ahead was only darkness. At the same instant boots pounded up ahead. There was a dull thud of wood striking flesh, a groan, then silence.

Robert raced forward. Dimly he could make out a shape sprawled on the dirt. Another shape, bending over the first, tossed aside a club; moonlight glinted on steel raised high.

Robert hit in a shallow dive; the assassin grunted. Robert grabbed the other's knife hand with both of his, fighting to keep the gleaming blade away. They rolled to a halt in the only light on the street, from a window high on a boarding-house wall. Robert stared into the contorted face of the man he knew as Vance, and he saw Vance sense his recognition. Arms knotted, the two men poured all their energies into the knife; slowly, inexorably, it began to move toward them, chest to chest in the street.

Robert could feel the sweat pouring down his face. There was sweat on Vance's face, too, and now a certain desperation in the eyes. Vance convulsed in a furious attempt to gain control of the blade, and Robert added his own strength to Vance's.

The would-be murderer screamed as the blade socketed home in his chest. He stared at their clasped hands, pressed tightly against his chest, then looked at Robert with fury. "Damn you!" he said hoarsely. "Warbeck will still get him. One of the others . . . " His eyes went wide. Blood spilled out of his mouth, and his head fell back, staring sightlessly into the night.

Robert pried Vance's hands loose from his, rose, and walked back to Burr. Miller and Kemal had helped him to his feet and were supporting him.

"What happened?" Burr asked fuzzily. He was feeling

gingerly at his skull. "Footpad?"

"Captain Vance," Robert said simply. Burr stared at him. "He's dead. With the knife he meant for you."

"At least that threat's done with," Burr murmured. "I thank you, Mr. Fallon."

"It's not done. He said 'Warbeck' would still get you. And he mentioned 'others.'"

Burr shook his head, and stopped with a wince. "Warbeck? Wilkinson's aide is a Lieutenant Warbeck."

"You see, then? God knows who these 'others' are, or how many they are. You must return East immediately, tonight, or your may not live to leave Natchez."

"Yes, Mr. Fallon. I believe you're right." Burr shrugged off the support of Miller and Kemal. "To run out on my bond . . . but you are right." He paused. "All the roads east from Natchez are probably already being watched."

"Well, you certainly can't go downriver to New Orleans."

"Ah. But I will go south. To Mobile. Or better yet, to Pensacola. I can take ship from there for Washington City."

"I'll wish you good luck, then," Robert said, offering his hand, "and, as you wished your men, Godspeed."

Burr gripped his hand firmly. There was a trace of the old grin on his face. "Considering who I am, it seems more likely the devil will give me what winds I get. Farewell, Mr. Fallon." And he was gone, into the darkness.

XXXV

Robert's return to Charleston was uneventful, but there he found that the nation was agog with news of Burr. The Vice-President was arrested on the road to Pensacola and carried to Richmond, Virginia, for trial. The charge was treason against the United States. John Marshall, Chief Justice of the Supreme Court, was to sit the bench. Army officers were given the powers of U.S. Marshals to search out witnesses and Burr's fellow conspirators. From secret sessions of Congress word leaked that the President had attempted to have the right of *habeas corpus* suspended. Jefferson, it was whispered, was read ready to tear down the Constitution and erect a military dictatorship to get Burr. It was said he went into apoplectic fits at any "malicious insinuations" against Wilkinson. Burr was the culprit. Burr must be destroyed. There were open attempts to stack the jury.

Burr, however, was not defenseless. Edmund Randolph, who had been Attorney General under Washington, and Charles Lee, brother to Light Horse Harry Lee and the Attorney General under John Adams, led the team of lawyers who would defend him. John Adams himself, never a lover of Burr, proclaimed that the charges were suspicious, and the methods of the government "irregular."

In the midst of preparations for the trial, the U.S. frigate *Chesapeake,* Captain James Barron commanding, sailed. All her guns but one were dismounted until she should be at sea. Inside U.S. territorial waters she was hailed by the British frigate *Leopard*, whose commanding officer demanded to search the *Chesapeake* for Royal Navy deserters. Barron refused; the British ship opened fire and pounded the defense-less *Chesapeake* into submission. Four sailors were taken off as deserters. America screamed for war.

Thomas Jefferson's answer was to issue a proclamation ordering British warships out of American waters. He announced that America had first to "scotch the snakes in our midst." Destroying Burr was to take precedence over war.

On the first of September, the jury found Aaron Burr not guilty of treason. Jefferson brought charges of mounting an invasion of Spanish territory from American soil. The public was beginning to tire of Jefferson's pursuit of Burr. Burr was found not guilty again. The same charge was brought again, with the trial site changed to Ohio. Burr, finally realizing that Jefferson would indeed cut down the Constitution to destroy him, went into hiding.

With Burr disposed of, Jefferson turned his attention to the British problem. On December 14 America was forbidden to import British goods, or any goods in British ships. A week later he protected American ships from the British Navy by forbidding them to leave ports for any foreign country. America was successfully being isolated from the rest of the world.

February of 1808 had been mild, Robert thought as he crawled over the misshapen barge moored at Carver's Bridge. He tried not to look at the idle ships tied up to the Bridge. The harbor was full of them.

"How's the pressure?" he called to Miller.

Miller peered at a gauge in front of him. "Says a hundred and fifty, captain," he called back, then added in a lower tone, "If you can trust the damned things." Kemal sat nearby, suspiciously watching the firebox that Miller bent to stoking.

"Cast loose!" Robert shouted.

Nervous men on the dock tossed the barge's lines onto her deck and back hurriedly away before it all exploded. Robert took a firm grip on the tiller. "Open the valve, Miller."

With a quick glance at the heavens Miller twisted the lever that opened a valve below deck. There was a rushing hiss, and the great paddle wheels on either side of the barge began to revolve. Slowly the barge moved away from the Bridge, under the power of steam.

Robert guided the chuffing, fifty-foot barge out into the

Cooper and pointed it upriver. The tide was running out, and on the last run against the tide the barge had made no headway at all, barely holding its own. He had poured over every word he could gather about steam boats and steam engines. Finally, he had made an adjustment that would allow the paddles to rotate faster. This was to be the test.

Near the middle of the channel, he swung the barge head on into the outgoing current. The paddle wheels churned the water; the barge slowed; but it continued to move.

"Open the valve all the way!" Robert shouted. "And pile more wood in the firebox!"

Miller looked at the stack above him, pouring out gray-black smoke, then motioned for Kemal to feed the fire while he took care of the valve. The huge Turk shook his head vigorously and moved further from the boiler. He had refused even to board the barge at first, until he realized Robert meant to leave without him. Miller sighed and pushed the valve lever all the way over, then bent back to throw wood into the firebox.

The paddles rotated faster, churning the water beneath them into white froth. And the boat began to move upstream, against the tide, a plume of smoke trailing behind it. From the banks came yells, some of greeting and some of derision, but Robert ignored them all. Others might have been first, but he had his steamboat, and that was all that mattered.

His practiced eye measured the speed at which the bank passed. Six or seven knots against the tide—Nothing to sneer at, he thought. It might even be faster than Fulton had been, back in September.

"Stand by to come about!" he shouted, and the other two took a firm grip on the nearest thing to hand.

Robert pulled a lever in front of him straight to the back and simultaneously put the helm over. The starboard paddle ground to a halt, dragging in the water while the port wheel keep turning. That, and the helm sharply over, spun the fifty-foot barge in almost its own length. As the barge completed a hundred-and-eighty-degree turn to face downriver, he pushed the lever forward again. The starboard paddle wheel grated and lumbered to life again, and the boat sped back toward the city, hastened by the tide.

"What do you think, Miller?" Robert called over the chuffing boiler and the clunking gears below.

"It's against nature, captain!" Miller shouted back. "It ain't no way for a man to travel!"

The balding bear of a man was glowering. Robert laughed. Miller would fight to keep his place aboard.

Back at the bridge, docking was simply a matter of shutting off the steam valve and throwing lines to the handlers on the wharf. The barge was drawn snuggly into place, and Robert scrambled up the ladder to the dock.

"It hardly looks like the *North River Steam Boat,*" Langdon Cheves said. He leaned casually on his walking stick as he studied the barge.

"Hello, Langdon," Robert said. "It's not supposed to. Fulton is after river traffic. There's none of that here. This is just a test. When I'm ready, I put this engine in a coaster. Then I'll get a bigger one for the real prize. A steamship that can cross the Atlantic."

Langdon whistled. "That's a large dream, Robert. Your whole cargo would have to be fuel for the boiler. And I understand some people aren't so eager to travel on Fulton's steam boat, even with the river banks handy if something goes wrong. How are you going to convince them to sail out to sea in one of these contraptions? They're dangerous, Robert."

Robert gestured such problems away. "I'll sail without passengers. And I'll just build the ship big enough to carry fuel *and* cargo." He pointed down the river. "*That's* the problem." From the Bridge they could see five hundred ships at anchor. "I'll never get a steam ship to see if Jefferson has his way. Sometimes I think I should have done like the New Englanders. Sent everything I could load out before the embargo went into effect."

"Let the Yankees be scofflaws, Robert. We'll do our fighting within the system. There isn't a planter south of Maryland—rice, cotton, or tobacco—who isn't opposed to the embargo."

"But you'll all go along with it, you planters. Jefferson is a Virginian, and a planter. As soon as the Yankees oppose him you all leap to his defense. Us against them. North against south. And you never stop to consider that just because he's a planter doesn't mean he's right.''

"That's the first time I've heard you use that construction," Langdon said slowly. "'You planters.' If you want to be particular, I'm a lawyer, not a planter. And you most certainly are a planter by birth.''

"It doesn't work that way, and you know it." He stepped to the edge of the dock. "Miller, bleed off the rest of the steam and douse the firebox. We'll not be going out again today.''

"Aye aye, captain," Miller growled.

"Robert," Langdon said, "I didn't come down here to talk about politics. Catherine's back.''

Robert didn't turn from watching Miller on the barge. Finally he said, "I didn't know." It was a lie; her note had arrived yesterday. He had taken a house on Legare Street when he returned to find Catherine still gone. He hadn't been near the East Bay house since. A year should have been enough time to make him free, but he had felt the familiar curlings of lust in his stomach. "The foundry," he said, trying to take his thoughts off her. "That's one thing the embargo will actually help. The orders for iron stock are up already, and I've begun the alterations necessary to make steel.''

"Did you understand what I said? Your sister's back. She's been back for two days. She adopted a baby up there in New England.''

"A baby?" Robert said. He leaned down to give Miller, and then Kemal, a hand up to the dock. "After gallivanting around New England for a whole year, I'd think she'd be eager to see her own daughter instead of bringing home a strange baby.''

"If you've any understanding of women, you're one up on me, Robert. Look, now that you know she's back, will you go to see her? She prevailed on me to come to you. I don't usually interfere in personal matters, but this looks dashed odd, you know. After all, you were so close.''

Robert winced. "I'll go see her, Langdon. I just . . . I'll go see her.''

When he presented himself at the East Bay house that evening, Robert knew his resolves were failing. The coat that fit snugly over his chest and shoulders, the tight, fawn-colored shirt and the white silk cravat had all been chosen with the care of a man dressing for his lover. When the thought first came, he had loosed a shout of denial that had brought Kemal on the run and scared his valet half to death, but he had not changed his care.

Ezekiel opened the door, and a smile bloomed on his face. "Why, Mr. Robert! It's been near forever since we've seen you. Come in, Mr. Robert. Come in."

"Uncle Rob!" came a squeal as he stepped through the door. A chubby, blonde, five-year-old whirlwind in a pink dress scurried across the floor to hug his knees. Just as quickly she backed away. "I wasn't supposed to do that. It's not ladylike."

He dropped to one knee to hug her. "That's all right, Charlotte. You can be unladylike with me any time you want to."

Charlotte dimpled and giggled. "Mama is home," she said. She gave a conspiratorial look around. "She brought me a baby brother to play with. Edward."

Suddenly Catherine was on the stairs. "You've taken up enough of your uncle's time for now. I'm sure he'll see you later. Cora." The child's mauma, who had been watching fondly, hurried to lead Charlotte away.

Robert slowly got to his feet. "You look well, Catherine. Beautiful." And she did. She seemed lovelier than ever, more radiant. And more desirable.

"Come into the study where we can talk," she said. He followed her half in a trance. She closed the door behind them, and then she was in his arms.

All of his good intentions went flying. He crushed her to him; his lips descended on hers hungrily. It was she, finally, who broke the kiss and leaned against his chest, breathing hard. Her hands stroked his shoulders. "So broad," she murmured. "So strong."

"A year is a long time, Catherine. Things change. I've changed. And I've decided it has to be over between us."

She laughed throatily. "You say that after that kiss? My lips are still burning from it." She traced a C on his cheek with her fingernail, hard enough to leave a mark. "I have my brand on you, Robert. You think I don't know the effect I have on you? If I flung open that door and wanted to make love in the middle of the entry hall, you'd do it. You'd argue, you'd protest, but you'd do it. If the servants were watching, you'd do it. I know the fires you light in me, and the fires I light in you, but I'm the only one of us who will admit it."

"Damn you!" He groaned. "You're the one should be branded. I ought to burn WITCH across your backside."

"Not witch. Your initials. Mark me for your property, and I'll bend over for it myself." She looked up at him fiercely, her hazel eyes blazing, and grabbing his lapels. "Damn *you*, Robert Fallon. You're the only man I've ever wanted to be weak and submissive for, and I can't, or you'll try to escape me. Damn you to hell."

He managed to pull away from her. "I came to tell you it's over, Catherine. It's over. It has to be."

"Never." She smiled, and her hands went to the laces of her dress. "You'll see."

"Edward," he said, desperate for something to divert her. He was surprised to see her flinch. "I understand you adopted a baby in New England. What sort of parents did your Edward Holtz have?"

"Fallon," she said slowly. "Edward Fallon. Karl had no part of him, of choosing him, I mean, so I gave him our family name. Edward Fallon."

"There's nothing wrong with that, I suppose." He was relieved to see that she seemed nervous. She was no longer trying to seduce him. Her discomfiture would protect him; God knew his weakness was as great as ever. "Can I see the boy?"

She hesitated. "He's sleeping. I told his mauma to put him down for a nap."

"I won't wake him." He opened the door and stepped halfway through. "Come on. I'd like to see my new nephew."

For a long moment she stared at him, then nodded stiffly. Her face was blank. Head erect, back rigid, she swept out of the study and up the stairs.

The child was in a room on the third floor. "Leave us,

Opal," Catherine said as they entered. The child's mauma flickered a glance at Robert and went out. Robert stood without speaking, looking down into the cradle. The infant had a tiny hook to his nose, and strong cheekbones sharpened his face.

"I thought he looked as papa might have as a child," Catherine said rapidly. "That's what first drew me to him, I suppose. I thought it would be wonderful to watch papa grow up."

The baby's eyes opened for a moment and stared at Robert, as sapphire blue as his own. "Oh, God," he breathed.

"His parents were Irish," Catherine hurried on. "Of a good merchant family. They. died of a fever, and there were no relatives. They must have been of the same stock papa always talked about. Black Irish."

"You've branded me, all right, Catherine. You've put a worse mark on me than the mark of Cain. And God help me, because I helped you."

"I don't understand, Robert."

He slapped her. With a small cry she spun and fell across the couch by the wall. She put a hand to her face, and licked her lips hesitantly.

"Don't lie to me," he said wearily. "On top of all the rest, don't lie to me. Do you think I don't know who this boy's mother is? Who his *father* is?"

"Robert. Please, Robert. It's not as bad as you think."

"I should have been stronger. If I'd said no to you that first time, walked away." He looked down at the child. "You poor little bastard, you. Will God mark you for it, too?"

"Don't call him a bastard!" Catherine snapped.

"He *is* a bastard. Just as I'm a bastard. But he's the bastard son of incest, and that's a double blow. Lord, Catherine, he's as much as marked for hell before he's left the cradle!"

"Damn you! Stop your whining about what you should have done. It's past, and you're not God. You're just a man. You can't change it. I've lived with it for over a year. Now *you* live with it!"

"I'll be going away," he said slowly. "Leaving Charleston. I doubt I'll be back."

Catherine sneered. "In the end, you men are all the same. You run away and leave a woman to carry your load."

Anger flared in him for the first time. "How in hell are you going to make anyone believe your little lie if I'm around? Chance resemblance to the family? Hell! The whole city will know the lie before he's ten. Because he'll be a Fallon, won't he, Catherine? We've seen to that. He'll have the marks of the Fallon blood and the Fallon pride on him for all the world to see."

"All for him," she said sarcastically. "You're running away, and it's all for him."

"You never take the responsibility for anything, do you, Catherine? Not for what you've done to me, or to the boy, or even to yourself. But you're right. I'm going away for me, too. And for you. You see, I'm thinking about taking a strap to you till you can't scream any more, then waking you up and starting over again. I don't like thinking like that. It's half what you deserve, but I don't like it. Thinking like that is liable to push a man over the edge. I might just end up putting a pistol ball right there." He put a finger between her eyes. She tried to pull her head back from it, but he followed till her head was against the back of the couch. "That's the kind of thoughts I'm having. Putting you out of your misery. So I'm going."

Abruptly he turned and stalked out of the room and down the stairs. He was taking hat and walking stick from Ezekiel when Charlotte came dashing from some hiding place down the hall.

"Uncle Robert! Aren't you going to visit with me before you go."

"I'm sorry, dumpling," he said. "I have to go away for a while. But listen," he went on as her face fell, "I've got a job, and you're the only one who can do it for me."

Her smiles blossomed again. "I'll do it, Uncle Robert."

"You must promise to look after your new little brother, dumpling. You're going to have to protect him the way a good big sister is supposed to." He looked up and saw Catherine on the stairs, pale and regal. She seemed about to reach out to him. Abruptly he realized that all the lust he'd felt for her had been cut out, and the wound cauterized. "You're the only one I can trust, Charlotte. The only one who'll look after him the way he needs to be looked after."

"I'll look after him," she said. "Uncle Robert? When are you coming back?"

He brushed her cheek with a kiss. "I don't know, dumpling," he murmured, and walked out of the house without a backward glance.

BOOK THREE

XXXVI

1807 flowed into 1808, and 1809. France invaded Spain on the pretext of protecting her coasts from the British; the British responded by invading Portugal. Thomas Jefferson declined a third term, and his protégé, James Madison, defeated Charles Cotesworth Pinckney of South Carolina for the Presidency. Napoleon divorced the Empress Josephine and married the Archduchess Maria Luisa. In Spanish America a revolutionary named Francisco de Miranda, who had once gotten arms from Michael Fallon, seized control of Venezuela. One of his lieutenants was a young man named Simón Bolívar. The French Marshal Soult was defeated at the Battle of Albuera, sealing the fate of the French in Spain; and in America, on the Wabash River, the Shawnee under Tecumseh were defeated in the Battle of Tippecanoe by William Henry Harrison, sealing the fate of the Indians in the Ohio valley.

Robert Fallon knew of none of these things. *Staghound* fled down one coast of South America, rounded the Horn in a tempest, and sped up the other coast. From the markets of Mexico to the fur-trading Indians of the Northwest Coast, to the Japans and the Mandarin courts of China, to the pagan temples of Indonesia and the dying splendor of India, to Zanzibar, to Madagascar, round the Cape of Good Hope and north again, *Staghound* ran like her namesake, away from the world Robert had left behind. Until . . . .

May was usually a gentle month in Ireland, and the people of Belfast expected no different in the year of 1812. There were soft winds down from Antrim and Lake Neagh, and rains enough to settle the dust on the cobblestones.

Belfast was a port city, a seafaring town, and its people had seen more than one strange sight, but the three men who walked up from the docks that Wednesday morning the last week of the month, gained a second and even a third look. Even from those who had seen them before.

The leader was a tall man, sun-darkened, with broad shoulders and a hooked nose and cheekbones that named him Irish as his clothes named him sea captain. He wore a sword, a strange thing in peaceful times, all decked with ivory and silver. A heathen marking, a serpent, peeked from under his left cuff; in his left hand he held a polished wooden case. There was a scar on his left cheek, and many a man who thought himself hard stepped out of this man's path after one look at his eyes.

His companions were also dressed as seamen, but the first was a swarthy giant, with a shaven head and a sword by his side that was as long as some men. The other, as bald as the first but bearded, seemed almost ordinary at first. Until the watchers realized that only the giant next to him made him look a normal size. Until they noted the scars on his face, the missing top of his right ear, the sunken knuckles, all the signs of a man who has seen a hundred hard fights.

Kemal and Miller took places on the McConnels' front step as Robert tapped on the door, then waited impatiently.

"Sakes alive!" Mrs. McConnell said when she opened the door. The diminutive woman, her gray hair drawn back, stood aside to let him in. "We weren't expecting you, Captain Fallon! I thought you sailed last night."

"I was planning to, ma'am," Robert said awkwardly. "I changed my mind. Is Moira about?" He hefted the polished case.

"I expect she's about somewhere," Mrs. McConnell said with a smile. "You join himself in the parlor, and I'll go see if I can find her."

"There's no need, mama."

Robert turned with an eager smile. Moira McConnell of the angel's face, he thought, once again admiring soft black hair framing an upturned nose and clear gray eyes. And the man in him couldn't help but notice that she was full and round of breast and hip, slender of waist and thigh. At twenty she was still single, because the young men of Belfast had learned to be wary of her sharp wit and her strong will.

"I brought you a gift, Moira," Robert said.

"Is *that* why you came back, then, Robert Fallon? Last evening you were telling me you had to go. You had to sail away somewhere. You're a man of the sea, you said, Robert Fallon. A man of the wild, free, untrammeled spaces, who cannot be held on land by four walls and a woman's arms."

"Moira!" her mother said, scandalized.

Robert smiled. "There's always another tide, Moira."

"Is there, now? And you say you've brought me a gift. Well, you've brought me gifts before, Robert, but you weren't hanging on the edge of the next tide, then. But that's just like a sailor, now, isn't it? In with one tide, barter his cargo, then out with the next tide. But what is it you intend to barter this cargo for, Robert?"

"Moira," her mother said, "that's more than enough. You hush, now. The both of you. And follow me."

She led the way to the front parlor, Robert following in her wake, Moira smiling up at him mischievously at every step. The girl had some more acid wit ready for him, he was sure. But he thought he had the way to cut her short. Perhaps even, for a wonder, leave her speechless.

Thomas McConnell, Moira's father, was poring over the London papers when they entered the parlor. He looked up with a smile. "Why, Captain Fallon! What a surprise. I thought you—"

"Not now," his wife broke in. "Captain Fallon wants to talk to Moira."

"Well, he can be saying a word or two to me, can't he?"

"The reason he didn't sail," his wife said, one word at a time, "was so he could talk to Moira."

Mr. McConnell darted a glance at his daughter, then at Robert. Suddenly a huge smile split his face. "Oh! Like that, is it? Well, now." He bustled to his feet, folding the papers, then stopped. "Those heathen that follow you about, Captain. Would they be sitting on my steps as usual?"

"Miller's a Christian, Mr. McConnell," Robert said. "But they're out there."

"Christian!" McConnel snorted. "The man's a Papist! Still, he knows good whiskey when he tastes it. And so does the other heathen. I think I'll share a drop with them." He disappeared, chuckling, and his wife followed, closing the door behind her.

"You'll have to be forgiving my parents, Robert," Moira said. "They've had me on their hands so long they're desperate."

"I don't mind," Robert said quietly.

"I mind," she said darkly, but in an instant her mood was light again. "Come, Robert. You were going to tell me something. How you got that fearsome dragon on your arm. No? I know! The Emperor of China. Chia Ch'ing. Did I say the name right? You're going to tell me about his lithe concubine who was visiting the great city of Canton, and how you climbed over the wall."

"How did you . . . there was no . . . ," he blustered. "Where did you hear a story like that?"

"I like to listen to your man Miller, boasting to my father about you. What about that dusky native princess in Zanzibar, or the sinnuous temple dancer in Calcutta? I know! That Spanish diplomat's wife in Manila. The Dutch diplomat's wife in Djakarta. And his daughter! Robert Fallon, I do think that was terrible of—"

He silenced her in the only way he could think of. By kissing her. Her arms slowly went around his neck, and her lips softened under his. Finally she drew back with a sigh.

"Robert, you shouldn't do that to an innocent girl. You've no idea what it does to me, and I'm no good at dissembling."

"Perhaps you're ready to listen, then." He sat her down in a chair, and put the box on her knees. "There, now. Open it."

She eyed the box, then him. Finally, she swung up the lid. Her eyes went wide at the contents, and she gasped. Nestled in their carven niches were combs and brushes in sterling silver and ivory, with designs were picked out in pearls.

Moira sat staring into the box, and suddenly her face twisted up. "I wish you hadn't brought it, Robert."

"Well, I suppose I should have given it to you afterward," Robert said slowly, wondering what had happened.

"Afterward," she repeated. "What is it you think to be buying with these fine trinkets?"

"Buy! Why, you fool girl, I thought you understood, what

with the way your parents were carrying on. I'm asking you to marry me, Moira McConnell.''

She sat up straight. "I'm twenty years of age, and there's no man wanted to marry me since I was seventeen. I have a sharp tongue and a willful nature, and if you meant to break me to wife you must use a heavy hand. And I'll fight you every step of the way, if you do."

"I've no intention of breaking you," he said softly. "I want to marry you, not ride you. Listen to me. When I dropped anchor in Belfast, I meant to stay no more than a week or ten days. That was three months ago, and it's all because of you. Yesterday I tried to leave. I couldn't give the orders. Now. Will you marry me?"

"Will you go out nights and get drunk?" she asked, and he smiled.

"Only if the occasion demands it."

"Will you chase after other women?"

"Only if I think you won't find out."

"Will you beat me?"

"Only if you deserve it. Moira, what are you doing?"

"I trying to think of more questions to ask you," she said seriously.

"The important question's been asked," he shouted. "Will you marry me?"

A radiant smile bloomed on her face, making her more beautiful than ever. "I will marry you, Robert Fallon. And the good Lord have mercy on your soul for the miserable wife I'll make you."

He was about to gather her into his arms when her father cleared his throat in the doorway. "Your mother, Moira—my wife, Captain Fallon—assured me there were important things to be attended to this morning, and I can see she was right." He paused to clear his throat again, and his wife darted a look around the door. "It seems to me I heard something mentioned about marriage."

"I asked Moira to marry me," Robert said.

"And I said I would, papa," Moira said in a tone that brooked no nonsense.

"That's all very well," her father said, "and I'm not one to be standing in the way of my daughter's last chance, but—"

His wife poked him in the ribs; Moira's face flooded scarlet. "Well, after all, she's twenty and still not married. How many more chances—all right, wife, all right. I'll get on with it." He tugged at his coat and put on a serious mien. "Captain Fallon, what sort of life do you offer my daughter? Will you be expecting her to go gadding about the world with you on your ship? Or do you mean for her to be waiting years at a time for you to be coming back? If you do."

"I'll sail with him, papa," Moira said quickly, "or wait ashore as he wishes."

Robert hesitated. He hadn't thought much beyond the fact that he was in love, long after he thought he'd never be so again. "Neither one is a proper life for her," he said slowly. He nodded with sudden decision. "I'll give you a home ashore, Moira, as you deserve. I can't tell you I'll never sail, but it will be measured in weeks or months, not in years. That I promise."

She smiled at him, shyly at first, but then with mischief. "If you break that word, Robert Fallon, I'll be coming after you to drag you back, if it's halfway around the world."

"Well, now," Mr. McConnell said. "That's settled." He sniffed and pursed his lips and studied the rug. "I have six daughters. May God bear witness. Six daughters and never a son. Well, five of them are married off to fine, strapping lads with businesses of their own. And my chandlery . . . well, it's the biggest in Belfast. I built it up from a pushcart, I did. But I've got no son to leave it to, and my daughter's husbands have no need of it. Now, owning a ship is a fine thing, and I must say yours is the finest I've seen. Still, a man with a wife can never have too many strings to his bow. I've room in my business for a partner, someone who'd take it over when I grow old. McConnell and Fallon doesn't sound so bad, now does it? And you'd be able to give Moira that home ashore you were speaking of, without worrying about pirates or some such."

Robert shook his head. It was clear to him now that there was only one way to give Moira the kind of life she deserved, the kind of life he *could* give her. They had to return to Charleston. Four years and more had passed. It *must* be all right to return.

"I'm sorry, Mr. McConnell, but I intend to take Moira to

the United States, to Charleston in South Carolina. I don't know what's left, but when I departed some four years ago, I had a warehouse and twenty ships, a cotton mill, an iron foundry, and a plantation. Tir Alainn no longer makes a crop, because I freed the slaves there, but the rest is enough to give Moira the sort of life I want to give her.'' He realized they were all staring at him. ''What's the matter?''

''Twenty ships,'' Mr. McConnell said faintly.

Moira faced him accusingly. ''You never told me you were rich.''

''Would it have made a difference?'' he asked.

''Perhaps not, but a woman likes to know these things about the man she's going to marry. What other surprises do you have for me?''

Suddenly he was assailed by doubt. Catherine. Little Edward. Could he really go back? ''Moira, I want you to listen carefully. I'm forty-one, old enough to be your father. That's something you may not have considered, and here's something else. I have not spent those years well. If the good and bad of my life were totted up, your minister would probably deny me the church door. And he'd be right in it. I'll not recount my sins to you, now or ever, but you must realize the kind of man I've been. I'll do my best to be a good husband to you, but think on it, and if you change your mind I'll understand.''

''Moira,'' her father said, ''you can't be expecting a saint.''

''Hush, papa,'' she said quietly. Her gray eyes rested on Robert serenely. ''The first day you walked into the chandlery, the first time I saw you, I knew you were a man filled with wickedness. But when you looked into my eyes I melted inside.''

''Moira,'' her mother admonished softly.

She went on as if she hadn't heard. ''I thought to myself, if this man doesn't ask me to marry him, I'll die. I knew it for a childish thought, and I tried to get rid of it. But I couldn't, and I still can't. If you want to back out, with your foolish talk of ages and sins, I will not stop you. But I will never marry another. And I will never stop loving you.''

''Then it looks as if we're going to be married,'' Robert said gently. He took her small soft hand in his large, hard one. ''Because I love you and want to marry you no matter what kind of sinner I am."

"Praise the Lord," Mrs. McConnell said, and Robert started. He had forgotten there was anyone else there. Mr. McConnell beamed at them from the doorway. "I thought the two of you were going to talk each other out of it. Now. Your return to America, Robert. I can call you Robert, can't I, now that you're going to be one of the family? I've been thinking on it, and I think it's a good idea. This may not be a good place for an American when the war comes."

"War?" Robert said blankly. "You mean Napoleon?"

"No, no, no! Don't you know what's been going on with your own country, man?"

"It seems not," Robert said.

McConnell puffed out his cheeks and shook his head. "Shameful, it is. Well, now, where will I start? You know that it's only a fortnight gone that Spencer Percival, the Prime Minister himself, was assassinated?"

"Vaguely," Robert said. "I haven't been paying much attention to much except Moira. You don't mean an American killed him?"

"I mean no such thing. Was a poor sot of a bankrupt named Bellingham who thought Percival should help him. Insane, most likely. But you see, Percival was going to revoke the—what are they called?—the Orders in Council. No more stopping neutral ships at sea. No more pressing foreign seamen. It's been in all the papers. With him dead, there's no telling when, or if, there'll be any change."

"Well, then," Robert said.

"Ah, but your United States has changed. Men in your Parliament, Congress, you call it, have started shouting for war. Henry Clay. John Calhoun. Langdon Cheves. Others, too. Even your own papers are calling them the War Hawks."

"John and Langdon," Robert said. He felt very foolish. How engrossed he had been in his own troubles, and then in Moira, not to have learned the state of the world. Not to have learned the state of his own friends. "So the United States may declare war."

"Exactly. I was perusing the *Times* and the *Observer* this morning, and there is disturbing news. Your Congress has voted war bonds, and authorized your President Madison to

call up a hundred thousand men. I've no doubt the next thing
we hear will be war.''

''So Jemmy Madison is President,'' Robert murmured.
''You may be right, Mr. McConnell. Jefferson wouldn't have
gone to war unless the United States was actually invaded, and
perhaps not then, but Madison is a different story.''

''You sound . . . well . . . you sound as if you welcome
it,'' McConnell said.

Mrs. McConnell clucked disparagingly. ''Hush now,
husband. The good captain isn't welcoming any war.''

Robert hesitated, but kept his silence. He did welcome the
war, welcome it for a sign that the rabble who had won their
independence thirty years before might finally be becoming a
nation. Moira squeezed his hand.

''Will you go, Robert?'' she asked. ''In the war, I mean? If
it comes?''

''If my country's at war,'' he replied, ''I can hardly sit at
home, can I?''

''The devil with all this talk of war!'' McConnell broke in.
''We have to be planning how to get you married and gone as
quickly as we can.''

''The banns!'' Mrs. McConnell cried.

''You leave the banns, and the dominie to me, wife,''
McConnell said. ''Now, here's what I propose . . . . ''

The wedding was held on the first day of June, at the
Reverend Henry McGregor's Presbyterian Church. The
Reverend had discovered that the banns had been read the
preceding three weeks in an outlying church. Robert was the
picture of a handsome groom, the ladies of the church agreed,
in his snug black suit with snowy linen at throat and cuffs.
And Moira, draped in pristine lace, was the very form of a
bride.

Robert could barely make out her face through the veil, and
her replies to the minister were quavery. And when the veil was
thrown back for the kiss, her face was as pale as the lace.
Throughout the reception that followed, Moira moved as if in
a trance, at times staring past people who tried to greet her.

Then, suddenly, Moira was gone, whisked away into the
McConnell house by her giggling sisters. Robert tried to

follow, only to find his way blocked at every turn by another smiling man with a mug or glass.

"Here, Fallon, man. Have a sip of this."

"Ah, Fallon. Here, drink this down, now."

"Captain Fallon. A sea captain, is it? Well, don't tell the ladies, but I've a jug of rum over in the corner."

Robert made his way from man to man, smiling and drinking and moving on as quickly as he could. At last he found his way into the house, vacated for the night by the McConnells themselves, who said they were visiting friends after the wedding.

Moira was standing in the middle of their bedchamber, draped in a shapeless white nightgown, twining her fingers. She darted one glance at him when he entered, then stared resolutely at the floor.

"Moira," he said gently. "Moira, I won't hurt you."

She shot a surprised look at him. "I should hope you wouldn't, Robert Fallon. It's just that I've never done this before." A flood of scarlet poured into her face. "I mean . . . I don't know much . . . that is . . . but . . . Oh, for the love of heaven, Robert, get on with it!" She gave a dismayed moan and shut her mouth tight.

"Oh, Moira," he said with a smile. He undid the buttons of the lawn nightgown and slid it off her shoulders. The gown dropped to the floor, and he gasped. Her body was perfection in cream and pink. Pear-shaped breasts tipped with upturned nipples seemed larger for her diminutive size, and the tiny waist below them. Her hips flared, round and womanly, then flowed into slender thighs and long legs.

"My mother," she said suddenly, "says I have good hips for bearing children."

"And other things, my love," he laughed, as he snatched her up in his arms and deposited her on the bed. As his mouth descended on her nipples, she gasped.

"That feeling," she panted. "Robert, I feel . . . I don't know how I feel. So good."

He didn't answer, beginning an exploration of her satiny skin with fingers, lips, and tongue. She moaned as he traced a trail across her stomach, wailed softly as he kissed his way up the insides of her thighs. When he returned to her now stiffly erect nipples she tangled her fingers in his hair, and lifted her shoulder to press her breast more firmly to his mouth. The only sounds she made now were incoherent fragments of words. Her body seemed to move of its own accord.

Moving over her, he parted her thighs and thrust into her. Immediately she came alive. Her legs whipped around him, her teeth clamped into his chest. She writhed against him as he moved in her, soft silken flesh forcing itself harder against hard muscle. When he gasped his release, she screamed against his chest and drummed her heels on his back.

Afterwards, she traced red ridges her teeth had left. She giggled. "I put my mark on you, Robert Fallon."

He felt a sudden chill. Catherine had said the same, or nearly. "So you have, Moira. And yours is the only one that counts."

"Of course." She stretched langorously and sighed with contentment. "I wonder if it will be a boy or a girl."

"What?"

"Our baby. The baby we just made. Will it be a boy or a girl, do you think?"

"Well, you may not be with child after only once, Moira."

"But I thought . . . ."

"Sometimes it takes years, you know."

"Years? Then we have to do this lots of times?"

"Lots of times," he laughed. "But you'll have to let me rest a bit."

She snuggled in against him, making swirls in the hair of his chest with her finger. "Do you think my father's right, Robert?"

"About what?" He settled deeper in the pillows.

"About the war. Do you think there will be a war?"

"Perhaps."

"If there is . . . well, a man with ships and all, he wouldn't need to actually go himself."

"He would," he said gently. He went on as she tried to speak. "Do you know, I think I've rested long enough." And he rolled into her waiting arms.

XXXVII

The bells of St. Michael's were sounding as Catherine left the church after Sunday service and made her way to her waiting carriage. Its top was down to catch whatever breeze was available in late June. Mary hurried to hold a parasol over her.

A liveried black footman held the carriage door for her, but she paused as her children were bundled out of the church by their maumas and into their own carriage. Catherine refused to be crowded by having them in her own. They were beautiful children, she thought. Young Edward, only four, did his best to walk with a manly swagger. And at nine Charlotte was a tiny lady in blue lawn, with graceful movements and just a hint of coquetry in her smile. Already she was being marked by mothers with sons of a suitable age. Her and the Fallon wealth.

"Such lovely children," Anne Waring said, pausing next to Catherine.

"Beautiful children," Louise Thibodeaux agreed, then added cryptically, "Men fashion crosses, then leave us women to bear them."

Catherine acknowledged the comments briefly and hurried into the carriage. "Home, Jacob," she said, and settled back beneath Mary's parasol.

Louise had been one of those who had seen through Edward's parentage, she thought. At least, part way. She, like the others, assumed that Edward was Robert's illegitimate offspring, and that Catherine had concocted the tale of adoption to protect him from his bastardy. After all, Robert Fallon was something of a ne'er-do-well, gone from Charleston for years now, with no hint of when he would be back. Catherine chuckled throatily. The same people who were condemning Robert regarded her as something of a saint. She could imagine their shock if they knew that she had a discreet sucession of lovers, each carefully chosen to maintain his silence.

As the carriage pulled up at the East Bay house, she frowned; another carriage stood in the drive. "Thomas DeSaussure," she muttered to herself, and hurried into the house. "Mrs. Holtz," Ezekiel said with a bow as he opened the door.

"Where is he?" Catherine broke in.

"Miss Catherine," Mary said, darting into the house, "you got to watch that getting out in the sun. A minute here and a minute there, at your age."

"Hush up," Catherine snapped. "Ezekiel, where is he?"

"Mr. DeSaussure in the study, Mrs. Holtz."

Catherine smiled to herself as she swept to the study door and flung it open. He still thought to gain some advantage by holding this meeting in a supposed male sanctum. "Mr. DeSaussure," she said, "how good of you to call. Especially so early. On Sunday."

DeSaussure blinked awkwardly. "I'm sorry, Mrs. Holtz. But news just received this morning makes it imperative that I speak to you."

"The same thing again?" she asked wearily. "When I asked you to shut down the mill and the foundry, it was because I deplored having my family name so vulgarly associated with trade. When you refused, in the absence of my brother, and I resorted to the courts, the magistrate agreed with me. It was degrading and humiliating. I have not heard that the court has changed its ruling, and I have not changed mine. I only wish the judge had felt the same way about the ships. Owning ships is *not* a genteel occupation, no matter what he said."

DeSaussure took a deep breath and made a visible attempt to gain control of himself. "Mrs. Holtz, you must let me reopen the foundry at least. The nation needs it."

"What are you talking about?"

"We're at war, Mrs. Holtz. That's the news I spoke of. Tuesday last the Congress declared war on England. Riders from Washington City arrived this morning. Before he left, your brother had ordered machinery for making musket barrels. We're going to need muskets, Mrs. Holtz, and with sea trade disrupted as it likely will be, a thousand other things from iron. There'll be a need for cotton cloth, too, for uniforms and such.

"There are many places in New England where they have no scruples about manufacturing. Let them make the uniforms and the muskets. I will have no part of it."

"But, Mrs. Holtz—"

"Ma'am!" Ezekiel said, suddenly appearing in the doorway. His face was split by an excited grin. "Ma'am, he's home!"

"Ezekiel," she said angrily, "you know better than to interrupt!"

Her frown didn't dent the butler's wide smile. "He's home, Miss Catherine. Mr. Robert is home."

Catherine took a shaky step forward. "He can't be. He's dead this time. He's dead and gone."

But suddenly he was in the door. "I'm sorry to disappoint you, sister, but I'm very much alive. I brought *Staghound* across the bar this morning." There was a scar on his cheek and a touch of gray at his temples, but there could be no doubt it was him.

For the first time Catherine noticed the girl behind him. His usual taste, she thought. Too young for him, with breasts too big. What port had he picked her up in? "You haven't introduced me to your friend."

His smile had an edge to it. "Sister, may I present my wife, Moira McConnell Fallon. Moira, this is my sister, Catherine Fallon Holtz."

"It's pleased I am to meet my husband's sister, Catherine," Moira smiled.

From the back of the entry hall there was a sudden burst of children's laughter and the sounds of running feet. Charlotte and Edward, somehow free of their maumas, appeared racing for the steps. They skidded to a halt at the sight of the adults. Charlotte stared at Robert quizzically, then a great grin swept her face.

"Uncle Robert!" she squealed.

He dropped to one knee and flung his arms wide, and she ran into them. "How's my dumpling?" he chuckled. "You've gotten to be such a pretty girl, I'll have to stand in line for my hugs now.''

She dimpled, but almost immediately motioned vigorously for Edward to come forward. ''I took care of him, Uncle Robert. Just like you said.''

Edward held out his hand solemnly. ''My name's Edward,'' he said.

Robert shook hands with equal dignity. ''How do you do, Edward.''

''Enough,'' Catherine said, and had to stop to clear her throat. Robert—a wife—his son! There was a burning behind her eyes. Angrily she shook her head. ''Cora! What are these children doing running loose?'' The errant maumas appeared guiltily from the back of the house, quailing under her gaze. ''Take the children upstairs. I'll speak to you later.''

DeSaussure had gained Robert's elbow. ''Mr. Fallon, I need to speak to you urgently.''

DeSaussure drew Robert across the room. Catherine was about to follow when she noticed that Moira was staring after the children. Something in her gaze prompted Chaterine to say, ''Charlotte is mine. Edward is adopted.''

Moira looked at her in surprise. ''I would have thought otherwise.''

Catherine smiled maliciously. ''One can't leave one's brother's bastard to roam the streets, can one?'' She watched, puzzled, as the shot seemed to miss entirely.

''Men are no saints at the best of times,'' Moira said. ''There's little telling what the best of them can do at his worst.'' She sounded amused.

Catherine was shaping a sharp retort when Robert broke in.

''Mr. DeSaussure has been telling me about your help in managing my affairs while I was away, Catherine.''

''You know my opinion of trade,'' she said sweetly.

''My father is in trade,'' Moira said suddenly.

Catherine gave her most condescending nod. ''I'm sure.''

There was an angry light in Moira's eyes, but Robert, the one she wanted to reach, to tear at, faced her with arrogant amusement on his face.

''Didn't you know,'' he said, ''that I set aside part of the income from the mill and the foundry for Edward? They seemed the most likely to flourish with the embargo and all the rest.''

Her face tightened. "I don't need any of your money to take care of Edward." She was aware of Moira watching her curiously, and that added to her rage.

"You've answered one question for me," he said, still looking at her with that half-smile on his lips. "Considering the state you've put my affairs in, I can't afford to stay out of this war. Mr. DeSaussure, I assume the government's issuing letters of marque?"

"No!" Catherine shouted, and was irritated to realize that Moira had shouted the same thing at the same time.

"They have announced that intention, Mr. Fallon," DeSaussure said. He ignored the women's interruption, as did Robert. "It may be some weeks yet, however, before one can be produced."

"Just as well," Robert said. "That will give me time to put things in order here."

"Robert," Moira said, "you promised me you would consider this carefully, and here you're going at it on the moment."

Catherine shot her a sidelong glance. Why didn't the little snip shut up? She could convince Robert to stay if the stupid woman stayed out of it. "Robert, there's no need for you to go yourself. In fact, it's foolish. The country needs the foundry and the mill now." DeSaussure's jaw dropped; she hurried on. "You must stay and put them to rights. Send a ship out privateering if you want to, send all your ships. But don't go yourself."

"Such concern for the country," Robert said mockingly. "From that tremor in your voice, a body would think the country was almost as important as the price of cotton, or the newest modiste in town."

"Don't let her be goading you," Moira said quickly. "In a minute you'll be committing yourself to something just because she's saying don't."

"Why don't you shut up!" Catherine snapped. "I'm his sister. I can talk him out of it if you'll just keep your mouth shut, you miserable vulgar little snip."

"It's his wife that I am," Moira spat back. "His wife. It's my place to keep him from harm. From what I can see, you've done what you could to destroy him. Now you're trying to goad him into going away to be killed."

Catherine's eyes glittered, and her fingers curled into claws. "Why, you little . . . ." Moira faced her with her teeth bared, her own nails ready to claw.

"You two cats take the arch out of your backs." Robert growled, "or I'll throw a bucket of water of you."

Catherine turned on him, infuriated that Moira did the same.

"Cats, is it!" Moira said. "It's trying to protect you I am, and you're calling me a cat?"

He took Moira's face in his hands. Catherine felt a stab of jealousy. "Moira, my love," he said gently, "you *are* a cat. So fierce in defense of me; so soft otherwise. But I only promised you to consider, and my consideration's done. You must understand that and accept it."

Moira sighed and put her hands over his on her cheeks. "Go if you must, Robert Fallon, but if you get yourself killed I'll follow you to hell to make your stay there miserable."

"You fool!" Catherine said. "You'll let—"

"And as for the manufactories," Robert broke in. "Is McGregor still around?"

"He's upstate," DeSaussure said. "Building another cotton mill."

"Get him back. He can run the mill and the foundry better than I could."

Catherine took a deep breath to try again. "Robert—"

"Sister," he said, ostentatiously putting Moira's hand on his arm, "my wife and I are tired from the journey, and I still must arrange rooms. This will have to continue later." Moira leaned lightly against Robert and smiled up at him. It was doubly angering to Catherine that she could detect no triumph in the smile. The foolish woman didn't even know she was doing battle for her man. But she would.

"Nonsense, Robert. There's no need for you to go looking for lodgings. I have a huge house here, and there are always rooms ready. Most certainly for you."

He paused and looked at Moira, then patted her hand. His voice softened. "Thank you, Catherine. We accept your offer. It's most kind."

She returned his smile. Did he think marriage would make him free? He was mistaken. Fatally so.

XXXVIII

Jeremiah dropped the piece of sharkskin with which he had been smoothing the table leg and regarded his work sourly. No air stirred among the carefully displayed furniture in his shop, the fine pier-tables, the beautifully grained sideboards, the highly polished chest-on-chests. Sweat dripped down his face in the August heat.

He wondered why he was finishing the table. No one had ordered it; no one was likely to buy it. The diplomacies of Washington City had hit him hard. In the North, he understood, ships still sailed despite the Non-Intercourse Act, despite, some whispered, the war. From Chesapeake Bay south it was otherwise, and had been since the beginning. The planters had, to a man, put their rice, cotton, and tobacco into warehouses. Some still shipped to New England and New York merchants, and doubtless some was resold in Europe, but the trade had slowed to a trickle. And so had the flow of dollars. No planter was buying fine furnishings.

His thoughts turned to Robert Fallon. Back little more than a month, the man had worked wonders. The weeds were gone from the foundry yard; bars of pig iron had already taken their place. At the mill, the first cotton cloth was coming off the looms. Fallon was a human whirlwind. That seemed to give added weight to his offer. With a child on the way, perhaps it was time to reconsider.

Even as the thought formed, the door banged open and Denmark Vesey strode in. "What's this I hear?" he said without preamble. "You're going off to fight in the white man's war?"

"Not to fight," Jeremiah said. He picked up the sharkskin and busied himself on the table leg. "Robert Fallon's taking out a privateer. He's offered me the post of ship's carpenter. That's not a fighting job.''

"Don't pick nits with me, boy!''

"I'm not a boy, Denmark. I'm twenty-six years old. I have a wife and a family. Two little girls, and a third child on the way. My wife has been laundering these past two years for us to make ends meet. You think I've been feeding them with this shop? Most of what I make comes from odd jobs, fixing and mending, even hiring out as a laborer. I've been doing a lot of fishing the last couple years. We've been eating a lot of fish.''

"I didn't know it was that bad,'' Vesey said awkwardly. "You should have come to me. I could have found you some work.''

"I've noticed how flush you've been,'' Jeremiah said drily.

"All right. So I haven't been working that much myself. That's no reason for you to go get yourself killed in the white man's war. It's none of your business, Jeremiah. Whatever comes out of it, it won't make your life one bit better. You'll still be a black man.''

"I'll be a black man with three and a half shares. That's the split, Denmark. Half to the owner, and he intends to give up the captain's share for the crew. The six shares to lieutenants, four to the gunner, three and a half to gunner's mates, sailmaker, boatswain, and carpenter. That's me. Carpenter. That's a lot more than most of the whites will be getting. A share and a half to able-bodied seamen, one share to ordinary seamen. It might be a white man's world and a white man's war, Denmark, but this is one black man who's going to do damned well out of it.''

"You'll get your fool head blown off.''

"It's better than watching my wife work herself to death.''

"You've made up your mind, then,'' Vesey said flatly.

"I suppose I have.''

"Looks like I wasted my time. If you change your mind, come by the shop. Maybe I can find something for you.'' And he disappeared as quickly as he had come.

Jeremiah frowned at the table. He had rubbed across the grain, roughing the surface instead of smoothing it. He *had* decided.

His brother Billy stumbled out of the back of the shop,

yawning. "Who was that I heard?"

"Vesey," Jeremiah answered curtly. Billy ran to the front of the shop, trying to spot Vesey in the street. There was something unhealthy there. Billy took anything Vesey said as Gospel. Anything.

"Why didn't you wake me?" Billy complained. "You always trying to keep me away from Denmark. I don't understand you. *You* listens to him enough."

"I know enough to tell what to listen to."

"What that suppose to mean?" Billy scrubbed at his face with both hands. "You got any money? I gots to get me a drink before my head busts open."

"It was drink got it like that in the first place." When Billy continued to stare at him, he sighed. "No, I don't have any money."

Billy sneered as he ran his eye over the displayed furniture. "All this fancy work, all this hard work, and you ain't got no money neither. What will it gain you now, brother?"

"I'm going away for a while," Jeremiah said. He was pleased at Billy's surprised grunt. "I'm going to be the ship's carpenter on the privateer *Shrike.*"

"*Shrike!* That a Fallon ship."

"That's right. If you need anything while I'm gone, Billy, you go to the Fallons. You hear?"

"I ain't going to beg from no white folks. Denmark, he say—"

"You go to Denmark, and he'll try to put to work. I know you won't work, Billy, and if it comes to begging or stealing, I'd rather have you beg."

"You go on," Billy said. "You go be the Fallons' nigger. I ain't going to beg for nothing."

"That's fine." Abruptly Jeremiah put down the sharkskin and put on his coat. Herding his brother before him into the street, he locked the door firmly.

"What you doing?" Billy asked. "You don't ever close up this early."

"I'm closed up till the war's over," Jeremiah replied. "I'm a ship's carpenter now. Not a cabinet maker. You'll have to find some place else to sleep off your drunks."

"You always got the hooks into me," Billy scowled. "You

doing this just to get at me, ain't you? Well, I don't need you. I got plenty friends with places I can sleep.'' With a sneer he swaggered of down the street.

Jeremiah watched him disappear into the traffic with a frown. Billy had to live his own life, make his own mistakes, however bad they were. Jeremiah shrugged; he had all he could do to live his own life. He began to whistle as he turned up East Bay. *Shrike* was moored up that way.

Robert stood in his shirt sleeves on the bank where the tall marsh grass began and watched the men on the sunken steam barge. They were plying the pumps. At each seesaw sweep a gout of water spouted over the far side of the barge, but still there was no sign of motion from the hulk. Its smokestack was the only thing showing. Men had lived to patch the holes. Why wasn't it rising?

In a clatter of hooves, three horsemen galloped up behind him, stopping next to his own mount. One, Louis Middleton, in the high-collared blue uniform and cocked hat of a lieutenant-colonel of South Carolina Militia, dismounted.

"They told me at the foundry you'd be here," Middleton said, with a curious stare at the pumps. "What is it?"

"My steam barge. Remember? For some reason I had it on the books of the foundry. The machinery, I suppose. When Catherine got the foundry closed down, the barge sat out here untended till it sank."

"How could I forget?" Louis chuckled. "Huffing and puffing up and down the river. Scared hell out of the horses, as I recall. But why raise it, Robert? Wasted effort, you know. Rot and rust probably have it full of holes by now."

"Perhaps," Robert said irritably. How could he explain that the sunken barge was a symbol of what Catherine had done to his life? He had stared at it day after day as he rode up to the foundry, and finally he had known he must raise it. If he could, then he would salvage his life from Catherine. "What did you want with me, Louis?"

"The same as I wanted yesterday, and the day before, and the day before that. The muskets, man. You got the order because everybody would like some of the militia's muskets to be made here in the state. And I keep saying you'll deliver. Well, you know Joseph Alston isn't going to pressure you, but there are others, and they're worried." He settled into an uncomfortable silence.

"I don't know how many times I have to explain it, Louis. The iron I'm making now is good enough for some things, but not for the muskets. Inside a month, though, the foundry will be turning out good cast English steel. A month after that, you'll have the first of the muskets. Explain that to Alston and anyone else who wants to know. God, I don't remember him being such an ass before he became governor."

"I'll try, Robert. But—are you sure?"

"I'm sure," Robert said wearily. Suddenly there was a shout from the pumps. He whirled just as the steam barge bobbed to the surface with a splash. It was covered with the green slime of long immersion and streaked with black mud, but it floated. "I'm sure," he said more strongly.

Louis followed Robert back to the horses, watching with pursed lips as Robert tugged on his coat. "What will you do with it? The barge, I mean."

"They'll tow it up to the foundry, clean it up, haul it up on the bank." He swung into the saddle. "I have to ride down to the Bridge. Will you ride with me?"

"Um? Oh, Delighted. Gaillard! Lockwood! I'll see you back at headquarters." The two lieutenants saluted and rode away. Louis scrambled into his saddle, and he and Robert turned toward the city. "I have some news, and it's not for general consumption," he said with a nod to the departing lieutenants.

"Such as?"

"Well," Louis said slyly, "the governor of Massachusetts has declared a fast to protest the war."

"Is that all? The last I heard they were talking secession. And *that's* known in any tavern you care to choose."

"Yes," Louis said smugly, "but they don't know the British have revoked the Orders in Council."

Robert jerked in his saddle. "Are you sure? Why, this could mean the war's over before it's begun."

"I'm afraid not, Robert. There's been fighting already."

"Where? A naval action? I heard the frigates were being ordered to sea."

"I don't know anything about the Navy. This is up in the Northwest Territory. A General named William Hull surrendered Detroit to the British without firing a shot. And some British-led Indians massacred a lot of people up at Fort Dearborn. I don't think there's going to be any quick peace after that. Do you?"

"No," Robert said thoughtfully. They clattered past the fortifications that were being built across the peninsula, some of them following the British and American lines of the Revolution. Then, he remembered from his father's tales, every man in the city, rich and poor alike, had turned out to work. Now this work was mostly being done by slaves. The few soldiers standing about seemed to droop in the August heat.

They merged with the traffic on East Bay, mainly carts under hire to the militia. Some had expected the war to revive trade, but New England was still trading with the British, and no one was willing to try running the English blockade into France.

"We're circling the harbor with fortifications," Louis said. "If the British come, they'll get what they got the last time."

"Surely you mean the time before last," Robert said drily. "The last time they took the city."

At the Bridge, Robert took Louis out to *Shrike*. A topsail schooner with the sharp hull called a Baltimore clipper, she was seventy feet long with two raked masts, and pierced for eight guns. Kemal hurried down the gangplank as soon as they appeared. If *Shrike* was to be ready for sea as soon as possible every experienced man was needed, but even so it had taken every ounce of his persuasion to make the huge Turk leave his side.

"Eight guns," Louis said, shaking his head. "You won't face down much of an opponent with that. I've heard of privateers with twenty guns or more. You should take the *Staghound* instead. You could mount twenty guns on her."

"Too big," Robert said. "A privateer must be able to dart and cut, and *Staghound*'s not made for that."

"But still, Robert. Eight guns. What will you do if you meet a warship?"

"I'll run like hell!" Robert sobered. "Things are different

now. We aren't going to fight any warships. You know, I thought this war was going to bring the country together, unite us and make us strong. Instead it seems to be dividing us. New England is talking of leaving the Union, and even those who support the war are only lukewarm. No, this lot won't fight any warships." He shook his head. "God, I wish my commission would come. This waiting is grinding me down."

"Your commission?" Louis said, his face suddenly vacant. He dug beneath his coat and produced a packet with a large red seal. "This came to headquarters for you. I was bringing it to you, but it slipped my mind. Perhaps it's . . . . " He let his voice trail off as Robert snatched the packed from his hands.

Robert didn't need the seal of the United States to tell him what it was. He tore it open.

> The President and Congress of these United States of America do hereby authorize and direct the private armed vessel *Shrike,* out of the port of Charleston, South Carolina, to seek out the vessels and commerce of Great Britain wherever they may be found on sea or land, and seize or destroy the same.

As the *Shrike* sailed out of Charleston the first day of September, Catherine stood on the front portico of her East Bay house watching through a spyglass.

"He's gone," Moira breathed, lowering her own glass.

Catherine's mouth tightened. "You did little enough to stop him." Having them stay with her had seemed such a good idea when Robert was there.

"He wanted to go," Moira said. "When a man wants to do a thing as much as Robert wanted to do this, a smart woman lets him do it. The other's the way to losing him, as you no doubt discovered."

"What?" She looked at Moira curiously, but the other woman avoided her eyes.

"I've heard of the like happening before, though most often in the country, where other girls and boys might be a long distance of. Still, Robert is the kind of man even a sister could have dreams about."

Catherine stood staring blankly out at the harbor. Her feet

seemed frozen to the spot. "I don't understand," she said faintly. Moira's reply was like a knife.

"I didn't either, not in the beginning. There was something in the air between you, though. Then there's Edward. Your smile at him is a mother's smile, Catherine. The way your fingers caress his cheek, the way you scold him. You're not a woman to be that way toward your brother's bastard waif."

"What you're suggesting—"

"I'm suggesting nothing," Moira broke in, but immediately her voice softened. "I'll not be speaking of it again, Catherine, but it had to be brought out between us. You see, I truly can understand. I ask myself how I would feel if I were Robert's sister, and the answer I get each time is I'd want him just as much as I do now. I know it's called a sin, but some of the . . . some of the things Robert and I have done are called sins, too, married though we are. And how can I call it sin? I might well have done the same thing were I in your place."

"You're making horrible accusations. Horrible! You're simply making things up out of whole cloth!" Moira turned to face her for the first time, and though the smaller woman's face held no animosity Catherine found herself shying away.

"I don't mind you denying it, Catherine. I suppose I would, too. But I want you to know that Robert's mine. You can't have him back."

"This is ridiculous," Catherine insisted. "This is Charleston, not some Turkish bagnio."

Moira went on as if she hadn't spoken. "I'll be staying here, because to leave as soon as Robert's gone would only set tongues to wagging. And I do love being near little Edward. Catherine, I don't know if we will ever be friends, though I think you're a woman I could like, but I'll call a truce, at least, from this moment. If you'll have it. Edward is Robert's child and yours. And Robert is my husband. I think I'll go in now. The breeze from the river is chilly. You should come in, too, Catherine, and have a hot cup of tea."

Catherine remained frozen where she stood while Moira went into the house. She felt as if she were going to be ill. She pressed her palms against her ribs and felt her heart beating wildly. She had to get away, away from the house, away from Charleston, away from the state. As far away from Moira as possible. But there had to be a reason for the trip, a good reason. She wasn't about to let Moira think she was running from her. Theodosia Alston. Theo had been talking of going to New York after Christmas. If she could prompt Theo into an invitation to accompany her . . . .

Thoughtfully, she turned and walked into the house.

XXXIX

Shrike knifed into the long gray rollers of the North Sea, sending icy spray dashing down the length of her deck. The sails were taut from a stiff December wind that howled out of a sky as gray as the sea. Robert, on the quarterdeck, turned up the collar of his heavy coat, but it was already soaked. He buried his hands deep in his sodden pockets, keeping his eye on the fleeing sail ahead. Much rested with that sail.

The first prize they had taken, a month ago, had been a brig loaded with lumber, and the next two had been laden with odds and ends equally worthless of a prize crew. He had put the crews in boats and burned the ships, though his own crew was grumbling by the last. Even a rundown brig, they complained, was worth something.

Kemal appeared on the quarterdeck, a steaming mug in his large fist and a dry coat over his arm. Gratefully Robert shrugged out of his sodden coat and worked into the fresh one. His joints felt stiff, and his knuckles hurt as he forced them to bend around the hot mug. The taste of hot chocolate and rum spread through him. The sail ahead was closer; it was a brigantine. Miller was crouched over the fore gun of the starboard battery, and the crew watched both him and the doomed merchantman hungrily.

There had been other prizes in the Irish Sea, many of them. Seven fishing smacks, stinking of their cargos. A smuggler's lugger, empty. Two snows flying the flag of Norway. A schooner with the flag of the Russias. Three merchant vessels with British flags had managed to dart into a handy port, and another had been lost in the night. Twice, just as the *Shrike*'s long dry spell seemed about to be broken, a warship had hove over the horizon. Each time he'd run, leaving warship and prize alike. There had been more than grumbling, then. Some had talked openly of leaving ship at the first port where they might sign on with another privateer. One with a "luckier" skipper. His decision to leave the Irish Sea, to sail the icy waters above the British Isles, hadn't lessened the rumblings. But then, he hadn't made his decision because of the crew's complaints.

"We could fire now, captain," said Hogarth, the thin-faced first mate. He stood on the other side of the helmsman from Robert.

"Not quite yet, Mr. Hogarth," Robert said. He took another swallow of the chocolate and rum. It was beginning to cool already.

"We've been in range for five minutes," Hogarth protested. "If another prize gets away . . . well, the crew are going to be disappointed."

"If any of the crew are disappointed," Robert said levelly, "they can leave the ship when we reach Norway."

"I was merely pointing out that we've lost more than one prize already, captain."

Robert sighed. Benteen, his first mate on *Staghound,* had been offered a privateering commanding of his own, as had Danneman, the second. He had had to make do with new men, Hogarth, and fat Copes, and Dacoin, who never stopped smiling. "The more we fire, the more we fire and miss, as we're likely to in these seas at anything more than point-blank range, the more heart we put in that brigantine's captain. I intend to fire one shot from close enough to make sure of cutting rigging, and hope the captain will think about how he's right under our guns."

"Yes, sir," Hogarth said uncomfortably.

Robert looked at the crew gathered in the waist. They all had cutlasses or boarding pikes in hand, though they would most likely be used only to intimidate the merchantman's crew. Jeremiah, his carpenter's apron on over his heavy coat and his tool chest at his feet, watched the proceedings coolly. Kemal reappeared with his silver-and-ivory-hilted scimitar, and he belted it on absently.

"Miller," Robert called, "what do you think of the range?"

"I can put it in her captain's ear, sir," Miller shouted back.

An approving murmur went through the crew.

"Close over the bow will do," Robert replied. "And try to cut some rigging. When you're ready. Starboard your helm, Putnam."

The wheel went over and *Shrike* veered to bare her starboard side to the running brigantine. Miller bent quickly over the twelve-pounder, tapped a quoin in a trifle, and touched linstock to the vent. With a roar the piece slammed back against its restraining tackle. The wind whipped the acrid smoke away immediately. On the brigantine the fore topmast staysail was suddenly slack, and then the wind tore it away. In the same instant her flag came fluttering down. She turned into the wind and came to a stop in the water.

"Shall I put a boat over the side?" Hogarth asked eagerly.

Robert didn't mention the heavy seas. "Take us alongside, Mr. Hogarth."

"Aye, aye, sir," Hogarth said, and turned to give orders to the helmsman.

Shrike was maneuvered alongside the larger vessel, and grappling hooks secured them rail to rail. A dozen of the privateers swarmed onto the brigantine as if expecting a fight, but Robert merely climbed over the rail onto the other vessel's quarterdeck.

"What vessel is this?" he said.

A plump, chesty man who kept pushing his lips in and out stepped forward angrily. "The *Anna,* out of Bristol. I'm Captain Oliver Harcourt, and I want you to know this is an outrage. You may rest assured that piracy will not be tolerated in the very waters of—"

"You know of the war," Robert broke in. "Else you wouldn't have run when you saw us. I'll have your manifest, if you please."

Harcourt worked his mouth, then nodded sharply and went below. Amidships, the *Anna*'s seven-man crew huddled under the watchful eyes of their guards. Others of *Shrike*'s crew could be heard below, searching for contraband. Jeremiah climbed up from below and came to Robert.

"I sounded the well, captain. There's more water in it than should be, but I made a quick check of the hull and I couldn't find any bad timbers."

Sounds as if the owner's been skimping on repairs,'' Robert used. "Well, we'll save him even that cost in the future. Thank you, Jeremiah.''

Harcourt puffed up the ladder, but before Robert could read the papers, *Shrike*'s masthead lookout sang out.

"Sail ho! South-south-west and bearing this way!''

Hogarth jerked. "A warship! Another damned man-o'-war to rob us!'' Harcourt beamed maliciously.

Robert tipped his head and cupped his hands around his mouth. "What kind of ship?''

"Sloop!'' came down the howled reply. "Topsail sloop!''

Harcout's smile faded a trifle. Hogarth shook his head. "It could be a revenue cutter.''

"A revenue cutter's not a warship,'' Robert said. "It's a toy with popguns. We could pound it to flinders for target practice. Send up a distress flare, Mr. Hogarth.''

"A distress flare, sir?''

"That's right. And get *Shrike*'s port battery loaded. Don't run out, and keep back from the guns, but stand to. What sort of battery does this tub have? Well, Hogarth? The merchantman's guns?''

"Uh, four-pounders, sir two to a side. Scarcely worth the bother of carrying.''

"Christ! Well, load the starboard ones anyway. Same as with the *Shrike*'s guns. Crews to keep back until I give the order.'' Both Harcourt and Hogarth were staring at him with their mouths open. "Hop to it!'' he said. "The flare, man. The flare.''

A yellow rocked arced into the air, and the lookout called excitedly. "She's turning this way!''

"You're mad!'' Harcourt said in a strangled whisper.

As the sloop approached the two vessels, it swung its stern toward *Shrike* and the wind went out of its sails. Robert picked up a speaking trumpet.

"Halloo!'' came a hail from the sloop. "What seems to be your trouble?''

"Run out,'' Robert said quietly. The gun ports crashed open and the cannons rumbled forward to poke their iron snouts at the sloop. "This is the American private armed vessel *Shrike!*'' he called through the leather trumpet. "You have one minute to surrender or receive a broadside!"

From the sloop there was complete silence. And then the British flag drifted down from the masthead. Robert turned to look at Harcourt with a smile. "You were saying?"

Later, when the crews of both captured vessels were gathered on the decks of the *Shrike,* he had a chance to peruse the manifests. The *Anna* was laden with cutlery and ironware, worthy of a crew, but the sloop, the *Stout Heart*, was rich. Her cargo, in its entirety, was sugar—worth a small fortune in any European port.

Jenkins, the *Stout Heart*'s captain, was twice as fat and twice as fiery as Harcourt. He stalked to the foot of the quarterdeck ladder, ignoring the cutlasses of the *Shrike*'s crew. "I still demand to know the meaning of this! These are practically British waters! Who in hell are you?"

"The American private armed vessel *Shrike*," Robert said. "As I told you.''

"American private armed vessel? A damned pirate is what you are?"

"So I've been told," Robert said drily. "You men," he went on, addressing the captive crews over Jenkins' head. A few looked at him dispiritedly. "That's right. You. Your ships will be taken in prize, your fate is likely to be confined below till I can put you ashore, or find a worthless ship to turn into a cartel. For a few of you, though, there's a chance to help crew the prizes, and get a half share of the prize money for it. You'll be free to walk away or sign on, as you please, once the prize is in port."

Furtive glances passed among the huddled sailors.

"You'll not seduce my men, you bloody American bastard!" Jenkins shouted. "Their loyalty can't be bought!"

"You scurvy swine," Harcourt growled. "You Jonathons are all alike. You think any man's for sale."

As if unsure of his own words, Jenkins rounded on the British seamen. "You stand fast, hear! Take this offer and it's the first step on the walk to the gallows."

Robert ignored the captains tirade. "Who's for it?"

Two men from the *Stout Heart*'s five and one from the *Anna* stepped forward without looking at their fellows, then quickly took a few paces away from the rest.

"You'll hang!" Jenkins screamed. "I'll tie the bloody rope myself!"

"Get the rest below, Mr. Dacoin," Robert ordered. "Mr. Hogarth, take four men and that one from the brig aboard the sloop. Mr. Copes, you'll take the two from the sloop and three of ours, and take the brig. We'll separate now, to avoid notice, and meet in Bergen as planned." Everyone started to move except Hogarth.

"Captain," the first mate said, "the British have probably cut off the supply of sugar to the United States. That's where the best price will be, don't you think?"

"No, I don't, Mr. Hogarth." For once he was unable to keep the irritation out of his voice. A prize captain bringing a rich prize into an American port this early in the war was certain to be offered a command of his own. Well, Hogarth would have to wait. "If the British have managed to cut off the sugar supply, they've so blockaded the coast you're not likely to get through at all. Besides, I don't want to send any of my Americans off. We'll be filling up with the sweepings of Europe's ports soon enough without that. Now get your men aboard the *Stout Heart*, before a man-o'-war *does* show up."

"Aye, aye, sir," Hogarth said, clearly disgruntled.

Robert watched him gather his men with a jaundiced eye. With faint hearts and self-servers, and those who were willing to change coats, with such were they trying to cripple a giant's trade.

XL

"Watch the decorations," Catherine called, and grimaced as the slaves knocked two more wreaths of smilac and holly off the wall.

As they took the last of her trunks out the back door, she sighed. They'd likely drop it twice before it got to the wagon, whether she was standing over them or not. It wasn't worth the additional aggravation.

It had been an irritating three months since Robert had sailed Moira had been everywhere, into everything. Just being in the same house with her was bad enough, but she insisted on spending time with the children. Especially Edward. She had found an old miniature of Robert and given it to the boy, and she continually made up heroic stories for him. Always the hero was Robert Fallon.

At last it was coming to an end. Three more days to the last day of 1812, and she would sail with Theo on the *Patriot* from Georgetown. Today's wagon would carry her trunks there ahead, and she would have only to bring a few small personal items and the children.

A knock sounded at the door. Ezekial had been sent on an errand. She smoothed down her dress, put on a smile, and opened the door. "Yes?"

Her smile slipped a trifle. The man on the portico had been tall once, but now was stooped, and leaned heavily on a cane. His face and hands were painfully gaunt, and there was an unnatural glint in his eye. Still, his coat and pantaloons were well cut and his boots gleamed with a high polish.

His face cracked in a semblance of a smile. "You must be Catherine," he said in a gravelly voice.

"I am Catherine Holtz," she replied. "I fear you have the

advantage of me, sir."

"I am your Uncle Justin," he said. "My name is Justin Fourrier."

Catherine realized her mouth was open and shut it with a snap. *This* was Justin Fourrier? This weathered, sickly old man? This was the villain who had battled her father through the Revolution and before? This was the man Robert insisted was the devil incarnate? *This?*

An icy whip of wind swirled across the portico, and she saw him shiver. Whoever he was, she couldn't let him freeze on her front step. "Come in."

He gave a small bow, and stepped across the threshold carefully. The cold, she thought. She led him to the study, where he sank gratefully into a chair, and poked up the fire.

"Would you care for some wine?" she asked. How *did* she address him?

"No, thank you," he said in that gravel voice. He rubbed his chest with a grimace. "My doctor allows me no wine or spirits. My doctor allows me little that I enjoy."

"I'm sorry to hear that. Have you been ill?"

"I am dying," he said. She started, both at his words and at the glitter in his eye. "I could not die without settling with the Fallons. Making my peace, that is. I have come to make a final peace."

"That . . . that is very good. To make peace, I mean," she added quickly. *That* was what seemed so strange about him. Dying, and come to make peace. "I've heard stories, of course, about the feud between my father and yourself."

He looked at her sharply. "Yes. There were wrongs done. Wrongs on both sides. I did my share. As did your father. I was saddened to hear about his death." His eyes brightened momentarily. "I had always hoped to meet him again, face to face. Still, his children will do. Yes. I will know peace when I got to my grave."

"Catherine," Moira said as she walked into the room, "Edward has broken his toy horse. Do you suppose—oh, I'm sorry. I did not know you had company."

"Don't go," Catherine said quickly. "Mr. Fourrier, may I present Mrs. Robert Fallon. Moira, this is Justin Fourrier, my . . . my uncle. My mother's brother."

Moira stopped and stared. "I have heard of him," she said faintly. "Robert told me . . . he told me . . . Catherine, in God's name, what is he doing here?"

"Moira, please," Catherine snapped. "Mr. Fourrier is ill. Very ill. He has come here to make peace between our families."

"Before I die," Fourrier said. "I am dying, Mrs. Fallon, and there are some things that must be done before I die. Your husband, Robert, will I meet him today?"

Moira didn't speak. Catherine shot an angry glance and answered. "Robert is at sea, Mr. Fourrier. He's let himself be caught up in this foolish war, and taken a privateer to sea."

"A privateer," Fourrier muttered. His black eyes skittered across the far wall as if searching for a pattern in the panels. "A dangerous profession. Who can say if he will return? Or when? I can hold on till then. I must." His gaze focused once more on the women. "I have taken a house in the city. On Broad Street, not far from my family's old home. I look forward to getting to know both of you. And awaiting Robert's return."

"Catherine," Moira said. "Your trip."

Fourrier's blank gaze rested on Catherine. "You are going away?"

"I plan a trip to New York," Catherine said slowly. "I leave in three days from Georgetown."

"Dangerous times for sea travels," he said softly.

"The *Patriot* is very fast, I'm told," she said. "It's a privateer, though the guns will be dismounted and hidden till the ship reaches New York. I'm assured there are papers to satisfy the British if we're stopped. But of course, with you here . . . . "

"I wouldn't hear of spoiling your trip," Fourrier said. He used his walking stick to lever himself to his feet. "I must be going, now. I really only called to let you know I was here and why. There will be time for us to become acquainted when you return, Catherine. Have a pleasant journey on the—*Patriot*, wasn't it?"

After he was gone, Catherine shook her head. "Imagine. Coming to make peace."

"So it's believing him that you are," Moira said. "You grew

up in this family, Catherine. I only married into it, but I know that man tried to have your father killed more than once, and he has tried the same with Robert. I know him for an evil man, with the truth not in him.''

''Father told a lot of stories,'' Catherine said. ''Men usually do, and who can tell how much there is to them? As for Robert . . . well, for God's sake, Moira, Robert is the bastard son of that man's wife. You can hardly expect them to lack bad will. I expect it's as Mr. Fourrier said. There was wrong done on both sides.'' She moved to look out at the sky. The wind was still whipping the treetops, and dark purple clouds were drifting over the city. ''Why does December have to be rainy? The roads to Georgetown will be impossible.''

''You're going on with your trip, then?''

''I'm going down there to tell Theo I can't accompany her. I owe her that much for pulling out at the last minute.''

''And that means you believe him,'' Moira said flatly. ''I don't know which is worse, you taking the children away, or believing that man.''

''You heard him,'' she said. ''He wants to make peace before he dies. And if a man ever looked as if he was dying, it's that man. I don't know why you don't believe him. Listen. It's going to be a very long ride to Georgetown, and Ezekiel is off on an errand. Please ask one of the maids to have the carriage brought around? I must go up for a cloak.''

''Certainly. But I wish . . . go slowly with Justin Fourrier, Catherine. That man is dangerous.''

Catherine watched her go with a small smile. Dangerous? Perhaps. But for whom? If she could arrange a peace, a reconciliation between Robert and Justin, it might be the wedge she needed to pry him away from Moira. Her smile took on the look of a cat as she went up for her cloak.

The Union Jack whipping at *Asad*'s masthead was disguise enough in these American waters, Murad Reis thought. Already the sloop ahead—the *Patriot*—was coming into the wind, letting her mainsail drop. *Asad* ran down alongside the smaller vessel. Timbers grated, and the sloop's rail splintered in one place. Her crew stared in sudden consternation as the expected red-coated Marines resolved into baggypantalooned Barbary pirates. Roughly the pirates began herding the passengers and crew together, searching them for valuables.

Murad strode onto the captured ship, Akmed Mahomet, his first mate, at his side. One of the passengers, a well-dressed man of middle years, broke free and grabbed at Murad as he passed.

"My name is Timothy Green, sir. A ransom will be paid—"

One of the pirates, thinking Murad attacked, drew a pistol and shot the man. Murad pushed the slumping body aside and proceeded to the quarterdeck.

"The captain?" he said.

"A thousand pardons, *effendi*," Akmed said, "but he was so foolish as to resist."

Murad sighed. "You must learn, Akmed—"

A sudden excited babbling broke out amidships as a woman was dragged up from below. Quickly she was brought to Murad. Pretty, he thought, and drew out the sketch Fourrier had sent, but he knew she was the wrong woman even as he asked, "What is your name?"

"I am Theodosia Burr Alston," she answered arrogantly. "If I am delivered safely to New York, a fair ransom will be paid."

He turned away from her. "Find the other woman," he ordered. "Find her!"

Theodosia grabbed the sleeve of his burnoose. "You don't understand."

He slapped her to the deck and stared around him angrily. "Is it such a large thing to ask? To find one woman on a small ship?" He bent and tangled his fist in the woman's hair. "Where is she?" She raked her nails down his face, and he slapped her again, harder. "Where is Catherine Holtz?" Again he slapped her and shook her by the hair. "Where?"

"I don't know!" she sobbed. "She didn't come! I don't know where she is!"

With a roar he straightened, drawing her roughly to her feet. "Catherine Holtz is not on this ship? Not, you say!"

"No," she quavered. Her eyes were wide and moist. One hand kept touching the cheek he had slapped as if she could not believe it.

Abruptly he released her hair and seized the front of her dress. She shied back, and her breasts trembled in the open air as the dress split to the waist. In shock she stared at him.

"I like large breasts," he told her in English, and smiled at the tremor that went through her. He touched his cheek and examined the blood on his fingers. "Take her to my cabin," he ordered in Arabic. "Strip her and give her the bastinado. Fifty strokes. Half on the soles of the feet and half on the buttocks. Go." As the uncomprehending woman was pulled away, he turned to Akmed. "Well? Is the correct woman aboard?"

"No, *effendi*. The vessel has been searched even to the bilges. There is no other woman."

He muttered a curse. Fourrier wanted that woman badly. The price he offered was worth an Indiaman's cargo. The other woman's screams began to drift up from his cabin. Briefly he considered trying to claim that she was Catherine Holtz. An accident . . . . Regretfully, he decided not. If the woman was not on the *Patriot,* he could trust that Fourrier knew where she was, or soon would. He climbed back on his own ship. "Are the prisoners secured below?"

"All," Akmed answered, "excepting only the nightingale even now singing in your cabin."

"Then burn the ship." And he went below to enjoy himself with the woman he had.

There was a roaring fire in the study of the Holtz mansion, but Justin Fourrier could not forget the drizzle that was peppering the roof. Another twinge in his chest; defiantly he took another swallow of brandy. Damned doctors. Damned fools. He'd live as long as he had to live.

He looked around the study and chuckled to himself. Moira was off visiting somewhere, and the servants had let him in without question. He was, after all, "Miss Catherine's uncle." The servants and the house would fetch a pretty penny after . . . After.

Murad should have her by now. If he knew Murad, she had already been raped more than once. But the important thing was that she was almost in his hands. A day or two more and a messenger would appear. A launch would take him to Murad's ship with the outlandish name, and he would spend days making the bitch regret the Fallon blood in her veins, regret even more the Fourrier blood that was mingled with it. Then the return to Charleston, and to Moira. He needed a lonely place for Robert's wife, a lonely place and a long time. Watching her break, bit by bit, knowing she was his woman. He chortled till he slopped brandy over his wrist. And the children. No death for them; that was too easy. There were plantations in Spanish America that weren't too particular about light skins on slaves. He might even travel to see them, if he lived that long. If he lived that long. If only he lived long enough for Robert to come back.

The study door began to open, he started up with an angry retort. He had told the servants not to disturb him on any account. "You!" The word had to be forced out. "You can't be here!"

"Mr. Fourrier," Catherine said. "My servants told me you were here. I regret not being here to greet you, but the rains were so bad it took two days to reach Georgetown and four to return."

He felt strangled. "You didn't sail," he managed.

"Not and leave you." She smiled at him graciously. "Are you all right, sir?"

Breath wouldn't come to him. His lungs seemed to have stopped working. With a groan he collapsed. She ran to him, screaming.

"Have—to—do—"

"You be quiet," she told him, smoothing his brow. He wanted to strike at her, but his arms wouldn't work for the pain in his chest. "Ezekiel!" she called. "Ezekiel, send for the doctor! Quickly!"

From somewhere he found brief spurts of breath. "Have—to do it—myself. No time—for others."

"Of course," she told him soothingly. "Once the doctor gets here, everything will be all right. You'll be able to do whatever it is you want."

He wanted to laugh at her assurance. If she knew what it was he wanted to do. He wanted to laugh, but the blackness rolled over him.

Catherine realized that she had been staring at the same page for at least ten minutes without reading a word. In fact, the entire thought of reading had begun to pall. She put the book aside with a sigh. She hadn't done much of anything since Justin Fourrier's seizure. Read, embroidery, plan the menus; read some more. Six weeks of it, while she waited to see if he was indeed to expire under her roof. The windowpanes rattled in another gust of wind, and she shivered. Ezekiel claimed a big storm was coming, and from the waves marching across the habor to crash not a hundred feet from her house, she believed him.

"Catherine?"

She looked up to find Moira settling her cloak about her in the doorway. "Are you going out in this, Moira?"

"The children are out at Seven Pines with none but their maumas and the housekeeper. It's not a trip I'm relishing in this weather, but they shouldn't be alone if Ezekiel's big storm does come."

"It's your own fault," Catherine sniffed. "You insisted they be sent to the country. And in the middle of winter!"

"Would you rather be having them in the house if that man upstairs dies?" She looked at the ceiling and shivered. "I wouldn't even want them in the house with him alive." Catherine refused to let herself be drawn. "How is he this evening? I went up to his room just after noon, and he was awake. He didn't say anything. He just watched me. I'm not sure he *can* say anything."

"He's sitting up in bed," Moira said. "And he can talk. He had one of the maids bring him Robert's robe. He watched me, too. Those black vulture's eyes followed every move I made." She frowned at the ceiling. "I'm not certain I should leave, now he's awake."

"Well, you'd better make up your mind. It's almost dark. If you're going to the children, you must leave now." A thunderclap punctuated her statement, and it seemed to make up Moira's mind.

"I'll go now," she said. "But don't you be turning your back on that old man."

With Moira gone Catherine tried to interest herself in the book again, but the rattling windowpanes and the drumming rain brought a lassitude that was little short of sleep. She drifted in and out of wakefulness, never making it off the page she started on. Amidst the wet howling of the storm a metallic click brought her awake. The book fell off her lap as she sat up. Justin Fourrier was just shutting the study door.

He wore Robert's lounging robe, red velvet that dragged the floor. His face was blank, his black eyes unblinking. When he saw her looking at him, he thrust his hand into one of the robe's pockets. In the other, she realized, he was carrying a short pony-cart whip. She wondered if he had misplaced his walking stick.

"It's good to see you up," she said, "though I'm not sure Doctor Reed would agree that you should be out of bed. If you've lost your walking stick, I can lend you one that's certainly better than that . . . ." He had produced a pistol from the robe pocket. Now there was a second metallic click as he cocked it.

"You are a stupid little bitch," he said.

A flash of lightning accompanied his words, and the thunderclap followed so closely on their heels that she wasn't sure she had heard correctly.

"Uncle Justin," she began uncertainly, "perhaps your seizure has confused you a little. I'm—"

"You're a stupid little bitch, as I said. And don't call me 'uncle.' Mr. Fourrier will do. Or 'master.' Or 'my lord.' Anything but 'uncle.' That sticks in my throat."

She chose her words carefully. "Mr. Fourrier, I don't understand. Why threaten me with a gun?"

"Stupid and foolish. You really believed I came to make peace. Peace? The only peace I want is the peace that comes from knowing the Fallons lie in hell. That's my peace." A dry grin cracked his face, but went no further than his lips. "Now, Catherine, it's time for you to take off your clothes."

Stunned, it took her minutes to find speech. "Mr. Fourrier, I'm your niece."

"I wouldn't care if you were my sister," he snapped. "You're Michael Fallon's daughter, and Robert Fallon's sister, and that's all that matters. I may not be alive when Robert comes back from the wars, but he'll find I've done his sister in a fine style. Strip! Or would you prefer a ball between your eyes?"

She licked her lips; they were suddenly dry with fear. The pistol barrel loomed at her as large as a cannon, and she realized that, more than anything else, she did not want to die. Slowly her hands went to the fastenings of her dress.

He kept up a discourse, punctuated by thunder, as she shed her garments. The pile of satin, velvet, and lace around her feet grew as he spoke.

"Yes, Robert will find his sister has gotten the training of a Limehouse whore. There are going to be things done to you that you won't believe, Catherine, even while they're happening. You'll find a sick craving remains in you, a desire to have them done again, even though you deny it on the outside. Others, you'll beg me to stop. You'll offer your babies, your soul, but I won't stop. And do you know what the prize is? If you please me very much, if, by the end of the evening, you're properly humble and eager to please, I'll let you live." He giggled suddenly, and a shiver of pure terror ran down her body. "Isn't that wonderfully kind of me? I'll let you earn your chance to live."

Her fingers faltered with her chemise, and she muttered, "Please," but he kept on as if he hadn't heard.

"And then there's his wife. I saw her leave from my window, but she must be coming back. The servants are still huddled in the quarters, afraid of the storm. There will only be her and me here." He giggled again. "Which is better? A man's wife, or his sister? I've tried both, and they're different, but which is better? Ah, you're done. Look at yourself in the mirror, there. Your skin looks like satin. Go on, look."

She squeezed her eyes shut. Alone with Moira? That meant he would kill her. Quiet, hopeless sobs wracked her. Something burned across her hip. She jumped, and opened her eyes just in time to see him drawing back the whip.

"I told you," he rasped, "to look at yourself in the mirror. If you want to live, obey me."

Slowly she turned. Lightning lit up her naked image in the large mirror. She was thirty-two, but she had always prided herself that her body was that of a woman ten years younger. The waist was still trim, the stomach still taut. The hips were round and firm, the breasts high and full. She stared at her shivering nudity. If she could only live a little longer, something might happen to save her. Just a little longer. To hell with pride. Deliberately she put one foot slightly ahead of the other and bent her knee. She drew her shoulders back and let her fingers rest delicately at the top of her thighs.

"Slut!" he spat. "Bitch! Whore!" Spittle ran from the corner of his mouth. "Ready to buy your life with your body, are you? Ready to crawl and grovel and try to expiate the Fallon in you?"

She flinched as he slid the whip across her skin, using it like a hand to caress her breasts and belly and thighs. She managed to keep her pose, but a desperate sob slipped into her voice. "I. . . I want to live. I'll do anything you want. Just don't hurt me. Let me live."

His insane giggle ripped the air. "Let me live," he mocked. "I'll do anything. So you will." He gestured with the pistol. His black eyes seemed to have captured some of the lightning's sharp light. "Over there. Bend over the back of that chair. Now! Move!"

She stumbled to the large, padded chair he pointed out. Taking a deep breath she draped herself across the back. Roughly he pushed her face down into the seat cushion. Desperately she grabbed the chair arms. Her feet were off the ground, now, and she was afraid of falling. She wanted to giggle at that sudden fear.

"Not ready," Fourrier panted behind her. "A little sweetner."

Suddenly a line of fire bloomed across her elevated buttocks. With a strangled cry she arched up and looked back in disbelief. He was already raising the whip again. She buried her face in the cushion as the second burning streak was placed beside the first. She couldn't stop the frantic kick her legs gave at every blow, the rolling twist of her hips as if to throw off the pain, but she could stifle her sobs and screams by digging her teeth into the velvet cushion, and she did. Anything to live. Her tears rolled down her cheeks and soaked into the blue fabric beneath her face.

As abruptly as they began, the blows stopped. Bony fingers began to caress her back. And the pistol barrel. Fourrier was breathing heavily. Remember," he grated, "if you please me, you live a little longer." With a grunt he fell across her back, the hand with the pistol sliding down to dangle over her shoulder in front of her face.

Weeping seized her. The gun was too much.

"Are you just going to lie there with that man on top of you?"

Catherine jerked her head around in surprise. Moira was standing there in her dripping cloak, a heavy candlestick clutched in both hands like a club. The base of it was smeared with red.

With a strength she didn't know she possessed Catherine levered herself out of the chair. Fourrier fell to the floor, the untied robe spilling open to reveal his scrawny nakedness, but she didn't even spare him a glance. Words and emotions bubbled up inside her, tumbling over one another.

"I knew someone would come. I just had to stay alive, and someone would come. And you came. Oh, God, thank you Moira! Thank you. He was going to, to rape me, and then kill me, but you came." Tears of relief and gratitude welled up in her uncontrollably, and she collapsed against the smaller woman.

"There, now," Moira whispered, stroking her hair as she would a frightened child's. "It's going to be all right. It'll be all right, Catherine. You cry it out."

Catherine sobbed against Moira's shoulder, in the shelter of Moira's arms, and felt as safe as it she were in her mother's embrace. Somehow Moira had managed to snatch up Catherine's dress and wrap it around her. A part of Catherine seemed to stand off and watch. There had been a change in her, a change in the very fabric of Catherine Fallon Holtz. From this day forward she would do what was necessary to survive, and no pride or arrogance would get in the way. She didn't know if she would be stronger for it, or weaker, but she knew that was the way it would be. And there was Moira.

"Why did you come back?" she whispered.

"I couldn't stand the thought of you being alone with him, with no one here but the servants. At the landing I paid off the boatman without even getting in his boat."

"Thank God you did," Catherine breathed. "If you hadn't come back, he—" She looked at Justin, and the breath caught in her throat. "He doesn't seem to be breathing."

Moira knelt beside him reluctantly, shifting his robe to cover his nakedness. Gingerly, with a grimace of distaste, she pressed her ear to his chest, then straightened, her eyes wide with fright. "He—he's dead. I killed him. I'm not sorry I did it, but . . . we'll have to send for the constable."

"No," Catherine said. She suddenly felt very cool and calm. As if in her boudoir, she gathered her clothes and began to dress. "If we send for the constable, there will be a terrible scandal. My rich uncle from Jamaica comes to Charleston for a visit and is killed by my brother's wife while trying to rape me. A story like that will follow us the rest of our lives. That's if we're believed."

"But it's the truth!" Moira protested.

"It's bizarre," Catherine said. "It doesn't sound like the truth, and that's worse than being caught in a lie."

"But what would we do?"

Catherine took a deep breath. Everything seemed laid out with crystal clarity. "We dispose of the body." She ignored Moira's cry. "After a storm like this there are always one or two bodies found in the harbor. One more won't draw any attention."

Moira nodded with obvious reluctance. "But how, Catherine?"

"You go to the stables and get a horse. The stableboys will be with everyone else. I'll get the body ready." Moira didn't move. Catherine dragged her to her feet and settled the cloak about her shoulders. "The horse, Moira," she said.

An hour later, the two cloaked and hooded women staggered down the rain-slicked front steps, carrying an old rolled carpet. Waves broke high against the peninsula less than a hundred feet away; the wind drove spumes of spray all the way to the houses. The night was an all-soaking wetness, and the windy rain tugged at them and at their burden. Somehow, though, they got it across the horse.

"What if we're seen? Moira shouted against the wind.

"We won't be," Catherine shouted back. She tugged her hood back into place. "There's no one out in this, likely no one looking out a window. Let's go."

She led the way, one hand keeping her cloak together, the other for the reins. Moira walked beside the horse, gingerly balancing its grisly bundle against the wind. Heads down, they moved through the storm-swept streets looking like ancient monks in a drawing of hell. And then they had reached the docks.

Waves running up the river pounded the outer reaches of the docks and churned the waters between them. The horse put one foot on the trembling timbers and balked, but Catherine tugged at the bridle and Moira pushed and poked till he took one step, then another, and another.

Halfway down the dock Catherine stopped. "Here," she shouted. Any further, and they might be washed into the river themselves.

She went to help Moira with the carpet-wrapped body, and together they lowered it to the rough planking. Immediately the horse, free of restraint, whirled and dashed back the way they had come. Moira took a step after him, but Catherine grabbed her arm. The horse could be found after the storm, after what had to be done.

The wind seized their cloaks again, sending their hoods streaming behind them, but the two women managed to roll the carpet to the edge of the dock. Catherine looked at the younger woman and wondered if she were as pale. As if at a signal, they each took an edge of the carpet and straightened. The carpet unrolled, and Justin Fourrier's body flashed white in the night before it was swallowed by the waters.

Without a word they folded the carpet, adjusted their cloaks and left the dock behind them.

Jasper Trask pulled his collar closer against the driving rain and shivered as he watched the two women leave the dock. He thought he knew what he had seen, but he was curiously reluctant to make sure.

He had arrived in Charleston a month earlier, close to destitute. It had been desperation that drove him to the Fallon house; he could always make up some tale about Fourrier for a few dollars. But the old devil was there, in the house with the Fallon women. Sheer terror had driven him into hiding for a week. The servants said Fourrier was confined to bed; they said he was dying. Jasper Trask would believe that when he saw the nails go into the coffin lid and the dirt cover it. But the fact that Fourrier was in the same house as Fallons meant that something was happening, something that could mean money for Jasper Trask. He had been watching the house for weeks, trying to discover what. And now, just when the storm was about to drive him to shelter . . . .

He hunched against the wind as he made his way across the dock. A smile flickered on his face when he saw the pale, scrawny body floating face down on the churning waters. Even there, in the relative shelter between the docks, it was being pounded against the pilings so that it would soon be unrecognizable. They'd dumped a body; that meant that had murdered him. But who was he? That might be the bit that was needed to pry a few dollars out of them.

He found a boathook between the two crates and reached down with it. The hook slipped free, then caught, and he managed to lever the body over. The vagary of the waves caught the turning body, and for a moment Justin Fourrier stood upright out of the water, his snarling rictus staring at Trask. Trask screamed and staggered back.

He shook himself, suddenly aware of the rain soaking through his clothes and the howling wind that chilled to the bone. There was warmth in the city, though, and Justin Fourrier, dead at last, was going to help him get it.

Billy Carpenter, warmly ensconced on dry straw in a tight-seamed crate, peered through a knothole as the white stranger left the dock. First the two women, Catherine Holtz and Moira Fallon, coming to dump something in the river. Then that man, skulking around. Whatever it was, it had scared that white man. Billy grinned. He hadn't heard anybody scream like that since Ned Bennett sat on a live coal. Whatever it was, though, it might be worth a dollar to know about it. He kicked open a board in the lee side of the crate and wriggled out into the wet and cold.

Shivering, he darted to the dock's edge and stood staring down, open-mouthed. The body had caught against a piling so that it floated face up. Even as he looked it ripped loose and rolled over, slammed against the pilings again and again, but that glimpse of the face had been enough. He had seen Justin Fourrier going into the Fallon house just after Christmas, and had heard his name.

He rocked back and forth thoughtfully. The rich white folks had disposed of a body and were going to get off. That was worth a whole lot more than a dollar, but he had a feeling it might be worth his life to collect.

With a start he realized that other things might be worth his life. If he was found hiding in that crate when the body was discovered, he'd probably hang for the killing those white women had done. He hunched his shoulders against the rain and wind and trotted off the dock. First he'd find a new place for the night; then he could try to think of how to use what he knew.

Catherine stared into the fire, wondering whether Justin's body had been one of those unidentified after the storm. So far, it seemed, they had managed to make him disappear without a trace.

"The fire's hardly necessary," Moira said. She frowned intently at her embroidery frame. "It's warm for February."

"He won't be found now," Catherine said flatly.

"Damn," Moira muttered, sucking her fingertip. "Don't bring that up so sudden. You made me prick myself. Lord, I wish Robert were here."

"Well, he isn't," Catherine answered irritably. She glared at Moira, then back at the fire. Robert was another problem. How could she take Robert away from the woman who had saved her life? "He's not here, and we are."

"He gave up his rented house after his attack, so that's taken care of," Moira said wearily. "We've told the servants he wanted to move now that he was better, so they're not wondering where he is. And now that we know his body won't be found and identified, we tell anyone who asks that he sailed for New York, and we're poor little women without a wit in our heads who can't remember. You see, I remember it all perfectly. Shall I be reciting it again?"

"No need, my dear," Catherine laughed uneasily. "I know it as well as you. But I'm not easy in my mind—" There was a knock at the door. "Yes?"

Ezekiel stuck his head in uncertainly. "Miss Catherine, there be a man to the door. He ain't a gentleman, and I normal wouldn't bother you, but he won't go away. He insist I tell you he got to talk to you about Mr. Fourrier, and the way he left town. Do you want I should tell him to be about his business?''

"Oh, my God," Moira murmured.

Catherine gripped the arms of her chair. "Show him in, Ezekiel. Then don't disturb us for anything till he goes." When the butler backed out, she rounded on Moira. "Buck up, damn it. This may not be what you think." She took a deep breath and tried to take her own advice.

The man Ezekiel showed into the drawing room was tall and skinny, his face almost hidden by bushy black whiskers streaked with gray. His coat was worn, and he twisted his hat nervously in large, spidery hands.

"I don't believe I know you," Catherine said coldly.

"Name's Trask," he said. "Jasper Trask, but you can call me Mr. Trask." He grinned slyly.

"I will call you nothing," Moira said in a low growl.

"Moira!" Catherine said sharply. Trask's face had dropped into a sullen lower. "What do you want—Mr. Trask?"

"I want money. If I don't get it, I'll have to talk about Justin Fourrier, and just how he left this city."

"Extortion?" Catherine said coolly. Her heart felt as if it would burst any moment. "You will find this family does not take to threats. You may leave now, or I will send for the constables and see you taken away in chains."

"You will?" He sneered. "And I will tell them how I saw the two of you dump Justin Fourrier's body in the river. I don't know which one of you bashed his head in, but I expect the other one will start babbling to save her neck when the chains go on."

Moira shifted angrily, but Catherine didn't dare take her eyes off Trask. "Tell that preposterous story and you'll be locked away as insane. Remember you are speaking of two ladies of position and gentle birth."

"Fourrier was what some call a gentleman, too. I expect even two ladies can't get off with murdering a gentleman. It ain't like it was some poor sot in the street."

"You have no proof," Catherine snapped. At his triumphant smile, she realized she had made a mistake.

"I can prove enough. Fourrier ain't in this house any more. He just went, poof, in the middle of the night, and no one saw him go. They'll check around and find out he didn't rent a carriage, and he didn't take passage on a ship. You might have got rid of his belongings here, but I'll wager he didn't bring all his trunks here, him sick as he was supposed to be. I'll wager they're stored somewhere, and then can be found. You think I won't be believed?"

"Tell your story!" Moira said. "Tell it and be damned to you! We'll not—"

"Moira," Catherine said quietly, "Let me handle this." She had to stop to let her nerves settle, but she was careful to let none of it show on her face. "You spoke of money."

"That's right," he said eagerly. With success in sight, his tone became ingratiating. "I won't try to bleed you dry. I don't want much. Just a tifle now and again. Say, five hundred dollars to start."

"Five hun— Do you think I have that kind of money lying around the house? There are ship captains who don't make as much in a year."

"You're rich. You can get it easy enough. Say by tomorrow. I'll come back then." He grinned mirthlessly. At the door he paused. "And if you figure on doing me like you done Fourrier, well, don't. I've got all this writ out, and it'll be sent to the constables if anything happens to me." He smiled again, insolently, and was gone. Catherine went quickly to the window to watch him leave the house. He went down the broad front steps with a jaunt to his walk.

"You're going to pay him?" Moira asked.

Catherine sighed. "What else can we do?"

"Robert would know how to handle him. God, how I wish he were here."

"So do I," Catherine said. She turned from the window with bleak eyes. "So do I."

XLI

"Sail ho!" the masthead lookout cried. "Two points on the starboard bow!"

Robert kept pacing the quarterdeck silently. Copes stood by the helmsman, his nervous eye flashing from Robert to the lookout to the point where the sail should appear.

"It's the *Lady Susan!*" the lookout shouted. "*Yankee Girl* is close behind!"

Robert released a breath he hadn't realized he was holding. This wasn't the first rendezvous at sea he had had with other privateers, but now, in March of 1814, he was nervous over any sighting.

In half an hour the other two privateers were sailing alongside *Shrike,* and Timothy Walters, captain of the brig *Yankee Girl,* and Henry Rogers, captain of the schooner *Lady Susan,* were on the quarterdeck with Robert.

Walters, short and balding, hawked and spat over the side. "I hear we lost a frigate last summer."

"Which one?" Robers asked. A lanky Virginian, he seemed perpetually surprised and always slightly rumpled. "I thought we were winning those frigate battles."

"*Chesapeake,*" Walters said sourly. "Got her captain killed. She was towed into Halifax by H.M.S. *Shannon.*"

Robert kept quiet. The other two always began by exchanging gossip and tidbits of news. He would wait till the important talk.

"We had any successes lately?" Rogers said.

"Seem to be doing all right up to Canada. Some general named William Henry Harrison beat the British on the Thames. Killed that Indian, Tecumseh."

"I figured we'd be about done with trying Canada. I heard

414

the Governor of Massachusetts won't even let American troops cross his state to get there.''

Walters, who was from Boston, looked disgruntled. Robert stepped in before an argument started.

"The only news I've heard that's important," he said, "is that Napoleon's bottled up in Paris." The other two looked at him in consternation.

"What in hell's that have to do with us?" Walters said finally.

"He's almost done," Robert explained patiently. "Once he is, the British will turn everything on us." While they ruminated on that he swept the horizon, eyes squinted to pick out a sail from the distant glare.

"I expect you have a suggestion," Rogers said, "or you wouldn't have brought it up."

Robert nodded. "I left home eighteen months ago, and since then I've sailed out of Norway, and France, some, while they still controlled their ports. I've taken forty-one prizes worth the name. You two have done about as well. I think it's time to quit.''

"Quit!" they shouted at the same time.

"We can't quit now," Rogers said.

"We're still at war," Walters growled.

"We are," Robert said, "but how many of our countrymen are? I've stopped two Americans going into British ports in the last month. Both had sidmouths."

There was a moment's silence at the mention of the British Naval passes named after Lord Sidmouth.

"You should have taken them," Rogers said at last.

"And be condemned as a pirate? They were American ships. But that's not all. Even with Napoleon still hanging on, the British are shifting more ships against us. How many prizes have you been chased off in the last six months? I've nearly fallen to frigates three times, and I've outrun a dozen other warships. I made this rendezvous because I said I would, but when I leave here, I'm sailing from Charleston.

Walters and Rogers looked at each other uncomfortably.

"To tell the truth, Fallon," Rogers said, "we were hoping you'd sail with us on a little, ah, hunting trip we have planned."

"The Irish Sea," Walters said.

"You're both crazy," Robert said. "I tried the Irish Sea when I first came out and got nothing but splinters and dust. Half the vessels you sight will be worthless fishing smacks, and half the rest men-o'-war."

Rogers grinned eagerly. "Aye. All those warships. Think Fallon. With no privateers there, they must have shifted the Navy elsewhere, where it's needed."

"Right," Walters said. "You yourself said they've been as thick as fleas where we *have* been operating."

"It'll be open, Fallon. We'll be a wolfpack in the sheep fold."

"You're set on this," Robert said slowly.

"We are," Walters said.

Rogers squatted to sketch with his finger on the deck. "You see, we'll spread out in a line abreast so that each masthead can just see the next ship. We can cover forty miles of width that way, and scan the sea for eighty."

"We'll sweep up everything in our path," Walters said. "Just one pass through, and we'll sail out the other end with a convoy of prizes. You'll go back to Charleston richer than Croesus."

"And if I don't go with you?"

Again the other two held a silent conference with their eyes.

"In that case," Walters said, "we'll go alone."

"And likely get snapped up by a frigate," Robert muttered. "All right, then. I'll come. But we'll plan this thing carefully. One pass down the Irish Sea and out. That's it. Agreed?" The other two nodded, and he went on. "Rogers, *Shrike* and *Lady Susan* stand the best chance of getting away if we're caught against the coast, so you take the Irish side and I'll take the English. That leaves *Yankee Girl* in the middle, Walters, and that's good. Your mainmast's tallest, so you'll have the longest view. Now, if anyone sights a warship, hoist the Swedish flag. That'll warn the rest of us. Walters, if you see that flag go up on either one of us, hoist a Spanish flag to relay."

It took only a short time for the details to be ironed out, and the other captains made ready to return to their own ships. As Walters went over the side, he paused.

"Fallon, wasn't William Hogarth your first mate?"

"He was," Robert grunted. "Till he took a prize to New York when I told him to run it into Bergen. Got himself a privateer out of it, and took six of my best men with him."

"He doesn't have it any more," Walters said. "He was caught on a lee shore up in the Orkneys by a pair of frigates. Ran aground on Stronsay in high seas. No survivors, I hear."

Robert watched them go with a sense of foreboding. Before he went to his cabin, he issued orders. "Mr. Copes, south-south-east. We'll be leading the way through the North Channel."

The three ships proceeded in line past the Mull of Oa, past Rathlin Island and through the North Channel into the Irish Sea. At the Mull of Galloway they formed a shortened line abreast, and as they passed the Isle of Man lengthened it to the full spread of their plan. But the green sea remained as bare of ships as a glass table.

With Holyhead in sight and Caernarvon Bay curving to port, Robert began to study the horizon ahead. A dark mist seemed to stretch across the sea and up into the sky. Occasionally there were flashes along its length.

"Squall line," Copes said.

Robert shook his head. "Worse than that. That's a full-fledged Atlantic storm. I'll wager they've not seen anything like that in these parts in many a year. There have probably been riders and semaphores up both coasts since it was sighted. That's why we're alone out here."

"I suppose we'll not take any prizes, sir."

"It means we stick out like sore thumbs." He made a worried sweep of the horizon, but from the deck he could see little. "Masthead!" he bellowed. "Keep a sharp eye."

"Sail astern!" the masthead lookout shouted. "Two of them! They be frigates, sir! I can make them out plain! Big ones!"

"Damn!" Robert muttered. "Someone on the British shore must have spotted us, or someone in Ireland saw the *Lady Susan*. Ships out when everything's staying in because of the storm. Of course, the Navy's investigating. Bend on a Swedish flag, and hurry."

Copes was turning away when the lookout sang out again.

"Swedish flag on the *Yankee Girl!* No! That's down! It's a Spanish flag!"

Robert measured the distance to the storm and cursed again under his breath.

"Both flags?" Copes said. "Have they spotted a warship, or has the *Lady Susan?*"

"Both!" Robert snapped. "Damn it, get that flag up. And I'll have the guns over the side."

Copes had leapt to hand the Swedish flag to McLellan, the boatswain, but at the last he stared. "The guns, sir?"

"Yes, you fool. Do you expect to fight a pair of frigates with eight twelve-pounders? Twelve tons less to carry might have us hiding in that storm before they reach us. Now move, man!"

Copes half-fell down the ladder to the waist, shouting for men, and Robert went back to studying the storm. Already the winds were beginning to affect them, forcing *Shrike* deeper into Cardigan Bay as she passed Braich-y-pwll, the Welsh headland. The swells were longer and deeper, now, their tops whipped to froth by the wind, and the crash of thunder from the dark mass ahead rolled across the deck.

The guns were going over the side, one by one. Miller and Kemal, stripped to the waist, wielded axes, chopping away bulwarks above the gunports. As each was hacked away, they moved on to the next, and others darted in with levers, handspikes and ropes. Slowly the guns rose and toppled into the sea; each time *Shrike* seemed to lift.

The frigates were closer. They could handle the heavy seas that now pounded *Shrike*'s razor hull. First the topsails could be seen, white patches resting on the horizon. Then the mainsails, and finally the hulls, great heavy hulls with the bone in their teeth, gouts of spume flying as they battered through the waves the schooner had to struggle against. Smoke bloomed at the lead frigate's bow, instantly whipped away by the gale and replaced by another gray-and-fire billow that also disappeared. The ranging shots of the bow-chasers were lost in the wave-wracked sea behind, but even as the guns fired the reason came clear. Rain deluged the deck of *Shrike*. In an instant the frigates were hidden from sight.

"We're safe!" Copes cried, and the storm laid its hand on the ship.

Suddenly the bow began to rise, up and up a towering wall of water that loomed into the darkness, till the deck was almost straight up and down. Men, tackle, gear, anything that wasn't lashed in place crashed and slid down the deck until brought up short with the sickening crack of wood or ribs. A hollow shriek ripped from Copes as he hurtled back over the sternrail and into the sea.

With the same abruptness the giant wave was gone, passed beyond *Shrike,* and the schooner dropped sickeningly to smash into the trough. The crack of timbers and the screams of men could be heard even over the shriek of the banshee wind that tore the sails to shreds in an instant and made the rigging hum like guitar strings and the masts sway like reeds.

Robert scrambled across the pitching deck to seize the spinning wheel. Where the helmsman had gone he did not know, and as with Copes there was no time to find him. Feet braced, he fought with every ounce of his strength, but the sea sent the ship where it would. The wheel jerked and twitched like a thing alive. Then Kemal was there, putting his great back into the fight, and Miller, and Jeremiah, the four of them fighting the wheel and the sea.

Robert found himself staring into Miller's face, and he realized with a start that the man was smiling. "Where away, captain?" Miller shouted. "What course?"

"Into the wind, you bald-headed bear," Robert yelled back at the top of his lungs. "Keep her head into the wind or the only course we'll steer is for hell."

Then there was no time for words. All their strength, every ounce of muscle and sinew and will, had to be forced into the wheel, to keep *Shrike* headed into the wind that ripped at the tattered sails and clawed men from the deck. Ahead there was only the blackness of the storm, the walls of black water crashing across the deck in hip-deep foam, sucking the warmth from a man's very bones. The four men were welded into one at the wheel, but through the hours the battle became for each of them a personal one; the man, the ship, and the sea that was trying to kill him.

Robert had no idea how much time had passed when he suddenly felt a difference in the ship's motion. Miller cocked his head as if listening for something behind the howl of the wind and opened his mouth. As he did a shudder wracked

Shrike, hurling the strongest of them to the deck.

"She's struck!" Robert shouted. Again *Shrike* was slammed into the land by the remorseless sea, her timbers splintering like kindling. "Over the side!" He struggled to his feet, and shouted to the few men still clinging to the ship. "Over the side! Miller! Jeremiah! Kemal! Where's Kemal?"

"He went below!" Jeremiah called.

Robert stifled a curse, "Go on! Over the side with you!" He raced to the companionway as *Shrike* lifted and dropped once more, this time with the sickening sound of her back breaking. He started down, only to be pushed back on deck by Kemal, hurrying up with something hidden beneath his coat. Robert felt himself seized by the giant Turk's free arm, and then he was sailing through the air. He hit the water, and there was no time for anything but survival.

He had no hope of swimming, nor any idea of what direction to swim in. All his energy went to keeping his head above the pounding waves. His sodden clothes were dragging him down, but to stop and pull them off would be to drown. His eyes burned with the salt water, his mouth filled with it. Breathing was a happenstance in a world where there was air one moment and water the next. And then he felt bottom beneath his feet.

Desperately he struggled, fighting toward the shallows, but the sea still had its games to play. He was picked up, hurled into the shallows he sought, then dragged back to the deep. Time and again he found himself in water to his waist, to his knees, shallower, and each time the next wave drew him out again, forced him down till his lungs were ready to burst for the want of air. Then he was thrown on his face, water running over the backs of his hands, and with desperate, agonizing slowness he clawed his way across the wet sand toward safety. He could hear the next wave coming, feel it rearing over him. It crashed, and the afterwash rolled around his ankles. His fingers dug into the beach, and he felt dry sand. Dry sand! Even as the thought came, exhaustion rolled him into darkness.

A sharp pain at his ear woke Robert. He jerked away, and watched a crab scuttle across the sand. Shorebirds circled and swooped overhead, cawing shrilly. The sun was high, and the sea washed calmly against the beach. There was no sign of *Shrike,* or of any other survivors.

Mentally he flipped a coin. Heads. South. He clambered to his feet, dusted off as much sand as he could, and set out walking. The beach was empty, high dunes topped with tufted shore grasses, and there wasn't as much as a pinnace on the sea. He counted his paces as he walked. His stride was only a bit more than a yard, so approximately seventeen hundred strides should be a mile. He had reached one thousand six hundred fifty seven when Miller slid down a dune to his left.

"Morning, captain," the big man said. "I was hoping you made it." Kemal and Jeremiah scrambled down after him. The Turk diffidently handed Robert his scimitar from Derna.

"So that's why you went below," Robert murmured. "Thank you, Kemal. Thank you. Miller, have you seen any more of the crew?"

Miller shook his head. "Not alive. Kemal and I buried McLellan in the dunes about a mile south of here. That's where we found him. Then we met Jeremiah and holed up here till we could decide what to do."

"Where are we?" Jeremiah asked Robert.

"This ought to be Cardigan Bay, in Wales."

Jeremiah dropped back on the sand, staring at the sky. Few clouds marred the blue. "You know, Captain Fallon," he said, "it's a long way back to Charleston from this Wales, too far to walk. I don't think we're going to make it."

"We're going to make it," Robert said sharply. "China is a lot further from Charleston, and I made it back from there."

"Begging your pardon," Jeremiah said, "but you had a ship, then."

Miller moved angrily, but Robert motioned him back. "But Wales is on the same island with England. In England there's a city called London. In London, unless the British have shut it down, there's an office of Fallon & Son. And even if they have, there's still a man named Tom Jarvis who should be able to get us on some sort of ship."

Miller shook his head. "Captain, it's not so short a way to London. We've got no money, and we will attract attention."

"Then we'll try to attract more," Robert said. "The way to hide something conspicuous is make it more conspicuous." He whipped out his sword and flashed through a set of presentations. "I will do fancy bits with the sword, and I can play a tin whistle, if we can get one. I've seen Kemal bend an iron bar with his bare hands, and I'll wager there's no man between here and London can lift more than he can."

Miller chortled and presented his fists. "And I can take on all comers, fists, or no holds barred. Except for that Chinee with his funny grips, I haven't been beaten since I was nineteen, and that heathen fellow taught me a few things, after."

They all looked expectantly at Jeremiah. He shrugged doubtfully. "I can juggle. A little bit."

"That's it, then," Robert said. "We'll be the best traveling raree England's ever seen. We'll be so damned conspicuous, no one will think about us a second time."

XLII

With a patch over his left eye and his left arm strapped beneath his coat to look crippled, Robert tootled his tin whistle for the small crowd gathered on the London street. Jeremiah, whose turn at juggling hadn't been well received this time, lounged behind Kemal, who was bending iron bars, then letting men in the crowd try to unbend them.

There was an appreciative murmur as Kemal finished, but only one coin clinked in the cup. Robert got his canvas bag from their ragged pack and drew out his sword. He watched the covetousness light up some of the watching eyes. It always did. Until he did his act.

At his nod, Jeremiah threw an apple into the air. The blade flashed out of the scabbard and two halves of the apple dropped to the pavement. A surprised gasp went up. Two apples went up and fell in four pieces. Another gasp. Three apples became six halves, and were greeted with wondering silence.

"Let's try the melon," Robert whispered.

Kemal gave him a doubtful look, but produced a somewhat shriveled melon. The crowd frowned intently, sensing some great effort as Robert limbered his sword arm. The melon rose in a graceful arc, and Robert's sword flashed. Two cuts only, the second following immediately on the first. Four pieces of melon dropped, and a ripple of applesauce ran through the watchers. Half a dozen coins clattered into the cup. There was no covetousness in anyone's eyes.

Robert was bowing to the crowd and putting the sword away when Miller hurried up. The small crowd was already dispersing.

"Jarvis is there," Miller said quietly. "I watched the house

as you said, and a man drove up in a carriage not twenty
minutes ago. Way the servants acted, it had to be him.''

With no waste motion they gathered the small packs moved
off toward New High Cardiff Street and Tom Jarvis' house.
The crowds jostling them were no different from dozens
Robert had been in, but London seemed filled with unwashed
odors that the June heat cooked into smells of dank decay. It
couldn't be that he was fresh from the sea; nearly three months
of English barns had filled his nostrils with the smells of cow
manure and horse dung. London was worse, though.

Blowzes and trulls, pickpockets and cutpurses, sharpers and
grifters rubbed elbows with the peddlers and hawkers that
filled the streets. And the broadside sellers. They were
omnipresent, it seemed. Just then one caught his ear.

''Burning of New York! Storming of American city!
Jonathon taught a lesson!''

Robert tossed the man a penny, snatched the sheet and
hurried on. It was a bit of doggerel on an imagined taking of
New York. Imagined? There had been too many of those the
last weeks. And the rumors everywhere had an element of
sameness. The British were going to strike at New York,
Robert felt sure. They were going to teach the Apple Johns a
lesson. Baltimore was to burn. How dare those American
renegades declare war on Great Britain when the British were
fighting for the freedom of the world against Old Bony?
Washington City was to be sacked. That would teach that
scurrilous villain, Jemmy Madison. Charleston was to be
stormed. Let those southerners with their phony aristocracy
see what true aristocrats were. The British Grenadier and the
British bayonet—somewhere along the east coast of America,
they would fall with a hammer blow.

''We're there, captain,'' Miller said.

Robert realized with a start that they were on a quieter
street, tree lined, where the few people afoot stared curiously
at his odd band. He hurried up the stone steps of number 129
and rapped on the door.

A butler cracked the door and raised a supercilious eyebrow.
''Yes?''

''Tell Mr. Thomas Jarvis that I have a message from Robert
Fallon.''

The eye shifted down to the other three on the sidewalk. "Wait here," it ordered, and disappeared. Before Robert had time to worry, it was back. "The servants' entrance is in back," it said stiffly, and disappeared again.

The servants' entrance was a small door that led into the kitchen from the mews. A puffy-faced woman opened the door for them, and Robert found himself staring past her at a well-dressed, well-padded man a few years older than he.

"Yes," the man said faintly. "Yes, I knew from the description it had to be you. I'm Thomas Jarvis. Follow me, please."

The servants watched, mouths open, as the peculiar four-some followed their master out of the kitchen. A babble broke out behind them, but Jarvis led the way without speaking to a study overlooking the street. There he turned with a sigh. "You must forgive me, Mr. Fallon—Mr. Robert Fallon, is it not?—but one cannot be too careful in these times."

"Of course not," Robert said. Jarvis, he knew, had been his father's bugler boy in the Revolution, the boy who had saved the colors of the Irish Legion at the fall of Charleston. He could see no traces of that gallantry in the stuffy man before him.

"I, ah, I was not aware that you'd been injured, Mr. Fallon."

It took Robert a moment to realize he meant the arm. He himself was so used to it, he sometimes forget. "A part of my disguise. If I look too healthy, I might find myself pressed into the Royal Navy."

"I don't know why you're here, of course," Jarvis said. "I can only hope it isn't spying. I do make my home here, you know. Can I offer you wine? Brandy?"

"Nothing now," Robert said. "We were shipwrecked. I was hoping you could help us get out of the country, back to America."

Jarvis was visibly relieved. "As to that, now, there might well be a chance. I managed to get all the Fallon ships out as soon as I thought war was coming. All but one, a sloop called the *Seagull*. She's at a dock on the Thames right now, with an Admiralty seal nailed to her mast. No cargo, of course. Only ballast. But no guards, either. I know where there are a few American seamen hiding, men caught here by the start of the war and afraid of being imprisoned. The four of you, two or three of them, and it's all done. Sure I can't interest you in some brandy?''

"Yes, thank you." He took the glass Jarvis offered and waited till the man had poured his own. "Now, about that spying."

Jarvis slopped brandy onto the floor. "I hope you aren't serious."

"I'm as serious as I need to be. And maybe it's time you remember you're an American."

"I remember, Mr. Fallon. It's just that I live . . . oh, very well. What is it you want? I can't promise anything."

Robert pulled out the handbill; Jarvis stared at it curiously. "I hear the British are going to attack America. Some major city along the east coast, according to the rumors. What do you know?"

"As far as I know, they're just rumors. If you want to know where the British are going to attack, you'll have to ask Admiral Sir Peter Montfort."

"Montfort? Who's he? The name sounds familiar."

"A joke," Jarvis said hastily. "And a bad one. Admiral Montfort is something or other in the Foreign Ministry, something to do with North America. He has a house just down the street."

"But he'd know?" Robert insisted. "Where is his office? Does he bring work home?"

"Burglary! Out of the question. Not because it's dishonorable, Mr. Fallon. It's impossible. He does *all* of his work at whichever residence he's occupying at the moment, in this case 170 New High Cardiff Street, but there's a ball or a rout there every night. The house and grounds will be filled with guests, servants, and entertainers."

"What sorts of entertainers?" Robert asked curiously.

"Oh, a bit of everything. A string quartet in the ballroom, a wind ensemble in a drawing room, acrobats somewhere else, jugglers and puppeteers and mountebanks in the gardens. He always offers his guests variety."

"How do we go about getting hired as entertainers for tonight's ball?"

"You!"

"Us," Robert said patiently. "We worked our way here putting on street shows."

"But it's damned dangerous!"

"I know, but Montfort being just down the street makes it too much to pass up. If I find nothing, at least I've tried. But if he does have some paper saying where the British are going to attack—"

"You're like your father, Mr. Fallon. You have too much daring for your own good. You won't even consider the possibility that you might fail, tonight or anywhere else. When you do fail, I fear your fall will be a great one. I'm sorry, I didn't mean to preach."

"I would hate to see you when you do mean to," Robert said, softening his words with a smile. "Are you going to help us?"

"I said I would. Whether you discover anything tonight or not, I think it best if you steal back the *Seagull* before morning. The sooner you're out of England, the better. As for tonight's rout, all I can suggest is that you present yourself at the gates . . . ."

A liveried gateman appeared at Robert's shout, glaring at the motley group. "Get away with you, now. Ain't no beggars allowed here. Get on with you."

"We are here to entertain," Robert cried, and they began. Miller tossed the apples for Robert's blade, while Kemal bent a horseshoe straight and handed it to the surprised gateman. Jeremiah capered around them, juggling three brightly colored balls.

When they stopped the gateman disappeared, to return with another man, this one in a dark suit, with the air of an upper servant. The second man examined the horseshoe with interest, then requested an example of Robert's swordsmanship. Afterward, he nodded.

"Be here at six o'clock," he said.

As they left Jarvis' house that evening, Robert felt sudden compunctions. "Listen, Jarvis, I haven't been thinking about the trouble we may be giving you. Even if we get away, your servants talking to the Admiral's servants might tie you to us."

"Never fear," Jarvis replied. "The same social distinctions

apply in this country for servants as for masters. Sir Peter's servants don't mix with mine. Just make sure you reach the docks on time. The three men I found you are eager enough to return to America—two of them have been begging in the streets—but they are frightened, too. They won't stay much past midnight if you don't show up. And the tide—''

"I know. The tide swings then." Robert gripped Jarvis' hand. His other was strapped down, and his eyepatch was in place. "We'll make it. And thank you."

Jarvis gave a short laugh. "It's the least I could do for a Fallon."

The four of them filed out through the kitchen, as grim as they had ever been. There was a damn fog in the streets that fit their mood, but torches and lanterns blazed all over the grounds of the admiral's house, burning the fog away. The same gateman let them through sourly, and a liveried footman took them to the garden nook where they were to perform.

Almost as soon as they arrived, a strolling group of guests paused to watch them, and the night became a montage of gaily dressed women and uniformed men. As one group drifted away into the night, another appeared. Most of the men were military officers, and some tried to duplicate Robert's feats with their dress swords. None succeeded, and they, too, disappeared, taking their colorfully gowned companions off for laughing consolation. Robert began to fear that they might spend their night in truth entertaining, slinking away without a try at the admiral's papers.

The man who had hired them appeared. He was the butler, Robert decided. "You," he said, flicking a hand at Robert. "Come wih me. Bring your sword. The rest of you remain here," he added as Kemal got to his feet.

"Stay here," Robert said, and gestured for the butler to lead on.

He was taken directly to the main ballroom, where the assemblage seemed to await him. As he entered, an anticipatory murmur ran through the room. Crystal chandeliers cast dazzling reflections from the mirrored walls, and the pale expanses of bosom, the clusters of uniforms, made almost as glittering a show.

One man, plainly dressed and gray-haired, with freshly

shaved and powdered cheeks, seemed the center of it all. The butler led Robert to him and faded away.

"What's your name?" the plain man said.

"Richardson," Robert replied.

A red-coated Army major laughed. "Richardson! With that face? He's a Spanish dog or an Irish pig."

The plain man pursed his lips disapprovingly, but kept his eye on Robert. "I'm Sir Peter Montfort, Richardson, and I understand you do tricks with a sword. Would you favor us with a few?"

"I will," Robert replied. He unwrapped the cloth covering his sword.

"That's no mountebank's sword," the major said loudly. "I'll wager he stole it. The bailiffs should have this one in hand."

"The sword is mine," Robert said grimly. "I took it from a man who tried to kill me."

"I'm sure," Sir Peter said smoothly. "I understand that some of those swords are sharp enough to cut a silk scarf." He produced a white square from his sleeve. "Like this." The scarf dropped.

A gasp rose as the blade flickered out and two pieces of white silk drifted to the floor. There was scattered applause from the women. Robert thanked God he made it a habit to sharpen the blade each morning.

A bewigged servant appeared with a silver bowl of fruit, and Sir Peter took out an apple. He had the pleased look of a host who has provided something out of the ordinary. "Your chosen target, I believe," he murmured.

The apple was thrown, and split, then two, and three. At each the applause and appreciative gasps increased. Sir Peter was lifting a pineapple from the bowl when the major suddenly stepped forward.

"Swordplay with apples is just that," he said. "Play." And he whipped out his ornate hanger.

Robert had no time to dodge. His blade darted around the major's, caught in the hilt, and tore the sword from the soldier's grasp. He was able to pull his following cut so that only the front of the major's jacket was slashed.

The major staggered back with his mouth hanging open,

and several other red-coated officers gathered around him.

"He tried to kill Hagland!"

"Major Hagland!" Sir Peter's voice cracked like a whip. Everyone froze. He went on in icy tones. "I can only credit that you have had too much to drink, and so must leave. At once."

There was a stunned silence, and then Hagland, accompanied by his coterie, left wordlessly. The crowd parted to let them pass.

Sir Peter eyed Robert curiously. "Drunk or sober, Major Hagland is one of the finest swordsmen in England. Perhaps the finest." When Robert didn't speak, he continued. "Your accent sounds peculiar. Where are you from?"

"Nova Scotia, sir," Robert said. "In Canada." He could feel the sweat running down his back.

"Canada. Well, yes." He took a purse from his pocket and tucked it into Robert's coat. "There are five guineas in that. I had meant to have you do a few more tricks, but not all of Major Hagland's friends have left. And of course, should one of them fall under your blade, I should have to see you hang. You had better go."

"Yes, sir," Robert said, and hastily sheathed his sword. He was already in the hall when he realized that no one had been set to show him out.

One quick look around; he was alone. He took the stairs two at a time. If Montfort's office was on the first floor, he'd never be able to get to it amid all the partygoers. It *had* to be above.

The first door he opened revealed a bedchamber, as did the second. The third gave onto a drawing room. He hesitated at the sight of a tall walnut secretary against the wall, but decided finally that the admiral would have a true office. The next room had walls covered with books and ships models, and a huge desk set near the windows. Light from the garden lanterns flickered in the room, and a fire burned against the admiral's return.

Quietly closing the door behind him, Robert headed for the desk, but something struck him about the models. His sailor's eye was trained to recognizing the lines of a ship once seen, in whatever light. It was a skill that could mean the difference between a prize and prison for a privateer. He moved to examine them more closely.

The one dead in front of him—he could scarcely credit it—was the *Shua*, Jasper Trask's slaver that had burned in the Stono River. And that one over there was the nameless black ship that had pursued him from Tripoli with Louis aboard. Suddenly Robert recalled the voice of Eugene Leitensderfer, telling him that one of Fourrier's partners in the slave trade was a British admiral. An admiral named Montfort.

The information was as useless now as it had been in the North African desert. He had to get on with the business at hand.

The desk was unlocked, and the drawers yielded papers by the ream. Whatever Montfort's position with the Foreign Ministry, it brought him correspondence about naval stores on the Great Lakes, reassignment of infantry regiments stationed in Jamaica, and the value of prizes taken on the American coast. There were letters about the market for seized tobacco, documentation of the naval passes—sidmouths—sold to American merchants, and speculations that New England would voluntarily return to England as a colony. Then, in a folder marked Cochrane, he found what he needed.

Cochrane, it seemed, was commanding a British fleet aimed at the coast of America. His letter was uncompromising.

> I shall give these wretches the blow that will end their wretched capital of Washington City, named appropriately enough, after the traitor, and burn it. Their treacherous leader, Madison, I shall return in chains to England. It will be the finish of them.

"You shan't find any money in there."

Robert turned, letting the paper drop back into the drawer. Montfort stood in the doorway, a cocked pistol in his hand.

"I began to think about your accent," Montfort went on in a conversational tone. "There are any number of Americans in London, living by theft. You should have been satisfied with the five guineas." He turned, as if to call the servants.

"Justin Fourrier wouldn't like me to be arrested." Robert's words arrested Montfort.

"What do you know of Justin Fourrier?"

"I've done a job or two for him, at Fernando Po, and other places."

"A slaver." Montfort was the picture of contempt. "Slavery is outlawed in England, and everywhere that England's realm holds sway."

"So is owning the ships that carry slaves." He watched the bolt go home. "Nice models you have, Sir Peter. I recognize a few of them. The *Skua,* for instance. Jasper Trask's craft. Of course, Trask burned her down in South Carolina. I expect Fourrier will kill him for that, if he hasn't already." Montfort nodded; his gun hand twitched. "I wouldn't," Robert said quickly. "I've friends in the city who know I came here tonight. If I should turn up dead, or disappear . . . well, some of them don't give a fig for Justin Fourrier. They'd ruin him as well as you to avenge me."

"Fourrier is noted for paying poorly," Montfort said hoarsely, "unless it's something his heart is set on. Certainly not the sort of information you'd find here. I, on the other hand, would pay well for the services of a man with boldness and courage. If that man was accountable only to me."

Robert rubbed his chin as if thinking. "I'll have to consider that."

"Where can I reach you?"

"I'll reach you," Robert said. "Tomorrow." He took a step toward the door. Montfort lowered his gun and nodded.

Robert walked out as if he had a perfect right to, ignoring the curious guests in the hall below. In the garden he quickened his pace, hurrying to the niche where the others still put on a desultory show for a few onlookers.

"We're leaving," he said, and they packed up despite the protests of their small audience.

Once through the gates and enveloped by the swirling fog, they broke into a trot. Just loud enough to be heard over their pounding feet, he gave them the bare bones of what had happened in the house.

"Captain," Miller said suddenly, "we ain't heading for the—"

"Montfort gave in too easily. At the next corner, turn right.

And keep going, no matter what I do.''

The turning loomed quickly in the gray mist, and they all veered to the right. As the others pounded on, Robert darted into a doorway, pressing himself into the shadows.

In moments the sound of trotting feet came up the street they had turned off. A shape, indistinct in the fog, stopped at the corner, head cocked to listen. He started in the direction Kemal and the others had taken. As he passed the doorway, Robert lunged out, the full weight of his fist smashing against jawbone. The man dropped as if poleaxed.

"Miller!" Robert called. "Kemal!" By the time they returned, he had the straps that bound his left arm to his chest undone, and his shirt and coat on properly. He bent to check the man in the gutter. It was Sir Peter's gateman, still breathing, but soundly unconscious. "Now for the docks," he said.

The oily black waters of the Thames were slack when they reached *Seagull*. In minutes the tide would turn. The sloop, only fifty feet long but with a sixty-foot whip of a mast, lay deserted, looking long abandoned. Robert tore the Admiralty notice of seizure from the mast.

"Looks as if the men Jarvis found didn't stay. Miller, you and Jeremiah put some sail on her. Kemal, undo the shore lines."

There was a clatter from the forecastle. In two strides Robert kicked open the companionway and dropped through, sword first. Three men in worn clothing, faces drawn and unshaven, cowered against the bulkhead in the dim light of a lantern.

"Please," one with a notched ear whined, "we was only looking for a place out of the wind."

"Who sent you?" Robert asked grimly. "Quick now. Who?"

"Fallon!" one of the others gasped. "He said his name was Fallon."

Robert grinned to himself. Jarvis was covering his tracks well. "On deck with you. Miller! Put this lot to work."

Seagull had already been carried away from the dock by the tide when he reached the quarterdeck. Miller and Jeremiah had the triangular mainsail and a jib on her; he took the rough wood tiller from Kemal. A light wind in the sails and the pressure of the tide on the rudder made the craft alive. Now to drop down the Thames to the Channel, and then to Washington City. Good fortune was smiling on them at last.

XLIII

Seagull slipped into Chesapeake Bay in the latter part of August, 1814, without having seen a British sail during the crossing. Off the mouth of the Potomac River, though, a storm blew up out of nowhere, and Robert, eager to get his news ashore, diverted north toward Baltimore. As he entered the Patapsco River, caution came on him. The British might already have launched their attack; Washington City, and Baltimore, too, might already be in the British hands. Well short of the city he dropped anchor in a branching creek. Kemal and Jeremiah rowed him the rest of the way, past the star-shaped brick bulk of Fort McHenry, to the city itself. The sight of an American flag flying over the fort's parade ground brought a sigh of relief.

At the dock he motioned Kemal to stay in the boat, then spoke to Jeremiah. "I intend to ride on to Washington City as soon as I can rent a horse. Tell Miller to keep those fellows aboard. If they get ashore now, we'll never see them again. Tell them they'll be paid off in Charleston."

Ashore the city seemed possessed of a fever. People hurried everywhere, looking almost driven. The few Robert asked for directions shrugged him off without a word. Finally, he saw what he wanted. A livery stable.

Inside the barn, a blue-coated U. S. Army officer waited impatiently while the hostler finished saddling a large bay. "Just a minute, Major Armistead," the wizened man grunted. "Have him ready in just a minute more."

"I need to rent a horse," Robert said. "To ride to Washington City."

"In a minute," the hostler said irritably. "Can't you see I'm busy?"

The major regarded Robert with interest. "Washington City, sir? I'm on my way there myself. Perhaps we can give one another company on the ride. My name is George Armistead."

"Commands the fort, he does," the hostler said, leading out the bay. "Fort McHenry."

"Robert Fallon, Major Armistead, presently captain of the sloop *Seagull*. I escaped from England less than a month past, with news that must get to the President or the War Department as soon as possible. The British are going to attack Washington City."

The hostler snorted, and Armistead shook his head. "You're late with your news. They landed at Benedict, on the Patuxent, three days ago. Since I can get no information as to whether they are aiming for Washington City or Baltimore, I intend to ask Mr. John Armstrong, the Secretary of War, face to face. We are frankly in a dither as to whether to send our forces there or keep them here. I don't like leaving my command, but the orders I receive from Washington City change by the hour."

"I can tell you where they're going," Robert said. "In England I saw letters from an Admiral Cochrane, saying he intended to burn Washington City."

"Cochrane? The British admiral commanding is named Cochrane."

"Then perhaps you'll give me an introduction at the War Department."

"At any rate, I'll get you in to see someone. Leonhardt, trot out a horse for this gentleman. Captain Fallon, if we take the Bladensburg road, we can be in Washington City before four this afternoon."

From the Bladensburg Bridge on into Washington City, the road was choked with refugees heading in, carts piled high with furniture and mattresses, children settled on the bedding. Some adults rode, but most walked, herding cattle or sheep, or carrying crates of chickens.

Washington City seemed no better than the road. A horde of refugees wandered the streets, sweat-stained and dirty. Many stared in bewilderment about them, waiting to be told what to do, where to go, how to find safety.

At the government buildings near the President's House, conditions were as bad, but there the shifting crowds wore uniforms. The building that housed the Departments of War, State, and the Treasury seethed like a broken anthill, for all it was near seven when they reached it. They jostled their way inside to find a single lieutenant at a table, surrounded by supplicants.

"No, sir, I don't know where Commodore Barney is. Sir, General Winder is with the army at Long Old Fields. No, sir, I don't know where those requisitions are to be presented."

"Lieutenant," Armistead said, pushing his way to the table. "Lieutenant, this man has information on the British intentions."

"Corporal," the lieutenant called over his shoulder, "take this man upstairs."

Robert followed the corporal up to the second floor, where he ducked inside an office for a moment, then returned and motioned for Robert to enter. Inside he found a gaunt, stern-faced man seated behind a large desk.

"Have a seat, Mr. Fallon. Captain Fallon. Anyone with hard information about the British is brought to me. I'm John Armstrong."

The Secretary of War himself! The fates were smiling on him. "My name is Fallon, sir. Robert Fallon, of Charleston, South Carolina. I'm captain of the sloop *Seagull*. The information I have is that the British intend to take Washington City and burn it."

Armstrong nodded thoughtfully. "I see. And the source of your information?"

"Letters from Admiral Cochrane, who commands the British fleet here, to Admiral Montfort in England."

"Letters!" Armstrong said incredulously. "To an admiral in England?"

"Yes, sir. Perhaps I'd better explain. I was recently ship-wrecked in England while on a privateering cruise. During my escape I came across these letters from Admiral Cochrane. He stated his intentions clearly, sir. To burn Washington City and carry President Madison to England in chains."

"Fantastic," Armstrong murmured. "You say you 'came

across' these letters? How does one 'come across' letters containing such information?''

Robert drew breath. "Mr. Armstrong, what does it matter how I got it? The information is factual. You can arrange your forces to meet the attack, here. Not at Baltimore.''

"I do not order the disposition of troops," Armstrong said stiffly.

"But you're the Secretary of War.''

"General Winder disposes of troops here." Irritation crept into hs voice. "His uncle is the Governor of Maryland, you know.''

"Then I must find General Winder," Robert sighed. "I understand he's at a place called Long Old Fields?''

Armstrong snorted. "You'll not find William Henry Winder so easily, Captain Fallon. He runs everywhere, without rhyme or reason, like a chicken with no head. And he does about as much that's useful.''

"Mr. Armstrong, I must reach someone. Help me to an officer who can give orders, else the British may be in the city within seventy-two hours.''

"Very well," Armstrong said, sounding as if it were of no importance to him. He scribbled a note and pushed it across the desk. "That should admit you to President Madison. He's the only one giving orders besides Winder." He began to shuffle papers on his desk.

Back downstairs Robert found Armistead getting ready to leave. "I was just waiting to say goodbye, Captain Fallon. I'm returning to Baltimore tonight. I'm afraid I found out little, and that little depressing.''

"As did I. Secretary Armstrong says he hasn't the authority to do anything. General Winder is the man to be seen, but the general's whereabouts aren't known. Finally he's given me a note for the President. I'm beginning to think no one here knows what's going on at all.''

"It wouldn't surprise me if they didn't. You heard the lieutenant mention Commodore Barney? I was told that he was ordered to burn his gunboats without even firing a shot. To make certain none of them were captured.''

"And he did it?" Robert said incredulously. "It sounds as if he fits right in with this city.''

"Don't let *him* hear you say that, Fallon. Joshua Barney's as tough as they come, hard enough to walk on. But he knows enough to obey orders, and those were his orders."

"Thank God nobody's given me any. Now I must go to the President's House. Perhaps someone there will listen."

"And I must take the road to Baltimore if I'm to reach Fort McHenry tonight." He checked his watch. "It's near eight o'clock."

"If I'm wrong," Robert said, "if the British do attack Baltimore, that fort of yours should withstand anything they throw at you."

Armistead shook his head sadly. "I'll tell you something no one else knows. The magazine at Fort McHenry isn't bomb-proof. One solid hit on it from a good-sized mortar, and the entire fort becomes nothing but a large ruin. Good evening, Captain Fallon. I wish you luck."

"And I you, sir," Robert called as Armistead rode away into the gathering dark. As Robert swung into the saddle for the short ride to the President's House, a commotion caught his ear—shouting, the sounds of men in panic, the rumbling of gun carriage wheels. It couldn't be the British already, he thought. But it could be the remnants of a battle. It could be what was left of the American Army. He galloped down Pennsylvania Avenue, past the still unfinished Capitol Building, toward the Eastern Branch.

The roads were clogged with soldiers, tunics undone, dust-caked and drooping with exhaustion. They tumbled to the ground as soon as they were across the bridge, barely waiting to get out of the way of the men shambling behind them. Robert leaned out of the saddle to grab a passing corporal. "What happened? How badly were you beaten?"

"Beaten?" the man said blankly. "There wasn't no battle." He jerked loose and stumbled away into the dark.

A field piece rumbled across the bridge, accompanied by two young mounted officers. Robert reined up next to them. "What happened?"

"I don't know," one replied wearily. "The order came to fall back to Washington City. Then someone started to run, and somebody else panicked, and then everybody was running. I don't know, mister. I don't know." He trotted off, slumped in the saddle.

Robert turned toward the President's House thoughtfully. Disaster, without the enemy even being met. Whatever had happened in the three days since the British had landed, he was beginning to doubt that anything could be salvaged. Barring a miracle, Washington City was as good as in British hands.

The President's House was lit at every window. A dapper man with thin mustaches let him in. "Yes, *monsieur*?"

"I'm here to see the President," Robert said. "I have a letter of introduction from the Secretary of War."

"I am Jean Pierre Sioussa," the small man said, "the major-domo. If you please . . . . " He held out his hand, and Robert reluctantly placed the letter in it. Sioussa trotted upstairs.

There was only one other person waiting in the entry hall, a dreamy-eyed man with a long nose, sitting against the wall and sketching at the marble floor with a stick. Robert began to pace, his stride quickening as time passed. Abruptly, the seated man held out his stick.

"Stop. Don't step on the Capitol."

"I beg your pardon?" Robert said.

"The Capitol. It's right there," the man said, tapping a spot on the floor in front of Robert. "I'm mapping out strategy. Or is it tactics? I always get them mixed up. At any rate, you see, we place a large reserve inside the Capitol. As the British attack, we fall back slowly, blunting their attacks until we reach the Capitol. At that point, the men inside rush out, surprising the British, and we all counterattack."

"I see," Robert said. It was madness. The men he'd seen couldn't blunt an attack by washerwomen, and if the British troops were veterans of the Napoleonic War, as they almost certainly were, the men rushing out of the Capitol would achieve only their own deaths. "Are you one of the generals?"

"Um? Oh. Not exactly." Long-nose grinned, offering a hand. "Francis Scott Key. Aide to General Walter Smith, of the District of Columbia militia."

"Robert Fallon, captain of the sloop *Seagull*."

"A ship captain?" Key said interestedly. "Tell me, captain. How does the sea look at night? I mean, out of sight of land, with the moon shining, and—"

"Excuse me," Robert broke in, "but do you think that man took my letter directly to the President? It's been twenty minutes."

"French John? Oh, he took it up all right. There's no need to worry about old French John."

The front door banged open, and a fox-faced, harried-looking man in a general officer's uniform strode toward the stairs.

"That's General Winder now," Key said.

"General," Robert called, moving toward Miller. "General, I have important information."

"Not now," Winder said, and disappeared up the stairs. Robert stared angrily.

"You might be able to find him later at McKeowin's Hotel," Key said, "on Pennsylvania Avenue. It's become a sort of unofficial headquarters when he's in the city."

"The last time I was in this city," Robert said, "it was inhabited by lunatics. It still is."

"Captain Fallon?" came a woman's voice.

Robert turned to face Dolley Madison. The vivaciousness he remembered was masked by worry, but she still managed a smile.

"Mr. Key," she said. "It's good to see you again. You don't mind if I speak to Captain Fallon alone for a moment?" Key bowed, smiling, as Dolley put her arm through Robert's and walked him down the hall.

"Mrs. Madison," Robert said, "I must see your husband immediately."

"Captain Fallon, I am so forgetful! Pray forgive me, and refresh my memory. When *did* we meet?"

"Once, ma'am, briefly. On the steps of this house, while Mr. Jefferson was President. I must see President Madison, or at least give him my message. The British are definitely moving against Washington City. Baltimore may come later, but I've seen proof that the capital is their prime target."

She drew a deep breath. "What chance have we? For days my husband and Mr. Monroe and General Winder have been moving men about, almost at random it seems to me. Now they are talking of staking everything on one big battle."

"If it all comes to one battle," Robert said hesitantly, "I

don't believe we have much chance at all. Perhaps you'd better give some thought to leaving the city, Mrs. Madison.''

"I cannot leave while my husband remains, Captain, and he cannot leave until that last chance is lost.''

"Will you at least prepare, ma'am? Put a few things in whatever carriages or wagons you have. When the end comes, there won't be much time.''

"But, of course, it may never come to that. We may win.''

"Of course, ma'am,'' Robert said. He hoped he sounded confident.

"I'll see that my husband hears your message, Captain. What decision will be made, I don't know, but I will do my best. Captain Fallon. Mr. Key.''

Robert watched her up the stairs, her back straight and her head high. "A gallant lady,'' he said.

"Exactly, sir,'' Key said.

"Mr. Key,'' Robert said suddenly, "what can you tell me of the lay of the land? I don't know my way around this area.''

Key seemed delighted to make further use of his stick. He began to sketch briskly on the floor again. "This is the Potomac River. The fork to the east is the Eastern Branch. Where the two forks meet is Washington City. There are two bridges across the Potomac to the west, and two across the Eastern Branch. There's another about seven or eight miles up the Branch, at Bladensburg.''

"I crossed that one on the way here from Baltimore,'' Robert said.

"Yes. Well. About five miles east of the city is Long Old Fields, where the main part of the army lies.''

"Not any longer,'' Robert murmured. "Pray, do go on.''

"Another seven or eight miles east of that is Upper Marlboro. The British were camped there last night. They've come straight up the Patuxent from Benedict, some eighteen miles to the south. If they continue as they have, they should march straight on to Baltimore. Or they could veer to the west, and come for Washington City.''

"What sort of scouting do they have? Do you know? Have they moved as if they knew the terrain?''

"I don't know for certain,'' Key said doubtfully. "But there have been reports that some people have given them a warm welcome. Food, wine, that sort of thing. I suppose guides, or information, aren't out of the question.''

"Then they won't come directly west," Robert said.

"Why not?"

"The Eastern Branch is perhaps half a mile wide here at the city. If the bridges are burned, they'll have to use boats to cross it. Up at Bladensburg, even if the bridge is gone, they can wade across. They'll come that way. How many men do we have at Bladensburg?"

"General Stansbury *was* there. An order was sent for him to march here, or else he decided to march here, but I believe he has been ordered back."

"Christ," Robert muttered. They were worse than amateurs; they were fools. "It should be full dark in another hour or so. I intend to scout toward this Upper Marlboro. Care to come along?"

Key blinked. "A scout? I'm not sure."

"It may give the lady upstairs a chance to escape," Robert said quietly.

"Then I'll go, of course," Key said.

When they rattled across the North Bridge about ten o'clock, the lone sentry watched them sleepily. Trying not to think of what would happen if the British made a forced march by night, Robert followed Key down the road that led to Long Old Fields and thence to Upper Marlboro. There was little moon, and scudding clouds cut its scanty light. The warm Maryland summer night was filled with chirping insects, and the occasional cry of some night bird.

Just as suddenly the night was filled with the rattle of musketry. Robert dropped low in his saddle as he whipped his mount around and galloped back the way he had come. Key close behind.

"Sergeant of the Guard!" someone shouted. "Post number nine!" Musket fire split the night, but none came close. Eventually even the shouting faded behind them, and they drew rein.

"That was the British camp," Robert said.

"Impossible," Key retorted. "That was Long Old Fields. It's another eight miles to Upper Marlboro. Perhaps it was a scouting party."

"He called for the sergeant of the guard! That was a full-scale camp."

"Oh. Then they *are* going for Washington City."

"Yes. Come on. They've settled down by now. We'll find a place to watch their camp."

As Key turned to follow, he asked, " But we *know* what they're doing. We must ride back to the city! Tell General Winder, or somebody."

"Those fools will ignore anything. From what I can see, they've successfully ignored logic ever since the British landed. The one thing they might believe is if the two of us tell them we saw the British do thus and so with our own eyes." He stopped and strained his eyes into the darkness. There seemed to be just the hint of paleness that might indicate tents ahead. Moving off the road, he dismounted and led his horse into some bushes that would screen him from the camp when dawn came. Key followed. "We'll spend the night here, wait till the British make their move in the morning, then ride like hell to Washington City. I'm betting they'll move toward Bladensburg."

Key was silent; they stood peering toward the British camp.

The night went slowly. Its gentle warmth added to the difficulty in staying awake. In the early hours, between two and three, Key suddenly grabbed Robert's arm and silently pointed back toward Washington City. The night sky was tinged with pink and flickers of red.

"The bridges," Robert said comfortingly. "They're just burning the bridges across the Eastern Branch."

"For a moment I thought . . . If they've burned the bridges, Captain Fallon, how shall we get back?"

"By way of Bladensburg."

The night at last began to lighten; there was a stir in the camp. Robert bent to shake Key, who was asleep against a tree. "They're getting ready to march, I think," he whispered.

"Um? What? Oh." Key scrambled to his feet, rubbing his face. He peered blearily toward the encampment, then suddenly stared at the graying sky, fully awake. "It's almost light! They'll see us when we ride away."

"Then we'll have to ride fast," Robert said shortly. "Watch."

Briskly the camp was struck, tents folded away, cook stores stacked into carts. The red-coated soldiers formed in the road. Their motions were spare, Robert saw, the men laconic. They were bored. Veterans, he thought. Up against Washington City's ragtag of militia, who had never heard a shot fired in anger.

A drum began to beat the cadence, and the first battalion stepped out, every musket sloped precisely, every left foot coming down solidly on the beat of the drum. They turned down the road toward the Eastern Branch.

"You were wrong," Key said excitedly. "They're not going to Bladensburg. But didn't they see the bridges burn last night?"

Robert didn't reply. The long red snake of the British army curved toward the Eastern Branch. He recognized some units by their uniforms as the light increased. The 21st Regiment of Foot. The 85th. The 44th. They swung down the road toward Washington City and the destroyed bridges. Suddenly mounted officers were galloping the length of the column, shouting. The column drew to a halt. Then, officers shouting and haranguing, the British army wound back down the road toward camp. At the road junction, the lead units swung north, and the others followed. Toward Bladensburg.

"Let's go," Robert said, swinging into the saddle. Key scrambled onto his own horse, and they burst from the trees at a dead gallop. Shouts rose behind them. Robert lay low in the saddle, using his cap to whip the horse. Seven miles to Bladensburg Bridge, according to Key. An easy march for the British. Even if they galloped all the way there would be precious little warning. He could only hope there were troops in Bladensburg already.

The road led into a dense tangle of woods, and then they were in the village of Bladensburg, neat brick houses, some abandoned. No soldiers. They trotted across the narrow wooden bridge, no more than ninety feet long.

Some three hundred and fifty yards from the bridge and off to the right, a high embankment of fresh dirt dwarfed the battery of cannon poking their snouts through embrasures. A scattering of militia infantry rose up from behind a rail fence near the embankment as they crossed the bridge, and a few more appeared near an old tobacco barn upstream.

"Find their commander," Robert told Key. "Tell him the British will be here today. I'm going on. Good luck, Key."

"Good luck, Fallon. And Godspeed."

As Key trotted toward the embankment, Robert turned south again, toward Washington City. Six miles away; an easy march. He flogged his horse with his cap, kept him at a dead gallop.

The roads into the city were empty. There were no refugees, and there were no soldiers marching north. Surely, with the Eastern Branch bridges burned, it was clear the British would come through Bladensburg. That handful at the village couldn't possibly hold the bridge. He galloped into the city, past the gaunt poplars that lined Pennsylvania Avenue, not pulling rein till he reached McKeowin's Hotel. He rushed inside and collared the first man he saw, a militia captain.

"General Winder?"

"The dining room," the captain said.

Robert burst into the dining room to find the fox-faced Winder behind a table. Two dozen men, mostly in uniform, milled around him. "Take this to Commodore Barney," Winder shouted, handing a note to a major. "He's to guard the south bridge." He seemed as harried as the night before.

"The south bridge!" Robert burst out. "Weren't the bridges burnt last night?"

"Just the north one," Winder replied, then caught himself. "Who the devil are you?"

"Robert Fallon, General Winder. I've spent the night across the river. The British were camped last night at Long Old Fields. This morning they marched for Bladensburg."

Winder hurled his pen to the table. "God, everyone spent last night across the river! I've one report that they're camped at Long Old Fields. Then one of Laval's dragoons comes pounding in here: the British are at the Old Fields, all right, and coming on for Washington City. My own surgeon, Hanson Catlett, comes back from a little ride across the river. He says there are no British on the road from the Old Fields, and none at the Old Fields. Now you say they were there, but they've gone to Bladensburg. What am I to believe, sir?"

"General, I saw the British on the road to Bladensburg with

my own eyes. Mr. Key stopped at Bladensburg to warn the commander there, but I saw nothing to indicate they can stop them. If they get across the Eastern Branch, General, the city is finished.''

Winder hesitated, looking at several of the other officers. Before he could speak, a dusty corporal burst in and swayed to slovenly attention.

"General Stansbury's compliments to General Winder, and I got a message for the general, sir.''

Winder held out an impatient hand. "Well, let me have it.''

"Wasn't time to write it, sir. General told it to me, and told me to tell it to you, I mean, to the general, sir.'' He took a deep breath. "General Stansbury has sent a scout down the road to the Old Fields, and the redcoats is coming hell bent for leather for Bladensburg. The General says he can't hold with the troops General Winder gave him. He says if General Winder don't get him some rein—, rein—, some more men fast, he's going to pull back to Washington City like he wanted to in the first place. Sir.''

"Well," Winder said. "Well." He suddenly shook his head and got to his feet. "This is decisive. We must move at once. Major Biscoe, write orders for Lieutenant Colonel Laval. His dragoons are to move to Bladensburg immediately. Major Peter and Captain Burch will move out with their artillery. General Smith is to march with the District Militia. Colonel Scott's regulars, Captain Stull's riflemen, all to go. Come, gentlemen, there's a battle to be fought.'' He strode for the door, trailing a cloud of advisors and staff.

"General," Robert called. "May I march with you as a volunteer?''

"Certainly not," Winder replied without slowing or looking back. "War is for the professionals, sir. The professionals.''

Stunned, Robert watched them leave the hotel and gallop off. Professionals? They weren't even talented amateurs.

It struck him hard that there was to be a battle, perhaps a decisive one for the nation, and he would have no part in it. There was, however, one service he could render.

Outside the President's House, three carriages stood waiting, with Sioussa overseeing their loading. A pair of cannon stood like a forlorn hope on either side of the drive. Dolley

Madison appeared at the door with two servants carrying a trunk.

"Careful with that," she said. "It's china." She saw Robert and smiled. "Ah, Captain Fallon. You see, sir, I'm taking your advice."

"I could wish you would take the rest of it, ma'am. General Winder is finally marching to meet the British, but I doubt he's going to get there in time. Even if he does, I don't hold out much hope of stopping regulars with militia."

"I won't leave, Captain. My reason still obtains." She smiled warmly, and put a hand on his wrist. "I thank you for your concern over my safety. I will always remember it."

"It seems I'm not wanted as a volunteer, ma'am, so I'll ride out toward the battlefield and bring back the news to you. Good or bad."

"You're not wanted?" she said incredulously. "Whatever can the Army be thinking of?"

"I don't believe they're thinking at all, ma'am. Even now that he's convinced the British are marching on Bladensburg, he's left Commodore Barney to guard the bridge over the Eastern Branch."

Her head came up sharply. "I know Joshua Barney, and if there's one man I want in the fight for this city, it's him. You wait here."

She bustled inside while he sat his horse impatiently. In a few minutes horses were led around front. Almost immediately after, a cluster of men in civilian clothes hurried out. President Madison, short and stooped, was heavier than when Robert had met him as Secretary of State. He seemed wearier, too. Armstrong was with him, and George Campbell, the Secretary of the Treasury, with a pair of huge pistols belted on, William Jones the Secretary of the Navy, and Richard Rush, the Attorney General. A handful of aides swarmed after them. Dolley Madison waved at him from the doorway as they mounted. Armstrong saw him and glared dourly, but Madison nodded. "Captain Fallon? I thought I remembered your name, sir. If you'll accompany us, we're riding down to the Eastern Branch."

At the bridge Joshua Barney met them.

"Mr. President," the square-jawed, curly-haired

commodore said with a curt nod. "I obey orders, Mr. President. When I was ordered to pull my gunboats up the Patuxent without fighting, I did. When I was ordered to burn them, rather than fight, I did. But this is too much, sir. I have four hundred tough flotilla men here, a hundred and twenty Marines under Captain Miller and five field guns. And I've been ordered to guard this damned bridge while a battle is taking place up river, and burn it if the British show. Mr. President, it's a damned waste of good men. A criminal waste."

"Yes, yes, Commodore," Madison said soothingly. "General Winder was concerned for the safety of the city." Barney snorted dangerously, and Madison hurried on. "In any case, as Commander-in-Chief, I am issuing new orders. Leave what men you consider sufficient to burn the bridge if the British do appear, then march to Bladensburg. I will need every man there today."

"You, sir?" Barney said.

Madison nodded. "As President and Commander-in-Chief, I intend to assume command of the forces in the field."

"If you'll excuse me, Mr. President," Armstrong said drily, "I had better be off for Bladensburg."

"Of course," Madison said, and the Secretary of War galloped off north.

"Captain Creighton," Barney called, "tell off a corporal and four men. If the redcoats show, fire the bridge. Captain Miller, limber up the guns. Get the men fallen in. We're marching." The men at the bridge broke into furious activity, the Marines swarming over the field guns, the sailors from the gunboats falling into rough ranks under their officers.

"Commodore," Robert said, "I would appreciate it if you'd allow me to march with you as a volunteer."

"And who are you?" Barney asked.

"Robert Fallon. I've commanded a privateer, the schooner *Shrike,* and I took the full-rigged ship *Staghound* to China, with plenty of pirates along the way. I was also with Eaton and O'Bannion in North Africa, at Derna."

"It seems you know what powder smoke smells like, Mr. Fallon. Get yourself a musket and bayonet."

"Mr. President," Campbell said suddenly, "I don't know

what good a Secretary of the Treasury can do in a battle, but here." He unbuckled his pistols and handed them to the President. On Madison they seemed even larger, making him look like a child going out to play at war.

"I will see you on the battlefield, commodore," Madison said heartily. "If the city is lost, gentlemen, we will meet at Frederick, Maryland. God be with you." And he galloped away, followed by his Cabinet.

Minutes later Commodore Barney's command was on the road, the Marines leading at a crisp march, the five field guns coming next with the jingle and clatter of harness, and the four hundred sailors from the gunboats bringing up the rear. As they reached the limits of the city the rumble of cannon fire rolled down the road from Bladensburg. Without an order, the pace picked up.

They marched toward the pounding guns, the crackle of muskets, and the whistling roar of the Britishers' newfangled Congreve rockets. Robert impatiently gripped the musket he had gotten from a sailor, but the column could move no faster. The men afoot were already nearly at a trot, and there was a fight yet ahead.

Suddenly they were forcing their way through a panic-stricken flood of men shedding packs, canteens, muskets as they ran. He recognized some of the dusty, wide-eyed men. Some of Laval's dragoons rode down a cluster of Sterret's 5th Regiment, who left the injured where they fell, and ran on. Men from Schurz's regiment, from Ragan's, Doughty's, and Pinkney's, mingled together in a common wash of terror. Overhead the Congreves shrieked, and the rat-a-tat-tat of drums ahead told of the steady British advance.

Madison appeared out of the fleeing mass, the two huge pistols still belted to his waist. "Thank God I've found you," he shouted at Barney. "There's a second line ahead. For the love of God, we have to stop them."

"Double time!" Barney shouted. "Guns to the fore!" And the weary men broke into a trot, raising the dust higher as they forced their way through the fleeing men toward the battle. Captain Miller managed to get the field pieces and their caissons to the front of the formation. The civilian drivers of the ammunition wagons looked nervous, but they obeyed the command to follow. Before the charging guns the tide of men parted, and Barney's command ran toward the fighting ahead.

The second line was evident when they came on it, and pathetic in its weakness. Scott's regulars, Peter's artillery, and a large number of the District Militia were formed to the left of the road on a wooded slope. To the right, on a hill, waited Beall's regiment from Annapolis. Kramer's Maryland Militia had formed down the road. Barney drove into the empty center with the cry of, "Action front!"

As smoothly as if there was no turmoil ahead of them, no panic behind, the three twelve-pounders and a company of Marines took up positions squarely in the middle of the road, with the rest of the Marines and the flotilla-men grouped as infantrymen. Robert tied his horse to a tree and checked his musket as he joined them.

The noise from the bridge faded. There was silence at Bladensburg. Five minutes. Ten minutes. Fifteen, and then, far down the road, an oncoming mass of red, slanted bayonets gleaming in the sun. A little more than a quarter of a mile from the second line, the British advance rippled down into a shallow ravine. Kramer's militia opened fire. There was a sharp crack of return musketry, and in an instant the Marylanders' formation had scattered like quail.

With a roar the British came on. They could smell another rout in the making. As they came out of the ravine, Peter's guns raked them from the left, and Barney himself touched off an eighteen-pounder right into the center of them. The British staggered and came on. Peter's guns redoubled their fire, and the pair of eighteens laid down a methodical barrage at point-blank range.

The British began to fall back, but then their officers were out in front, waving their swords and shouting for the advance. Gaps were appearing in the red lines, but they moved with parade-ground precision into the field to the right of the road. They would outflank that worrying artillery.

Unseen until the moment they opened up, Captain Miller's three guns suddenly hurled cannister and grape into the advance. Gaps a dozen men wide were ripped in the British line. They wavered, tried to reform and advance despite the three batteries now zeroed on them, but it was too much. They broke and ran. Through the pall of powder smoke their officers could be seen, rallying them at a rail fence that bordered the field.

"Hit them!" Barney shouted. "Boarders away!"

With a howl the flotilla-men rushed the fence. Robert roared with exultation. He parried an officer's saber thrust with his musket and bayoneted him, caught a private in the face with his musket butt, and then he too was over the fence. A redcoat, his face streaked with grime and powder smoke, faced him, bayonet ready. Robert feinted, and the man twitched in that direction. Robert feinted the other way, and had to dance back from a thrust. Warily they circled, probing and feeling each other out. Suddenly the man thrust again. Robert dropped to one knee, letting the bayonet pass over his shoulder. His own thrust caught the soldier just above the belt.

And then he was caught up in the flow of sailors back to the guns. The British had been driven back to the ravine; some had fallen back all the way to the river. It was time to regroup.

The British advance came on again, but Barney's guns kept a heavy fire, and the Marines and flotilla-men worked their muskets as smoothly as the regulars. Robert fired and reloaded so many times that his teeth ached from tearing open the cartridges; he thought he might for the rest of his life taste nothing but powder. Their deadly fire was doing its work, though. The British were caught in the ravine.

Then, without warning musket balls began to fall among the Americans from the hill to their right.

Abruptly Barney's horse screamed and reared, falling to catching the Commodore's leg. Robert rushed to pull him free. There was a wet patch on Barney's thigh.

"Say nothing," Barney ordered when he realized Robert had seen the wound. Gesturing with his cutlass he hobbled back to the guns. "Get those pieces trained on that hill! Lively now!"

Had the Annapolis militia gone mad? There had been no sounds of fighting from their direction; they couldn't have been driven off. Then he saw that a few of the Annapolis men were crouched among the sailors.

Robert grabbed one. "What are you doing here? Why aren't you up on that hill?"

"Let me go," the man answered angrily. "At least I come back to try to help. Winder ordered us to retreat. Us, and the regulars on the other side of you. Don't you understand? You're out here all alone! Let me go!"

Stunned, Robert let him go. He took off at a fast trot, slowing only to sling his musket into the bushes. It was over. He looked for his horse; it was gone, strayed or stolen during the battle. "Commodore," Robert called. "Commodore Barney!"

"Bring up more ammunition!" Barney shouted.

But the hail of fire was proving too much for the civilian drivers. First one, then another, leaped to the seat of his ammunition wagon and whipped up his horses. Back toward Washington City. Two minutes after the first driver broke, they were all gone. Barney stared after them.

"Commodore Barney," Robert said. "It's over. General Winder has pulled everyone else off the line. I don't know why we didn't get the order, too, but we're by ourselves. Listen. You'll not hear any firing except from here."

Barney nodded bleakly. "If we had ammunition . . . . God damn it to hell!" He took a step, and his wounded leg collapsed under him. Robert caught him and eased him down. A cluster of officers gathered around. "Miller," Barney said between clenched teeth. The Marine captain was nursing a shattered arm. "Miller, spike the guns. Get the men out that you can."

"What about you, sir?" Miller asked.

"I'm going nowhere," Barney said, "unless one of you has a horse under his coat. All right, then," the Commodore went on gruffly. "Off with you. I expect the British will be along any minute to look after me."

The officers began to argue, saying that they could carry Barney, but Robert remembered his promise to Dolley Madison. Where her husband had been swept in the day's storm he had no idea, but he could see that she received the warning he had promised. Leaving his musket with one of the officers he set out walking.

For a mile or so he saw no one. Those fleeing the battle had already gone further; Barney's men were just beginning their retreat. Then he came on a horse. Its rider lay nearby. From his blood-drenched coat it was plain he hadn't been able to go any further. Robert took the mount gratefully.

On horseback he caught up with the flotsam of the battle, the stragglers and the runners who were too tired to run any more. Some tried to seize his horse; he kicked them away or ran them down.

The dusty poplars along Pennsylvania Avenue seemed already dead, foreshadowing the doom of the city. From the southernmost tip of the city came the glow of flames. Burning the Navy Yard, Robert thought. From time to time there was a distant explosion.

At the President's House the carriages still stood waiting, teams hitched and drivers mounted. Inside, Dolley Madison met him in the front hall, her hands clasped anxiously.

"It *is* over, then? Captain Fallon, when they began destroying the Navy Yard . . . . " Another explosion shook the windows; the crystal chandelier tinkled above their heads.

"It's over, ma'am. Commodore Barney almost held the field, but General Winder . . . . What happened doesn't matter now. You must leave Washington City immediately. The British will be here in a matter of hours."

"I had dinner set," she said almost to herself. "I've loaded what I could in the carriages. My husband's papers. Most of the silver. But all the things I must leave! It took hours to get George Washington's portrait out of the frame, and it's still too large to fit in the carriages. I told Mr. Barker and Mr. de Peyster—they're the gentlemen helping me—that it must not be allowed to fall into British hands. It must be saved or destroyed. I . . . I suppose they will destroy the house themselves."

"It's time for you to go, ma'am," he said, and she nodded numbly as he led her out to the carriages.

Suddenly, as she was getting in, she stopped. "You've done a very great service to your country today, Captain Fallon. You should have a reward."

"I did nothing for my country but run from place to place."

"Then you did a great service to me." She smiled at him. "And you can't deny that without offending a lady, something I'm sure no Carolinian would do." She ducked into the carriage, and backed out with a large and heavy bag. She took it from her before she dropped it. "That, I fear, is all the gift I am able to give you, Captain. It's our tea service, and I fear it has the Presidential Seal on it. If we lost too many battles that may make it dangerous to own."

"I will treasure it, ma'am, no matter how many battles we lose, as I will treasure the memory of the gracious lady who gave it to me. But now," he said firmly shutting the carriage door, "you must be off. Driver!"

The carriage lurched down the drive, followed quickly by the other two. Robert was sure a feminine hand waved from the first as they rolled out of sight.

Grimly he mounted his horse again, fastening the bag behind the saddle. Time for him to save himself. If he could make it out of the city to the north, he might be able to work his way around the British to Baltimore. If he was lucky . . . .

XLIV

The night was already lit by fires by the time Major Gerard Fourrier reached the President's House. The Navy Yard still burned, and the fort at Greenleaf Point. The houses north of the Capitol were a solid mass of flames. The Capitol itself was burning well; he'd helped in starting that one. His "souvenirs" had been the portraits of Louis XIV and Marie Antoinette. It was like these Americans, he thought; for all their talk of republicanism, their Capitol had been a far grander building than the Houses of Parliament.

He dismounted tiredly and went inside.

"Ah, Fourrier," General Ross said. "Have you the information?" The commanding general of the attack on Washington City was watching chairs and tables being piled in the Oval Office. A few soldiers appeared to be grabbing what loot they could.

"Yes, sir," Gerard replied. "Madison seems to have fled north into Maryland. A town called Frederick."

"Not too rough on the people you questioned, I trust," Ross said with a grin. Gerard grinned back. They had served together before, in the Peninsular Campaign.

"Too bad," Ross said. "Would have liked to bring Madison out. Best souvenir of all, eh? Did you know we found the table set for forty when we got here? Think they were expecting us?"

"If they were smart, sir," Gerard said. "As for Madison, sir, I could take a contingent in civilian clothes and haul him back."

"No time," Ross replied. A Navy lieutenant appeared in the door with a torch, and Ross's smile deepened. "Ah, Pratt. Just the man. Stand away there," he barked at the enlisted men stacking the furniture, and they retreated from the room. "Care to do the honors, Fourrier?"

"Thank you, sir," Gerard said, taking the torch. Carefully he thrust the burning end into the heap, watched the cushions and curtains catch, the runners flare across the pianoforte and lick at a huge sideboard. With a sudden burst the room was engulfed. Ross said something to him, but he didn't hear. As always with a fire, he was imagining a Fallon twisting in the flames.

Catherine put down the paper with a shudder. The Charleston *Courier* was bad enough, but the papers from Baltimore and Philadelphia, the *Federal Gazette* and the *Advertiser* were horrifying. "Moira, have you seen these? Will you stop reading that book and listen to me?"

Moira shut her book with an irritating patience. "I've seen the papers, Catherine, and the news is depressing. This book, on the other hand, is quite entertaining. It's called *Pride and Prejudice*, written by an anonymous."

"Be damned to the book," Catherine snapped. "Washington City's been burned, one paper says razed to the ground. The population routed from their homes, maidens' dignity offended. That's a polite way of saying rape, Moira. And these papers are two weeks old. Why, they could fall on Charleston any day."

"If they attack Charleston," Moira said patiently, "we'll remove to Riding Green, or to Tir Alainn. It isn't the British that's worrying you. Out with it."

"You're right, of course. It's Jasper Trask."

"Why? For a blackmailer, he's more than discreet. And the sums he's asking are never so large as to cause distress."

Catherine nodded tiredly. "That's what worries me. He seems a greedy man to me, yet he's held back. Why?"

As if the mention of his name was a conjure, Jasper Trask walked into the study, Ezekiel hurrying after him. "Miss Catherine, I'm sorry, but he just pushed his way on past me."

"That's all right, Ezekiel," she said. "You may go. And close the door." She gave Trask her coldest eye. "What do you mean, barging into my house?"

Trask had been spending some of his money on clothes; his

taste ran to brocade vests and yellow trousers. They made him look far from a gentleman. His eyes flickered to her, pausing at her décolletage, then fell to the floor.

"I'm getting out of the city," he began. "Them British will be coming here next. Yes, sir."

"We will regret to see you go," Catherine said drily. She had discovered that sarcasm was a safe way to prod him; he didn't seem to recognize it.

"That's as may be," he said. He looked around the room approvingly. "I'm going to have one like this where I'm going. All I need from you is enough of the ready, and I'll be able to set myself up. Give me a year or two, and I'll be as rich as the two of you put together."

"How much of the, ah, ready, do you need?"

"That's what I can't be sure of. I could ask for a big figure, but supposing what I got was just five hundred or a thousand short of what I need." He scratched his whiskers and shook his head. "No, the only way is for you two to come with me to New Orleans."

Catherine felt her calm slip. "Go with you to New Orleans! You must be mad!"

Trask seemed offended. "You think I'm a fool? I leave you here, and what do I get if I need that extra thousand dollars? Nothing! This game don't work so good at long range. You got to be right there in New Orleans where I can keep an eye on you. When I'm set up, you two can go on your way."

"Go on our way?" Moira said bitterly. "Do you think we're fools enough to go anywhere with you?"

"Moira," Catherine warningly.

"You're not mad," Moira said. "You're stark, staring insane."

"Now just a minute," Trask began angrily.

Catherine lunged out of her chair to catch Moira's arm in an iron grip and lift her bodily to her feet. "If you'll excuse us, Mr. Trask, I must speak to my sister alone for a moment."

Moira let herself be dragged to the far end of the room, then stopped with a jerk. "Now, what—"

"Be quiet," Catherine commanded. Her voice was low, but full of iron. "Turn so he can't see your face, and listen to me. Now. Ever since this started, I've met Trask with all the arrogance and coldness I can muster. It's the only way I could keep from screaming. You've been cutting, slashing at him at every opportunity, goading him into fighting back."

"It's the only way *I* can keep from shrieking. Are you thinking he'll get so angry he'll tell what he knows? He'll not be throwing away our money so easily."

"When Trask came in, I realized what's been worrying me. I had been keeping distance between us, but the more you argue with him . . . well, he's begun thinking about us as women." Moira gasped and was silent. "You must remain cool, remain above him. Remember, he can demand more from us than money."

This time Moira growled. "If he as much as suggests . . . why, I'll murder him."

"And dispose of another body?" Catherine asked wearily. "Or find that he really has written out his information? No. We will hang on until Robert comes, or until we figure a way out. Until then . . . ." Her voice failed; she had to swallow to regain it. "Until then we give him *whatever* he wants."

After a long moment Moira nodded.

Catherine stared at her intently. Despite herself she had come to like this woman. First Moira had saved her from Justin, and then she had been there through all the trouble with Trask, giving support, lending strength, while Robert was off playing at his war. Despite it all, despite the fact that he was Moira's, she still desired Robert, but he was a lot of trouble, more trouble than he was worth. Men were always trouble.

"Courage, Moira," she said. "Their maumas can take care of Charlotte and Edward, and we can take care of ourselves."

Moira smiled with something of her old strength. "Courage."

When they turned to go back to their seats, Catherine saw her eyes bright with unshed tears.

"Listen," Trask began brusquely, "I ain't going to argue. I've reserved two cabins on the *South Wind*, sailing for New Orleans tomorrow morning. You're either coming with me, or . . . ." He gave an ugly laugh.

"We will go with you," Catherine said, and saw Moira's hands clench in her lap.

Trask seemed almost surprised. Immediately he became placating. "You won't be sorry. I have contacts in New Orleans. Important people. Jean Blanque is one of the most respected lawyers there. Of course, he smuggles a few slaves on the side. Once I'm set up—"

"Mr. Trask," Catherine said coldly, "we do not care to know the details of your business, just as I'm sure you do not wish us to know them. Now. If you will leave, we must begin preparing for our journey."

"Oh. Yes, of course." Trask seemed deflated, looking at her sideways again. "I'll be going, then. But I'll expect you at Chalmer's Wharf at eight o'clock in the morning. Or I'll send a letter to the magistrates before I go."

Then he was gone. The two women sat staring at the door.

"What will we do?" Moira asked finally.

"Survive," Catherine replied. "We will survive."

Robert sat up in bed and blearily checked his watch. Six-thirty. The morning of Tuesday, September 13. He might as well wake Kemal, Miller and Jeremiah. It was time for another day's work on the defenses on Hampstead Hill, east of Baltimore. Miller had hidden *Seagull* deeper in the creek, then brought the Turk and Jeremiah ashore to help defend the city. As Robert swung his feet over the side of the bed, there was a huge cannon roar from the harbor. He realized it had been another that had wakened him. The others were rolling from their pallets as a third sounded, and then they were all at the window.

The huge garrison flag waved over Fort McHenry's red brickwork, but not serenely. Five bomb ships and a host of frigates and sloops opened fire. Ranging shots had wakened them. Now a short, squat vessel suddenly began hurling Congreve rockets to burst over the star-shaped fort. Fort McHenry's bastions were swept with smoke and flame; its guns roared back.

"There'll be no work on the trenches today, captain," Miller said.

"No. It looks as if there'll be fighting. Since we're considered good for no more than digging, I suggest we find a good spot to watch the battle."

"Like where, captain?" Jeremiah asked.

"The roof." An hour later the four of them were firmly ensconced among the gables of the boarding house with spyglasses and a hamper of cold meat pies and wine. It was a strange experience for Robert, to be watching a battle as if it were a play. Other rooftops were filling with other eager watchers.

For the civilians of the city it was no doubt exciting, Robert thought. At least, they oohed and aahed at every bomb burst. To men who had been in battle, it had the deadly monotony of all battles.

At nine o'clock sails were let out on the British fleet. Stately they sailed out from under the guns of the fort and dropped anchor some two miles down river, out of range of McHenry's guns. For most of the British ships, too, the range was too great. Only the bombs kept pouring their shells in. Robert counted, and calculated that each bomb ship was working her two mortars at the rate of fifty rounds per hour. Two hundred and fifty of the two-hundred-pound bombs were falling on Fort McHenry every hour. Many of them burst over the fort, showering it with iron fragments. Already the great flag was showing rips and tears.

At ten the fort's guns fell silent.

"They aren't done?" Jeremiah said worriedly.

Robert kept his glass to his eye. "They've just stopped wasting powder."

Five hours later the pounding was still going on, but now three of the bombs and the rocket ship began to creep closer. Two miles. A mile and a half. Across the city a cheer went up as every gun in the fort fired at the same instant. The waters of the Patapsco were whipped to a froth by an iron hail. The four vessels shook and quivered under hit after hit. Back with the rest of the fleet, signal flags rippled aloft on H. M. S. *Surprise*. Slowly, being raked all the while, the four ships retraced their course down river, out of range of the fort. As they dropped anchor, all firing ceased on both sides. An unnatural stillness settled over the city.

Robert stretched, cursing that a few hours on a rooftop should make him stiff. "That's it for now, it seems. I'm getting off this roof before my joints seize." He took one last look toward the fort before he swung down through his window. Armistead and his magazine had had a day of luck. He wondered how long it could continue.

As he dropped through the window into his room, his landlady squealed and jumped, clutching her apron with both bony hands. "My word, Mr. Fallon! You should give a body some warning before you do that." She started again as the others followed him into the room.

"Did you want something, Mrs. Williams?" he asked.

"Why, yes," she said excitedly. "Yes, I did. There's a gentleman downstairs says he's been looking for you for three days." Her voice was suddenly drenched with awe. "He says he's the Secretary of War."

It was indeed John Armstrong, waiting for him grumpily in Mrs. Williams' parlor.

"I understand you've got a ship," Armstrong said without preamble, "one that's not bottled up here in the harbor."

"That's right," Robert replied curtly.

Armstrong made a visible effort to control his anger and only partly succeeded. "I've been everywhere searching for a ship that hasn't been taken, burned, or boxed in. I've been three days trying to find you. Three wasted days."

"Then I assume you don't want me or my ship."

"Don't fence with me," Armstrong snapped. He opened his leather case and drew out an oilskin packet. "This must be carried to General Andrew Jackson at once. I believe he is in New Orleans, but you may have to search him out along the coast, or even in the backcountry, for that matter. But he shouldn't prove difficult to find."

Robert didn't take the packet. "What message will I be carrying?"

Armstrong's face began to empurple. "You're being hired to deliver this packet. That's all you need to—"

"Find another ship," Robert said. He turned to go.

"Wait, Fallon! There *is* no other ship. Not here. The government is willing to pay any price you ask."

"I won't hire my ship," Robert said. He went on before Armstrong could protest. "I'll do it in return for knowing what message I'm carrying. No gold. Just that."

Armstrong's mouth was drawn up in disapproval; then his

shoulders slumped in defeat. "Very well. I suppose you'd rip the packet open if I don't . . . .We've lost Washington City. We may lost Baltimore. It looks as if we may lose any city the British care to attack. If we don't want to lose the whole damned Second War of Independence, the British must be induced to move their troops somewhere else. We must buy time for John Quincy Adams to get us good terms at the peace talks at Ghent."

"What does all this have to do with Jackson?"

"These are orders," Armstrong lowered his voice and glanced anxiously at the door, "for Jackson to mount an invasion of Canada."

Robert shook his head. "Seems to me we've tried invasions before, and they've all been failures."

"It doesn't have to succeed. Don't you see? If Jackson prosecutes it strongly enough, the British will be forced to send troops there instead of against another American city."

"All right," Robert said. He took the packet.

Armstrong sighed with relief. "Thank you, Captain Fallon."

After he was gone, Robert smiled at the packet. He didn't know if the plan was a good one or a bad one, but he was glad Armstrong hadn't realized how much he wanted to be of use again.

"Miller!" he shouted up the stairs. "Kemal! Jeremiah! We're through digging trenches!"

That night the four of them left the city on horseback and rode south in a wide arc that took them around Ridgely's Cove and the Ferry Branch to bring them back to the Patapsco again some three miles downriver from Fort McHenry. The city was dark. Only a few lanterns on the British bombardment fleet, a mile upriver, competed with the stars.

They swam out to the *Seagull,* found her as they had left her, and Hastily poled her out of the narrow, tree-lined creek. As the *Seagull* reached the waters of the river, Robert took the tiller, while the others raced to put sail on her. The wind and the tide were with them.

Suddenly, from the fleet upriver, came the heavy cough of a mortar. Robert looked back just in time to see a bomb burst redly above Fort McHenry. In an instant a fiery rain was falling, continual explosions roaring above the fort. In their illumination he could see the huge garrison flag, still flying defiantly, rippling in the wind that pushed *Seagull* downriver.

There were fools back there, he thought, like Winder, stiff-backed men like Armstrong who would destroy the country for their pride and punctilio, cowards, poltroons, profiteers and scavengers. And there was also Joshua Barney, fighting till there was nothing left to fight with. And George Armistead, holding the fort that he alone knew could blow up any minute. And Dolley Madison, refusing to leave the doomed city till all was lost. That flag covered all of them.

Seagull ran for the Chesapeake and the sea.

XLV

On the first of October, *Seagull* dropped anchor at New Orleans. The city was as Robert remembered it, the same pleasant streets, the same sullen dampness to the air. Kemal rowed him ashore, while Miller and Jeremiah remained with the ship.

"General Jackson?" a wizened oldster on the levee said. "His headquarters be a couple blocks over on the Rue Royale. Number 106." He fielded the coin Robert tossed and made it disappear.

The streets were filled with uniforms in every hue of the rainbow, their numbers getting thicker as he got closer to 106 Rue Royale. His knock was answered by a bushy-haired young lieutenant in the tight-fitting dark blue coat of a regular.

"I have a message for General Jackson," Robert said. "From Secretary of War Armstrong."

The lieutenant shook his head. "The general isn't here. To the best of my knowledge, he's over toward Mobile somewhere. You won't catch him. He's been wearing out horseflesh lately. Your best bet is to leave it here."

With a sinking feeling he thought of Winder, riding everywhere before Bladensburg and doing nothing. "Isn't there any way to get it to him faster? The President wants him to invade Canada. Washington City's been burned, you know, and Baltimore was under seige when I sailed."

"I know about Washington City, sir, but, hell, we've got our own invasion to worry about. The British are getting ready to hit us here, probably at Mobile the general thinks."

"How many soldiers do they have?" Robert handed the packet through the door. "You might as well take it. If the British are coming, though, I don't suppose it matters."

"Sir," the lieutenant said as he turned away, "would you mind leaving your name, and where you might be reached? The general will probably want to talk to you if you know anything about what happened at Washington City."

Robert left his card and directions that he could be reached through Esteban Lopes, just down the street. When he got to Lopes' house, a black butler opened the door.

"Yes, sir?"

"Tell *Señor* Lopes that Robert Fallon is here to see him."

"I'll tell him, sir. Would you step inside to wait?" He gave Kemal a curious stare as they entered, then disappeared up the stairs. He was back in two minutes. "Mister Lopes, he say you go right on up. His study is the second door on the left, sir."

Kemal took his position at the foot of the stairs as Robert went up. Lopes was not alone. Jean Lafitte was the only one he recognized, but all had the dark eyes and haughty stares he had come to associate with Creoles.

"*Señor* Fallon!" Lopes said, hurrying forward to offer his hand. "Let me introduce you to these gentlemen. *Señor* Denis de La Ronde. *Señor* Alexandre Declouet. *Señor* Jean Daquin. *Señor* Jean Baptiste Plauche. And of course you know Jean."

"Hello, Fallon," Lafitte said.

"This is *Señor* Robert Fallon, owner of Fallon & Son shipping and Tir Alainn plantation in South Carolina."

"I must insist," Declouet said, "on 'Colonel.'" He was a slender whip of a man who seemed to walk on his toes.

De La Ronde, the oldest of them, sighed. "Come, Alexandre. Jean Baptiste commands the Battallion of New Orleans Volunteers, and he does not insist on his rank. We are friends here."

"Jean Baptiste is but a major," Declouet said as if that explained matters.

"You come at a good time, Fallon," Lafitte said. "Everything is going to hell."

"This Jackson isn't seeing to the defenses, then? I heard the British are expected."

"This Jackson—" Declouet began angrily.

"Easily," de La Ronde said. "Easily, Alexandre. *Générale* Jackson has perhaps not understood the people of New Orleans so well as he might, Mr. Fallon. Most especially those of us of Creole blood.''

"I'm not sure I understand," Robert said. "You mean he doesn't let you help in the fight against the British?"

"With soldiers, yes," de La Ronde replied gravely, "but not with advice or counsel. He listens but little to what we can tell him of the terrain, for instance, and the lands along this river are most complicated."

"At least he lets you fight," Lafitte said sharply. "At least he does not burn you out." He settled back in his chair, swirling his brandy angrily, while the others looked awkwardly anywhere but at him.

"You cannot say you were not pirates," Lopes said gently.

"Pirates! We were, and are, privateers of the Republic of Cartegena. We prey only on Spain and her pig of an ally, England.''

"But America is not at war with Spain," Lopes said, "and here that makes you a pirate."

"*Mon oncle* Renato commands an American privateer," Lafitte said sullenly. "One would think that would gain one some consideration. But do you know what these Americans did, Fallon? They burned everything on Grande Terre, and they have put Dominique and eighty of my Baratarians in chains."

"Perhaps an offer to enlist in the militia," Robert said, "to fight the British."

Lafitte leveled a finger at him. "By damn, I have made that offer before this ever happened. The British Captain Lockyer came to me and offered gold for the aid of my Baratarians. I fobbed him off with words, and sent a letter to Jackson and Claiborne offering to fight by their sides. At the same time I began moving men and stores from Grande Terre, for I was sure the British would attack when the truth was known, leaving Dom and five hundred men behind to fight off the British if they came too soon. But it was the Americans who came. Commodore Patterson with his miserable schooner and his few gunboats. But Dom would not fire on the American flag. He had the men disperse into the swamps, but he himself was among the captured. I and the rest of my Baratarians are proscribed. I think I should take the next British offer."

There was an angry murmur, but only Lopes spoke. "Jean,

do you mean this Captain Lockyer has made contact with you again?"

Lafitte shook his head. "No. It was another one, a Major Fourrier who comes without a uniform."

"Fourrier!" Robert exclaimed. "Gerard Fourrier?"

"You know this man?" Lopes asked.

"I know him," Robert said. "Jean, you can't trust anything that man says. He's the sort that likes to hurt, especially those who can't fight back."

"I did not say I was accepting the offer," Lafitte muttered. "I can talk no longer. After all, I am proscribed. I must go now."

As if Lafitte rising were a signal, the others all made their apologies and left, shaking Robert's hand warily on the way out.

"They trust few of English descent," Lopes replied. "Forgive them." He offered a glass of brandy and Robert took it gratefully.

"I can't get over Gerard being here, *Señor* Lopes. Whenever a Fourrier shows up, it generally means danger for the Fallons. All I need now is for Justin himself to appear, or Jemmy Carde, or Jasper Trask."

"Trask?" Lopes said. "There is such a man in the city, *señor*. He appeared a few weeks ago and has already become the partner of Jean Blanque in the smuggling of slaves, though it is not generally known."

"He was smuggling slaves when I first met him," Robert said grimly, "but the last time I saw him he was begging a few dollars to get out of town before one of Fourrier's men killed him. I wonder where he got the money to become a partner."

"Trask most certainly has money," Lopes said. "He has taken a great house and rides behind one of the best teams in the city. But I do not believe he was able to buy his way into partnership with money alone. Many have that. I have heard rumors. No, less than that. A fragment of a whisper. Jean Blanque has interests in several of the ships that once sailed from Barataria. He is a man who likes to play both his cards and yours, and he knows many people who are close to Governor Claiborne. If he discovered that Grande Terre was to be raided, and that he would lose not only those ships but the Baratarian pilots who have taken his slave vessels safely past the U.S. Navy patrols, he might have considered it time to take another partner."

"But Trask? I can't believe he's an expert pilot."

"Ah, señor. That is where the fragment of a fragment comes in. It is possible that somewhere he came into possession of maps made of the Louisiana coast during the Burr affair. I have seen such maps, and they were the finest ever made. Very nearly as good as a Baratarian guide."

"That's how you think he got his partnership with Blanque?"

"It is possible. He is said to carry an oilskin packet beneath his shirt at all times. If I had such maps and was in a partnership with Jean Blanque and Cordelia Applegate, I would keep them on my person in such a manner."

"Cordelia Applegate," Robert murmured. He felt a chill such as not even Gerard's name had brought. "So she's in this, too?"

"Yes, señor, she is in it to her pretty neck. Claiborne abandoned her after the affair of Señor Burr, though she has convinced most people that it was she who ended things. It was not hard for her to do. She is still the most beautiful woman in New Orleans. I think that he realized that having a viper in his bed was not good for the health."

"I'd as soon steer clear of Cordelia, if I can, and Trask will have to wait. There's going to be a battle here, Señor Lopes. A big battle. I can smell it. I intend to do something to help win this one. Can you arrange another meeting with Lafitte?"

"I can try, senor, but today was most unusual. Normally he has a great care to avoid being taken."

"Try hard. If I can stop him from going over to the British it's almost as good as having him on our side. Now, what else can I do? The militia must need muskets."

It was early December before Lopes could arrange the meeting with Lafitte. Robert was on the levee watching the river steamboat *Enterprise* chuff to an anchorage, her tall, single stack pouring out black smoke.

"A year of peace and I'll have one of those, Kemal," Robert said. He was about to expound further on the craft when Lopes came trotting down the levee. Robert frowned. The dapper Spaniard never ran.

"*Señor* Fallon! Señor Fallon, it is arranged!" He stopped, painting.

"What is arranged?"

"The meeting." Lopes cast a wary eye around, and whispered, "With Lafitte! You must hurry. He will be gone from the city in an hour. Come." He made off at a fast walk, and Robert fell in beside him.

"At last. I've been expecting a summons from Jackson, but he's been back in the city for over a week and I've heard nothing. Not even about my offer of the muskets."

"At least he is talking to the Creoles," Lopes panted. "Be thankful for what we have. Here it is." He hurried up the steps of a house near the corner of Rue du Quartier and Rue Bourbon.

A dignified butler opened the door, but once they were inside a dozen roughly dressed Baratarians quickly searched Robert and Lopes. Kemal they eyed carefully, and apparently decided he needed no weapons beyond his muscles. The shaven-headed Turk folded his arms and stared back at them impassively. Robert and Lopes were ushered into the study.

Lafitte, dressed as roughly as his men, sat with his feet on the desk, balancing a knife on the arm of his chair. With him was Gerard Fourrier. He had some of their mother's featues, giving him almost too sensual a look for a man, but Justin's dead black eyes told the true nature of the man.

Gerard was startled. "I was told this was to be a private meeting," he said, his eyes on Robert's face.

"The meeting is private," Lafitte said smoothly, "because I say who comes to it. And I say he comes to it."

"Very well, then," Gerard said. "If you don't mind him hearing. This is our final offer, Lafitte. The patience of His Majesty's government is at an end."

Lafitte was unruffled. "The offer, good major?"

"One hundred thousand dollars in gold, a captaincy in the Royal Navy, a pardon for all crimes committed against Great Britain or her allies, and he lives and freedom of your brother and his compatriots as soon as we take the city."

"You know that Dom is my brother, eh?"

Gerard smiled faintly. "We know many things, Lafitte."

Lafitte nodded, and raised an eyebrow at Robert. "Lopes says you want to stop me from going to the English. What kind of offer do you think I can expect from Jackson?"

"Nothing," Robert said quietly.

"Nothing?" Lafitte echoed.

"That's right. For one thing, we don't need your knowledge of the waterways, as the English do. For another, we don't bribe people to fight with us."

"You say 'we.' What are you doing in this fight, Fallon?"

"I've raised a company of forty men, seamen mostly. Colonel de La Ronde says we can march with the militia regiment he's raised."

"Militia," Gerard snorted. "There you are, Lafitte. You know how long these militia will stand against regulars. And remember that the second part of our offer remains as Captain Lockyer delivered it. If you don't give us the aid we require, the entire force of the Caribbean Station will be used to hunt you down. There will be no Frenchies to distract them. Only you."

"You think they're going to let you go?" Robert scoffed. "You've taken a lot of British ships, not to mention Spanish ones. The Spanish are very good allies of the English these days. When the Spanish complain about you not being hung, do you think they'll consider one ex-pirate more important than their good ally? But you've never taken an American ship."

"And the Americans spit on me," Lafitte erupted. "I have done nothing to them, but they put Dom in jail and refuse my offer of aid. At least the British offer something."

"I'll get you in to see Jackson," Robert said desperately. He ignored Lopes' start. "You can put your case to him personally."

"Putting your case to Jackson won't help," Gerard sneered. "If you aid the Americans, we'll hang you once the city's ours."

"You can get me a safe-conduct pass?" Lafitte asked quietly.

"I'll get it," Robert replied.

"Then I will come."

Gerard leaped to his feet, a small pistol appearing out of his hat. He froze at that point, though, and Robert saw that Lafitte's free hand now also held a pistol.

"That is very tricky," Lafitte said admonishingly. "You may give thanks that I have pledged my word to return you alive to your British ship." He gestured expressively with the dagger in the other hand.

"You can't let him go," Robert said. "He's likely scouted the city while he was here. He'll take back a full report on what troops we have and where."

"I gave my word," Lafitte said simply. "Claude! Charles! Arnaud!" The door flew open and three Baratarians spilled through. "Take this gentleman back to his boat."

"Fallon," Gerard said as he was being taken out, "it pleases me to have all of you together. It pleases me very much."

Even as Gerard was being hurried out, Lafitte made preparations to go himself. In minutes the last of the Baratarians were leaving by a back exit, and Robert and Lopes were in the street. Robert was puzzled over Gerard's parting remark. All of them together? What could that mean?

"Señor Fallon," Lopes said, "how will you arrange this thing you have promised?"

Robert realized the Spaniard was half-running to keep up with him; he slowed. "I have no idea, Señor Lopes. Perhaps I will send a note to Jackson suggesting he use that steamboat that arrived today to go upriver for powder. I know he's desperate for it, and I know he admires initiative. Perhaps that will get me the pass I need for Lafitte."

"A slight hope," Lopes said. "Perhaps I have a better one. I am a friend of Bernard de Marigny. He is a friend of Dominic Hall, who is a judge. And a judge may issue the pass."

"We'll both try," Robert said. "We have to get that pass some way. Just because Gerard has been sent back downriver is no reason to think he's given up."

A thought struck him. Had the pistol been meant for Lafitte, or him?

On the fifteenth of December, word reached New Orleans that the American gunboats on Lake Borne had been captured

or sunk. The next day Jackson declared martial law. And that
night, a Friday, Lopes delivered a pass to Robert signed by
Judge Hall. A messenger was sent to Lafitte; they would meet
the next morning.

Robert felt strange walking down the Rue Royale with
Lafitte at his side. The usual Saturday morning strollers, the
carriages of pretty women, were gone, swept away by fear.
Exactly what would martial law mean? In place of civilians
were soldiers, the tight dark-blue coats of regulars from the
44th Infantry, the paler tunics of the Louisiana Blues.

Lafitte, his coat a credit to the finest tailor in New York or
Charleston, strode beside Robert with an air of defiance,
clutching the pass tightly.

As they approached 106, a man suddenly hurried down the
steps and into a waiting carriage that sped away. Robert let out
an involuntary exclamation.

"Do you know that man?" Lafitte demanded. "Does he
mean some problem?"

"No," Robert said slowly. "He means no problem." It
couldn't have been Martin Caine. Louisiana was a large place,
and what would the former overseer have to do with Andrew
Jackson?

Robert's knock was answered by the same busy-haired
lieutenant as on his first visit, but before he could speak
Lafitte brandished his pass at the lieutenant.

"I am Jean Lafitte," he intoned. The lieutenant's jaw
dropped. "I have the safe conduct. I am here to see General
Jackson."

The lieutenant took the pass as if it were a snake. When he
finished reading he looked at Robert. "And you, sir? I recognize you, but I can't recall your name."

"Robert Fallon. And I'm with Mr. Lafitte, to see General
Jackson."

"I see, sir. Won't you come in? I'll take this to the general at
once."

Inside the word spread quickly after the lieutenant disappeared upstairs. A constant stream of officers put their heads
into the hall to stare at the visitors.

"Jackson," Lafitte said suddenly, "he will honor the pass?
You are certain?"

"I'm certain," Robert said, and wished he was. Since martial law had been declared, how much weight did a civilian judge's pass carry?

The lieutenant appeared at the top of the stairs. "Gentlemen? General Jackson will see you now."

Jackson was standing at the window when they entered the study, his back almost to them. His iron-gray hair was combed straight back from his face, and that face was spare, almost gaunt. Robert remembered rumors that the general was sick. Jackson strode to his desk and sat down, picking up a pen as if to busy himself with the mounds of paper on it. "You wanted to see me," he said without looking up.

"I am Jean Lafitte," Lafitte announced.

Jackson threw the pen on the table and glared at them. His deep eyes were like a physical force. "So the hell you are. And you, Mr. Fallon. You turn up everywhere. It was you that brought that damned fool dispatch from Armstrong. And you who sent the suggestion about using the steamboat. That was a good idea, by the way. I've already sent Captain Shreve on the *Enterprise* upriver."

"I know, general," Robert said.

"I'm not finished. You attached a request to your suggestion that I found strange. You wanted a pass for Jean Lafitte to meet me. And then Dominic Hall approached me and said *he'd* been asked to grant a pass to Lafitte. I got names out of him. Marigny. Lopes. And Fallon again. Mr. Fallon, why are you so interested in Jean Lafitte meeting me?"

"I think it's better he fight with us than against us, general."

"Short and to the point," Jackson grunted. "Others have asked me to accept Lafitte, and I've turned them all down. I asked questions about you, and if half what I hear is true, you're an interesting man."

"You asked Martin Caine?" Robert said.

"I don't know any Martin Caine," Jackson said levelly. "You, Lafitte. What do you have to say for yourself?"

"You have refused my services," Lafitte said.

"I have," Jackson replied grimly. "I decided it was time to meet you face to face, but it might interest you that once this trouble with the British is over, I intend to see you hung as a pirate."

"I am an American," Lafitte said.

"You are a brigand, and you lead a hellish group of cutthroats."

"We feel alike about the British. I hate the Spanish because they drove my family from Spain, and I fight the British because they are allies of the Spanish. I hear that you too hate the British. One of them cut you with his sword when you were a boy because you would not polish his boots."

"Leave my boyhood out of this."

"I want to fight the British. Why do you continue to refuse me?"

"Why should I trust you?"

Lafitte put both fists on the desk and glared back at Jackson. "I can put two hundred men on the march when you fight, perhaps three. And I have enough powder hidden to fight a dozen battles."

Jackson leaned back. "Powder," he said. "Your men know the terrain between here and the sea?"

"As a husband knows the body of his wife," Lafitte said.

"And they will agree to be under military discipline? To obey the officers I put over them?"

"Agreed."

"Done," Jackson said. Lafitte offered his hand; after a moment Jackson took it.

"*Mon générale*, you have made me pay to fight on your side. Do you have any idea what the British offered for me to fight on theirs?"

"Don't expect my praise for refusing a bribe," Jackson said. "Now, let's test that knowledge of yours." He unrolled a map across the desk. "I already have Major Reynolds blocking beyous west of the city. What is there east of the river the British could make use of?"

"This is not a very good map," Lafitte said. "For instance, it does not even show Bayou Bienvenue coming from Lake Borne."

"I've been on that," Robert said. "If it goes all the way to Lake Borne, the British could move troops right to the outskirts of the city."

"What?" Jackson exclaimed.

"Only canoes can get so close," Lafitte said. He traced with his finger. "Boats large enough to carry soldiers would have to leave the Bienvenue and perhaps take the Bayou Mazant. They could unload at the Villère plantation, or the La Costew.''

''Damn!'' Jackson growled. ''That's no more than two miles below the city, and clean above all the river forts. Major Gabriel Villère owns that plantation. I'll have him block the bayou. Lafitte, you've proved your worth already. How soon can you start that powder toward the city?''

''As soon as my men are freed from your jail, I can issue the orders.''

Jackson hastily scribbled on a paper and handed it to Lafitte. ''There's the order for their release. You can take it over yourself, but I'll want you back here. After your demonstration today, I intend to keep you at my side. And to you, Mr. Fallon, my deepest appreciation for bringing about this meeting.''

In the street outside Jackson's headquarters Lafitte took out the paper and read it again as if he didn't believe it. ''So I have freedom for Dom,'' he murmured. ''For that you have my thanks, too, *Monsieur* Fallon. Will you accompany me to see them let loose?''

A shot cracked against the wall by Robert's head. Lafitte dragged him to the ground as another ripped the air above them. The door to the headquarters burst open, and men came running from all parts of the street.

''What happened?''

''Is he shot?''

''Did anyone see who fired?''

Robert dusted himself off and ignored the men clustered around them. ''I have other business,'' he said grimly. ''I'll meet you later at Lopes' house.'' With a purposeful stride he set out for the address Lopes had given him for Trask.

It wasn't hard to find, a large house on the Rue L'Dauphin, three stories high with wrought-iron balconies and a high-walled garden to the rear. The butler, who answered the door, stared when Robert pushed him back inside and closed the door behind them.

''Where's Trask?'' he grated. The man flinched.

''Mr. Trask ain't here now, sir? Maybe . . . maybe one of the ladies can help?''

''Ladies?'' Robert sneered. ''I know the kind of women

Trask is likely to have around. Where are they?"

"In the drawing room, sir. I'll see if they—sir?"

Robert strode to the door the man had indicated. He shoved it open, and stood struck dumb. Catherine and Moira sat in front of the fireplace doing needlework.

"I knew you'd find us," Moira breathed, and ran to throw her arms around him. Catherine sat as if turned to stone.

"What . . . in God's name, what are you doing here? In New Orleans! With Jasper Trask!" Moira shrank against him without speaking, and he stroked her hair. From rage, he had gone to wondering if he was still sane.

"A few months after you sailed," Catherine began, "Justin Fourrier came to Charleston." She went on in a flat voice, detailing a story that made him shrivel inside. Moira clung to him as if he was the rock of salvation, and he held her wishing he'd never sailed from Charleston.

"Justin dead," he muttered when Catherine was done. Moira sobbed softly against his chest. "And Trask a blackmailer. I'm sorry. Moira, Catherine, I'm sorry. I should have been there to protect you." A sudden thought slithered into his mind. "He didn't . . . I mean, if he touched either one of you, I'll make him pray for hell before he dies."

Catherine faced him calmly. Altogether too calmly, he thought. "Your wife is unharmed," she said.

"And you?" he asked softly. Moira suddenly pushed free of his arms. She ran to Catherine, taking the other woman's hand. Catherine gripped hers very tightly.

"I made an error," Catherine said. "Too late I discovered that Jasper Trask is fascinated by the woman so far above him he cannot ever hope to reach her. The icier and more haughty, the larger his attraction. To have such a woman in his power . . . ." She drew a shuddering breath. "He takes great delight in breaking down façades."

"I promise you, Catherine," he said, "he'll beg to die before I'm done."

"Because I've been despoiled," she snapped. "Because your pride is offended? Well, you can kill him all right, but not for that."

"Catherine," Moira said, "don't be putting yourself through this."

Catherine pressed Moira's hand, but she kept her eyes on Robert. They blazed like amber in a flame. "Two weeks ago Trask brought a man here. Trask was terrified of him. I was— loaned out for the night."

"Oh, God," he breathed.

"The man wasn't feminine, but he was pretty. Except for his eyes. Black and lifeless, like his soul. That man hurt me." She squeezed her eyes shut. For the first time she seemed truly shaken. "He made me sweat with my own fear. I wanted to die rather than let him touch me again. And for that you can kill Trask. And the other man, if you can find him."

"Gerard Fourrier," Robert said. "You've described Gerard Fourrier. And he's here, or was."

"Heaven help us," Moira said faintly. "Then he knows how his father died. He must. There's no end to it, is there?"

"There's an end," Robert said grimly. "First you'll pack up your things and come to Señor Lopes' house. Then I'll dispose of Trask, and I'll find out what arrangements he's made about his story in case something happens to him. That can be taken care of, too."

"That still leaves Gerard," Catherine said.

"Let him do his damnedest. The Fallons are strong enough to face it." He realized suddenly that the two women facing him were strong enough to face it, stronger than they had been when he left them. What fires they had walked through to reach that strength! The knowledge tore at him. "I'll finish Gerard Fourrier. I swear it." Suddenly the pain was too much. He stumbled to his knees, throwing his arms around both of them. Sobs welled up inside him, and he couldn't stop them. "I should have come sooner. Oh, God, I should have come sooner." They leaned against him almost protectively, and their tears joined his.

Robert installed Catherine and Moira with Lopes' house-keeper, then summoned Miller and Kemal.

"Someone tried to kill me," he said. Kemal leaped to his feet. "Wait, Kemal, I have my suspicions as to who it was. A man named Jasper Trask. He's partnered in slave smuggling with a woman named Cordelia Applegate."

"That the same woman who tried to get you to kill General

Wilkinson and Governor Claiborne, captain?'' Miller asked.

"The same. Kemal, tuck a couple of knives under your coat. Miller, get a brace of pistols apiece. We'll see what the lady can tell us about Jasper Trask.''

The tall stuccoed house where Cordelia Applegate lived seemed deserted, though. No servant answered Robert's repeated knocks. He took a quick look up and down the street. There was no one in sight.

"Kemal.''

The Turk's bulk crashed against the door, and the lock splintered free of the doorjamb. Inside, there was no sign of Cordelia. The house didn't seem abandoned. It was as if she had gone out for the day, and taken all her servants with her.

Hurriedly they began emptying drawers, rifling papers, pulling the books off shelves, looking for anything that might give a clue to the whereabouts of Jasper Trask. On the top floor, Miller started through a door and suddenly stopped.

"Captain.''

Robert pushed past him. He had found Jasper Trask. A man's boot and part of a pants leg were just showing from under a large bed. Robert grabbed the boot and pulled the body out. As unpleasant as he had been in life, Trask was worse in death. His eyes bulged almost completely out of his head, and there was a gaping, powder-rimmed hole in the back of his head. The hair was matted with blood.

"Christ!'' Miller said. "You think she did this, captain?''

"I think she'd kill her own mother if there was profit in it.'' Hastily he went through Trask's clothes. There was no oilskin pouch. "She won't leave this body here to lead to her. Sooner or later she'll try to move it. Miller, I want you to get some good men to watch this house. If anyone comes here, one is to come for me, and the other is to follow why they leave.''

They hurried out of the house.

XLVI

For all Robert's watchers, the body disappeared. But Cordelia didn't return to her house. Uneasily he left one man to keep an eye on the empty house. Except that both had had contact with Jasper Trask, he had no proof of any connection between her and Gerard Fourrier, but more and more he was certain there was one. That meant she was a danger to the city, but to protect Catherine and Moira he could not tell Jackson. Mired ever and ever deeper, he went on working with the Lafittes and the Baratarians.

On the twenty-third of December Robert was at 106 Rue Royale with Pierre Lafitte. Jean's older brother was twice as heavy as the first time they met, but he still had the same devil-may-care attitude. He sketched on a map of Lake Borne as he spoke.

"You see, *Monsieur* Fallon, if we Baratarians are given back the vessels the American government has so outrageously seized, we can ourselves drive the British from the *lac*." He looked up as a man rushed in from the street and dashed up the stairs. "That is Augustin Rousseau. I wonder where he goes in such a hurry? No matter. My plan, it is possible. Is it not?"

"Not," Robert said. "Pierre, put your Baratarians back on their ships, and half of them would disappear."

"*Sacré bleu!* You offend—"

"Lafitte!" Jackson bellowed from the head of the stairs. "Where's your brother?"

"He is with the good Major Reynolds," Pierre said, "as you have commanded."

"Then you'll have to do. Get up here."

Robert followed Pierre. Jackson glared at him, but didn't

480

order him to leave. Rousseau sat panting by Jackson's desk, where the map of lower Louisiana was once more unfolded.

"This man claims to have ridden through British troops at the de la Ronde plantation," Jackson said. "Lafitte, how could they have gotten there?"

"A few may have poled through the swamps in canoes," Pierre said doubtfully. "If they had a guide."

"They were not a few," Rousseau broke in. "There was fifty, perhaps a hundred. In green uniforms."

"That means more like twenty," Jackson said drily. "But how in God's name did they get there?"

"There are more than twenty," Denis de la Ronde said, pushing into the room. Both he and the dark young man behind him were breathing heavily, their uniforms sweat-soaked and mud-stained. "Gabriel—Major Villère was captured last night at his plantation, but he escaped. He saw many men, in the uniforms of at least three regiments."

"Villère," Jackson growled, "how did they get there? Did you block that damned bayou like you were told?"

"It is possible some part of it may have escaped my attention," the young man said uncomfortably.

Pierre laughed. "It is possible you did not wish to lose such a fine route for smuggling."

"I assure you," Villère began stiffly, but Jackson cut him off.

"Both of you be quiet. Three regiments. That can't be the whole of the force, not if they're meaning to attack here."

"If the general will pardon," de la Ronde said, "but Major Villère thinks it is." Villere stood sullenly and said nothing. "He says they spoke of caution until their reinforcements arrived."

"If that's true—" Jackson said. He banged his fist on the table. "—If they've split their army, I'll destroy it piecemeal. Mulgrew!" The bushy-haired lieutenant appeared in the door. "Write orders, Mulgrew. Coffee's Tennesseans, Hinds' Dragoons, Jugeat's Choctaw, and Plauché's battalion are to leave Fort St. John for Fort St. Charles. They're to force march, if necessary, but they're to be there before dark. Then orders to the regulars; 7th Infantry and 44th will make ready to march. Also Beale's Rifles and Daquin's Haitian Coloreds.

And send for Commodore Patterson. I'll want to use the *Carolina* for artillery support. The Feliciana Dragoons will scout the enemy immediately. Well? Move, Mulgrew!''

The lieutenant dashed out, leaving the others staring at Jackson.

"You intend to attack?" de la Ronde said. "But we are not sure how many the enemy are."

"Lafitte, you and Colonel de la Ronde will guide us." Jackson pointedly ignored Villère. "How many, colonel? The Felicianas will discover that. In any case, I do not intend the British should have any rest on American soil this night."

The night deepened, and the smell of the cypress swamp to their left rolled over Robert and Pierre. Only five hundred yards away the British campfires blazed. The sentries walked their posts unaware of being watched. On the river the dark shape of a ship dropping anchor could be seen.

"The *Carolina*," Robert said softly.

Lafitte nodded. "It is time for us to go."

Quickly they moved back to their horses and mounted. As they started toward the left side of the British camp, a file of horsemen followed them out of the trees. Coffee's Tennesseans were lean, silent, unshaven men in woolen hunting shirts, with fur caps pulled down over their long hair. Beale's Rifles were middle-aged merchants from New Orleans, dressed in a strange mix of hunting clothes and everyday garb. Only Hinds' Mississippi Dragoons had uniforms. Robert checked his pistols and the Derna sword. The Tennesseans and Beal's Rifles dismounted once they were in position on the British flank, the plump merchants making so much noise that Robert wondered why the sentries didn't hear. Kemal, Miller, and Pierre Lafitte clustered close to him as they waited. On the river the ship suddenly blossomed in flame, and grapeshot swept the British camp.

"At them!" somebody screamed, and the Americans charged.

In the camp, blazing logs were hurled from the fires by the grapeshot. Cook kettles overturned as men rushed to snatch at stacked muskets and rifles. Artillerymen managed to get to their posts, and Congreve rockets began to roar overhead.

And then the charge from the swamp rolled into the British camp.

Robert heard a bugle begin as he reached the first tents, but whether it was British or American from Jackson's attack down the river, he could not tell. The *Carolina*'s cannon still tore at the far side of the camp.

In the midst of red-coated troopers Robert laid about him with his sword, hacking to right and left, kicking side bayonets. The Tennesseans had no knowledge of bayonets, but they knew how to fight hand-to hand, with knife and tomahawk. More than one redcoat rolled to the ground with a dingy rifleman, and the Tennessean was always the one to rise. The British fell back, but in the same moment their officers were rallying them. With leveled bayonets they charged.

The Tennessean's rifle volley shattered the front line of the charge, and Hinds' Dragoons hurtled into the British flank. With a roar the Tennesseans rushed forward, and the British began to fall back again.

A musket ball tugged at Robert's coat sleeve, and another burned his neck. A British captain who seemed to have mounted a downed Dragoon's horse rode at him, saber swinging. For five hot minutes Robert and the captain sat their horses thigh to thigh. There was no art in it, just hack and cut and slice, chopping at the other man as if he were a log. There was a sudden opening, and the captain's body rolled bloodily from the saddle.

Abruptly there were fresh British troops facing them. The fight settled to a stalemate of bayonet and musket butt and tomahawk, neither side advancing or retreating.

Suddenly John Coffee, a tall, powerful man, was striding down the line. "Fall back! Back to the swamp! Fall back!"

With a curse Robert gathered up Kemal, Miller, and Lafitte, all untouched despite the fierce fighting, and galloped back toward the swamp. The British followed the retreating Americans no more than a hundred yards before falling back into their camp. Blazing tents lit the night, and between the roars of the Congreves and the blasts of *Carolina*'s broadsides, the moans of the wounded drifted across the field.

Robert found Mulgrew, his tunic awry and blood trickling down his face. "Why were we pulled back?" he demanded.

"Another push, and we'd have had them all the way to the river."

"Right under *Carolina*'s guns," Mulgrew replied. "The general hasn't been able to get word to Commodore Patterson to stop firing. You'd have caught as much as the British. Besides, the British are getting fresh troops in. Either they had reserves the general didn't know about, or more of the main army has arrived."

"Damn," Robert said. He touched the shallow gouge on his neck gingerly. "What are our orders now? We aren't falling back to the city?"

Mulgrew shook his head. "Only about two miles upriver to the Rodriguez canal, between the Macarty place and the Chalmette plantation. We're digging in there. The general says he's going to stop them there."

Robert nodded sourly. He had heard that before. He turned north, up the river.

XLVII

The Rodriguez canal was only a ditch, twelve feet wide, perhaps four deep, dry and grown over with grass. The ground was too damp for trenches, so everything had been built up above ground. The defenses were as good as they could be made under the circumstances, Robert decided, but it was still going to take a lot of luck to hold them. Stakes had been driven along the nine hundred yards from the river to the tangled cypress swamp, and dirt embankments built behind them. Cotton bales had been brought up to form a firm foundation for the gun batteries, and there were as many of them as there was room for. Robert had found himself assigned to a battery of two twenty-four-pounders, with Dominique You and Renato Beluche. From the two-gun battery he eyed the narrowing fields that stretched downriver to the British. There might just be a chance.

"Eh, Fallon," Beluche called. "You think they going to come again?" In the twelve days since the first battle, the British had attacked their line twice, once at night and once, on New Year's Day, with a long artillery duel.

"They'll come," Robert said.

"I think me they will come, too," Beluche said. He shifted his bulk to a more comfortable position against one of the long twenty-fours. "I figure it up. How much there is in New Orleans for the loot. Just the tobacco and the sugar and the cotton—I think maybe thirty million dollar. And then there is all the silver on the sideboards, the gold hidden under the floorboards. I think me they will come."

"You think only of money, *mon oncle*," Dom said reprovingly. "Sometimes I think you would like to loot New Orleans yourself."

"Of course I would!" Beluche laughed. "Eh, Fallon! I see your sister today. Very pretty woman. How you like to have me for a brother?"

"Catherine?" Robert said. "Here?"

"Yes, here. Where you think I been today? She ride a nice horse with a sidesaddle, all up and down the line. I don't think she had no maid with her, either."

Robert frowned worriedly. Had she been looking for him? She could have asked where he was. Unless she was scared to. Unless it was something about Trask, or Gerard Fourrier. "Dom, I have to go into the city."

You shook his head doubtfully. "The British, they may come again any time."

"I think my sister may need me."

"Eh, Dom," Beluche said. "You let him go help his sister. I go, too, to make sure he come back. As commander of this battery, give us a pass."

"Very well," Dom sighed. Quickly he wrote out the pass. "You keep *mon oncle* out of trouble, Fallon. And if you hear shooting, you get to hell back here damned fast."

"If we hear shooting," Beluche laughed, "we will sprout wings."

Robert dropped over the back end of the emplacement, where the gun crews rested. Kemal, Miller, and Jeremiah huddled around a small fire brewing coffee. "Kemal, come with me. Miller, you and Jeremiah stay here. I'll be back before dark."

"Trouble, captain?" Jeremiah asked.

"I hope not."

They rode the five miles to the city at a gallop, Robert thinking that once more he hadn't been there when they needed him.

At Lopes' house, though, Catherine sat calmly in the front drawing room. "Need you, Robert?" she said. "Of course I don't need you. I simply rode out for the air."

"To the lines?" Robert said incredulously.

She delicately pushed the needle through the hooped material before answering. "I ride where I choose, Robert. With your approval or without it."

"Tell him the truth," Moira said, stepping in from the hall.

She closed the door behind her with a glance at Beluche and Kemal.

"I pricked my finger," Catherine said, absently sucking it. "I didn't know you were there, Moira."

"Tell him the truth, Catherine, or I will."

"What truth?" Robert said. "What were you doing, Catherine?"

Catherine sat silently, her sewing on her lap, and Moira sighed. "Then I'll tell him. She made a sketch, a map of the defense line, showing all the guns, the numbers of men. She bribed one of Lopes' servants to carry it to the British."

"He hasn't gone yet," Catherine said abruptly. "If I send a message before ten tonight, he won't go."

"*Sacré bleu!*" Beluche breathed.

"In the name of God, Catherine!" Robert took a deep breath. What's the message, and how do I find this man you've bribed?"

"I intended to fabricate an emergency," she said. "You would have been sent back from the lines. You'd have been safe."

"The message, damn it, Catherine! How do I stop that man?" She sat with her hands folded.

"Why?" Beluche asked. "Why would this pretty woman do this thing?"

"Yes," Robert said. "I'd like to know that too."

"It was Cordelia Applegate," Moira said. "She came here last night."

A chill spread through Robert. "Go on," he said.

"She said she wanted to see us, so the butler never even told *Señor* Lopes. Once she was alone with us, she took a gun from under her cloak."

"Are you trying to say she threatened you? I don't believe it. You'd have laughed in her face."

"She had a letter," Catherine broke in angrily. "A letter written by Trask. It said that we had murdered Justin Fourrier, and told how to prove that Fourrier disappeared in Charleston. It said Trask had helped us, and that we had fled to New Orleans because we were afraid of being found out in Charleston. Trask claimed to be writing because he was filled with remorse, and because he was afraid you were going to kill him to cover our crime." She shuddered and regained control of herself. "The letter had blood on it. She said there was a man ready to testify that he saw you shoot Trask in the back of the head, and that you left the letter because you ran when this man surprised you."

"And she threatened to turn it over to the authorities unless you spied for the British," Robert said quietly.

"Yes," Catherine said quietly. "Unless the information is delivered by noon tomorrow. I told Emanuel to wait, hoping some miracle would occur, but there is no miracle."

"You're ready to deliver a whole city to the British!"

"Yes!" she shouted back. "Or you, Moira, and I all hang."

"Keep at her, Moira," Robert said grimly. "I'm going to find Cordelia Applegate."

Kemal and Beluche followed him into the hall, the latter saying, "How you expect to find her by ten o'clock? You been watching for her almost a month and you don't find her."

"I don't know. Where's *Señor* Lopes?" Robert asked the butler.

"In the study, sir. He ask you to see him before you go."

Lopes didn't look around when Robert, Kemal, and Beluche walked into his study. He stood frowning at himself in the mirror above the sideboard.

"I do not look old, *Señor* Fallon," he said. "I am not yet seventy, and there is no gray in hair. But when I went with my musket to offer my services, I was told to go home. I was too old. The young fool called me grandfather."

"*Señor* Lopes," Robert said, "if you wish to take part in the battle, we would be honored to have you in our gun battery. But right now it is urgent that I find Cordelia Applegate."

"That woman," Lopes said. "I discovered from my butler that she was in my house last night, and I did not know it. It makes my blood run cold. You may rest assured I have given orders no one is ever again to be admitted without my being informed. As to finding her, *señor*, that is most difficult. I know that your man watching her city house has seen nothing. My men have heard nothing of her, and I am sure she has not rented another house. All that is left are her plantations, and one is abandoned while the other is behind the British lines."

"A second plantation?" Robert said. "I only knew about the one downriver, where she took me."

"The other is above the city a few miles, purchased with the profits of her slave smuggling. But it is abandoned, *señor*. I have had men check it, twice, and they saw cloths on the furniture and dust over everything."

"Beluche," Robert said, "can you get hold of some of your Baratarians quickly? Since she's taken to spying, she may have guards."

"I get you a dozen in half an hour," Beluche said.

"And I go too, *señor*," Lopes said.

"Of a certainty," Robert replied.

Despite their haste, it was after five when they pounded out of the city, Kemal, Lopes, and Beluche, with his dozen rough Baratarians, galloping at Robert's heels. He closed his watch with a snap. Five hours left to stop the messenger. He bent low in the saddle and laid on his riding crop.

There was no light in the plantation house when they reached it. Moss-hung oaks lined the drive and obscured the house in the purple with twilight.

"You see," Lopes said with a regretful sigh. "There must be light at this hour if anyone is here."

"I want to make sure," Robert said. He rode a few paces up the drive and stopped. "Kemal," he said, and slipped from the saddle. The big Turk joined him swiftly.

"Wait, Fallon," Beluche said, tossing his reins to one of the Baratarians.

The three men ghosted along the drive, slipping from tree to tree, shadow to shadow, hugging the massive oaks and freezing when the gathering darkness shifted with the clouds.

"I think me," Beluche began in a hoarse whisper, but Robert cut him off. He smelled cigar smoke.

He stayed frozen, searching across the front of the house, among the trees that screened it from the road. Next to an oak at the corner of the house he found a faint red glimmer that glowed brighter for a moment. With grim satisfaction he motioned for Kemal to circle around. The giant Turk faded into the darkness. Quietly, straining to feel the branch beneath his foot before it cracked, Robert moved to come up behind the guard.

A lone man squatted beneath the tree, puffing on his stubby cigar, a musket across his knees. Robert eased out one of his pistols. In a quick step he had his arm around the sentry's throat, jerking him to his feet. The gun muzzle pressed to his temple and the snap of the hammer going back froze him. The man jerked when Kemal loomed out of the night, a foot-long dagger in his fist. Robert's pistol stilled him again.

"Answer my questions soft and true," Robert whispered, "or I'll give you to him and the knife." He felt the man jerk again; Kemal gestured with the blade and grinned ferociously. "All right, then. Where's Cordelia Applegate?" He loosened his arm and the man drew a ragged breath.

"Second floor. Drawing room in the back. She's got blankets up to the windows to hide the light."

"How many guards besides you?"

"Two. Sam, out back, and Jack inside. Mister, you ain't going to let him at me with that knife, are you?"

For a reply Robert reversed the pistol and cracked him across the head.

"That will keep him for a while," Beluche said from the shadows.

"It'll keep him long enough," Robert replied.

"If you say. Let me take the one in back, else I don't get no fun." Robert nodded, and Beluche disappeared with a grin. Five minutes later he was back, slipping his knife back into its sheath. "That one don't bother us."

"Go back to the road, Renato. Bring Lopes and the Baratarians. Kemal and I will deal with the guard inside."

Once more Beluche faded into the night. Robert slipped toward the house and went up the broad front stairs. He tried the front door, found it open, and slid through, the pistol leading the way.

From out of nowhere a massive hand seized his arm and jerked. He had a glimpse of a bearded, gap-toothed man, even larger than Kemal, before he crashed into the wall and fell to the floor.

Fighing for breath, he managed to push his way to his knees. His eyes were blurred, and his lungs burned with every effort to breathe. He struggled to his feet and had to grab hold of the banister to keep from falling.

In the middle of the hall a silent, titanic fight went on. Kemal and the bearded man, a head taller than the Turk, were locked together, hand to hand, each straining to move the other. Suddenly the bearded man's knee smashed into Kemal's side, then again. The Turk staggered back, and a huge fist hammered him to his knees. But as the other closed in, Kemal surged to his feet, arms locked around the larger man's chest, shaven head buried against the man's shirt, lifting him clear of the floor. Robert could see the muscles knot in his huge arms. The bearded man grunted, but he gripped Kemal's head with one hand and pounded the other against the base of the Turk's neck. Kemal quivered with the strain of tightening his arms. The bearded man groaned, and pounded at Kemal again. And again. And again. Suddenly there was a crack like a thick branch snapping. As if all their strength had gone, both men fell to the floor.

Robert staggered over to him. "Kemal. Kemal, my old friend, are you all right?"

With a shudder Kemal rolled over his back and lay panting. He put up both hands to rub at his neck, then with a groan he sat up. Robert pulled him to his feet. Kemal nodded gratefully and put out a hand to steady Robert, but he bent to check the huge guard. The man was dead; his back was broken.

The front-door opened, and Beluche and the Baratarians came through to stop and stare at the strange tableau. Without speaking Robert picked up his gun and started up the stairs. Kemal followed at his heels, and so, after a moment, did the others.

There was a line of light under the door to betray Cordelia's hiding place. Robert kicked the door open with a crash. Cordelia froze by the fireplace, her eyes wide as first Robert, then Kemal, Beluche and Lopes entered the room. At Beluche's muttered order, the Baratarians remained in the hall. Her pale skin above the blue velvet dress was alluring, but not to Robert.

"I want the letter," he said without preamble. Her lips tightened, but she pointed to the table. It was lying there in the open. He didn't know Trask's hand, but it said what Catherine said it did, and there were dark brown stains across the bottom. He thrust it into the fire, held it till the flames licked his hand. From the regretful way Cordelia watched it burn, he was sure it was the only copy.

"That damned Trask," she said bitterly. "If he hadn't bedded your sister, you'd never have caught me."

"By damn!" Beluche exclaimed. "This one murders Trask, then blames him for her troubles."

"It was self-defense," Cordelia said, very sincerely. Robert would have believed her if he hadn't seen the hole in the back of Trask's head. "He tried to force me—"

"Shut up, Cordelia," Robert snapped. "It's clear as glass what you did. Clear as glass, and as twisted as a sack of snakes. You decided to steal Trask's maps, to rid yourself of an unwanted partner. Then you found out about his blackmail scheme. Maybe he tried to bargain with it when you had your gun on him. So you forced him to write that letter; then you shot him. The bloodstains just added authenticity. The only thing I don't know is when you started working for the British. Before or after you killed Trask?"

"Oh, before," she said brightly.

Robert was taken aback. "You don't seem reticent about it."

"Since you know so much," she replied, "you might as well know the rest. I met Gerard Fourrier through Trask, oddly enough. Trask was frightened of him for some reason, and let slip that Fourrier was a British officer. I always did like to be on the winning side, so I told Fourrier about the maps, without telling him Trask had them, of course, and he offered to buy them. I delivered them the same day Trask was shot."

"So that is how the British knew of Bayou Bienvenue!" Beluche roared. "I hear rumors they hire some by-damned fisherman for a guide, but all the time I wonder, how did they find it in the first place."

"*Señora* Applegate," Lopes said suddenly, "you worry me. You as much as condemn yourself out of your own mouth."

To everyone's surprise, she laughed. "I don't think there's anything you can do to me. If you turn me over to the military authorities, why, I can still spin a web around most of you. Spying? Well, Catherine Holtz was riding out at the American lines yesterday. And she and Moira Fallon were living with Jasper Trask, who disappeared mysteriously. *I* killed Jasper

Trask? Why, he was my business partner! You might as well let me go.''

"By damn,'' Beluche rumbled, "she is right. This one will enjoy trying to make the mud stick on every one, and the man she killed was no friend of mine, or yours, Fallon.''

Robert shook his head. "She's dangerous. Can you post a couple of guards on her here, Renato?'' She glared at them furiously, but Beluche nodded.

"*Señors*,'' Lopes said, "I think it is time we get back to the city. Even now we may have trouble with the curfew.''

"Time!'' Robert shouted, hauling out his watch. He had forgotten there was still the servant Catherine had bribed to be stopped. It was five of nine, and there was almost an hour's ride back to the house in the city. "I have to go! Kemal, stay here. You don't need a hard ride now.'' And he dashed out of the house.

He leaped onto his horse and went pounding down the drive, rounding onto the river road at a dead gallop. He did not spare the horse. At the edge of town there was suddenly a soldier in his way.

"You there! Halt!''

Robert bent low over his horse and didn't slow. The soldier had to leap back to keep from being trampled. A musket cracked, the soldier's shouts faded behind him, and he was on the empty cobblestone streets of the city. The moon was the only light as he rode into the garden at Lopes' house, leaped from the saddle and dashed inside. Catherine met him in the hall, Moira close behind her.

"What's the matter, Robert?'' Moira asked. "You look pale as death.''

Robert grabbed Catherine by the shoulders. "Where's this Emanuel? How do I stop him?'' She hesitated, and he shook her. "Beluche and Lopes have Cordelia! The letter's burnt! Damn it, how do I stop Emanuel?''

"He's at a tavern called Salem's Pit, on Rue Girod. You tell him Mrs. Holtz says the weather has changed, and he should come in before it rains.'' The clock in the next room chimed the hour, and she gasped. "It's too late.''

Without answering he raced out of the house and threw himself back in the saddle. Horseshoes struck sparks from the stones of the street. There were only shadows, and the flitting shapes of scurrying dogs. Even Rue Girod, center of the district known as the Swamp, was still and lifeless, the drunken music stilled and the whores in their beds, alone or not. His eyes twitched to read every sign he passed. The Bucket o' Blood. *Le Coq d'Or*. The Hellspout. And then there it was. Salem's Pit, with a picture of an old woman being lowered into a fiery pit. Robert jumped to the pavement and began pounding on the door.

"Go away!" a gruff voice inside shouted. "It's curfew."

"Open up!" Robert shouted back, and beat at the door till it shook on the hinges.

"God damn it!" the gruff voice said, cracking the door, "go away!"

Robert pushed through. "I'm looking for Emanuel." There was one man in the place beside the gruff proprietor, a dark, slender man. He started for the back of the tavern. "Emanuel?" Robert said. The man's eyes flickered, and his pace picked up. "Mrs. Holtz has sent me. The weather's changed. You're to come in before it rains." He was aware of the tavern keeper staring at him as if he were crazy.

The dark man paused. "The weather has changed?"

Robert nodded. "And you're to come in before it rains."

Emanuel let out a long breath and pulled a sealed paper from his coat. Robert took the paper, ripping it open. When he saw the map, he heaved his own sigh of relief. "Good, Emanuel. Good."

XLVIII

The night of the seventh of January brought no rest to the men in the American lines. In the cold dampness British work parties could be heard. The word spread along the mud ramparts that they would be coming at dawn.

Robert huddled beside one of the long twenty-fours, the one commanded by Beluche. Kemal, Miller and Jeremiah were among the Baratarian crew. To their right, along the embankment to the next battery, crouched part of the 7th Infantry, regulars in their tight blue jackets. Plauché's battalion, the New Orleans Volunteers, and Lacoste's Battalion of Free Men of Color held the stretch to the left. Their colorful uniforms were sodden and dingy after a week at the ramparts.

Jeremiah peered through the darkness toward the Lacoste battalion. "Every time I look at them, I can't believe my eyes. Black men with guns in their hands."

"What do you expect?" Robert said sleepily. "It's their city, too." He checked his pocket watch and put it back with a sigh. After two o'clock.

"You believe that?" Jeremiah asked. "You believe it's really their city, too?"

"Look sharp," Dom hissed suddenly. "Jackson."

Before any of them could move, Jackson had climbed up into their emplacement. Over his iron-gray hair he wore a leather cap, and a short blue Spanish cloak was drawn about his shoulders. His high dragoon's boots looked as if they had never seen polish. "How are you men?" he asked.

"We are fine, *mon générale,*" Beluche said. "You have one hundred men so fine as me, and we beat the whole damned British army by ourselves."

"If there were a hundred men like you, Beluche," Jackson said, "they'd steal the world. And you, Fallon. I expect right now you're wishing you had kept that company of seamen together."

"The men fit in just fine with the Baratarians, general," Robert said.

Jackson nodded as if he hadn't really heard. He looked toward the British. "Tomorrow, you keep your men cool. Just make sure they serve the guns and don't get caught up." He grinned at them suddenly. "We're going to beat hell out of them tomorrow." Then he climbed down and walked to the first of Plauché's battalion, stopping to talk a few minutes before he moved on.

"I think," Dom said, peering after him, "we are going to catch one God-damn big hell tomorrow."

At dawn Robert saw a blue rocket rose into the gray sky, and the skirl of bagpipes advanced along the river.

Through the early morning mists they came, the 93rd Highlanders in their tartan trews, the scarlet-coated 44th Foot, the 21st and the 43rd, moving to a precise cadence, drums beating and flags flying, as if the marshy ground were a parade field.

"Fire!" the order roared down the American line.

Beluche and You touched slow matches to the vents of the long twenty-fours, and the view was obscured by acrid smoke as the guns thundered back against their carraiges. Immediately Robert leaped to sponge the barrel with the wet sheepskin on one end of his rammer. A solid roar hung over the ramparts; cannon fire rippled down the line. Kemal held a powder bag in place; Robert spun the rammer and shoved it home. A Baratarian followed with the wadding, then Jeremiah and Miller heaved the twenty-four-pound cannonball into place, and Robert rammed that home.

In the windless calm the smoke cleared slowly, but Robert could make out gaps in the British lines. But they still came on. Beluche pricked the vent. "Stand clear!" he shouted, and touched the gun off.

It was a frenzy of load and fire, load and fire. Serve the guns as fast as they could to pour shot into the oncoming. As the enemy came closer, muskets began to join in. The fire was beginning to have some effect. In the center some of the red-coated lines were slowing, and one battalion had stopped dead, firing their muskets despite the urgings of their officer to go forward. From the far left of the American line, though, the shouting and the sudden absence of cannon fire indicated that at one spot, at least, the British were in the lines.

Robert had bent once more to the gun when Dom screamed, "Coming up!"

He looked up to see a red-coated soldier scrambling over the top of the embankment. With a swing of the rammer he knocked him back down into the ditch, but there were more clawing their way up. From the far right came screams and the sounds of men in close combat. The British were into the line there, too.

Robert snatched his sword just as the attackers reached the emplacement. He slashed at the first man over, ducked under a bayonet thrust from the second. Then Kemal was beside him with a clubbed musket, smashing the head of the man with the bayonet. And then Miller was there, cutlass in hand, and Jeremiah with a musket and a bayonet. Beluche rushed in with a pistol in one hand and a saber in the other, and You with a dueling sword. The British clawed and hacked their way up into the emplacement, and the British died. The bagpipes suddenly broke into a tune Robert knew, "Monymusk," and the Highlanders roared and charged. Robert ran a captain through, slashed the throat out of a young lieutenant, and suddenly there were no more.

Desperately, wordlessly, the Americans threw themselves back to the guns, loading the heavy bags filled with grapeshot, buckshot, scrap iron. The Highlanders came at a run, bayonets leveled, a solid roar of sounding from their throats. The two twenty-fours drowned them out, and then other guns along the line were pouring their deadly hail into the Highland charge. Gaps were ripped in their ranks, which closed, and new gaps were torn. Riddled, the charge faltered, slowed, then died. Some of them tried to go to ground, to find a place to fire from, but the American cannon clawed at them, and slowly they began to fall back. All along the embankment the fire redoubled. The entire attack began to fall apart. It was retreating redcoats they fired at now, redcoats falling back, even redcoats running.

Robert pulled the sponge from the barrel, and Beluche put a hand on his arm. "It is over, Fallon." He sounded hoarse. "*Parbleu!* It is a charnel house."

Dazed, Robert realized that the other guns had fallen quiet also. He looked at Kemal and Miller, panting together against the back of the emplacement, Jeremiah wiping sweat from his face. Then he looked out across the field.

The sun had burned off the mist, leaving a clear view down the river plain. It had been chopped and churned into a morass of mud. And blood. Everywhere the bodies lay tangled, torn masses of red and tartan and green. Here and there something stirred; the only sound was the occasional cry for water.

Robert looked back as Jackson rode by on his gray horse. The general looked haggard. He stopped and stared at Robert. "Carnage, Fallon. A damned lot of brave men died out there. A damned lot."

"Do you think they'll come again, general?" Robert asked.

Jackson shook his head. "Not after this. This campaign is over. There may be skirmishing, but it's over." With a last look at the field, he rode on. "Carnage," he murmured.

The cries of gathering ravens sounded across the field, and in the sky the vultures circled.

XLIX

Church bells rang across the city of New Orleans for the victory, and the men in Rue St. Phillippe walked as if the sound buoyed their steps.

"I'm going to see my wife first thing," Robert said. "The rest of you can go get drunk if you want."

"I got the same thing in mind," Beluche laughed. "But I going to get me two girls from Madame d'Aumont."

"Wife," Jeremiah said, shaking his head. "I haven't *seen* my wife in three years. And my papa wasn't in good health when I left. He could be dead, for all I know."

"We'll be going home soon enough," Robert said. "What about you, Miller? What are you going to do?"

"Well, captain, I figure on going along with Renato. And I think Kemal does, too." Kemal nodded with an enormous grin.

Robert hooted with laughter. "All three of you'll come down with the French pox!"

From behind them came the crack of muskets; lead chipped the pavement and walls around them. Robert saw a dozen roughly dressed men with muskets, and something smashed the breath out of him. Then Jeremiah had an arm around him, dragging him toward an arched gate. They sagged in the small haven, and Robert looked back. Men were running from all directions. The men with the muskets were gone.

His friends were in a bad way, he realized. Jeremiah's face was contorted, and blood seeped between the fingers he had clamped on his thigh. A graze bled down Kemal's face, another marked on his shoulder. Miller sat cursing and awkwardly tying a kerchief around a left arm that hung limp. Only Beluche was untouched.

"By damn," the stocky old man growled, "those fellows try harder to kill us than the English. *Sacré bleu!* Fallon, how are you hit?"

Robert put a hand to his side and felt the spreading patch of wetness that soaked his coat. The others gathered to him. Gently Miller pulled his hand away; Jeremiah ripped his coat open and grimaced.

"You better get a doctor," he told Beluche quietly.

Robert looked from one face to the next. He felt strangely light. "Cordelia, or Gerard?" he managed, and darkness rolled over him.

When Robert woke, church bells were ringing. He looked around the room and saw Lopes by the window with Catherine and Moira.

"They brought me here," he croaked, and the three by the window rushed to his side.

Moira threw herself to her knees by the bed. "Thank God you're awake." She clutched his hand fiercely.

"I will tell you, *señor*," Lopes said, "that during the nights you raved I feared for you. The doctor said the bullet managed to miss both heart and lung, but I still feared."

"Be quiet," Catherine ordered. "Both of you. That's no way to talk to him when he's just come to. You'll scare him half to death."

"What are you all talking about?" Robert demanded. "How long have I been unconscious?"

The three looked at each other uncomfortably for a moment. It was Moira who finally said, "Two days more than five weeks."

His head spun, and he closed his eyes. "But the church bells. They were ringing them. They can't have been ringing five weeks."

"That was the victory," Lopes said. "This is for the treaty of peace."

"Peace," he breathed. He tossed the coverlet back.

"*Señor!*" Lopes gestured toward the women. "You are naked!"

He rubbed at the tight bandage that wrapped his chest. "My clothes, Moira. Get them for me."

"I'll be doing no such thing!" she said. "You lie back down there!"

"You've been unconscious for five weeks," Catherine said. "You're in no condition to get up. You'll tear something loose."

"If you won't get my clothes for me, I'll get them myself," he retorted. Lopes threw up his hands as he made his way, step by tottering step, to the clothes press.

"You're a stubborn man," Catherine said, "full of pride." Her tone was more of wonder than of anger, though.

"I can dress for the peace," Robert said. Lopes was helping him get into his clothes. "When did the news arrive?"

"Only a few days ago," Moira said. "There've been celebrations everywhere. Church bells every day. Fireworks. Balls."

Lopes nodded. "It was signed in Ghent, *señor*, the day before Christmas. It has yet to be ratified by the Congress or Parliament, so far as I have heard."

"The day before Christmas?" Robert said quietly. "That was the night the British landed. Two weeks before the battle. What effect is that going to have?"

"In England, *señor*, who can tell? But I think they are even more tired of war than we. We have been at war three years, they for twenty. And in America the battle is being hailed as a great triumph of American arms."

"It's true," Catherine said. "Even the most anti-war Federalist papers are saying it proves America can defend herself against any foe. They say we're ready to take our rightful place among the world's powers." She laughed. "The Federalists are beginning to sound like John Calhoun."

"I fear we are not yet exactly one of the world's great powers," Lopes said.

"That doesn't matter," Robert said. "I hoped once that this war would bring us together, and give us enough pride to stand up for ourselves. It seems to have done that."

"There is bad news as well, *señor*," Lopes sighed. "*Señora* Applegate escaped shortly before you were shot."

'That awful woman," Moira said.

Robert shook his head. "So she *could* have been responsible."

"An incredibly deadly woman, *señor*. She lured one of the Baratarians to her bed and stabbed him during, ah, an intimate moment. The other man was found shot with the first man's gun."

"Perhaps we're well rid of her." He finished tugging his coat on. "Where are Kemal and the others? Jeremiah. Miller. Beluche."

"They're down in the study," Catherine said disapprovingly. "All except Mr. Beluche. He spends half his time here, and the other half consorting with loose women."

"If we had let them," Moira said gently, "they would have been keeping a vigil by your bed."

"I'll go down to them," he announced, and after looking at each other despairingly the two women took places on either side of him.

He walked down to the study with as much jauntiness as he could muster, shaking off their hands when they tried to support him. In the study his appearance created an explosion.

"Captain!" Jeremiah whooped, then began to laugh joyously.

"Begging your pardon," Miller said worriedly, "but should you be up, sir?"

"Another word like that," Robert growled, "and I'll let you join the women as nursemaids.

Miller grinned. "Whatever you say, captain. God, but it's good to see you on your feet, sir."

Kemal reached out to touch his arm. The big man's eyes were damp. He gripped Kemal's arm and nodded. "I'm all right," he said gruffly, and Kemal nodded and smiled. "And it's mainly thanks to you, Jeremiah, that I am. You dragged me out of the street, or I'd be full of musket balls."

"It wasn't anything," Jeremiah said uncomfortably.

"I'll say whether saving my life is something or not," Robert said, "and I say it is. You can't pay a man for saving your life, but you had a good cabinet shop before all the troubles began. The least I can do is see you have as much again, and all the customers I can get you. And you, Kemal. You've saved my life more than once. What is it you want? A farm? A tavern?" Kemal touched his own chest, then Robert's. "Aye, Kemal. You'll always be my friend. But there must be something you want, and I mean to get it for you. A wife, maybe.'' Kemal laughed. "Every man needs a good wife to warm his bed.''

"Robert!" Catherine protested.

He rounded on her with a laugh. "And you, sister. What do you want?" His laugh died as he saw her looking at him.

A sad smile flickered across her face. She looked at Moira, and when she turned back there was a regal dignity in her face. "All I want is a good cotton crop and someone to buy it," she said at last. He knew she was lying.

There was a small silence; then Moira spoke up.

"My great lummox of a husband, you've not yet asked what your wife wants.''

"Anything you desire," he said quietly, and seized her in his arms, ignoring her protests about his wound.

He felt a warmth envelop him, a feeling of love and belonging he thought he had forgotten. "As soon as we can sail," he whispered, "I'm taking you home.''

Home, he thought, away from New Orleans. Away from Cordelia Applegate, away from Gerard Fourrier, away from blackmail and violence. Home to Charleston, where no one knew how Justin Fourrier had died, or cared. There was peace for the nation, and there would be long years of peace for the Fallons.

He hugged Moira closer.

More Bestselling Fiction from Pinnacle/Tor